"Max," I said sternly. "Valentina is your wife and where you go so should she. Why do you feel the necessity to explain your actions? It is ridiculous."

"Is it?" He moved closer still.

I held my ground. I could see the firm set of his chin, the movement of a muscle in his cheek. His eyes searched mine and then settled upon my mouth. There was a weighty atmosphere in the space between us, something intangible that I did not understand. Though Max made no movement, just his observation of me was a caress.

My breath picked up speed, and when his hand lifted to touch my cheek I could not stop the sigh leaving my parted lips.

"Dearest Ingrid," he said softly. "If only…"

"What are you doin' out there in the dark? You'll catch your death." Joan barked from the doorway and Max's hand quickly fell away.

Without turning to look at her I called. "Just getting some fresh air. I shall be there directly." Then I watched as Max gave me one lingering look before he stepped back into the night.

I made my way towards the silhouette of my maid in the open doorway, Max's words burning into my soul….*if only.*

Praise for Author

Jude Bayton

"*The Secret of Mowbray Manor* is an elegant historic suspense that does a beautiful job reminding us that when you scratch the surface of dignified family, you don't have to scratch hard to find blood. Jude's bold and crisply defined characters felt tangible. I loved getting swept up in the stunning settings, and the mystery and angst locked me in. I couldn't put it down. I went from trying to solve the mystery to just hoping that the noble heroine Kathryn isn't killed before she can uncover the secret and find out what really happened to her friend."

~Amy Brewer, Literary Agent

The Secret of Lorelei Lodge

by

Jude Bayton

This is a work of fiction. Names, characters, places, and incidents are either the product of the author's imagination or are used fictitiously, and any resemblance to actual persons living or dead, business establishments, events, or locales, is entirely coincidental.

The Secret of Lorelei Lodge

COPYRIGHT © 2022 Deborah Bayton-FitzSimons

All rights reserved. No part of this book may be used or reproduced in any manner whatsoever without written permission of the author, except in the case of brief quotations embodied in critical articles or reviews.

Contact Information: author@judebayton.com

Cover Art by *Diana Carlile*

Print ISBN 978-1-955441-05-6
Digital ISBN 978-1-955441-04-9

Published by redbus llc

Dedication

For Betty Hilda Bannister Stacey *'Squeeza Bet'*. My fabulous aunt.
A woman with such passion for laughter, clothes, chubby legs, and living-room lamps. I am so sad you are gone. Thank you, for being such an inspiration, and helping me learn how to be independent and fearless by your example.

For my dear friend Francis X. Schloeder.
One of a kind, smart as a whip and whose particular taste in good shortbread matched my own. Taken too soon and missed by us all.

To Karen McCoy. A lovely person, whose gentle soul now soars with the birds she loved so passionately.

And finally, to Richard 'Dick' Wessels. Loved and missed by his family. A brave veteran, and a hero to many.
Rest well.

Acknowledgements

To a wonderful author and my fantastic editor, Alicia Dean. You inspired and encouraged me to chase this dream. I am so grateful to count you as my friend.

To the members of the CROW writers' group. May we roost together for years to come! What a jolly murder of crows we are!

…and to all of you readers who make me feel so cherished. Thank you for spending your precious time reading my stories. I am truly humbled.

Chapter One

Town of Prinzenstadt, Germany, May 1895

THE BAYING OF A WILD *animal at my heels made my feet light as a deer as I ran for my life. Through dense thickets of pine trees, I fled, mindless of dry needles underfoot piercing my slippers. Dear God, let me find it before it was too late!*

Suddenly, there it was—the familiar wall, a fortress of safety in the terrifying black of night. I threw myself against the door, hammering on the wood with my fists. "Let me in!" I screamed loudly. "I beg you, please will you let me in!" The door slowly opened. Soft light spilled from the gap and chased the shadows away. Relief flooded my senses—I was safe at last!

I stepped inside where my rescuer stood, her hand still paused upon the doorknob. As she raised the lamp I observed the long sweep of her thick black hair, the dark mole to the right of her mouth. Then her eyes fastened upon mine, and I gasped in shock. For the person staring into my face was none other but myself!

I sat bolt upright in bed, gasping. Once my breathing slowed, I reached out a trembling hand for my glass of water on the nightstand and gulped it down. Curse this nightmare. Why did it haunt me whenever I was away from home? Was my mind so unsettled?

I had left London a mere two days earlier, spending

one night on the train and now this night, here at the hotel. It was not as though Germany was on the other side of the world.

I lay back in the bed, closed my eyes and automatically reached for the small gold pendant around my neck. The coin sized circlet was engraved with a Cornflower, the national flower of Germany, and had been a gift from my dearest mother on my tenth birthday. She had worn an identical piece herself until her death. Whenever uncertainty plagued me, the touch of the pendant brought me closer to her. I never removed it unless Father required my wearing another piece for a special occasion—but that was all in the past now.

I yawned, aware that I desperately needed rest, for tomorrow would be a challenging day. I plumped up the feather pillows and rested my head against them. Ordinarily my bad dream would plague me only once during the night. I hoped tonight it would be so. With that comforting thought, I drifted off to sleep.

HERR METZGER SPOKE LITTLE English but was able to ask for me at the reception desk of the hotel the next afternoon. He kept nodding and smiling as he gestured for me to follow him outside.

Slight of build, he was scarcely taller than me with scant hair poking out from underneath a well-worn cap. I wrinkled my nose. The fellow bore an unpleasant odour of onions about his person. I tried to hide my distaste as I was shown to the carriage and helped inside. Before long, we were underway.

Joan, my maid, had left the hotel that morning. The overseer of my possessions, she'd insisted upon going to Lorelei Lodge in time to unpack my belongings before I arrived. I was rather glad she would already be there, especially at an uncertain time like this.

As the carriage drove through the streets of Prinzenstadt, I paid little attention to the shops and businesses we passed. But when we reached the town's square, I could not help but note an impressive building declaring itself to be, 'Das Gro*ß*e Opernhaus', a grand Opera House.

It commanded one side of the square and was as fine a piece of architecture as many of London's beautiful buildings. The intricacy of the stonework, even from my vantage point, was marvellous. I would make enquiries about the place and plan to come back. Perhaps there would be events scheduled in the upcoming weeks? How fine that would be.

What was I thinking? I remonstrated. I was in mourning and not at liberty to socialise at will. There was much business to attend to. Since my father's death four months earlier, I had been immersed in all things legal. Though his affairs were handled by a competent firm of solicitors, there were still countless matters requiring my attention at home.

The unexpected telegram from Germany informing me of the death of an unknown relative, and a request to travel to *Prinzenstadt* for an important meeting with my mother's family lawyer had blindsided me. The past few days had therefore been somewhat hurried.

Prinzenstadt was a familiar name, of course. It was my mother's birthplace and where she had lived until marrying my father. But I had no previous knowledge of a relation still living there and was surprised when I received notification of her death.

Mr Francis, Father's solicitor, was of invaluable help to me. He quickly wired the German lawyer, a gentleman by the name of *Herr* Vogel, who informed him that Mother's home, Lorelei Lodge, was mine, and had been since her death, twelve years earlier.

This was news to me, until it was explained that Mother had willed her aunt, Gisela Bergman, the right to reside at Lorelei for the duration of the woman's lifetime. Upon Gisela's death, I was to be notified of ownership.

This past March, Gisela had indeed passed away and there were urgent matters to be discussed and settled. As owner and the last surviving family member, Mr Francis advised I travel to *Prinzenstadt* post-haste, meet with the Bergman family lawyers to finalize any legalities and claim the deeds. He assured me Father's estate in London was in secure hands, and I was not to worry.

I had no desire to travel, yet once I boarded the ferry at Dover it was rather a relief to put some distance between me and the events of the previous months. I planned to spend several weeks in Germany and learn about my mother's side of the family who apparently, I knew little of. Mother had left Germany before I was born, and to my knowledge had never returned. Whenever I asked about her German relatives, she'd always insisted there were none still living. How strange for her to say that when all the while someone dwelt in her home the entire time. Who was this unfamiliar aunt? Now I would never know.

THE JOURNEY FROM PRINZENSTADT was short, for within the hour we turned off the main thoroughfare and onto a gravel driveway. I roused myself from thought and tugged open the window so that I might see my destination.

My first sight of Lorelei Lodge was an unexpected delight. Set in the midst of beautiful parkland, the building resembled a massive piece of confectionary because the splash of colour amidst the greenery was breathtaking.

Three stories tall, the design of the lodge was blatantly Rococo—painted peach hued stonework and a green metal roof with no less than three spires that I counted from this viewpoint. As we approached, I noticed the abundance of different shaped windows, though they were all framed by the same white stone floral ornamentation.

The main floor was accessible through a grand front entrance, but on the second floor, in front of huge glass doors that suggested a ballroom, a magnificent staircase parted like a curtain, sweeping down either side of the house above the entrance. The entire effect was most pleasing, especially when I'd secretly expected a drab, monolithic building from the dark ages. Lorelei was by design a hunting lodge, by size a manor house and visually, an architectural wonder.

Herr Metzger drew the carriage to a halt in front of an impressive set of old oak doors. Simultaneously the carriage door swung open, and a hand reached inside to assist me out.

The liveried footman did not meet my gaze when I stepped down onto the driveway. But as I let go of his forearm, he clicked his heels together and nodded his blond head curtly.

"*Dankeschön*," I thanked him and walked towards

the building, where several people waited in a line to welcome me. It was usual to introduce the staff to a new owner, yet it was a novelty to me, for until recently I had always lived with my father.

An older man was the first to greet me. His black suited attire and confidence proclaimed him as a butler, his dour face pinched from years of frowning.

"*Guten Tag, meine Dame,*" he said politely. "*Ich bin Fritz. Wilkommen.*"

"Good afternoon, Fritz," I replied. "I am pleased to be here, though I am sorry it is under such sad circumstances." I could not tell if he understood me completely, yet he nodded, then turned to the others waiting patiently.

"*Das sind deine Diener.* Here are your servants," he announced with a heavy accent. The first was a woman who looked to be as old as the butler.

"My vife, Ursula. She is the *Köchin*, your cook." The woman nodded glumly. I greeted her with a smile, and then did the same for two footmen, three housemaids and one kitchen maid. None of them appeared pleased to see me there, neither did they utter a word. I assumed they knew no English, and I did not volunteer that I spoke German.

At length, Fritz escorted me through the entrance, past the staircase and into the drawing room, whereupon I asked him to fetch my maid. When he had gone, I took a moment to absorb my surroundings, for my head spun with the novelty of it.

The drawing room echoed the flamboyant Rococo style of the exterior. In here, the cherry-wood flooring was of a parquet design. The lower part of the walls decorously covered in a dusky rose marble while the upper portions were painted a creamy buttery yellow. Set at regular intervals, were inlaid areas in coloured pastels, where varying plaster of Paris designs had been placed. I had not seen their like before and found the overall effect calming and tranquil, in stark contrast to the dark reds and gloomy greens of our London home. *My* London home now, I realised. How strange that I should be the owner of two properties in such a short time.

A knock sounded on the door. "Come in."

Joan stepped into the room and closed the door behind her. She was a sight for sore eyes in this unfamiliar landscape.

"Blimey, Miss Ingrid. What do you make of this place?" Joan's eyes, usually the size of two small brown buttons, were as wide as when she received her Christmas box.

"It's all a bit much," I said. "Come. Let us sit," I gestured to a plump cushioned sofa of bright green.

"Well, I've never seen such fancy stuff, miss," Joan said, sinking down next to me. "It all looks a bit Frenchified if you ask me."

"That's because it is," I remarked. "The design of everything here is what they call Rococo, or perhaps it is Baroque? I don't really know the difference. Regardless, the style of it is meant to make things appear detailed and whimsical. Ornate, similar to Versailles."

Joan blew out a breath. "I call it over the bloody top." Her lined face crunched into a grin. She generally spoke her mind, usually peppered with a few curses. A privilege earned by years of service to my mother, and now to me.

"That's one way of putting it," I agreed. "Though I have to admit I'm relieved it doesn't look like a gaol. I know there are many beautiful palaces in this country, but the middle-class Germans aren't exactly known for their frippery."

"Their what?" her snub nose wrinkled.

"It means they don't like to adorn their homes with items that aren't useful and are just for show." I changed the subject. "Tell me, what do you think now you're here? Were the staff friendly when you arrived?"

She laughed. "I don't rightly know. I couldn't understand anythin' they said. Though one of the footmen, Dieter, now there's a handsome bloke. He winked at me, the cheeky beggar." She raised her eyebrows as though a maiden, when Joan McCullum owned every day of her fifty-seven years.

I knew which man she referred to, though I had only caught a glimpse of his face when he helped me from the carriage. "He's young enough to be your son," I admonished. Joan was such a shameless flirt. "I expect the servants feel uncertain about their future with my great-aunt gone. They're probably still quite upset about a new mistress taking over, and one that's foreign to boot."

"Oh, I doubt it," said Joan. "Most of them have only been here goin' on a year or so."

That surprised me. "How do you know that? I thought you said you couldn't understand them?"

"I can't." She gave a naughty grin. "But that Dieter, he don't half speak good English, an' he told me they were all new hires, every single one of them. Very odd if you ask me."

It was, especially since by all accounts Aunt Gisela

had lived here for such a long time. Why would her previous servants all be gone? Was she unkind to them?

Joan got to her feet. "Right then. I had better get busy. I'm startin' to worry about what we'll be eatin' for dinner. I hope it's not more of that pickled cabbage we had at the hotel." She stuck out her tongue and made a gagging sound. Joan liked to look forward to her meals.

I chuckled. "Why don't you show me to my room and then we'll go down to the kitchen and see if we can't persuade the cook to make something English."

THE REMAINDER OF THE afternoon passed with my spending time in what had been my aunt's small study. I sat at her sturdy desk and went through various papers and documents, all which were neatly stored and identified. Joan came to ask if I was ready for a tour of the house, but I declined and told her it could wait until the morning.

Dinner was tolerable, though there was the dreaded cabbage served with my main course. I ate a solitary meal in a modestly sized dining room, with Dieter loitering behind me to take the plates away after each course. By the time the clock struck nine in the drawing room, I was more than ready to get to my bed.

I had the nightmare again. This time it was so vivid, I awoke to find my bedclothes scattered on the floor and my breathing laboured as though I had been running, just like in the dream. I rose from my bed and walked to the window overlooking the front of the house. It was late, but the moon was bright, and I could see the driveway leading to the road.

Warm, I opened my window to let in the night air

and with it came the clean scent of fresh pine, coming from the forest nearby. I closed my eyes and inhaled the delightful fragrance, when something flashed through my mind so quickly I could not catch it, but it left a residual thought. The scent of the pines was so familiar. But from where?

MY MEETING WITH HERR Vogel the following morning went well. He arrived promptly at ten o'clock, looking more professor than lawyer. He carried a briefcase full of paperwork which he took out and placed upon the table, then went to great pains to explain the situation to me.

"You are the sole beneficiary of *Fräu* Marta Rutherford, your mother," he said in German accented English. "The assets consist of the Lorelei and its grounds, and a large sum of money." He passed a sheaf of paper and I read the numbers, mentally calculating the amount from Deutsche marks to British sterling whilst trying not to show how taken aback I felt. I passed the document back to him across the dining room table.

"Now, *Fräulein* Rutherford." His unruly grey brows knotted over round spectacles. "We must discuss your plans."

"Plans?"

"*Ja*. I understand your residence is in London and therefore you will probably wish to sell Lorelei Lodge? I must inform you there is already a buyer interested."

"*Herr* Vogel, I have only just arrived here and have yet to even see the grounds. I have no inclination of what I shall do with the place. After all, it belongs to a family I did not realise I had."

"*Entschuldigen, fräulein.* Forgive me, but I do not understand your meaning?"

I shrugged. "Until your telegram, I was unaware I had any living family at all. Mother told me she was from *Linnenbrink,* near *Prinzenstadt,* but since she never returned once she married my father, she seldom spoke of her home."

"How strange that you say this." The lawyer removed his spectacles and rubbed his eyes before perching the glasses back upon his prominent nose. "I did not know your mother well, but I can assure you she visited each year. *Frau* Rutherford met with me annually, to go over her personal accounts and those concerning Lorelei. I have documentation I can show you from our meetings."

I frowned. "That cannot be correct. Mother never mentioned coming back, not once." My memory raced inside my head, hunting for information to substantiate my statement. *Herr* Vogel was surely mistaken. Wouldn't I have known if Mother travelled abroad? Germany was far enough away from London that she would have been absent for many days. That would not have gone unnoticed. I held my tongue so he might continue.

"Your mother's family, the Bergmans, have lived in *Linnenbrink* for several generations. Marta knew many people here." He glanced down at his papers. "Were you aware that your aunt was preceded in death by her brother, Ludwig, who resided in Johannesburg, South Afrika?"

"I had a great-uncle?" Goodness, how many more relatives had lived without my knowledge? Why had my mother withheld this from me?

"*Ja.* He was your mother's uncle as Gisela was her aunt. But still, it is strange you did not know." He began gathering his papers together. One set he passed to me and then handed me a pen.

"*Herr* Vogel, was my aunt sick for very long?" No one had told me of her affliction and now I was here, I wanted to know.

The older man paused. His fingers tugged at his thin grey beard and then he glanced up at me. "You were not told?"

"Told what?" Did all Germans keep secrets?

"*Fräulein* Bergman was not sick, no, indeed. She was walking in the gardens, and they believe she took a nasty fall. Unfortunately, it was decided that as she fell, her head struck a large, jagged rock. By the time she was found it was too late. It was a sudden, tragic accident."

"That is terrible," I said.

"*Ja*, most unfortunate. But she is at peace now." He smiled. "*Fräulein* Rutherford, please be so kind as to sign these documents where indicated so that we may finalise everything? I shall be in contact with your solicitor in London, and between us, we shall complete all the necessary work and make the changes needed."

I signed my name on several papers and passed them back. I observed him as he placed them with the others. *Herr* Vogel looked like he needed a good meal. He was scrawny, and his large nose and bushy hair did nothing to improve his appearance.

"Where did you learn English?" I asked. "You speak it so well."

He smiled, and his face changed as though lit from within. "Ah, I am not unlike you, *Fräulein* Rutherford, in that my parentage is of two countries. My own mother was from Southampton. She taught me English, and we visited her family every summer for many years."

"That explains it." I said as I rose from the table.

The lawyer closed his briefcase with a snap and then stood. "I shall be in contact with you when I have more to report," he said. "Please think about your plans over the next few days and do not hesitate to send word if there is anything you require."

"*Danke für all deine hilfe,*" I said, thanking him for his help. He stopped at my use of the language.

"*Es ist meine Pflicht,*" he replied politely. And he was right, it was his duty to take care of these matters.

After *Herr* Vogel left the room, I wandered over to the window and stared out at the viridian front lawn which reached as far as the eye could see. I was filled with a sense of loss so strong it caught me by surprise. My parents were dead. Now I was aware there had been an uncle and an aunt, also gone, neither who I had seen or heard of. I felt robbed. Why had Mother never spoken of her family? It made no sense whatsoever. And if she did visit Lorelei Lodge as the lawyer insisted, why had she not brought me to her childhood home and introduced me to everyone?

It was infuriating. Though my life up to this point had been quite solitary, never had I felt more alone than I did at this precise moment.

Tears pricked my eyes, and I took a deep breath. Father had never countenanced crying and consequently I had been trained to keep my emotions tightly bound at all times. But for some reason I did not feel in complete control of myself.

I needed fresh air and some time to think. My life, which had once been so predictable had suddenly changed directions. I must consider all my options very carefully before picking a path to take.

I rang the bell to summon Joan. For now, I would start with the path leading away from the lodge.

Chapter Two

THE FRESH AIR WAS a welcome tonic when I stepped out and ventured around to the side of the building. As I walked, I studied my mother's home and found it ironic that the building itself was bright, welcoming and with the artistic flavour of its design, gaudy. Yet in contrast, the grounds were unimaginative. There were no flowerbeds, no ornamental bushes. Just a vast expanse of neatly trimmed grass, framed by the thick pine forest.

I turned onto a path running behind the lodge, then, halfway along, veered onto another leading away so that the building now lay behind me. Here the lawn narrowed, and the forest encroached yet was neatly dissected by the pathway.

In the near distance I spotted the back of the Saffron Palace, or the *Safranpalast* as it was called. Joan had told me all about it as I dressed for my walk. Much to her delight, Dieter enjoyed practicing his English, and it was from him she had gleaned a few facts about our temporary home.

Lorelei Lodge was originally built as the hunting lodge for the residents of the Saffron Palace in the previous century. From my vantage point the palace was significant in size, even though I could only see the rear of the building. Judging by the style of it, at first impression I assumed the architect was likely the same as the lodge's, so alike in design were they. But there all similarities ended, for the palace was exactly that…a grand palace.

The building was of a soft yellow hue and to my eye, every bit as large as Buckingham Palace. Though I could not see details, the ornate quality and character of the place was emphasised by its various spires and multiple towers. I was enthralled with the view, and marvelling at how many windows I could see, when there came a deep, menacing growl.

I froze. Then turned, terrified I may have encountered a bear or a wolf. But what I beheld looked like the evil offspring of both.

Standing not ten feet away from me was the largest hound I had ever laid eyes upon. The beast stood taller than my waist, its jet-black coat shining in the bright sunlight. Its massive head looked directly at me, its fierce jaws gaped while its pointed ears stood erect. The growling continued. I fought for composure and struggled whether to call out for help or just run for my life, when, much to my horror, another beast emerged from the trees and joined its companion. Now I faced two of them, though the second one remained silent and contemplated me.

When there came another sound of movement from the trees, I began to feel ill. Dear God, were there three of these despicable monsters come to maul me?

"Frido, Sascha, *komm jetz zu mir!*"

Thank goodness, it was a man. Relief flooded over me as he strode briskly in my direction. At his curt command, both animals bounded away, going directly to his side. I did not move but stood rooted to the spot with the remnants of my fear slowly dissipating as the stranger approached.

"Guten Morgen. Es tut mir leid, dass meine hunde sie erschreckt haben. Sie sind wirchlich sanfte kreaturen."

I understood his apology and that he said his dogs were harmless, but I did not let on. I said nothing—still shaken. Who was this person?

The man stared at me, waiting for my response. His bearing regal, his posture tall and straight, he was a striking fellow indeed. With dark brown hair, a close shaved beard and moustache, his thick lashed eyes currently look puzzled at my inability to say anything.

I gathered my thoughts. "The dogs took me by surprise."

"Oh," he said, switching to English. "You are British. I was apologizing for my dogs startling you. They really are not vicious animals, but they can be frightening if you don't know them."

His use of the language was exceptionally good. There was the trace of an American accent in his pronunciation. But I still bristled at his casual tone regarding the devil dogs. "I will have to take your word for it, sir. Though it is difficult to believe after having that one," I pointed accusingly to the larger of the two, "growling at me like I was to be his dinner."

The warmth in the man's brown eyes faded. He regarded me with a frown. "Again, my apologies. Frido would not have touched you. He was trying to keep you in one place to protect me as I was close by. Yet I can understand your being scared." He reached down and patted the guilty dog's huge head.

Had I not been so rattled, I might have appreciated the man's physique, admired the straight nose, and generous mouth visible through the facial hair. With two sentinels at his side, he looked every bit the master.

"Then I must take your word for it," I said, still annoyed. "Am I to expect an encounter with them the next time I take a walk?"

His brow furrowed. "This is where they live, *Fräulein*. Where else should they go?"

"That I cannot answer," I snapped. "Yet I also live here. Where do you suggest I take my exercise?"

Comprehension washed across his expression and his irritation instantly disappeared. "You are the new owner of Lorelei Lodge? Forgive me, I did not realise." He took a step closer, holding out a hand. "Allow me to introduce myself. Maximillian von Brandt. I am a neighbour."

Reluctantly I took the proffered hand. "Ingrid Rutherford."

"Marta's daughter?" he enquired.

"Yes."

"Then I am pleased to meet you. I met your mother on several occasions. Though I did not know her well, she and my own *mutter* were lifelong friends. Welcome to *Linnenbrink*. Is this your first visit to Lorelei Lodge?"

"Yes. Until recently, I did not even know of its existence."

His dark brows drew together. "Your mother never spoke of her home?"

"Very little. I knew she came from the area but was unaware she had family still living. This has all been a great surprise." I did not mention I had no knowledge of Mother's annual visits.

"How unfortunate you were never told of them.

The Bergmans have been here almost as long as my own family." He chuckled. "As a matter of fact, for many generations, our families were serious rivals. It began when one of your forebears was clever enough to win Lorelei Lodge in a wager. Something that rankled my family for decades."

"A wager? You mean gambling?"

"*Ja*. The Bergmans won your home from a bet on a horse race. Their horse, Lorelei, won. Hence the name. My family never quite came to terms with it. Of course, that was many years ago."

I frowned. The tale sounded ridiculous. "I don't quite understand," I remarked impatiently. "If the lodge was taken away from your relatives, where did they end up living?"

This time he gave me a broad smile and I was stunned how it brought such light to his face. He regarded me for a moment as though he inspected my face too. His eyes settled on the mole next to my mouth, and then swung back to meet my gaze.

"You misunderstand me. The von Brandts did not live at Lorelei. It was the hunting lodge situated in our grounds." He gestured to the magnificent palace I had admired earlier. "That is where I live."

HE WAS A BARON! Upon my return, I quickly sought out Joan and instructed her to question Dieter at the first opportunity. By luncheon, she had the entire tale.

Maximillian's story was indeed fact. The von Brandt family had lived in the *Safranpalast* for the better part of two-hundred years. There had been competitive bets placed upon horses owned by each family. We, the Bergmans, had won the bet, and the lodge became ours. Joan also remarked that the von Brandt family had spent years trying to purchase the property back. It was located so close to the palace, after all, and there was the issue with appeasing the von Brandts' wounded pride. Yet seemingly none of my family were willing to part with it.

I couldn't help wondering if the von Brandts were the buyers *Herr* Vogel had spoken of? How could I feel the same loyalty my predecessors felt when I was the last of a line I knew nothing about?

First things first. I intended to spend at least a month in Germany before returning to London. Surely there would be no need for me to keep this property when I lived in another country. Financially, I was comfortable, thanks to my father. Undoubtedly, with the sale of the lodge and Mother's money, my future welfare was well provided for. Yet, for the time being I wanted nothing more than to have some respite, perhaps do some sightseeing, and contemplate what I would do with the next part of my life. It was the first time I had any say in my future at all.

AFTER LUNCHEON, I DECIDED it was time to explore the lodge. I considered calling Joan to accompany me, but then remembered she had gone into *Linnenbrink* Village with *Herr* Metzger. I would be fine going alone.

I was already familiar with the ground floor. It consisted of the drawing room, a dining room and a study, all which I had been using. I had visited the kitchen, situated towards the back of the lodge, with access to the vegetable and herb gardens.

The second floor's wide hallway off the grand

staircase opened onto a massive ballroom, taking up the entire floor. As I entered the room, my breath caught in my throat.

The three-tiered crystal chandelier hanging in the ceiling's centre was as large as a carriage. As sunlight streamed through French windows, it caught the prisms of hundreds of crystal teardrops, showering the walls in a blanket of twinkling stars. It was magical.

The walls were decorated with ornate swirls of flamboyant gold paint, as majestic and whimsical as Versailles itself, with the exception of the front facing wall, which was multiple sets of double glass doors, the breadth of the lodge. Peering out, I saw they led to a huge balcony, with steps either side leading down to the ground floor. This I had admired from the carriage when I first arrived.

I turned back to survey the room. It was magnificent. I could easily picture a summer's evening, the doors flung wide-open to the night while an orchestra played for people dancing the night away. Sighing, I shrugged off the thought and continued my exploration.

The third floor was where my room was located, but as yet I had ventured no further. Now, I counted three other doors along the corridor and a set at the very end of the hall. I methodically looked around each of the bedrooms, finding them similar to my own. Unlike the ballroom, the bedrooms were more utilitarian, with less thought to decoration. This surprised me in comparison to the rest of the house. The furniture was Rococo in style, yet there was much less attention paid to bright colours and accessories.

When I reached the end of the hallway and the last

set of doors, I opened them expecting to find another bedroom, but instead discovered a schoolroom of sorts. Three small wooden chairs were tucked under a long table set in the middle of the room. On one wall hung a large, framed map of the world. There was no other furniture in the room, but I spotted something tucked into a shadowed corner and went to see what it was. As I reached the spot and saw the object, a strange constriction gripped my throat.

It was just an old rocking horse. Its off-white paint chipped and scratched, its mane, thready and thin. The saddle was worn and cracked, as though it had been frequently used. Again, I felt the rush through my mind as I had when I noticed the scent of pine on the wind.

I lifted a strand of the mane and held it in my fingers. It felt wiry and coarse, and ...familiar? I let go and my hand tightened into a fist. Did I have a horse like this as a child? If so, I had no recollection of it. With one last dismissive glance around, I retraced my steps and went back downstairs to the drawing room.

MY THIRD MORNING IN Germany and my second at Lorelei found me tired and irritable. Joan commented upon it when she brought me my cup of tea and pulled open the bedroom curtains.

She came to stand by my bed, her hands resting on ample hips. "You look a bit grumpy this mornin' if I do say so, miss." She indicated the teacup. "You'll feel better after a cuppa."

"Thank you, Joan." I sat up and reached for the drink.

"You've been dreamin' again, haven't you?"

I nodded. "Every night since leaving London. But

last night, the dream was far more vivid than usual." Joan knew all about my dreams as I had suffered with them for many years.

"That's not good," she said. "You're not gettin' enough rest an' it's catchin' up with you."

She was right. I did feel terribly drained. "Perhaps I shall rest for an hour or two this afternoon." I flung back my covers. "This morning I am meant to be 'receiving' should anyone wish to come by and meet me."

"Ooh," Joan said, fluffing the pillows on my vacated bed. "I'll bet you'll have a right bunch of nosey parkers lined up to take a *butchers* at you! The locals are bound to be curious who the new owner is."

She was right, of course. Though *Prinzenstadt* itself was several miles away, *Linnenbrink* Village was nearby, and I had no idea how vastly populated it might be. "Hopefully, none of the callers will speak English, and they'll all go away," I remarked.

I WAS WRONG IN my estimations. It had not occurred to me that affluent Germans likely travelled across Europe regularly and therefore had a strong command of my native tongue. Before an hour had passed, there had been seven callers, all women of middle age, and one hard to separate from the other. Dour matrons wearing dour clothing with barely a hint of lace at their sleeves.

Not only was I interrogated and bombarded by a multitude of heavily accented questions, I was also studied in such a fashion I could have been a piece of horseflesh. The manner of this German culture was so very stoic, so serious, that in comparison, I seemed lighthearted and flippant, though no one in England would believe that to be an accurate description of me.

My current guest was a grandmotherly woman in appearance, by the name of *Frau* Schneider. Short and stout, with bird-like intelligent eyes, she surveyed me with a frown.

"You look like your *mutter*," she commented. "Now that Marta, she vas a good girl. I see you haf the same mole on the face."

I took another sip of coffee from the demitasse cup. "Were you well acquainted with my mother, Frau Schneider?"

She sniffed. "*Ein wenig*, a little. Marta vas a pretty girl vith many suitors. She could haf picked a German husband instead of running off to England."

This rankled me. I set down my cup with a *clink*. "Perhaps. Yet she did not choose a German man. She fell in love with my father. Though I doubt it had much to do with his nationality." My tone was curt, and the older woman raised her eyebrows as though offended. I cared not. Frau Schneider was not the only woman in the room with German blood.

She put down her cup and abruptly got to her feet. I rang the bell on the table beside me and within seconds, Fritz appeared in the room.

"Fritz, please see Frau Schneider out."

With a disapproving last look at me, the woman left the room and I sank back on my chair in relief. I glanced around at the ornate décor, the brightly coloured furnishings, and wondered at the irony of such a light-hearted place being inhabited by gloomy individuals—myself included. If my guests were any indication of my aunt's personality, she must have been a dull and conservative person.

The Secret of Lorelei Lodge

Steps sounded out in the hall and inwardly I groaned. *Not another one.* The door opened after a knock, and Fritz stepped into the room.

"*Fräulein* Susanna Koppelman," he announced. I got to my feet as a rush of pale blue silk swept past him and entered the drawing room, bringing with her the scent of lilacs. No dull widow here in her black shrouds, but a young, strikingly lovely, blonde woman of about my own age.

"Miss Rutherford," she declared in a noticeable American accent. "I am beyond thrilled to meet you. The entire town is talking about you, and I just had to come and see what all the fuss was about." She sank down onto the sofa and settled her skirts.

I nodded at Fritz who quietly departed to fetch fresh coffee.

"Miss Koppelman. Please call me Ingrid. It is a pleasure to meet you. May I ask…"

She waved a gloved hand at me. "Oh, you won't have heard of me—I don't know any of your family. Saul and me, oh, Saul's my brother by the by. Why, we are tourists really. He's here on some tedious business with the Baron, and I am utterly bored out of my wits." She took a quick breath. "I've never been around such a glum group of folk in my life. I mean, back home in New York, there are plenty of unhappy people one sees regularly, but all you have to do is take a walk on Fifth Avenue and there's always someone with a smile. But who knew Germans were quite so…dull?"

She finally stopped speaking and I had a moment to respond. I did so by emitting a small laugh which surprised me more than it did her.

"Miss Koppelman."

"Susanna, please."

"Susanna. I am terribly sorry you are not enjoying your stay. I'll admit, the German people are quite reserved, but it is their nature to be cautious with others, at least until they get to know you better. Perhaps you are not frequenting the right places?"

She pulled a sardonic expression which still did not alter the prettiness of her face. Susanna Koppelman was fetching. With her fair hair and complexion, blue eyes, bow-lips and naturally rosy cheeks, she was everything I was not.

Fritz came in bearing a fresh pot of coffee which he placed on the table before me.

"*Danke*," I said in thanks. After a lingering look at my visitor, he retreated from the room. I determined it would not be unusual for men to study the American. She had one of those faces where a second look was necessary because her natural beauty was uncommon. Susanna, however, appeared not to notice as it was likely a frequent occurrence.

I poured the coffee and passed it to her. She accepted it with thanks, took a sip, and then placed it back on the table. Her bright eyes looked directly at me. "Miss Rutherford, or may I call you Ingrid?"

I did not have a chance to reply for she continued.

"I know you have only just arrived, but surely you must have noticed by the visitors you had today that there seems to be no young people living locally. Consequently, there's no one to talk to. I have made one acquaintance at our hotel in the village, which is merely a half mile from here. But they don't understand a word of English and just stare at me like I'm speaking nonsense. Honestly! I have been to visit the Baron in the palace. Oh, my goodness. Have you been there yet? I suppose you probably have as you are neighbours after all. He is quite an interesting fellow, don't you think? Of course, he and my brother Saul spend inordinate amounts of time chatting about mundane subjects like industry and steel and topics of that nature—they are so terribly dull. I find it tragic that the Baron has no sisters. I should like very much to get to know a German nobleman though. It would be a wonderful tale to tell when we go back to New York. Don't you think?"

I felt out of breath for the woman. I don't believe I had ever been around a person who spoke so quickly about so many subjects in one sentence. Susanna was a likeable sort, but different than anyone I had ever encountered.

"Susanna, I have not been to the *Safranpalast*. This is my first time in Germany. My mother was born here but never brought me to visit. I am only here now because my relative died and as I seem to be the last of the line, there is business to conduct. I have been here only three days, and other than my visitors today, including yourself, I haven't met anyone but the servants. Wait, I lie, I did meet the Baron yesterday out in the grounds. But that was the first time I had ever set eyes on the gentleman."

"Oh," she gave a little sigh. "He's rather a handsome fellow, don't you think? But just like all the other Germans, he is so very serious. I have tried to engage him in conversation countless times, but he never appears to be that interested. It is most tiresome. At home, I'm never at a loss for male companionship. What did you think of him? Did you find him dashing?"

I cleared my throat. "Not really. I was far too concerned his massive dogs were about to make me their next meal. Fortunately, I was quite safe."

"Are they not terrifying to behold? But they really are quite gentle creatures once you get used to them. Saul refuses to let me have dogs in our apartments at home. He says they are filthy beasts, and they bring in fleas and other nasty things from the outdoors. Of course, you haven't met Saul, have you? I shall have to rectify that immediately. Perhaps you could join us for dinner this evening at our hotel?" Her face lit up with excitement. "Oh, do say you will, Miss Ruther…Ingrid. It would be refreshing to have good company for a change, and Saul would enjoy it as well. I know he would!"

I hesitated. "Susanna, you are kind to ask, but I'm not certain I feel comfortable accepting. After all, we've just met, and I have never even laid eyes upon your brother."

"Please don't refuse," she begged. "My brother is very friendly, and as it will be at the hotel it wouldn't be formal at all. Besides, it would be good for you to see something of the village—although there's not much to see except for our hotel to be truthful. There are several little shops, but I don't go in them as the main road is always quite muddy and Saul encourages me to either stay in the hotel or take the carriage and go into town. You must have seen the town? What do you think of the Opera House? Is it not magnificent?"

Good grief, my head was practically spinning. How to stop this woman from prattling on? I determined the best solution would be to agree upon meeting her this evening. I told her as much, and she looked delighted.

"That is simply marvellous! I cannot wait to tell Saul we've met. In fact, I should dash right now and prepare. There is only one hotel in the village, so your coachman will know where to bring you. Let us meet at seven o'clock this evening."

Susanna got to her feet, and I followed suit. Then stepping forward, she reached across towards me, and, before I could stop her, took my hands in hers and gave them both a little squeeze.

"Truly, I cannot thank you enough for accepting my invitation. It will be wonderful to have your company this evening. I shall see you shortly."

Before I could ring for Fritz to escort her out, Susanna opened the door herself and marched down the hall. I watched her leave, still somewhat numb from our encounter. It was as though a little whirlwind had come into the house, stirred things up, and whisked right back out of the front door. Her energy, and the scent of lilac lingered in the atmosphere. As I contemplated my thoughts, Joan came down the stairs. She stopped when she saw me.

"You all right, miss?"

"Yes," I replied. "But I shall need your help. It appears I have a dinner engagement this evening."

My maid gave me a cheeky grin. "About bloody time. There's as much excitement in this place as there is in a bloomin' funeral parlour."

Chapter Three

HERR METZGER DROVE ME into the village that evening. I contemplated how unusual it was for me to socialise with my peers. In London, Father often had businessmen and their wives attend dinners at our home, but they were generally even older than him. I often found myself sitting awkwardly between matronly women whose children were around my own age.

Tonight would be different. Though I seldom became excited about anything, there was an underlying sense of anticipation noticeably present. Joan dressed me in a mourning gown of black silk. She'd insisted I break the monotony of the colour by wearing my mother's set of dropped emerald earrings with a matching necklace. The jewellery belonged to my maternal grandmother and were Mother's favourites. Joan made a thick braid with my hair and coiled it, pinning it up, much in the style of the German ladies.

The weather had turned cooler, as the sun sank on the horizon. I carried a black cashmere shawl to wear inside the carriage but would leave it there until my return home.

The *Linnenbrink* Hotel, was indeed the only large building in the small village. Once the horses came to a stop, *Herr* Metzger alighted to assist me from the cab. He hurried in front of me to open the door of the hotel, while I kept my distance, for his pungent aroma was still noticeable.

My arrival was anticipated. For when I entered the lobby of the hotel, the concierge ushered me into a busy dining room, astonishingly elegant for a rural location like *Linnenbrink*. I found the elaborate decor of statuary, chandeliers, and plush carpeting unexpected as I followed him through a maze of tables, aware of the eyes following my progress. The strangers in this dining room had the advantage of knowing who I was, while I knew not a soul.

Eventually, the concierge reached a set of open doors to a private room and gestured for me to enter. Here waited Susanna. Before I could utter a sound, she leapt to her feet to greet me, while I became aware there were two others at the table.

The first gentleman got to his feet. Judging by his features, which were so like the young American woman's, I gathered this would be her brother, Saul. When the other person stood, I was astounded to recognise Baron Maximilian von Brandt, who I had met so recently.

Being somewhat nervous meeting Susanna's brother, with the Baron also present, my confidence faltered at the prospect of spending time with people I barely knew. I confess to being rather overwhelmed.

"Here we are, everyone. This is my new friend, Ingrid Rutherford," said Susanna merrily. "Saul, you will have to be very polite as you have not met, but Max can be himself as he and Ingrid know each other and are neighbours." She tugged my hand and led me to sit across from the baron, while she took a seat opposite her brother.

The fair-headed gentleman gave me a welcoming

smile. "It is a pleasure to meet you, Miss Rutherford. My sister has spoken of little else this afternoon but you. I am Saul Koppelman, and I thank you for joining us this evening." His introduction came after we were already seated so I could not shake his hand, but we nodded at one another. Good looks ran in their family, for Saul had the same bright blue eyes and engaging face as his sister. Both Americans had an ease about them, a casualness in direct contrast to my strict and rigid upbringing. I was unused to mixing with commodious people. In actual fact, I was unused to mixing with anyone at all.

"*Guten abend, Fräulein* Rutherford. It is nice to see you once again." The baron gave me a polite nod while his dark eyes assessed me.

"Good evening, Baron," I replied.

"Oh golly," laughed Susanna. "You can't call him that when it's just us, for I shall giggle every time." Her eyes sparkled with gaiety. "We call him Max, and you must do the same. We shall all be on first name terms, or it will be such a bore."

"And there you have it," Max said. "Susie has spoken and so it must be." He smiled at our hostess, and I was pleased to see it appeared sincere.

"Good," she said. "That's settled. Shall we order dinner?"

THE FOOD WAS SURPRISINGLY good. We ate *Wienerschnitzel* with fresh vegetables and *spaetzle*, which were the dumplings my mother had Cook make every year on my name day. For our dessert, there was a delicious streusel cake with cherries, served with rich creamy sauce.

Having consumed a glass of wine, I was finally beginning to relax. Once the table was cleared of empty plates, we each enjoyed a small glass of schnapps, flavoured with pears. It was delicious, but I sipped it carefully as it was my first time drinking strong alcohol and I found it a little potent.

Our conversation remained light during our meal and thoroughly monopolized by Susanna. At least she was entertaining, though she often rambled along, and there were many occasions when she had us all laughing—even me.

"How long do you plan upon staying at Lorelei Lodge, Ingrid?" asked Saul, leaning back in his chair.

I studied him while considering my answer. His dark blue evening jacket complimented his tousled blond hair, giving his features a boyish quality. His complexion was probably fair, but his skin had the healthy glow of sun exposure. Saul exuded health and vitality.

"A few weeks," I replied. "But nothing is definite. And you? How long will you and your sister remain in Germany?"

"It feels as though we shall never leave," whined Susanna. "I thought we would be touring all of Europe by now. That's why I tagged along. If Saul had told me it would all be about stupid work, I shouldn't have come. After all, one of my friends is getting married while we are here, and I was supposed to be—"

"Please," begged her brother. "No more complaining, or Ingrid will wish she had stayed home tonight." He looked back at me. "I expect we shall be here for another month until Max and I conclude our business."

My curiosity got the better of me. "If you do not mind me asking, what line of business are you in?"

"Steel," said Max, meeting my eye. "Saul is part of a group of investors in New York, and he is here to invest in one of my companies."

"How utterly boring," said Susanna.

"What do you make with this steel?" I asked.

"We do not produce anything. We manufacture the steel to export to other countries as well as selling here in *Deutschland*. We have business contracts with many American and British companies."

"Max's steel works are the most efficient I have seen in my career," Saul remarked. "At this rate, I believe he, along with others in the country, will eventually out produce both Great Britain and the United States in steel production. I want to make sure that Koppelman steel is part of that growth."

"Honestly, Saul. I cannot believe you're ruining our pleasant evening talking about work. You and Max can speak of this all day long tomorrow. I insist you stop immediately."

Her brother rolled his eyes. "Oh, all right. I'm sorry."

"She has a point," said Max. "We should discuss more entertaining topics."

"Like what?" Saul asked.

"The opera!" Susanna announced. "There will be a performance next week." She looked over to me. "Ingrid, you must come with us. We would have such a wonderful time. I have only ever been to one opera in New York, and it was so interesting. I liked the music, well sort of, but the acting was splendid, and the costumes were gorgeous. We can all go together and perhaps Saul could reserve a box, which would be even better than when we went back home, as we sat in the public area and there was this annoying man in front of me who had such a big head."

"I would like that, thank you. Do you know what opera will be performed?" Father had disliked the opera therefore I had never attended one, but I had read much about them in the London newspapers and this idea appealed to me.

"Carmen," stated Max bluntly. His expression had turned serious, and a muscle ticked in his cheek. He really was a striking man. His dark features and serious countenance were in stark contrast to Saul, with his American charm, ready smile, and happy disposition. Max's eyes locked with mine as he caught me staring. I could not read what he was thinking, and I was the first to look away.

"Then it is agreed," announced Susanna. "Saul will purchase tickets at his first opportunity."

"No need for that," said Max. "My family have a box at the theatre, and you are welcome as our guests."

Susanna gave a squeal of utter delight, but I watched the baron's face. Though his tone was friendly and easy going, his expression was definitely pensive. Something had changed his mood at the mention of the opera, and I wondered what it was.

"Max, shall you invite your brother? He should join us," said Saul.

"You have a brother?" It seemed I was to remain ignorant of everyone's family, not just my own.

"Yes. I have three. But two of them live elsewhere. Wolfgang resides at *der Safranpalast*, as I do."

"Max, I insist you ask him." Susanna's blue eyes

shone. "Wolfgang is so much fun. Oh, he's nice and all, so very amusing and witty. His English isn't as good as Max's, but then he hasn't lived in America like his brother did. I often think Max sounds like a New Yorker sometimes…" she continued with her opinion while I remained engrossed in the study of the man sitting across the table from me. Why was I so compelled to watch him? I do not know. But since Mother died, I had become a keen observer of people, and specifically, their behaviour. It must stem from many years living under the control of my father. My incessant need to constantly read his mood so that I might not anger him unnecessarily.

When Susanna finally stopped talking, the gentlemen rose to leave the dining room and step outside to smoke. Susanna and I remained, and she regaled me with many stories of her life in New York while I half-listened. Though she was slightly annoying, one could not help but like the woman. She was a little bee, constantly buzzing and inquisitive, and never still.

At length, the men returned. I glanced at the time and realised *Herr* Metzger would already have come to collect me. I was tired from many restless nights of sleep, and I thanked my hosts and bade everyone a good night. Max insisted he escort me to the carriage, to which I did not object.

"Ingrid," he said as we walked through the hotel lobby and out into the evening. "Would you permit me to call upon you in the morning? There is a matter I should like to discuss with you."

We reached the carriage, and he opened the door. I felt the grasp of his hand, firm under my elbow as I got into the cab.

"Certainly," I answered.

"*Danke*. I will see you in the morning. *Gute Nacht*."

The carriage moved away. As we traversed the short distance from the village to the lodge, I wondered about the baron's request. Though I had little experience with men in my own age group, I knew a moment of pleasure that he showed an interest in speaking with me.

I sat back in my seat and reflected upon the evening. My life had always been so predictable. If it were a painting, it would be coloured in greys and browns. Yet in the space of a few days, I had met three new friends for dinner, had an invitation to my very first opera, and tomorrow would have a gentleman caller. My thoughts churned with a foreign sensation—was this excitement? At once I chided myself for being fanciful and silly. What did it matter that I met these people? Soon I would be gone back to London and a house that had never quite been a home.

THE NEXT MORNING, I awoke refreshed. My sleep had been dreamless for the first time in days, most likely due to the wine and schnapps I'd consumed at dinner. Joan had waited up for me last night, and she'd been most enthusiastic when I told her about my opera invitation. I also informed her the baron would be calling the next morning and asked that she help me dress for company.

After breakfast, I went into my aunt's study with a desire to read through some of the papers in her desk and learn about my mysterious family. I was unsure what records would have been kept, but perhaps births and deaths would be written down somewhere?

Rummaging through the desk drawers was unrewarding. I got up and walked over to one of the walls fitted with shelves and full of books. It occurred to me that families often kept a Bible, and there they often entered pertinent, familial information. I scanned the shelves but did not find a Bible, though there were several books I would be interested in reading at another time. Someone in this household had been an avid reader.

Glancing upwards, I noticed on the top shelf there were two thick books and what look like a framed daguerreotype. I could not quite reach that high, and I quickly glanced around the room to see if there was something I could step on.

I spotted a small end table next to a leather armchair and dragged it over to the shelves. When I stepped onto the table I hoped my weight would not be too much for it. I still could not see the surface of the shelf, but I could at least now reach it. That it had been untouched was obvious by the amount of dust that came away on my fingers. Although the maids worked hard to keep this house clean, it would be difficult for them to reach this high up, even with a feather duster.

I grasped the framed picture and stepped down to place it on the desk. It was a faded picture of a young girl who looked much like me. The same black hair, the same mole next to her mouth. It was my mother. My heart grew heavy seeing her as a youthful person, with her entire life before her. Little did she know how short it would be. I set the picture down upon the desk.

I went back to retrieve the books. The first was so

heavy I almost dropped it. It too went on the desk with a thud. As I lifted down the second book I lost my grip, and it slipped through my arms as I navigated my way off the table. In an effort to stop the book from falling, I wobbled, lost my balance, the table tipped, and both the book and I landed on the floor with a resounding bang, just as the study door opened to reveal Baron Maximilian von Brandt.

He rushed towards me. "Ingrid, let me help you." He leant down and put his arms underneath mine. While my cheeks burned with embarrassment, I grasped his shoulders and he pulled me to my feet. Then he bent to pick up the hefty book and set it on the desk next to the other, giving me a moment to compose myself.

"Did you hurt yourself?" he asked.

"Only my pride," I said. But I was sore. I had landed awkwardly, and my left ankle throbbed.

"Perhaps I can escort you to the drawing room? There you can sit comfortably?"

I nodded, and then accepted his arm yet again so he could lead me out of the study. Max was much taller than I, my head barely coming to his shoulders. It was comforting having him to lean on as I could barely place any weight on my throbbing ankle.

We encountered Joan in the hallway. "I heard a loud noise," she said. Her small eyes raked across me. "What has happened, miss? Are you all right?"

"I'm fine, Joan. But could you ask Fritz to bring refreshments to the drawing room?"

Joan's gaze flickered from my face to stare directly at the baron as though she was uncertain about leaving me in his care. I had forgotten she had not yet met Max.

"I hurt my ankle, Joan. The baron is helping me." I

gave her a hard glare so that she would stop fussing.

Reluctantly she nodded and left in search of the butler.

In the drawing room I sank down on the sofa, not even protesting when Max lifted my feet gently to get the weight off both ankles. After which, he sat down in an armchair facing me. He was dressed casually in a brown wool jacket and trousers. His appearance was well-groomed, and he had not a hair out of place.

I wondered if the hulking giant dogs lingered outside.

"Why on earth were you climbing up on a table, Ingrid? You should have sent for one of the footmen to help you retrieve those books."

"You're right," I acknowledged. "But I was impatient and not thinking clearly." I dusted off the skirt of my dress. "No harm was done, but I thank you for your help." I summoned my courage. "What was it you wanted to see me about?"

His dark eyes met mine. There were shadows beneath them. "It is a matter of business, actually. Regarding Lorelei. I realise you have only been here for a few days, but I wondered if you are considering selling the lodge when you return to London?"

Disappointment washed over me. I was foolish. What had I expected the man to want from me? I examined my thoughts quickly. I was not prone to fancy. I read no romantic novels and never daydreamed. So why did I feel 'different' when in Max's company? I barely knew the man. I shrugged it off and promised myself not to be so fanciful again.

He waited patiently for me to answer.

"It is certainly possible I might sell," I replied, my

voice tight with formality. "But I have not come to a final decision as of yet. I take it you have an interest in the place?"

The door opened and Fritz entered with a tray. He set it down on the table by the sofa and retreated. Once he had gone, I leaned forward to pour, but Max held up a hand.

"Allow me." He poured us both a cup and passed one to me.

"Yes. I have long desired to purchase the place, mainly to return the palace and its grounds to its original status."

"Ah," I said. "The victor who finally succeeds where no other has before. You would be a hero in the annuls of your family history, reuniting the properties once again."

"You mock me?" His eyes were piercing.

"Forgive me," I said apologetically. "I could not resist. I will certainly inform you of my decision once it is made. I have no qualms about returning the lodge to your family from whence it came. It is unnatural for me to have any loyalty to the Bergmans. I did not know them, and they apparently had no desire to become acquainted with me."

"*Danke*, Ingrid. You are most kind. Yet I hear such bitterness in your tone. You are, perhaps angry with your parents about this?"

He drank his coffee and returned the cup to the tray. I liked his facial hair, the trimmed beard and moustache which added such character to his face.

I grew bold. "Yes, I am annoyed that this place was kept a secret from me. To be frank, I wonder at the reason. I have no family on my father's side, and it grieves me to think I missed out by not knowing my aunt."

Max's expression changed subtly.

"What have I said?" I declared. "You were thinking something while I spoke."

He raised an eyebrow. "I shall be forthright, so please do not take offence. But your great-aunt, Gisela Bergman, was not such a nice person. Though I was never the target, there were many who considered her unkind."

"I see." At his mention of unkindness, my father's image filled my head.

"It might explain your mother's reluctance to expose you to a relationship with the woman. But I am sorry if it saddens you."

"Thank you. I suppose my sorrow is that I no longer have any family, and I should've liked knowing I was not entirely alone in the world. And here you are, one of four sons. I was surprised to hear of your siblings last night. Tell me, do you or your brothers have family?" I was unsure if Max was married. He certainly was old enough, though I saw no ring on his finger and he had joined us for dinner unaccompanied.

"*Ja*. Günther lives in Switzerland and has a new son. Kurt attends university in Bonn. My brother Wolfgang is married to Katja, and they have a boy, Jakob."

"And you?"

Max let out a deep sigh. "*Ja*. I am also married. Though there are no children." His voice wavered slightly.

I did not comment as disappointment swept over me, taking me aback. Why did I care about the man's marital status? It was an unsettling thought. I quickly posed another question. "Then I hope to meet your wife very soon. Will she join us at the opera next week?"

"She will certainly be there," he said with a bored tone. "My wife is Valentina Cavaletti, the Prima Donna of the performing company. I am married to a woman considered to be the best mezzo-soprano in the world."

Chapter Four

MY REPLY CAUGHT IN my throat. Why was I suddenly deflated? Max had not misrepresented himself. It was I who had made ridiculous assumptions.

In my muddled, bereaved state of mind, I'd distracted myself with notions of a silly schoolgirl's crush—a novel enterprise indeed. Something about the baron had kindled a part of me I had not realise existed. Now, I would ensure it returned from whence it came.

"That is marvellous," I forced a smile. "I shall look forward to hearing your wife sing. I had no idea."

His eyes met mine and held. "I do not often talk about her."

I quickly looked away, disliking his tone. I admired Max and did not care to bear witness to him displaying a lack of respect for his wife.

"Let me explain," he said, refilling his coffee. "Valentina and I are estranged. We have been for the past three years. I bear her no malice, but there is no love lost between us either. I choose not to speak of her because she no longer exists in my daily life and routine. My wife keeps her own apartments in *der Safranpalast* when she is not touring, and seldom do our paths cross. This arrangement suits us both. Valentina desires independence. She even refuses the title of Baroness." He gave a derisive chuckle. "She prefers retaining her own name as it is synonymous with her esteemed career. Therefore, my mother remains the current Baroness von Brandt."

I was astounded by his explanation. What a peculiar way of conducting a marriage. And what exactly did Max mean by estranged? I was not about to ask.

"Now you know a little of my life, perhaps you would like to tell me something about your own? I understand you have lived in London with your father. We were saddened to hear of your mother's death years ago. My mother was heart-broken, and I know it must have been very difficult for you."

"Yes, it was. Mother was a gentle soul. I learned much from her example. She spent a great deal of her time at a local orphanage where she was their benefactress. Mother always said that we lacked for nothing, therefore it was our duty to share our prosperity with others less fortunate."

"Marta Bergman was a remarkable woman. I wish I had known her better and not just when I was a child. My own mother is of a similar nature. She used to champion those with nothing. No wonder the two were such good friends."

A sudden thought struck me. "Would it be possible for me to meet your mother? I should like nothing more than to speak with someone who knew mine well. It has been so many years since she died, and I miss hearing her name spoken."

Max smiled kindly. "It grieves me to tell you this, but the baroness is not a well woman. She suffers with a malady of the mind that sometimes afflicts people of a certain age. Mother is only in her seventies, but her mind betrays her often and she is now housebound.

That does not mean you cannot meet her, Ingrid. Far from it. She enjoys receiving visitors and I know she would like you very well. But I do not know how much she will remember of your mother for her memory is hazy. I don't want to see you disappointed. Let me speak with her nurse. We can arrange for you to come very soon. Also, if you have any interest I'll give you a short tour of my home while you're there. We have an extensive library in English as well as German, which you can use whenever you like."

"Thank you. That is very generous." I smiled at his effort to accommodate me. "If you can send word when an appropriate time would be to call, I shall look forward to it."

Max finished his drink and set the empty cup back on the tray. "I have taken up enough of your time for one day, Ingrid. Why don't you call for your maid and let her examine your ankle and ensure it is not swollen before you put your weight on it. Please do not hesitate to send for me if I can help. I can organise a physician to visit you if needed." He rose to his feet while I stayed put.

"Thank you so much, Max. I appreciate all your assistance."

"It was my pleasure. Good day to you." He smiled politely and left the room. I picked up the bell and rang for Jean. if I did not see to this blasted ankle, I wouldn't be going anywhere.

SUSANNA CALLED UPON ME two days later. I had done little as my ankle had proved tricky, but the swelling had finally subsided. She arrived in high spirits.

"Ingrid. I had to come and check on you after Max

told Saul about your accident. And I've also some gossip to share." She sat down in the armchair, her blonde hair a froth of ringlets around her face and her blue eyes bright with excitement. She glanced at my foot which lay elevated on a thick cushion. "Does it hurt much?"

"Not anymore," I replied.

"Mine did," she said quickly. "I once tripped over a tennis racquet that my friend left in the garden, and I twisted my ankle. It hurt like the dickens, I can tell you. Mama was so mad with me as I missed a very important ball the Goodwins were having. I was so upset because I had this beautiful silk dress…"

I listened for the next five minutes as Susanna relived her terrible memory. We were so different, she and I, yet we were both privileged in our comfortable upbringing—though I envied her having a sibling, and that her mother still lived.

As she prattled on, Fritz brought refreshments and left again, Susanna never stopping, even at his interruption. But by the time she had gone back to recounting her coming out ball, I had suffered all I could take.

"Susanna, what did you come to tell me?" I said when she finally took a breath.

A sly grin played about her pretty mouth. "It's about Max's wife."

"Valentina Cavaletti?" I said blandly.

Susanna's smile faded. "Oh," she pouted. "You already knew?"

I could have told her the opera singer's existence had intrigued me since Max had told me about her. That I had commissioned Joan to question Dieter about the matter but none of the servants were familiar with the singer. They were new to the lodge, hired from other towns which I found peculiar. My aunt must have been a difficult woman if the locals refused to work for her. "I know who Valentina is. But I know nothing about her," I replied.

The gleam came back into Susanna's eyes. "Well, it is a fascinating story. Fancy being married to a famous opera singer and not being allowed by your church to divorce. It is true." She delighted in her role as informant. "Saul did lots of checking before we conducted business with Max's family and made the long trip to Germany. Of course, he never spoke of the findings to me. But after our dinner the other night, I waited until Saul retired and then I snuck a peek at some of the notes he had in his briefcase—though he doesn't know I looked, or he'd be mad as a bear." She took a sip of her drink.

I waited quietly, knowing Susanna would need no prompting to continue.

"Max met Valentina in Florence and they must have fallen madly in love because they married young, and against the wishes of the von Brandts. Being the son and heir, Max was expected to marry into German nobility, and his parents were not pleased with his choice. But they married anyway, and then just as Valentina's career began to blossom she became with child. After their son was born, she spent little time at the palace as she was desperate to focus upon her operatic career after all her hard work and training."

"Max has a son?" I was flabbergasted.

Susanna's face became solemn, which I had not seen happen before. "I don't know any details because that part was brief in Saul's notes. But Max's son died in a riding accident three years ago. It doesn't say if this dreadful event caused their estrangement, or if that had already happened. All I read was that Nikolai was six years old and the apple of his father's eye. I have no idea where or how the accident took place, but it explains why there is something very different about Max. He's such a private person, and I understand it better now I know what he's been through. The poor man must have been heart-broken from the tragic loss of a child." She gave a sigh and then looked directly at me. "How did you learn of her identity? Honestly, the people here are so tight lipped they probably wouldn't give you directions if you were lost. If I hadn't been so nosy I'd still be in the dark. Max has never spoken a word about Valentina in my company. Though he'll have to say something when we go to the opera. After all, he can't pretend she's not his wife."

"Max called here two days ago. He arrived at the very moment I had this ridiculous mishap and hurt my ankle. He stayed and had coffee with me, and we chatted. I asked him about his brothers and if he had a big family, and that is when he told me he was married. There was no mention of a son. Though I am not surprised. It would be a very difficult topic to share with anybody. Least of all a stranger."

"Yet he mentioned Valentina's being with the operatic company performing Carmen?"

"He did. I must admit he did not seem overly pleased at the prospect."

"From what my brother says, Max spends little time in her company. Though her staying at the palace when she is here means they must encounter one another," said Susanna. "But he won't need to engage with her at the opera house. We will be up in the box watching the performance, after all. And it's not as if anyone is forcing him to go." She gave a conspiratorial grin directed at me. "I think our Max might be a little bit curious about you. He's never shown an interest in socialising since we arrived. He just attends meetings with my brother during the day. But he was very anxious to join us for dinner the other night once he knew you would be in attendance. And now he's even coming to the opera! You are having a positive effect on your neighbour, Ingrid."

"Nonsense," I said quickly, feeling warmth rush up my neck to my face. "Max is merely being polite because our families are connected historically. It seems our mothers were the best of friends during their childhood. Max has shown kindness towards me based upon my recent bereavements. He recognises I have adjustments to make now I no longer have any surviving family. He also wants to buy the lodge if I sell, so it serves him to get on my good side. Please do not read anything into it other than that."

Susanna shrugged her narrow silk clad shoulders. "You are entitled to your opinion. I don't know the man well, but I have been around enough of his gender to recognise when there is an interest. I can tell by the way he looks at you." Susanna sighed. "Honestly, Ingrid, you must be more German than English, because I don't think you realise how pretty you are. I'd give anything for your thick black hair and your icy coloured eyes. Do you know women paint beauty spots by their mouths to look like yours? You shouldn't be surprised at Max's appreciation of you but be flattered. Though he's far too old for me, I'll admit he is rather dashing." She smiled, flashing small white teeth and promptly changed the subject. "I am just relieved you are here. I was going quite mad with just my brother for companionship. He means well, but Saul is quite dull. Anyhow, once your ankle is fully mended, perhaps we could take a drive into town and spend an afternoon there? The weather is so fine, and it would be a welcome reprieve from the hotel."

Compassion welled in me for the young woman. It must not be easy staying in accommodation where none of your personal belongings could be enjoyed. It would drive me insane.

"Susanna. You are welcome to visit Lorelei whenever you need to relieve the tedium of being confined to your hotel. I cannot guarantee that I will be available to socialise at all times, but you would have access to the grounds should you want a change."

Much to my amazement, the pretty blonde's eyes filled with tears, and she looked at me with something akin to surprise.

"Oh, Ingrid. I cannot believe you are so sweet to me. I know I am not alone in the world as you are, but I am so far away from home that I do miss Mama and Papa. Saul is a dear, but he's immersed in business and making deals to expand Father's company, and he cannot be bothered entertaining me. If I were able, I would go back home immediately. But my parents won't allow me to travel without him, and therefore I've to wait until his blasted business in Germany is concluded. But it means a lot to me, knowing I am welcome here. And don't be surprised if I take you up it. I wish we had met before because you are such a dear. I do believe we shall be great friends."

I smiled weakly. Susanna Koppelman was always generous with her words. There were just so many of them.

THE DAY AFTER MY visit from Susanna, I received an invitation from Max, to join him and his mother for tea at the *Safranpalast* that afternoon. He noted she was having an unusually good day, and that it was best to captalise on those times.

Joan insisted *Herr* Metzger take me, rather than my walking. She reminded me if I did not stay off my ankle as much as possible, I would not be able attend the opera, which was in three days. Reluctantly I agreed she was right.

Until now, my only view of the palace had been the rear of the building, though partially obscured by the forest of trees. Therefore, when the carriage turned into the palatial driveway, I gasped at the sheer majesty before my eyes.

The *Safranpalast* was neoclassical in design, just as I remembered the Palace of Versailles, so similar in fact, it could have been built by the same architect, though I knew that was unlikely. As we traversed the road, surrounded by beautifully manicured gardens, the butter-coloured stone edifice looked immense. A broad central building stood four storeys high, set back on a courtyard of red paving stones and flanked by two wings of the same height. The roof was reddish gold, the colour of autumnal leaves, with huge green metal spires protruding at regular intervals.

We pulled into the courtyard, passing a turquoise tiled tiered fountain. Each tier decorated with small statuary, I caught a glimpse of lions, eagles and deer among the animals depicted, with the uppermost being a large bear standing before the sun.

The vehicle came to a halt, and two liveried men rushed from the grand doors to assist me out of the carriage and escort me inside.

I was at once aware of the vastness of the place. As I stepped into its marble entrance I stopped in wonderment while my eyes feasted upon so much beauty it could not register it all simultaneously.

The floors and walls were carved from creamy stone, only interrupted by statuary of godlike creatures in alcoves. leading the eye up to a domed ceiling, complete with its fresco of blue sky and white clouds.

"Ah, there you are, Ingrid." Max walked towards me, impeccably clad in a dark morning suit. He glanced down at my feet. "Is your ankle healed well enough? We can wait for another time?"

"It will be fine. I shall tell you if it troubles me."

He held out his arm and gestured for me to take it. "Come then, let us have a short tour before I take you to see Mutti."

I took his arm and he led me from the hall. Everywhere I glanced I saw majesty, wealth and opulence. I was aghast and tongue-tied, a peasant in the midst of such grandeur. Max led me past so many rooms I lost count.

He gestured to the doorways. "These are of little interest, Ingrid. They are used for receiving guests and are mostly drawing rooms. One is much like the other." He stopped in front of closed oak doors. "But this room you will like, I believe." He relinquished my arm and pushed open the doors.

I gasped in utter delight. It was a library, so voluminous it was easily the size of two ballrooms. The room was long. Broken into segments by several cupolas, each dome decorated with a fresco repeating the one I had seen in the main entrance depicting skies and clouds. As far as my eye could see were white bookcases, inlaid with gold trimmings, every bit as extravagant as the Baroque and Rococo influences I had seen at Lorelei, only on a scale far grander. I stepped inside, absorbing row upon row of books. Breathing in the scent of paper, parchment and leather, an atmosphere of calm embraced my senses.

The floor was an arrangement of inlaid tiles the same buttery colour I had seen prevalent in the building but were interspersed with green and maroon tiles to form an intricate pattern. In the centre of the room, several tables and chairs had been placed which dissected the library, allowing room for one to sit and study. There were two sets of staircases at the end of the room which led up to a second floor.

"Do you like it?" Max asked, and I was startled because I had completely forgotten he was even there.

I turned to him. "It is the loveliest room I have ever seen." I sighed. "More than I can comprehend. The light is amazing." The room was swathed in afternoon sunlight.

"There are at least thirty windows in here," Max said, pointing up to the second floor. Though they are recessed, they allow a substantial amount of natural light to come in. The library is also situated to make the most of the daylight. Come." He gestured for me to follow him out of the library. "Let us go and see Mutti, and then I shall take you out into the gardens."

He led me back the way we had come and then down another hallway where we passed more rooms, my wandering eye catching the barest glimpses of their décor.

After ascending a magnificent marble staircase, replete with even more statuary, we reached the first floor. I noticed immediately that the cool stone so resplendent downstairs, was replaced with thick rugs spread across the floors. White painted walls were decorated with tapestries and paintings. Here and there were small tables or chairs nestled in alcoves should one want to sit.

I would never find my way out of the palace by myself if left to my own devices. It was like being in a small, encased city, with a network of corridors and hallways one much like another. As we navigated our way through the maze of corridors, Max explained some of his home's history, and occasionally pointed at one interesting piece or another. But frankly, I was so overwhelmed I absorbed none of it.

At length, we reached the end of a hallway, and arrived in front of tall white doors trimmed with gold. Max knocked lightly.

"*Komm herein*," came a voice.

Max opened the door and I followed him in. We were in an enormous bedchamber decorated in salmon pink and gold. The furnishings were so elaborate they made my head spin. It was as though I had stepped into a large embroidery box full of satins and silks and rich, vibrant fabrics.

Dominating the wall on one side of the room stood a massive stone fireplace, with seats arranged in a manner to engage company. There, seated in one armchair, was who I guessed must be Max's mother. A plain, uniformed nurse stood close by.

"*Guten Tag, Krankenschwester* Helga," Max said, greeting the middle-aged nurse. "*Du können für eine weile entlassen warden.*" He was dismissing her, and she nodded at him. But as she walked past me towards the door, our eyes met, and her expression showed a flare of interest.

"Come and sit, Ingrid." Max said. He indicated one of the chairs close to where the older woman sat, and I did as he bade.

When Lisbeth von Brandt looked at me, it was with the same dark brown eyes as her son. Yet without his thick black lashes, they were less striking. Her hair was dark brown, with ribbons of white and grey threaded throughout, and was pulled up into a tidy bun. She was no beauty, but her face was gentle, soft, with a touch of youthfulness, even though she bore the lines and wrinkles of a woman in her seventies. The baroness was dressed in a plain beige silk gown, with no adornments or jewellry other than her wedding ring.

"*Mutter, das ist Ingrid. Wir müssen Englisch sprechen.*" Max was telling his mother they would need to converse in English. I was half-tempted to admit I understood German, but chose to keep it to myself.

"Hello, my dear," Lisbeth said softly as her eyes met mine. "It is good to see you once again. Oh my, you are so like my *liebling,* my darling Marta. Such a pretty girl she was." She blinked heavily.

"Thank you, Baroness. You and my mother were good friends?"

She nodded slowly, and I recognised what was strange about Max's mother. She was sluggish, as though each action took a great deal of concentration and energy. Was this the disease Max had hinted at?

"Marta was my best friend in *die welt*," she continued, her gaze never leaving my face. "In the world." Her English was good but there was a thick German accent behind her enunciation. Out of the corner of my eye I saw Max take a seat.

"We had many adventures, the two of us. Then once we were older and I was a grown woman, she left for France."

"England, Mutti. Marta went to live in England with her husband." Max gave me a nod as though he wanted to remind me that his mother was frail and sometimes confused.

The baroness ignored him. "Marta came back though. But she had to, did she not? Someone had to make sure everything was as she wanted it. *He* wouldn't let her stay. No, not him. He was too ashamed. If he had not made her do it, none of it would have happened."

I didn't know what she meant. I looked over at Max. He shrugged his shoulders and raised a brow.

"I never liked him," Baroness Lisbeth von Brandt said passionately. Then she leaned towards me and held out a papery hand to grasp mine. "Everything would have been different if he had not made her lie." Her eyes filled with tears. "Boys do silly things. They cannot help it. It would not have happened if Marta had been here." Abruptly, she released my hand and slumped back in her chair.

Worried, I glanced at Max and saw by his expression that he was not alarmed.

"Ingrid is going to stay for a few weeks, Mutti.

Perhaps she can come back and see you soon?"

Before the woman could reply, there was a loud knock on the door and then it opened before anyone had a chance to answer.

"*Da bist du Max.*" Stated the attractive man striding towards where we sat, apparently looking for my host according to his comment. His glance moved from Max to land upon me, whereupon the colour drained from his face and his eyes grew wide with what looked like apprehension.

I frowned.

"Wolfgang," Max spoke English. "May I introduce my friend and our new neighbour, *Fräulein* Ingrid Rutherford, Marta Bergman's daughter from London. She has come to meet Mutti. Remember, Marta and she were great friends for many years."

The handsome gentleman visibly relaxed and came closer. Boldly, he stared at me, his light brown eyes curious and rather striking. His hair, like his brother's and mother's, was the colour of mahogany, and there was a familiarity in the shape of his nose, his cheekbones.

His face broke into a smile, and he came to stand before me, reached for my hand and pressed it to his lips. He let it go, but kept his eyes fastened upon mine with intensity. I felt as though he could see right through me.

"*Fräulein.* It is not often we have *eine Englische dame* staying here. It is a pleasure to meet you. You look much like Marta." His manner was unsettling and again I felt strangely vulnerable. He went to greet his mother, whose face underwent a sudden change.

"Mutti." He kissed her, but she moved to avert her

cheek, as though she did not want his touch.

Wolfgang ignored the gesture and then took one of the empty chairs next to his brother. I observed how their physical features betrayed their relationship, yet there the comparison ended. Wolfgang von Brandt was a confident fellow. From the cut of his clothes to his posture, he exuded self-assertion. Max was no shrinking violet. But his strength came from being a person of authority, a man always under strict control. I supposed it would be natural for him, with the responsibility of his family upon his shoulders.

"Tell me, *Fräulein* Rutherford. How do you find our little village?" Wolfgang's Germanic lilt made the English words sound more interesting. "I am sure it is not as exciting as your life in London?"

I smiled politely. "On the contrary. I believe it is far more interesting here than at home. It is also quite beautiful."

"*Sie war so schön,*" the baroness said. "*Niemand wird es jemals die Wahrheit erfahren.*" Then she began weeping softly.

Both men instantly got to their feet and Max gently coaxed his mother up and walked her to her bed, sending Wolfgang to find Nurse Helga. Respecting their privacy, I quietly left the room, passing the stern-looking nurse on my way out to the corridor. Again, I felt her eyes linger upon me. Perhaps she was unused to seeing an English person? I dismissed it and found a seat in one of the hallway's small alcoves, where I pondered over the baroness's distraught words.

'*She was so beautiful. No one will ever know the truth*', she'd said. I assumed she spoke of my mother. But what could she mean?

"Ingrid?" Max joined me in the hallway. "I apologise. I did warn you Mutti can get quite confused and upset."

"Please, there is no apology necessary. Your mother was lovely and very gracious. She did seem tired though and I am sure we overtaxed her." I rose to join him, and we walked down the hall towards the staircase. "Is the baroness medicated for her condition, Max? She seemed quite sleepy."

"Unfortunately, it is a byproduct of her powders. They keep her calmed, but they do make her drowsy, especially if she sits for too long. I am sorry if it made you uncomfortable."

"Absolutely not," I chided. "I felt far from it. I was glad to meet your brother, Wolfgang."

He made no response. As we reached the stairs I wondered at his silence. Did the brothers not get along? That would not be unusual. Saying nothing was preferable to saying the wrong thing, so I did not press the subject, and followed Max down the ornate staircase.

When we reached the first floor, he stopped. "Ingrid, if you have time, I should like to show you part of the gardens. You can see them from the lodge, but not in any detail. Would you like to come?"

I made a quick study of his face. He seemed distracted, as though his mind was elsewhere, and for a moment I considered turning the offer down so that he might attend to whatever troubled him. But then I changed my mind. I wanted to spend more time with Max. I enjoyed his company and was not ready to go back to the lodge and be alone.

"Yes," I said. "But only if your blasted dogs will

be friendlier this time."

"They would not dare be anything but," he replied, recommencing walking as he led me towards the rear of the palace. "Are you sure your ankle is recovered enough? I should not want to make the condition worse."

"I shall tell you if it causes me any discomfort, Max. I believe exercise is a good remedy if I do not walk too far."

Outside, the two beasts waited patiently for their master. Max introduced them as Frido and Sascha, and both animals behaved very differently than at our last encounter. They were still intimidating due to their size. For even in a sitting position, their heads reached as high as my ribcage.

"Are you certain these are not really a breed of horse?" I asked Max as the smaller of the two hounds nuzzled my hand.

He laughed. "No. But I can see why you would think that. The dogs are known as *Deutsche Dogge*, or more commonly in other countries, Great Danes. They were used for hunting dogs as far back as in the Middle Ages. Although they look fierce, and can be when necessary, they are actually incredibly loyal and gentle creatures."

I glanced down at the massive head currently resting on my palm and was not at all convinced.

"Come, Ingrid. If you are ready, let us proceed." We moved away from the palace and began walking down one of the pathways in the direction of the gardens, the dogs accompanying us. We had not got far when Max informed me his home had once been known as, '*Der Palast der vielen fenster,*' which meant '*the palace of many windows.*' I turned back to look at the building and could see why, for there were too many of them to count. But as my gaze followed them, my eye caught a sudden movement behind a window on the second floor. Was somebody watching us from inside the palace?

"Ingrid?" Max had stopped ahead of me and now looked around to ensure I followed.

"I am coming," I said.

But as he gave me a partial tour of the elaborate and beautiful gardens, I must confess it was not the pleasant excursion I anticipated. For no matter how I tried to control my fancies, I could not shake the feeling that someone observed every move we made.

Chapter Five

BY THE NIGHT OF the opera, my ankle was back to normal which was a welcome relief. After my visit to the *Safranpalast* two days hence, I had intentionally stayed off it. I could not decide if my anticipation was in seeing the Opera House and *Carmen*, or the famous Valentina Cavaletti. Upon quick reflection, it was indeed the latter.

Why was I so interested in Maximillian von Brandt and his family? I examined my thoughts daily to answer that question. After practically becoming a recluse following the death of my mother, I was unused to company, except Joan's. Being in a new place and meeting the Koppelmans and Max's family was exciting in comparison. No wonder I felt a lift of spirits whenever I was in his company.

Susanna had visited me the previous day and stayed all afternoon. I was surprised how easily I grew accustomed to the young American. Though her conversation was as long and consistent as train wheels on a railway line, I could not help but like her, for she was funny, and entertaining.

Tonight, the Koppelmans collected me in their carriage, and we planned to meet Max in his family's box at the Opera House. When we arrived in *Prinzenstadt,* it was as though the entire town had come out to enjoy the evening. The array of carriages, the throng of people walking the streets and then seeing those dressed for the evening's performance was a spectacle unlike anything I had seen. My eyes greedily absorbed every detail. The anticipation in the air was palpable.

Observing the other women in their finery, I wished I could have worn a more elegant gown. I felt like a crow in my black mourning silk in comparison to the beautiful designs and wonderful array of colours the ladies wore. Susanna was especially fetching in her sapphire gown, which served to enhance the lovely gold of her hair and the brightness of her blue eyes.

Making our way through the foyer, we were the subject of interested glances, no doubt because of our speaking English. Under such observation I wished I could have looked more elegant. It was ironic to dress in mourning for two people I truly did not mourn.

We were escorted to the von Brandt box, which, I noted, was closest to the stage. Max was not there, but an attendant quickly produced refreshments for us to partake of while we waited. The box was spacious enough to seat at least ten people. The chairs were large and comfortable, and I knew a sense of privilege, especially when I peered below and saw how closely the audience were seated together. Though Susanna and Saul kept a conversation going, I paid little heed. My eyes were locked on the bustling scene before me.

This social event was an opportunity for those who enjoyed being seen. There were bright lights throughout the entire theatre, but in its centre hung an enormous chandelier. According to Saul, *Prinzenstadt* was one of only ten Operatic Houses and theatres in Germany to have electricity fuelling the lights. From our high vantage point, the audience below resembled a flock of geese descending upon a river with much flapping of wings and honking, as they arrived and looked for their seats.

No wonder this building was the pride of the city. There was nothing provincial here. It was like stepping inside the interior of an ornate giant jewelry box. The ceiling's gigantic dome was a gorgeous fresco of what I guessed was a scene from a famous opera, and this theme was repeated on the outside of the prized private boxes. The brilliance of the electric lighting caught every fleck of golden paint and rich colour in the artwork so that one felt suffused in splendour. The opulence was breathtaking. As I looked out over the crowd I felt like a princess overseeing my people.

"Good evening, Max." I heard Saul say, and I turned my attention back to my companions.

Like Saul, Max wore evening dress. His suit was black and finely tailored, his waistcoat black satin, atop a crisp linen shirt and white cravat. But unlike Saul, who still looked boyish and a little untidy, Max was striking, cutting an imposing, dashing figure.

"Good evening, Ingrid," he said as our eyes met. His gaze lowered from my face as he absorbed how I was dressed.

"Hello Max." The way he looked at me caused my cheeks to warm. Though I wore plain black satin, my neckline was cut to expose my décolletage and my gown was sleeveless. Small red roses sewn onto the shoulders of the dress, and rubies in my ears were the only adornments I wore.

"Aha, here you all are." At the sound of another voice, I looked away to see Wolfgang von Brandt come through the door into the box. Like his brother, Wolfgang was dressed impeccably. He stopped next to Max, and I could not help but compare the men, as I am sure any female would.

Max was slightly taller than his younger brother and broader in the shoulders, but they were of a similar strong build. The dark colour of their hair was mirrored in their trimmed moustaches and beards. Even their facial structure was similar, though Wolfgang's eyes were lighter than his brother's. It was their countenance which separated them so vastly. Max's, so serious, thoughtful, and responsible, every bit a baron. While Wolfgang had a glint in his eye, a ready smile, and an adventurous demeanour. In comparison to Max, he appeared playful. But there was no denying the von Brandt brothers were a handsome pair and very much the object of many admiring female glances.

I watched the Koppelmans greet our new arrival and I did not miss the way Susanna's eyes lingered longer than necessary when Wolfgang pressed his lips to her gloved hand.

Then he turned to greet me. "*Guten Abend, Fräulein* Rutherford. You look as lovely as *Fräulein* Koppelman this evening."

"Thank you, *Herr* von Brandt." I felt uncomfortable as he made no attempt to hide his observation of my dress, but unlike his brother, his study felt more of an assessment.

Much to my relief, the lights were flashed and there was a buzz of eager anticipation while the audience quickly took their seats as the performance was ready to begin. The orchestra tuned their various instruments in the pit, and we settled into our box seats.

Susanna and I sat next to one another, she flanked by Wolfgang, while Max sat next to me with Saul at the very end.

The house lights dimmed and the stage lights came on. The orchestra struck up the introductory piece and I shivered with excitement. My very first opera! Who would have thought less than a week prior, my only engagement was with the board of Mother's charitable orphanage? Yet tonight, here I sat in a beautiful theatre in Germany, witnessing a wonderful spectacle.

The curtains swished open to depict a village scene with many people on stage. The chorus sang, filling the air with rich song. I was absolutely mesmerised by their brilliant costumes, their striking faces, thick with paint to emphasise their features. And just when I thought it could not be any more fascinating, Valentina Cavaletti walked onto the stage amidst thunderous applause.

Though my eyes were rivetted upon her, I sensed Max's body stiffen beside me, yet I could not turn away from the vision in front of me. The woman standing under the spotlight, soaking up the love and admiration from her audience was stunningly beautiful. Her hair fell in thick lustrous waves of ebony down her back, almost to her hips. She gave a sweeping curtsy, her arms open wide, palms up, and then she faced the boxes on the other side of the theatre and curtsied once again. I knew what would happen next. Valentina turned and looked directly up at our box as she dipped into another curtsy, then as she rose, her eyes fastened upon our group. I almost gasped aloud as I saw her breathtakingly beautiful face. Though she wore stage paint, there was no mistaking her undeniable perfection. Thick black brows, wide dark eyes, a Roman nose and full lips. Her slender neck accentuated the fullness of her bosom, and even garbed in the rags of her character, her voluptuous figure was hard to disguise.

I was at once filled with admiration, fascination, and jealousy. Suddenly, even more aware of my plainness, my lack of character, all I could think was how did a man resist a woman like that?

Then she began to sing, and I forgot all my thoughts as I was lost in the absolute perfection of her voice. She sang like an angel.

When the interval came, and the house lights brightened, there was a restlessness in the air from everyone sitting still for so long. The gentlemen in our box got to their feet and announced they would depart to smoke and bring back refreshments. I watched them leave and then turned to Susanna, who was peering through her opera glasses at the people below.

"My goodness, that man has a massive nose," she remarked.

"That is unkind," I said.

She set the glasses down upon Wolfgang's vacated seat. "It's just an opinion, Ingrid. You are so sensitive." Her eyes gleamed. "Well, tell me what you think so far?"

"The orchestra is marvellous, and the talent is—"

"No, silly," she interrupted. "What do you think about Valentina? Is she not fabulously beautiful? You know that Max has to be wildly in love with her still. I mean, look at her. Not only has she the face and body of a goddess, but her voice is magical." She sighed dramatically. "How is it that one person can be so gifted and yet the rest of us not?"

I frowned. "Susanna, you are a very pretty young

lady, and many would give their eye teeth to have your lovely hair and bright eyes. If everyone looked the same it should be a boring world." I did not acknowledge her comment regarding Max.

She gave a little grin at my compliments and then stared at my face deep in thought. "You are quite striking, you know," she said. "Though with your hair in a severe bun and no rouge, you're a little stern in appearance. But I do like your mole. It draws attention to your mouth."

I chuckled. "It's a family trait—my mother had one just like it." At that I remembered Wolfgang's surprise when we first met. Had he thought I was my mother? "In truth, I wish I did not have it for I dislike it."

"Dislike what?" Wolfgang reappeared in the box without the others. He stepped in front of us and leant back casually against the balcony wall.

"Ingrid hates having a mole on her face."

His eyes immediately went to my mouth where he contemplated for a moment. He smiled with one eyebrow raised. "I think it singularly fetching and unusual. You should be glad to have it." His eyes flickered away to settle upon Susanna. "What think you of the opera, Miss Koppelman? Is Carmen to your liking?"

Susanna blushed under his scrutiny, and again I thought her very taken with the man.

"To be perfectly honest I have been so absorbed watching miss Valentina, I haven't paid much attention to the rest of the company. Oh, the music is nice and all that, but she is by far the most interesting part of the evening. I had not realised she was such a beauty, and I am stunned to think that she and Max are no longer together. If I were a man, I would never let anyone like her out of my sight."

As usual, Susanna did not hold back. I watched Wolfgang's expression as she spoke. He seemed mildly amused by her youthful chatter. My thoughts about Max's younger brother were still not yet gelled. I wanted to like the man, and yet there was about him an element that kept a person on their guard. His winning smile and courteous regard were all extremely pleasing, and there was no question to his looks being easy to behold. What then did I mistrust about him? Was I being entirely fair?

Susanna chatted about an opera she had seen in New York with her parents, and my mind floated away from her conversation and went on its own journey as it often did when I was listening to my new friend. I looked out across the audience and marvelled at the variety of people before me and the spectacle of their beautiful gowns. How strange that I should be here of all places. And then it came to me that perhaps Mother had come to the opera when she lived here. I would have to ask Max and see if he knew.

"There you are, Wolfgang," said Max as he and Saul re-joined us. "Where did you go in such a hurry? I thought you were coming with us to smoke?"

Something flickered in Wolfgang's eyes before his expression changed. "I saw an old friend and wished to speak to him about a matter. I should have said something. *Tut mir leid, Bruder.* I am sorry."

It might have been my imagination, but to me it felt like the atmosphere changed slightly and there was a crackle of tension in the air. The lights flashed twice, and everyone resumed their former seats. The second part of the opera performance was about to begin.

THE FINAL CURTAIN CAME down after Valentina had sung one encore and then returned to face her audience three separate times to a standing ovation. Young men rushed up to the orchestra pit, throwing roses and other flowers onto the stage where they landed at the soprano's feet. I stood along with the audience paying my respects to her and the entire company. The opera had been absolutely phenomenal, and I was sorry it ended.

Finally, when the applause dissipated, people reluctantly began leaving their seats. Under Max's advice, we remained where we were so that the general audience could exit the theatre and we would not be part of the crush.

"I have a surprise for you," Wolfgang said with a charming smile directed towards Susanna. "I have arranged for you to meet Valentina Cavaletti in her dressing room."

"I don't believe it!" gasped Susanna excitedly. She clapped her hands with pleasure.

Beside me, Max's posture stiffened. "Was that necessary, brother?" He asked with a trace of irritation he did not disguise.

"Perhaps not, but I know Miss Koppelman thinks very highly of her performance, and as a visitor to our city I thought it a nice gesture."

"Indeed," Susanna exclaimed. "It was most kind of you. My parents will not believe my good fortune." Completely unaware of the men's tense exchange, the young woman continued.

"Father is a patron of the arts at home. He knows

all about Miss Cavaletti. Why, I believe he saw her perform once in New York."

There came a tap on the door, and it opened to reveal one of the theatre pages. Everyone rose immediately except Max and myself.

"Madame Cavaletti is ready to see you now," he announced. "Please follow me."

Susanna moved quicker than I had ever seen her move, hastily followed by Saul and then Wolfgang. I remained where I was. Wolfgang hesitated at the door and turned to look over his shoulder.

"Do you not wish to join us, *Fräulein* Rutherford?"

"Thank you, no. I believe I shall wait with Max and meet you afterwards."

Wolfgang glanced at his brother and then slid his eyes back to my face. With a sly grin, he followed the others.

An awkward moment passed, and then Max turned his chair at an angle so that he could see me better. "I am surprised you did not want to meet Valentina. Usually, people will wait hours for a chance to speak with her. Perhaps you are not as big of an opera fanatic as our friend Susanna?"

I smiled. "I doubt very sincerely if I am as passionate about anything as dear Susanna is. Indeed, I envy her boundless enthusiasm. I find myself cynical in comparison."

Max shook his head. "Ingrid, though we are recently met, I have already learned that you are your worst critic. For a young woman, you are extremely hard on yourself." His dark eyes held mine, and I found his expression difficult to read.

"I disagree," I replied. "I'm just being honest. My

upbringing and Miss Koppelman's were worlds apart. She is a delightful product of a family who no doubt has indulged her and brought her up in a manner that she believes herself to be treasured."

"And your upbringing was not like that?"

I could not help but chuckle. "Far from it. My mother was a good and loving woman, but she died when I was quite young. Father believed in running an efficient household. He considered people of Susanna's nature a bad influence upon his daughter. Consequently, I had few friends and did not leave the house often."

Max's face showed pity. "That is sad, Ingrid. It is a crime for any child to grow up feeling alone."

"I daresay. But loneliness is a curable situation. I was fortunate in that I had a warm, safe place to live and plenty of food to nourish me, not to mention nannies aplenty. How could I possibly feel cheated or disparaged, when there are so many less prosperous than I? My mother spent a great deal of time visiting orphanages in London. I saw first-hand what it really is to be in need. I am content, Max." I had another thought. "As for declining to meet Madam Cavaletti, I was not being rude. It is that I would prefer to do so in a different environment. One where I might actually have a conversation with her, and it not just be about paying her homage."

Much to my amazement, he burst out laughing. "Oh, Ingrid. You are such a character. Your forthright manner is more German than you realise. Yet you have a way with you unlike anyone I have had the pleasure of knowing before."

I could not look at his face for I was too

embarrassed. The man had paid me a compliment and I was unsure how to react.

"I am sorry. Have I offended you?" he said quickly.

I collected myself. "Not at all. Perhaps I should be less blunt. Society and its etiquette are not strengths of mine." I met his gaze and saw his eyes had warmed to the colour of molasses.

"I am no expert when it comes to society, Ingrid, as I leave that to Wolfgang. But if there is one piece of advice I can offer you," he said softly. "It would be to tell you never to change."

Chapter Six

THE NIGHTMARE CAME AGAIN and woke me in the early hours. With the house in complete silence, I put on my dressing gown, lit a gas lamp, and quietly ventured downstairs. I retrieved a glass of water from the kitchen and then made my way to the study.

It had taken me two days to read through one of the large books which had caused my fall. It had yielded little of interest to me as the time frame was the earlier years. Though I had discovered we were distantly related to the Kaiser, *very* distantly.

I was hopeful the second volume might prove more interesting. While the occupants of the lodge slept, I settled down at the desk with my lamp close by and pulled the book in front of me. Opening the cover, I was pleased to see the inscription on the front was dated Eighteen-hundred and thirty-one. This surely would be where I could find out more about Mother and her family.

I did not read the first pages. With my curiosity piqued, I wanted to move through history and learn about my mother as quickly as possible. I turned each page until I arrived at the year of her birth. There she was, Marta Louisa Bergman, born at home. My fingertips traced the ink of her name and the longing pulled at me relentlessly. Oh, how I missed her.

I turned the pages to read details of her early years,

first steps, first words, and then an engagement. She had been an only child. As I scanned the words, I found my father's name, Thomas Rutherford. The wedding date ended at the bottom of the page. I turned it in anticipation of seeing my name, and ...nothing? The next page had been torn out of the book, this evident by the ragged pieces still holding onto the spine. I flipped to the following page. It too was blank. I leaned forward, moving the lamp closer to be sure I was correct. Yes, there it was. The tell-tale jagged remnants of the page that should have been there.

I closed the book and sat back in the chair. How very odd. My emotions were a mix of disappointment and being put-out that I warranted no mention. It followed that I must have been in the book because I existed, yet why would the page be ripped out?

Defeated momentarily and finding my mind groggy from lack of sleep, I took hold of my lamp and ascended back upstairs to my room. Tomorrow, I would pay a visit to *Herr* Vogel. Though I had shown little interest in my German blood upon arriving at the lodge, I suddenly had a change of heart.

I DID NOT TELL JOAN of my late-night discovery. I did not want her fussing over my lack of sleep. At breakfast, I told Fritz I would need the carriage at ten o'clock that morning.

Herr Metzger, looking better groomed than usual, waited outside the front, and we set off for *Prinzenstadt*.

The main road was well maintained and busy, once we left the outskirts of *Linnenbrink* Village. It was a cloudless May day, and the windows of the carriage were wide open so the sweet scent of lilac blew in with the breeze. We passed farmland with rich green pastures and fields carpeted in yellow dandelions. Then the scenery abruptly changed as the flat land fell away to give room to thousands of Spruce and Pine trees as we passed a small forest. I felt a momentary rush in my head as the scent of pine pervaded my senses. What was it about the fragrance which caused such a response?

I spotted the large dome of the Opera House long before we arrived in the town. It was not as high as the many church spires poking through the sky, but the mere size of it was hard to miss. This time, as *Herr* Metzger navigated the cobbled roads of the town, I paid better attention to the shops that ran along the roadway, and people going about their business.

The sounds of the city were prevalent. Horses neighing, people shouting their wares, and from time to time I caught the scent of something delicious being cooked by one of the many street vendors.

Fritz had given *Herr* Metzger instructions where to take me, therefore I was unprepared when we stopped. I heard my driver climb down from his box, and the door swung open.

Herr Metzger nodded politely and then pointed to the building close to us. "*Herr* Vogel," he said and then gave me a grin. He held out a hand to assist me down the steps, and reluctantly I took it, hoping it was not too dirty.

"*Danke*," I said once my feet touched the ground. "Please come and collect me in two hours." I held up my fingers to show him two and then I pointed to where we stood.

"Ah," he gave another scary grin, "*Zwei stunden.*"

AFTER HIS INITIAL SURPRISE at my appearance, *Herr* Vogel welcomed me in and had his assistant bring me a glass of water. His office looked as though it had been ransacked and then everything put back in the wrong place. In front of a row of cabinets against one wall, his desk was covered in small stacks of papers. There were wooden boxes on the floor stuffed to the gills with folders, and even the few dull pictures hanging on the tobacco-stained wallpaper were crooked.

All in all, his lack of professionalism surprised me—likewise that my mother had engaged his services. His accommodation looked better suited to a moneylender. In contrast, he kept himself well dressed, and only the bushy brows, beard and hair gave him an eccentric look.

"*Wilkommen, Fräulein* Rutherford. I did not expect to see you here. If you had sent for me, I should have been happy to come to Lorelei Lodge."

"*Danke.* But I had other business in town, so I thought I would save you the trouble. I wish to ask you a few questions regarding my mother."

Herr Vogel nodded. "I see. What is it you want to know?"

"I would like to see documentation of her visits here since she married. Is that something you can help me with?"

He frowned and then got up and went over to the filing cabinets. He opened a drawer, retrieved a folder and brought it back to the desk. "Let me see," he mused as he looked at the various papers.

"*Herr* Vogel," I said impatiently. "Would it be

permissible for me to take that file with me so I might read through it myself?"

His bushy brows looked like hairy caterpillars as he frowned. "*Fräulein* Rutherford, that would be most unusual. I am not sure if I—"

"But the information there is in regard to my family. Where would be the harm in my reading about my own relative and her estate? I am the only one left, after all."

He considered this for a moment and then shuffled through the papers. "You do have a point, *Fräulein* Rutherford. The legal documents are kept elsewhere. All I have here are notations and a few accounting entries. But they are in German."

"That does not matter," I assured him. "I have a rudimentary understanding of written German, and a manservant who can translate if necessary."

He studied my face for a moment. "*Das ist gut.* I will let you take them but only on the condition I may collect them," he paused and looked at his open diary. "Today is Monday, hmm." He ran his finger down the diary page. "Let us say Friday, then? Will that suit you?"

"Yes." I smiled, pleased with the result. He passed me the file and I got to my feet.

"Thank you so much, *Herr* Vogel. Be assured I shall keep this safe. Until Friday then?"

I SPENT THE NEXT HOUR in a café close to *Herr* Vogel's office. I should have liked to walk around *Prinzenstadt* as I knew so little of the place. But I was too nervous I'd lose the papers he'd given me to read. So, when I spotted the small café, I went inside.

As none of the patrons knew me, I freely used my German, and it was enjoyable speaking it for the very first time in public. I ordered coffee and a pastry to eat with it. My fingers itched to open up the folder and start reading, but I waited until my drink and food was brought to me.

The café was painted a cheery yellow, with pictures on the walls of what I imagined were local areas of interest and dominated by a painting of the Opera House. There were five other people sitting at two different tables, three matronly women chatting amicably, and seated close to them, a young couple with eyes only for each other. No one paid attention to me. Convinced the other customers held no interest in my actions, my eyes turned to the file before me.

There were a variety of papers of different size and in no particular order. They were all handwritten notes, probably by *Herr* Vogel, some with dates written on the top. Without getting them near my food, I sorted them into chronological order, the newest on the top. Anything without a date I left at the back.

The first was dated only a few months before my mother's death, which instantly brought a lump to my throat. I still missed her desperately. I swallowed my sorrow and read the page.

Herr Vogel had noted Mother's arrival in *Prinzenstadt* and wrote of an appointment they would be having. The subject of discussion was an increase of an allotment of monies being paid to her aunt, Gisela Bergman. I paused and took a sip of my drink. Money? Why would my mother pay her aunt when she already lived in the lodge at her discretion? I read on.

There were notes made regarding bills that would

be settled while Mother was in town and not much more. I went to the next page and saw it contained much of the same information. The dates seemed to be in the frequency of at least once each year, sometimes more. This puzzled me, for I had no knowledge of Mother being gone, and surely I would remember that, perhaps not as a small child, but certainly later.

I closed the folder and turned my attention to my apple pastry. It was deliciously tart. I finished my coffee and left the café.

The day was glorious. Azure blue skies and a slight breeze with the promise of heat later in the afternoon. As I walked back to where *Herr* Metzger would collect me, I heard the town clock strike the half hour and realised I still had thirty minutes to wait for the carriage.

I passed the lawyer's office and went farther down the street where I spotted a small park. Curious, I made my way towards it, and once I got closer, saw it was an area fenced off with iron railings. There was a grassy area encircling a pond. Benches stood at regular intervals along the tree-lined pathway, and it was a popular spot judging by the people there—some reading newspapers, others taking a stroll.

I went through the gate into the park and decided to walk around the pond and then go back and wait for my carriage. I noticed a few children down by the water, out with their nannies or parents. Some excitedly threw pieces of bread to a handful of ducks and swans, while one lad had a toy boat he was trying to launch which kept getting stuck in the weeds. His father stood close, giving him advice.

I watched his endeavours, and almost cheered

aloud when the boat finally broke free and sailed away. The parents clapped in pleasure, and the young chap beamed. They congratulated the boy, and then as he ran alongside the pond to watch the boat's progress, the couple turned around.

"*Fräulein* Rutherford, is that you?" It was Wolfgang von Brandt not twenty yards away, a lady at his side.

"*Guten Tag, Herr* von Brandt," I said.

Wolfgang moved closer, "What a pleasant surprise to see you." He turned back to the lady, "Katja, *komm und triff unseren englischen nachbarn*," he told her to come and meet the English neighbour.

She came towards me with a polite smile on her face. She was petite of stature, especially next to her tall husband. Her light brown hair was swept under her hat, and her eyes did not meet mine as she spoke.

"*Guten Tag, Fräulein*. Wolfgang told me about you. *Wilkommen* to *Prinzenstadt*." Her accent was thick.

"*Danke*," I replied.

Wolfgang pointed to the young lad running alongside his boat. "That is my son, Jakob. We bought the boat just now and he could not wait to try it out."

"He seems to be having a wonderful time with it," I said pleasantly. I smiled at Katja, and she looked away.

Wolfgang glanced at the folder in my hands. "What brings you to town this morning?" His handsome face was guileless, but he was obviously curious.

"I had a meeting with *Herr* Vogel, my lawyer," I said. "He had some papers for me to look through." I glanced over my shoulder towards the street. "And I must be going as my carriage will be waiting." I looked at Katja von Brandt. "It was nice to meet you."

"*Danke*," she said and then turned her head to watch her son.

"Good day to you, *Fräulein* Rutherford." Wolfgang's eyes settled on mine, and he grinned. "We must invite you to the *Safranpalast* for dinner, very soon." With a nod, he led his wife away.

I left the park in search of *Herr* Metzger. As I hurried, I wondered why it was that I felt so at ease with Max von Brandt's company, yet whenever I was near his brother, all I wanted was to get away.

IT HAD ALWAYS BEEN my practice to share things with Joan. After all, she had been in my life since before my mother had died. When I returned to the lodge, I told her of my meeting with both *Herr* Vogel and Wolfgang and his wife but did not discuss the details or share my discomfort with the baron's brother.

After luncheon, I went into the study and sat at my aunt's desk. I picked up the framed picture I had removed from the top of the bookshelves and studied the image. Mother looked to be perhaps in her late teens. I did favour her greatly. The only characteristic I had from Father was the colour of my eyes. Joan called them ice blue, which I thought nonsense. But then whenever I thought about my father and his lack of kindness, perhaps his were made of ice, not unlike his heart.

I placed the picture to one side and reopened the heavy book with its pages missing. Then I took up the folder from the lawyer and began where I had left off. I wrote notes, marking the dates my mother had visited Lorelei Lodge. *Herr* Vogel was correct. The dates seemed to be annual. So why had I not known of her coming, and more importantly, why had she not brought me with her?

Impatient, I got up and rang the bell. After several minutes the door opened.

"Fritz, please send for Joan."

The older man's expression did not change. He nodded and stepped back out.

I went to the desk and sat down. While I waited, I picked up the objects situated on top of the desk, none which belonged to me. There was a large bear-shaped pewter paperweight, a pad with blotting paper and an inkstand. A potted fern which looked worse for wear, and a small wooden box I had not noticed earlier.

The door opened to reveal Joan.

"Hello, miss. Fritz said you wanted to see me."

"Will you come and sit over here?" I gestured to one of the chairs on the opposite side of my desk. "I want to ask you some questions about my mother."

Joan's face grew puzzled. "About Marta? Whatever do you want to know?" She sat down.

I pointed to the papers. "Why did Mother never tell me she came here every year? I have no recollection of her going abroad or even speaking about it for that matter."

"I had no idea she was doin' that," Joan said adamantly. "Your mother often went away for days at a time, an' that was never my business."

"But surely you would have accompanied her on some of her trips? Is that not what a lady's maid is supposed to do?"

Joan raised her eyebrows. "In the normal course of things, yes. But Marta did what she wanted in her own way, an' when she travelled, I stayed behind to care for you."

"Where did you think she was going?"

"Well," Joan said. "I did fancy she was off somewhere on the continent, one of those spa places, you know, to take the waters. She never said much about it to anyone, not even your father." Joan's expression hardened at the mention of my father. There was no love lost there. She was not in the minority when it came to the general feeling about Thomas Rutherford. His reputation was renown both upstairs and downstairs in our home.

She continued. "Do you remember how I took you to my sister Ethel's place in Brighton every year?" said Joan. "We'd spend two weeks at the seaside, an' you'd play with her son, Michael. We went every summer up until the year Marta died."

I did recall those holidays. They were indeed happy memories. "Yes, I loved going there. It was such a welcome change from London and Father's rules."

"Well maybe that's when your mum took her trip to Germany. We wouldn't have known any different as we were away ourselves."

Joan made a good point. I had not thought about my annual trip away to the sea. Of course, that would be the explanation. Yet it did not fully comfort me. "But that doesn't answer why she neglected to mention it to me, or you for that matter?"

Joan shrugged. "I s'pose not. But your mother was a private person, miss, very secretive about many things. I took it to be her German ways.

Life was hard livin' in London for your mother. She never did fit in with the other nobs. Goin' to the orphanages were what she lived for...an' you of course," she acknowledged.

But I was not mollified. "She was a lovely person. I just wish she hadn't kept her time here a secret from me."

"Well," said Joan getting to her feet. "She did, an' she must have had her reasons. Stop worryin' yourself about it." She gave me a cheerful grin as if that would solve everything. "If that's all, I've got some washin' to do. Idle hands make idle minds."

"Indeed. Thank you, Joan."

When she had left the room, I considered her comments. Did Mother tell my father about her visits here? Surely she would have. It was her home after all, and it would be natural for her to want to see her family, even a mean old aunt.

I returned to the folder, flicking through the next few pages until I got to the page dated the year of my birth, Eighteen hundred and seventy. The note stated that the sum of one-hundred marks would be paid on the first of every month to Gisela Bergman by Marta Bergman Rutherford. This was to be a private arrangement between the two women and the money would be sent from London to a *Prinzenstadt* bank account held in both women's names.

My mother was generous to help her aunt, but I wondered why it was a private arrangement? Then I considered my father and his controlling ways. Perhaps Mother preferred to keep him out of her business, and for that, I could not blame her.

This document was the last page of dated material. The remainder of the papers were a hodgepodge of notes and scraps. I pulled them out and spread them on the desk. Some were obviously things jotted down by the lawyer, and in terminology I did not understand. Then a pale-yellow sheet caught my eye. At the top of the page was an insignia that was vaguely familiar—a large bear standing in front of a bright sun. Where had I seen it before? Then I remembered, it was at the *Safranpalast*. It must be the family crest. Here was an offer for a property that was meant for my father. I studied the information and saw it mentioned Lorelei Lodge, along with my mother's name and date of death.

Upon the demise of my mother, the von Brandt family wished to purchase the lodge. This, they noted, was their sole right, as Lorelei Lodge was originally designed and built by their family.

The letter stated as the heir was a British child and still under the care of her father, a building of such great historical interest would fall into disrepair. If the lodge was conjoined once again with the palace estate, the building would be properly maintained. The letter was signed by the baron, who, at that time would have been Max's father. When I was finished, I placed the letter down on the desk. Why hadn't my father taken the offer?

It interested me that Max's family had such a strong desire to reclaim what had been my mother's home. I understood that to a degree, family pride was important in some cultures, and I believed it to be so in this particular case. How did I feel about that?

Though I had no real connection to the lodge, it was, nevertheless the childhood home of my mother, and one of the last links I had with her. If I should sell the place, I would offer it to the von Brandts. But I was not ready to do anything yet. I yearned to understand my mother's hidden history. With no one to tell me about her, other than the baroness, I desperately wanted to experience living in a place that had once been Marta Bergman's home.

My eyes grew weary from reading. A walk was in order. This time, however, instead of walking in the direction of the palace where I had encountered Max and his massive dogs, I would try another route—perhaps go down a perpendicular path which led away from the forest on the other side of the lodge. The weather was still fine, and I decided not to take my hat or parasol. I wanted to feel the warmth of the sun on my face.

I had not ventured far when the manicured gardens gave way to nature. The path led around the far side of the lodge, whereupon I saw a tall brick wall ahead of me. My feet came to a stop, and my breath quickened. I knew this place. My heart picked up a beat and I found myself drawn closer without any conscious decision to do so. I reached the wall and gingerly laid my hand against the sun-warmed bricks. An image flashed through my head, one from my terrible dream where I was running, desperate to get within the wall and its safety.

I took a deep breath to calm myself. There was nothing here to be frightened of. I was not dreaming but walking in the gardens on a beautiful spring day. Keeping that in the forefront of my mind, I walked slowly around the wall which was too tall to see over. When I discovered a wooden door, my mind flashed another image from my dream, only I was not hammering my fists against it to get in. *Stay calm*, I repeated in my head. *You are awake and this is not a nightmare.*

The thick planks of the door were worn with age, its hinges and doorknob brown with rust. I turned the handle. Nothing. It was locked. My curiosity piqued. I was not about to concede. Wasn't this the very same place mirrored in my bad dreams for so many years and now here I stood on the brink of discovery? I had to find the key! Perhaps I should hasten back to the lodge and ask Fritz?

All at once I became lightheaded. I blinked several times and waited for it to pass, then leaned against the door, scared I might faint. I concentrated on breathing deeply, and finally the feeling slowly subsided.

Dear God, what was wrong with me? Was I ill? This was the third time this had happened to me since arriving at the lodge. First the scent of pine, then the rocking horse and now this? I closed my eyes and continued to breathe slowly. When I finally opened them again, I glanced to the right of the door and upward, where an extra brick supported a tiny wooden birdhouse. Without a thought, I reached up into the little wooden box, took out a large metal key, put it in the lock, turned it and opened the door.

The door whined on its hinges as I pushed it open and went across the threshold, whereupon I stopped. It was a walled garden, or at least it had been, once. I stepped down several stone steps and saw the square courtyard of paving stones with weeds growing through the cracks. Around the courtyard were what must have been flowerbeds and remnants of a lawn. In one corner stood a large Weeping Willow tree, its branches drooping sadly to touch the ground.

Then I realised what I had just done, and I

trembled. Without conscious thought, I had retrieved the key to the garden's door though I had no prior knowledge of where it was kept. My legs shook, and I felt sick in my stomach. Gingerly I lowered myself to the ground and sat down on one of the steps.

This place was without a doubt the scene of my nightmare. But more importantly, I knew I must have been here before. The knowledge hit me in a thought so real, so raw that I knew it to be true. I lifted my eyes to look around the garden, and as sure as I knew my name, I had stood in this very spot. That strange feeling in my head I had experienced with the pines, the rocking horse, recognising the wall and now automatically knowing where to find a hidden key, all made sense.

But when? I had no actual memory of ever being at Lorelei Lodge, so how could it be? The answer came easily. Mother must have brought me here as a young child—it would account for it, surely? For I would not remember specifics, but there would be sensory memories, familiar smells, objects, and I had probably seen another take the key when I was too small to reach it myself.

I sighed with relief. I was not going mad then. Perhaps someone else would remember my being there? The baroness? She must have seen me with my mother. I pushed the thought aside. For the moment, I wanted to take in the scene before me and think about it. After a few minutes, I got to my feet and continued down the stone steps to the courtyard.

The paving stones were barely visible beneath the crocheted weave of grass and weeds. Were they familiar? Not really. I crossed the area and walked through the flowerbeds which had long gone to nature, then through waist high wispy grass to the corner where the solitary tree stood.

I knew this spot. Though everything was grown wild and unkempt, I knew this tree. Had I picnicked beneath it as a young child? It would be plausible after all. Then another thought hit me. A seat—there was some type of place to sit, I was certain of it. I moved closer, my eyes scanning through the tall blades of grass and then I saw it. A piece of iron poking out of the greenery.

It was an old wrought iron bench which had seen better days, its back rail barely perceptible to the naked eyes, so overgrown had it become. Tentatively, I reached out my fingers to touch the metal, as though by doing so, I might be transported back to another time where I could remember. But nothing came to my mind. I was not disheartened, for there was much to think about now I had learned something new.

I surveyed the forgotten garden. It was a sad place, whatever it might have once been long ago. But now it was mine, and perhaps I could remedy that.

Chapter Seven

Dieter, the footman, was more than happy becoming my official translator. He and Joan were now fast friends, and though I teased her about being a flirt, I could tell their relationship was more like mother and son.

The young German was from a small town called Minden. He had accepted the position at the lodge, because he'd never left home before, and the salary was better than he could make working locally.

With Dieter's help, within two days of my discovering the hidden garden, I had met with the gardeners and Fritz to tell them of my wishes. The work had already commenced, and each day I made a point of walking there to see the progress.

I kept the revelation about my memory of being at the lodge before to myself, though I carefully picked over Joan's mind at every opportunity, which was difficult to do without arousing her suspicion. I was frustrated she could not help me more, but then she had not been in Mother's employ that long ago.

This morning I was back in the study where I seemed to spend most of my time. I had discovered all the account books in a locked cabinet behind the desk and was busy scouring through every page. I was determined to find someone, anyone who might remember my being at Lorelei. Currently, I read one of the ledgers of household information—bills for food, and purchases made by the staff. In the front, I searched to see if there was a list of servants. I knew that was the practice in most homes. Yet none were mentioned here.

I reached for another ledger, this one a slim volume. The first page showed a very different hand to the others, the writing spidery and small. It was an account's book, but not of bills paid, but of monies coming in. My pulse quickened as I looked down the page. This must be my aunt Gisela's personal record. Each month, beginning in the year I was born, there were two entries, one amount which I assumed was from my father, and then one-hundred marks per month from what I now knew to be from Mother. Regular as clockwork, month after month, the entries were made and dated. I flipped through the pages, and then saw something which gave me pause.

January of Eighteen ninety-three, only two years ago, a third entry appeared. Just as the others, this amount was regularly entered, until the month of my aunt's death several weeks ago when everything stopped. I closed the book and set it down on the desk, sitting back in my chair with a sigh. How very odd? Gisela Bergman, by all accounts an unfriendly old woman, was being paid by three different people every single month. Why?

My father's money was probably to appease Mother by taking care of her only relative. With his propensity to be tight-fisted, I was not shocked my mother supplemented that amount, nor that her estate continued the payments after her death. But where was the other sum coming from? It frustrated me that there was no one to ask. Yet that in itself was strange too? I must find out who worked for my aunt. Only then would I get any answers.

I began a note to Herr Vogel, when Fritz knocked on the door and came in bearing an envelope on a small silver tray. I took it, thanking him, and recognised the now familiar bear crest of the von Brandts at the *Safranpalast*. It was an invitation to dinner for the very next evening. The thought pleased me as I had not seen Max since the night at the opera, and though I knew I should not allow myself to keep thinking about him, I found it difficult to stop. I accepted the invitation, rang the bell for Fritz, and then went in search of Joan to discuss what I would wear.

I DID NOT ENJOY wearing black. In truth, I had never been particularly interested in fashion before coming to Germany, and part of me felt foolish caring about my appearance—mainly because I knew the reason why.

My head had never been turned by a man before, and it opened a pathway in my mind that was unfamiliar and slightly exciting. I had no basis upon which to build my affection for Max. He'd behaved respectfully at all times. Yet I remembered the way his dark eyes lingered upon mine on several occasions. That, and the sadness he seemed to hold at bay intrigued my inexperienced feminine interest. There was nothing I could do to arrest it.

That he was still legally wed was enough to keep my imagination from running too far ahead. Perhaps that was part of Max's allure? For he was unattainable and therefore safe. This was a changing time in my life. I was far from home, recently bereft of all family members. Was it so terrible that I indulged myself in a little daydreaming? What could it hurt after all?

Herr Metzger drew up the carriage at the *Safranpalast,* and I delighted in how beautiful the fountain was, lit up in the darkness of night. The palace resembled a fairy land with all the brightness shining from within the open windows.

A footman helped me from the carriage and led me inside. Once in the magnificent hallway, another footman collected me and escorted me down the same corridor Max had taken me. But this time we stopped before reaching the library. The servant opened large double doors and I followed him in.

There were several people already in the room, most whom I did not recognise. I eagerly sought out the familiar face of Max, but he was preoccupied, stood with his back facing me, deep in conversation with an older gentleman. With some relief, I noticed Saul and Susanna were present, this eased my nerves considerably. But like Max, they were already engaged with others. I stood awkwardly, unsure what to do.

"*Guten Abend, Fräulein* Rutherford." The voice was instantly recognisable as Wolfgang's. He came up from behind me and I was not in a position to move away without appearing rude.

"*Guten Abend, Herr* von Brandt," I replied politely. Wolfgang was smartly dressed in evening attire. His waistcoat was a pretty shade of bronze satin, which emphasised the unusual shade of his light brown eyes. He gave me his roguish smile, yet I found it disconcerting.

"I am glad you have come to dine with us," he said. "I am sorry it has taken so long for an invitation, but at least we remedy that this evening." He glanced around the room. "Are you familiar with any of our guests? Of course, I know you are friends with the Koppelmans, but have you been introduced to anyone else since your arrival in *Linnenbrink*?"

"No," I replied. "I only know your family and the Americans. I do not count the ladies who have called upon me, as our meetings were brief and have not been repeated."

Wolfgang's face lit up as he chuckled. "I can imagine why someone as young and interesting as you would have little in common with the ageing matrons of our village. Perhaps you can visit the palace more often and acquaint yourself with Katja who is far closer to your age and, like you, starved of pleasant company."

I thought of his wife who I had met briefly in the park. She hadn't seemed interested in being friendly with me whatsoever. I doubted very much I'd be paying her a social call. But I was not about to tell that to him.

"How are you spending your time at the lodge?" Wolfgang asked. "Do you find plenty of activities to keep you busy?"

"Surprisingly, yes," I answered honestly. "As I was unaware of my aunt's existence I have been busy going through her study, trying to acquaint myself with the business of the place, among other things."

He smiled again, his eyes intent on my own. "It does not sound as though you are having any fun, *Fräulein*. I understand there are tasks that need seeing too, but there is also time for play."

I did not like the flirtatious tone of his voice. Wolfgang was a handsome man, used to charming any female. He did not impress me. In fact, his demeanour had quite the opposite effect. I was still trying to formulate a response when Susanna came to my rescue. She was dressed in a gown the colour of coral, and she looked lovely.

"There you are, Ingrid. Thank goodness you are come." She gave Wolfgang a shy smile and I would swear she fluttered her eyelashes. "Though it is a wonderful evening, and I am delighted to be here at the palace," she said to cover up her rude comment. "But I find myself unable to converse with anyone. The gentlemen are too immersed speaking about business and other boring subjects related to industry. I have tried to talk with some of the ladies, but they don't appear to understand English. Now you are here, you can rescue me, Ingrid."

Wolfgang seemed vaguely amused by her bluntness. He gave a short laugh. "We must not have our American guest getting bored. *Fräulein* Koppelman, perhaps you will allow me to give you a brief tour of this part of the palace? After which we will be called in to dine, and I believe you are seated next to me. I shall do my utmost to keep you entertained!"

Susanna's cheeks flushed. "That is too kind of you, sir." She was unable to disguise the rapt pleasure from her voice.

"Then please excuse us, *Fräulein* Rutherford," Wolfgang said holding out his arm for Susanna to take. "We shall see you at dinner." With that, they walked away. Rather than stand where I was, I moved over to one of the large open windows and looked out into the night. I could see the beautiful fountain and hear the spray of water. Was any of this familiar? I did not think so. Therefore, it was unlikely Mother brought me to the palace, even though the baroness was her dear friend.

That did seem strange. I would have thought she'd call upon her whenever she was at Lorelei.

"You are deep in thought, Ingrid." Max joined me at the window, and I turned to him with a smile already on my lips. He glanced at my face, and his eyes lingered as I watched him study me.

"You look very lovely, Ingrid. Your skin is radiant this evening. I believe the German air must agree with you."

I smiled, self-conscious of the compliment. "I believe it is less radiant, and more sunburned."

"Ah." He chuckled. "Then you have been spending time outdoors? That is good. You must not stay shut up in a dusty old building. Have you been taking walks? I haven't seen you when I'm out with the dogs."

A footman stopped by carrying a silver platter with several crystal glasses of sherry. I took one and thanked him.

"I have not been walking, but working, Max."

"In the grounds?"

"Indeed. Well, in one specific place. The walled garden."

"Oh, yes. I had forgotten about that little spot."

"It seems everyone had. It looked like a wilderness and quite forlorn."

"What are you doing to it?" he asked.

"The gardeners are tearing out the paving and clearing all the overgrown weeds. Beyond that, we are still discussing the plans."

"I haven't been in that place for many years—since I was a boy. My brothers and I used to try and climb the wall and sneak in there as it was always kept locked." He smiled at the memory. "I think it's wonderful you're resurrecting the place. I shall have to come and inspect it very soon."

A sudden eruption of noise filled the room as the guests began clapping their hands. Both Max and I looked away from each other to see what was happening.

Stood in the doorway, the vision of a Greek goddess draped in a golden silk gown, was Valentina Cavaletti. Her ebony hair was bound up in an intricate braid, and she wore thick rings of gold in her ears. She practically glided into the room on the wave of mutual adoration and reverence which permeated the atmosphere. I heard Max mutter something low and unintelligible.

"*Lieblings.*" Valentina had not even looked our way but greeted the other guests. "Would you mind if I invite myself to join you this evening?"

There was more applause, and the lovely woman beamed. She was breath-taking. Behind her, Wolfgang and Susanna came into the room, and I watched as the young American's face lit up with happiness while her escort frowned. Apparently Wolfgang was not happy to see his sister-in-law. Then before anyone had time to collect themselves dinner was announced. I turned to speak to Max, but he had stepped away, his expression thunderous.

Susanna joined me and together we found Saul who would escort us both into dinner. I was disappointed that my host had abandoned me without an explanation, but I forgave him for being uncomfortable at the unexpected appearance of his wife. Valentina must rarely mix with the family judging by his reaction and Wolfgang's as well.

Thankfully, Saul and I were seated together, Susanna several chairs down, next to Wolfgang. I had not seen his wife, Katja, and I wondered at her absence. Perhaps she was unwell? I counted fifteen of us around the large banquet table. Max was at the head of the table as befitted his status. There were several people between us, and I was sorry we would not be able to converse.

There was a sudden flurry of activity at the other end of the grand table, as a liveried servant seated Madame Cavaletti. She sat in the dining chair as though it were a throne, and gaily held court for her admiring public.

The tension in the room felt palpable to me, and I wondered if any of the others noticed? Yet looking around, it appeared they did not. It was odd Valentina had not been expected for dinner, at least that is how it seemed. I would have thought she'd be included whenever she stayed at the palace. Perhaps she had declined initially and then had a change of heart?

Over the first course, which was *Kartoffelsuppe*, a delicious potato soup, Saul and I chatted amiably about current affairs. We lamented the loss of a Spanish Naval ship, which had been sunk in a storm, taking four-hundred and twenty souls with it. This led to Saul's description of sailing from New York to Southampton, England. It sounded like quite the adventure.

By the time we were eating the main course, a stew made with tender beef, cabbage and potatoes, I was quite comfortable in the company of Saul Koppelman.

"She really is quite spoiled, you know." Saul was telling tales about his sister. "And I am as much to blame as my parents. See, my mother had Susie late in life, and we've all treated the little minx like a princess. I told them she needed a dose of reality, to see how other people lived, and that is why she accompanied me to Germany. The hope was she might quit being so concerned with balls and gowns and grow up a little." As if on cue, Susanna's pretty laugh rose above the chatter and Saul shook his head. "I don't think my plan has worked yet." He grinned at me. "She has a beau back home, you know."

This was a surprise. "Indeed? She has never mentioned it."

"Because she finds Henry boring. Though I am sure with her penchant for trinkets she will not find his fortune dull." Saul said, spearing a piece of meat on his fork. "He's a decent fellow, only a year older than Susie, but they will make a fine match. I think Father expects her to have a change of heart while she is away."

I looked down the table to see Susanna staring adoringly at Wolfgang, her face glowing in admiration. "I would not bank on it, Saul."

The remainder of the dinner passed without incidence, and at length, upon Valentina's suggestion, the ladies left the table so the men might enjoy their cigars. I found this custom irritating. I had no interest sitting in a drawing room listening to women chatting about fashion and society. Not that I blamed my gender for their lack of topics, more that they were so accepting of it. Why could we not discuss politics and economics, even war, as the men did behind closed doors while they puffed on their tobacco like little steam engines?

Once we were gathered in the drawing room, Susanna and I sat down together.

"Is this not the most wonderful evening," she gushed, her eyes bright and her cheeks flushed.

I studied her expression with concern. "I am glad you're enjoying yourself," I answered, holding back what I really wanted to say. I worried for the girl as it was clear she was enchanted by the flirtatious Wolfgang von Brandt.

"*Senorina*, did we not meet at the opera?" The rich timbred voice carried across the room, directed at Susanna. It was Valentina, holding court in a large velvet armchair, surrounded by her adoring guests.

"Yes," Susanna said enthusiastically. "And your performance was—"

"Yet I have not been introduced to your friend there." Valentina interrupted, gesturing towards me. "Would you do me the honour?" she asked Susanna, who jumped to her feet instantly and raised her eyebrows at me to do the same. Reluctantly I obeyed and followed her over to where the diva sat, resplendent in her shimmering golden gown.

Close up, the soprano was even lovelier than I had realised, and I felt such a conflict of emotion. For as much as I wanted to dislike her, I could not help but be fascinated. The woman exuded magnetism, her sensual mouth, her bold, unapologetic black eyes, her regal, Roman nose.

Valentina asked one of the other ladies to make room for us to sit.

"It seems your reputation precedes you, *Fräulein* Rutherford. You are quite the topic in *Linnenbrink,* and I have been meaning to visit your little home to see what all the fuss is about." There was a note of boredom in her words. "But rehearsals have kept me too busy." Her lilting voice held the flavour of her Italian ancestry. "Still, now we finally meet."

Initially I flinched under the impact of her judgmental stare. If the Italian sought to intimidate me, she would be disappointed. I'd had plenty of experience with those tactics from my formidable father. I sat up straight and looked at her directly. "I saw your performance, *Signora*, it was magnificent. My first opera, and an unforgettable one at that."

"*Perfetto*," she said and gifted me with a smile. "I am honoured. Now we are neighbours, I shall hope to see you again very soon." One corner of her full mouth turned up in half a smile. "Tell me. What do you think of this place? It is very different from London, is it not? How you say, a little *provinciale*?"

"I find it quite the contrary," I replied. "Indeed, the *Safranpalast* makes Buckingham Palace drab in comparison, and with the amazing Opera House, *Prinzenstadt* has much to offer."

She raised a thick arched brow. "This surprises me. A young woman such as yourself is better suited in a large city. Will you stay here permanently then?"

I thought it an odd question. Why should she care about my plans? "I have not yet decided, *Signora*."

She studied my face as though searching it for something, and then her eyes shifted and glanced over my shoulder. "Maria, *sono pronto per andare*."

An older woman who I had not noticed appeared. Our conversation was over. Her attendant waited for her mistress to rise. Then they linked arms, and the diva left the room to a repeat of the earlier applause. But as the beautiful soprano reached the door, she turned, and for one brief moment met my gaze. What I saw there was not friendship.

Once she had gone, the room was filled with chatter. Susanna assaulted my ears with a barrage of comments that were all uninteresting and mainly in praise of Valentina. But all I could see was the look she had just given me which was unsettling. What had I done to make the beautiful opera star dislike me?

With those thoughts tumbling through my mind, the adjoining doors to the dining room opened and the men came in, bringing the scent of brandy and cigars with them. I looked up just as Max von Brandt walked into the drawing room, and as I took in his well-built frame, his dark, handsome looks, I suddenly understood why the Italian diva disliked me and my heart sank. Valentina Cavaletti was still in love with her husband.

Chapter Eight

I SURPRISED HERR VOGEL at his office early the next morning. My sleep had been disrupted by my relentless nightmare, followed by fitful hours of tossing and turning while my thoughts chewed over my heritage, and the black eyes of *Signora* Cavaletti. My mood was not at its best, but I intended to get some answers. There had to be a link between something in my past and the nightmares which had plagued me for so long.

The lawyer almost dropped his pen when I strode into his room unannounced. "*Fräulein* Rutherford. What brings you here?" He got to his feet, but I waved at him to sit down.

I placed the folder he had given me on his desk. "Here are the papers, as promised. I thank you for allowing me to read them. I have many questions I should like to ask, if you are not too busy?"

By the looks of his desk, he probably was, but his pale eyes stared at me, and perhaps he saw the determination in my expression, because he considered for a moment, and then sat back in his chair. "What can I help you with?" he said kindly.

I steeled myself. "*Herr* Vogel, though I have researched much regarding my family, I still have few answers. It appears my aunt had no money and was dependent on funds sent by my father each month, and another private arrangement of money sent by my mother."

"*Ja*, that is correct," he agreed.

I laid the small ledger on his desk. He picked it up and opened it.

"I found this in my aunt's study. Do you have any idea where this other income came from?"

The older man frowned, and one hand stroked his wispy grey beard. "*Nein*. I have not seen this before. Your aunt kept accurate records."

"What has happened to her bank account? Would I have access to it as her heir?"

He shook his head. "*Nein*. Your name is not on the account. It will have already been closed and the funds put into her estate."

"Then I have no way to trace where this money originated?"

"You do not."

I tried to hide my disappointment. "*Herr* Vogel, have you ever met me before?"

"That is a strange question," he said. "What do you mean?"

"Did you meet me when I was a child? When I came to *Linnenbrink* with my mother."

I saw a flicker of emotion run across his face and that answered my question. "Please," I said. "Do not lie. I wish only to understand my past and there are so few people who can help me."

His long fingers continued toying with his beard. "As a lawyer, I am bound by oath to keep confidences of my clients. This is the case with your family, *Fräulein* Rutherford. Yet, as you point out, you are the only remaining Bergman, so perhaps as it cannot harm anyone nor will I be breaking my word, I can share what little I know."

My pulse sped up in anticipation.

"Your Aunt Gisela and your mother were not close. But when your mother married, Thomas Rutherford would not remain in Germany and insisted that she moved to England with him. Gisela had no income of her own, and so she took up residence in the lodge to care for the family home for which your father sent funds. However, your father was not generous, and Gisela complained to your mother that she needed additional monies, or she would not stay. Hence the 'arrangement'. I believe your father's wishes were to sell Lorelei Lodge, but as the property remained in your mother's name, he could not."

"What about my coming here?" I asked.

He nodded. "Your mother visited often, and she brought you on many occasions. Once you were four or five, she stopped bringing you."

"I knew I had been here before," I blurted. "I kept seeing things that are familiar."

"That is natural. Although you were very young."

"Why did my mother stop bringing me?"

The older man shrugged thin shoulders. "That, I do not know, nor did I ask. I am sure she had her reasons."

"I want to find out what they were." I said defiantly. "I need answers."

"*Fräulein* Rutherford, I believe you make this more complicated than it is. Travelling with young children is tedious. Perhaps your mother left you in London so your routine would go undisturbed—your lessons not interrupted?"

I shook my head. "No, that would not have mattered." I sighed. "Is there anything else you can tell me about the past, *Herr* Vogel?"

I watched him think. His brows furrowed and he took a deep breath. "I remember back in those days Gisela Bergman had a married couple who tended for the lodge and lived there with her. Let me see." He rose from the desk, his tall body unfolding like a piece of folded paper. He went to one of the file cabinets and opened different drawers until he finally found the correct one. He pulled out another file, squinted at it, grunted, and then brought it back to where I waited. He opened the file and flicked through several papers.

"In addition to handling your mother's personal affairs, I was also charged with the arrangement of payments to the staff at Lorelei, up until the new people were hired and then your aunt kept her own accounts. Ah, here we are." He opened a small black book and turned it to face me.

"As you can see, the entries start in eighteen-seventy, and are continued until, hmm." He turned it back so he could read better. "That's right, I recollect it now. Eighteen months ago, the couple were paid a large sum of three-hundred marks, and then replaced with the servants you currently employ now. Their name is here at the top." He pointed to the writing on the page.

"Gustav and Klara Krause," I read aloud. "I have never heard of them. Are they local, do you think?"

"I do not know." He squinted at the writing. "They were paid in coin and not a banker's draft. But if anyone could answer your questions, it would be them." He took a small piece of notepaper and wrote down their names. I put it in my reticule and got to my feet.

"*Herr* Vogel, thank you so much for assisting me. I do appreciate your help."

He looked so serious peering at me behind his round spectacles, his eyes pale, his beard and hair a mess. When he smiled at me, I was surprised by the attachment I felt between us. Because other than Joan, *Herr* Vogel was the only person I knew in Germany that I could count upon.

I WALKED IN THE GROUNDS in an attempt to shake off the strange mood which had plagued me all day. Though I tried to keep my mind occupied with thoughts of my plans going forward, I could not concentrate. Instead, I vacillated between the events at dinner the previous night, my strange encounter with Valentina Cavaletti, and my meeting today with *Herr* Vogel.

The lawyer had helped me tremendously by giving me a new thread to follow. This alone should have put me in better spirits because I was finally making progress. Yet it had not. Therefore, I reasoned, the culprit of my disposition must lay at the feet of the beautiful Italian opera singer. Why had *Signora* Cavaletti had such an impact on me? I knew the answer, and I felt foolish.

No matter what Susanna, or indeed Max, had said about his wife, there was no way in the world a man like the Baron would have any interest in someone as ordinary as me. Even allowing myself to think about it was a ridiculous notion, because Max was a married man. And no matter what my feelings or opinions were, it was a futile waste of my interest.

I arrived at the walled garden, noting, as I entered through the open door, that the workers had finished for the day. Although it still looked quite a wreck, the progress the men had made was impressive. The overgrown weeds were gone. The cracked flag stones had been removed, and the long grass surrounding the Willow tree scythed back, exposing the old iron bench I had seen poking through. The courtyard would be replaced in the centre of the garden, and I was considering the installation of some type of water feature, so taken was I by the beautiful fountain at the palace.

I wanted this garden to be a place of serenity, as it had remained hidden for so long which seemed sad. Perhaps my mother had played here as a child? And she had spent time in here with me as my memory of it was so strong.

Unfortunately, though I recognised the garden as a sanctuary of sorts, it was still prominent in my nightmare. I hoped my being here in person might eradicate whatever caused my bad dreams, but so far it had not.

The sound of running caught my attention and I turned in time to see Max's dogs bounding in my direction. For a moment my breath caught as I remembered how fearsome they could be, but their tails wagged, and they were excited to have spotted me. Where the dogs were, Max would be close behind. The thought of his company cheered me up.

Frido and Sascha greeted me with a friendly lick and immediately rushed past me into the garden where all the exposed soil would give them a banquet to sniff.

"I am sorry," said Max coming up behind me. "Once they caught your scent, the dogs were intent upon seeing you. I hope you don't mind?"

"No," I laughed. "They are most welcome now I know they won't eat me."

He stepped closer and looked around. "My goodness, look at all the work that has been done. I am very pleased you are undertaking this project."

"Indeed? Because you hope to purchase the lodge and therefore would have one less job to do?"

"Yes," he grinned. "You have read my thoughts exactly. No, of course not, Ingrid. I am just happy seeing something restored to its original beauty. This was always a unique and lovely place."

"Did you come here often as a child, Max?" Had he seen me here? Surely he would have mentioned that before now.

"Oh, yes, on several occasions. Mother brought us to visit when Marta was here. We would come for a picnic. I think both our mothers liked that it was safe because the door could be closed. My brothers and I were notorious for running off and getting lost in the forest."

"Do you remember ever seeing me as a child, Max?"

"Sadly, no, I do not. But I am several years older than you. Günther is closer to your age. He may have met you on some occasion. If he were here I could ask him, but alas, his work keeps him in Switzerland."

"What does he do there?"

"He is the clever one in the family. He is a chemist and works in a laboratory in Geneva," he said with pride. And then he looked at me thoughtfully. "It saddens you does it not, feeling like a stranger here and searching for those who knew you in your youth?"

"I suppose it does," I replied. "Being in my mother's familial home, I'm disappointed she did not introduce me to the people she knew when I was a child."

"It is odd. But your mother was an honourable person. Therefore, I would surmise she had good reason not having you associate with others. Of course, I do not include my own mother when I say that, because I know how dear they were as friends. I am sorry it upsets you, Ingrid."

"It shouldn't, yet it does. Mother was a wonderful person and generous with her affection. In London, she took me everywhere with her, and always acted as though she was proud of me. It's hard comprehending why she did not show the same courtesy in her homeland. I hate to think she was ashamed of me." Much to my horror, I heard the waver in my voice and knew tears were close. I was being ridiculous. I was never this sentimental. What on earth was the matter with me?

Max took one of my hands in his. His grip was strong, his skin surprisingly rough and warm. "Ingrid, seldom do we understand the actions of our families," he said, staring hard into my eyes. "If your mother was the person you believe her to be, then you must accept that whatever her actions, she had your welfare at heart. It would be far more beneficial determining what she did not like about the people she kept you from. Then you would better understand her motive, do you not agree?"

I considered his words, all the while conscious of my hand still held tightly in his. "That is sage advice," I said. "I appreciate your understanding. The past weeks have been tiresome, and my usual countenance affected by recent events. I am overreacting and shall do better. Thank you, Max."

Both dog's ears pricked up as they heard someone approaching. Max dropped my hand and called the dogs to his side. Moments later, Joan walked into the garden and let out a squeal of terror at one glimpse of the massive dogs laying at the feet of their master.

"Good God," she shrieked. "What are those monsters doin' here?" She quickly stepped behind me as though I could protect her.

I tried to reassure her. "I thought they looked terrifying when I first saw them. But they are actually sweet animals. They just need to know your scent. Come, Joan." I moved away from her, but she instantly stepped behind me once again.

"You must greet them by holding out your hand so they can smell you. That way they learn your scent, and understand you are a friend." I encouraged.

"Bugger that," Joan gasped, recoiling in horror. "I'm not puttin' my hand anywhere near 'em! It'll be bitten off an' swallowed in one gulp."

Max reassured her that would not be the case, but after stating he did not want to frighten the maid any more than she already had been, he made his farewells, whistled to the dogs, and set off back towards the palace.

"Blimey," Joan said when he had gone. "You must be mad getting' anywhere near those beasts."

"You were looking for me?" I prompted.

"Oh, yes." She collected herself. "It's that silly American woman." Joan's opinion of Susanna was unusually poor. She thought her shallow and had little tolerance for her conversation. Joan believed that anyone who considered being fashionable the most important goal in life, was a waste of time.

We walked back to the lodge, and I immediately went to greet my friend who waited in the drawing room.

Susanna was at the window staring out. She turned to face me as I came into the room, and I was surprised to see her looking so sombre. She was dressed in a dark blue gown, which was unusual as she always wore such flamboyant colours. The shade of it emphasised the dour look upon her face.

I walked over to her. "Good day, Susanna. I did not expect you. Is anything amiss?"

She did not answer but nodded her head and I saw her eyes were full of tears.

"Oh dear, what is wrong?" I was unsure what to do, not being used to caring for others I was at a loss.

"I hate my life," she said as tears rolled down her face. "I am so utterly miserable, and I cannot bear it."

"Come," I said. "Let us sit." I led Susanna to the settle and then rang for Fritz. By the time he appeared, Susanna had composed herself and I asked the butler to bring something cool to drink. Once he departed I looked at the young forlorn woman beside me.

"What has happened to make you so upset? Have you argued with your brother?"

"No," she said quietly. "Would that I had, then at least something would be happening." Her lovely blue eyes searched mine. "Ingrid, please tell me truthfully, am I ugly?"

"What?"

"Am I an ugly woman? Are my features ungainly, my colour peaky? Please, I beg you to be honest with me."

"You ask ridiculous questions, Susanna," I berated.

"You are perhaps one of the prettiest ladies I have ever met. In fact, had I not liked you as a friend, I should be jealous and never speak to you."

This brightened her spirits. "Really? Oh, Ingrid. Thank you so much."

There was a knock on the door and Fritz came in with two glasses of lemonade. He set the tray on a nearby table and then left us alone.

Susanna took up her glass and sipped her drink.

"Tell me," I asked. "What has brought this on?"

She set the glass on the table, and two pink spots appeared on her cheeks. "I should not really say. I do not want you to think badly of me."

"Nonsense," I encouraged. "We are friends. Therefore, I will not judge you."

She hesitated for a moment and then in a rush of words blurted, "It is Wolfgang. I am in love with him."

"I beg your pardon. Wolfgang von Brandt?" The incredulous tone of my voice was difficult to disguise.

Susanna flinched. "You see, you are shocked because he is so handsome, and you think me inferior for a man like him."

"On the contrary," I exclaimed. "My incredulity is based solely upon the fact that Wolfgang is a married man with a child, and if he is bestowing attention upon you *he* is the inferior. Susanna, you are a vulnerable young woman who is far from home. Tell me, has he encouraged you?"

Her face flushed another shade of pink. "I cannot say."

"Cannot, or will not? Susanna, men like Wolfgang are not the type of men for women of our age. Wolfgang should not have a flirtation with you as he is married, but neither should you be seeking one out knowing full well his situation. He is not available to you. Any dalliance you have with him will ruin you, and your family's reputation. A man in Wolfgang's position has nothing to offer a woman but the role of a mistress. Is that the measure of your value? How do you think your brother, indeed your parents, would feel about that?"

"I do not care how they feel. It is not their business how I live my life. I have no say in what they do. Why should they have a say in my own?"

Inwardly I groaned. This was not going to be easy. "Susanna, everything you do is most certainly your family's business while you are totally dependent upon them. Who pays for your living, your welfare? Are you prepared to lose that and care for yourself?" It was easy to see she had not given this very much thought. The girl was more immature than I realised.

I continued. "Has Wolfgang made promises to you?"

"No," She pouted. "He flirts with me and pays me compliments, but that is as far as he will go. I am convinced he does not find me attractive enough."

"And that is the source of your distress? That there is a possibility Wolfgang will *not* pursue you?" I could not hide my astonishment.

"Yes. And before you say anything else, do not lecture me. I have seen the way you look at Max and the way he looks at you. Are we really so different?"

She had me. The irony was difficult to deny. But I would not admit anything to Susanna when I could barely admit it to myself.

"There is nothing wrong with admiring a

gentleman, or indeed his admiration of you. It becomes a transgression if either one of you pursue a situation that should not occur. Susanna, I don't fault you for an attraction. Wolfgang is a very handsome man and would catch any maiden's eye. But he does not have the right to encourage you when he knows he can offer you nothing. You must stay away from the man."

Her body stiffened and her jaw set. I felt the concern of a mother, when in reality barely four years separated us in age. It was almost laughable that me, an unworldly, unsociable matron should be giving romantic advice to a beautiful socialite who had travelled and no doubt experienced far more than myself. But there it was. And judging by the stubborn expression on Susanna's face, she did not plan to take any notice of me. I had tried.

APPARENTLY IT WAS TO be a day of visitors at Lorelei. Not an hour after Susanna left, Fritz announced that Saul was here to see me. The young American came into the drawing room and declined the offer of refreshment as he took a seat.

I liked Saul's youthful face, for he always seemed to be in good spirits. Like his sister, Saul was gifted with handsome features, and the delightful quality of a person always ready to be jovial.

"Gosh, Ingrid. I really do apologise for turning up unannounced," he said. "But I've been meaning to speak with you for a few days, and somehow I never can get away."

"You're not interrupting anything," I assured him. "By coincidence, I spoke with your sister earlier today." I wondered if our topic was to be the same. I hoped not.

"Susie speaks of you frequently, and I am so grateful you've befriended her. I fear this trip has been terribly disappointing for her. At least with you she has someone close in age to spend time with. And, in fact, she is the very reason I am here."

"Indeed?" I braced myself.

He nodded. "Susanna will celebrate her twenty-second birthday in just a few days. With our staying in a hotel, it is hardly conducive for having much of a celebration. Therefore, I'm going to be extremely bold. I have a request I should like to ask of you."

"Let me guess," I said with relief. "You wish to have a dinner party in her honour, here at Lorelei?"

Saul's cheeks turned bright red. "Why, when you say it out loud, it sounds so impertinent for me to even consider asking. And, Ingrid, I do not ask lightly, I promise. If my sister were in her usual good spirits, I would take her into *Prinzenstadt*, buy her some new clothes or finery, and then end the day with a nice dinner. But lately, Susie's been a little withdrawn. To tell you the truth, I'm kind of worried.

I figured if we gathered the handful of folks she knows, it would make her so happy, and be more like her birthdays at home." He held up his hand. "Now, I know it's a lot to ask of anyone, and you won't insult me if you say no. In fact, I wouldn't blame you one bit 'cause I'm well aware it's a big undertaking."

My heart went out to him. I felt his distress. And that, mingled with my admiration for Saul being such a good, kind brother, had influenced my decision from when he'd uttered his first sentence. After all, it wasn't as though the work would be on my shoulders. My role was to play hostess. In any social event the responsibilities fell upon the servants. I would talk to them later this evening.

"Saul, don't worry yourself about it. I would be delighted to host such an event. It's about time I entered local society, and I can't think of a better reason to celebrate than Susanna's birthday. She'll be so pleased. All I will need from you is a list of those you wish to invite, and I'll send out invitations on your behalf." I had an idea. "I know. We'll serve American dishes! I'll ask Cook to bake a special cake in Susanna's honour as well."

Saul's face beamed with both pleasure and relief. "Ingrid, you're a very generous person and a true friend. I'll gladly accept your kindness, but only if you ensure that I'll cover all the expenses of the evening."

I gave a chuckle. "Don't worry, Saul. You'll hear no argument from me. What day would you like to have this dinner party?"

He thought for a moment. "Her birthday is next Wednesday. Is it appropriate to celebrate it then?"

"I don't see why not. But with little notice, you'll need to have a list to me by tomorrow morning. That will give me three days to notify everyone."

"I'll go back to the hotel and draft it immediately and have it sent around by this evening." He got to his feet, and I followed suit.

"Ingrid." Saul came towards me and took one of my hands in his. His blue eyes blazed into my face with such appreciation and gratitude that I smiled.

"If there is ever a time when I may do anything to help you, please know you can always count on me. One good deed always deserves another. You will always have my friendship."

I watched at the window as Saul mounted his horse and rode away. My mind worked furiously on how to plan for the party, but I turned when I heard someone come into the room.

"I reckon that chap's got his eye on you," said Joan cheekily. "He's a good looker, if you like the American type."

"He is a handsome fellow, Joan. But you're wrong about him liking me in that way. Saul's just grateful to have some help with an unruly sister who has a birthday coming up." I glanced at my maid who looked puzzled.

"We have some busy times ahead of us, Joan. I'm to host a dinner party on Wednesday."

Joan's eyes grew round with surprise. "Blimey, miss. I never know what to expect with you anymore. You spent all those years in London, shut up in a house and never wantin' to do anythin' since your dear mum died. Yet in the five minutes we've been in Germany, you've dug up an entire garden an' now you're havin' a blasted party. Whatever next?"

I could not help but grin. "You shall have to wait and see."

Chapter Nine

EMBOLDENED BY THE EVENTS of the past week and with a strong desire to get answers, I set off for the palace early Sunday morning. I had not requested an invitation, nor did I tell anyone I was walking over there. At least this time I would not be terrified should I encounter Max's dogs.

I had made a concerted effort not to think about the baron. Realistically, I had seen little of him to impact my day-to-day life. But I did miss our brief encounters and his company. He was not the reason for my visit today though. I intended to speak with his mother, Lisbeth.

I believed the baroness knew more about my past than any other, save the servants my aunt had used, whose location was still under investigation by *Herr* Vogel. It was disappointing that the baroness suffered a malady of the mind, but perhaps I could piece some of her comments together. It wasn't as if I had much to go on anyway.

When I arrived at the palace I was shown in without any hesitation. I asked the footman if it would be possible for me to see the baroness, and he requested I wait while he checked. He was gone for several minutes. Upon his return he explained the family were attending church in the village, but he had spoken with *Krankenschwester* Helga, and she had given permission for me to speak with her mistress.

The footman escorted me through the maze of palace corridors and then up the familiar beautiful staircase towards the baroness's apartments. This time, Max's mother was still in her bed, though she sat propped up, surrounded by a variety of satin pillows and cushions.

"*Guten Tag, Krankenschwester* Helga." I greeted the solemn nurse whose countenance was strange. She had not protested my visiting, yet I still felt unwelcome. There was something in her eyes which I found unsettling. It put me in mind of a cat, who wants your attention, but remains one step away from you.

The nurse suddenly spoke in broken English and asked if she could leave me alone for a short time as she needed to go down to the kitchen and speak with the housekeeper. I replied that I would stay with Lisbeth. She then explained to the baroness in German, that she would be right back.

As soon as the door closed, I pulled a chair closer to the bed while the baroness stared at me with a watery smile painted on her face. It was a cruel trick of nature to allow a woman of her age to retain the colour in her hair and a healthy complexion, yet steal away pieces of her mind. Lisbeth's dark brown eyes, so like those of her eldest son, had a cloudiness that suggested vacancy.

I sat forward and offered her my hand. I would speak in German to make it easier to communicate with the woman. No one would be able to hear anyway.

"It is so good to see you, Baroness," I said and was pleased to see her respond with a genuine smile.

"Dearest Marta," she sighed. "How I have missed you since you married that swine and went to England.

Life is not the same without you living close to me. I miss our chats and our walks. Tell me, how is the baby? Is she well? Have the doctors given you any hope?"

I was unsure how to respond. She mistook me for my mother, which was not surprising with the baroness's state of mind, and the fact I resembled my mother very much. I assumed she must be speaking of me as the baby. Lisbeth would have seen me on many occasions when Mother bought me with her to Lorelei. I did not recollect her telling me I had any serious ailment, though most babies often had illnesses of some kind or another when very young.

"And I have missed you too, Lisbeth." Was it wrong of me to maintain her mistaking my identity? The baroness did not look troubled. Quite the contrary. Believing herself to be with a dear friend seemed to make her content. It seemed the easiest route.

"He is cruel," she said with some anger. "How I wish you had never met him." Then Lisbeth reached out to take my hand, her bony fingers surprisingly strong. "It is unnatural for a man to behave this way. After all, he is supposed to be a father. I do worry so."

I presumed she still referred to my father. I was not shocked by her obvious dislike of him, for Thomas Rutherford was famous for being a difficult man. My feelings towards him had never been those of a loving daughter. I respected him and resented him in equal measure.

"You should stay here," she whispered, leaning forward to be closer." Otto will help you, I know he will."

She referred to be the former baron, Max's father.

"Yes," she hissed. "That's it. You can stay at

Lorelei and Otto will deal with Thomas. He will not bully him as he has you." Then all at once her expression softened as she stared at my chest. Her fingers let loose of my hand and instead found the pendant and laid it in her palm. "You still wear it? After all these years."

I jumped as the door opened.

"*Fräulein* Rutherford? What are you doing here?"

It was Wolfgang. At the sound of his voice, the baroness retreated back against her pillows and her face grew rigid.

I quickly got to my feet. "Hello Wolfgang," I said in English. "I was taking a walk and on an impulse came to see your mother. I hope it was all right? The *Krankenschwester* Helga knows I am here."

A flicker of displeasure crossed his face, I assumed he was annoyed with the nurse for leaving his mother alone with me.

"She went to the kitchen for a moment. I told her I would watch the baroness. She has been fine. We have had a lovely chat—reminiscing about my mother actually."

"Ah," he said coming closer. I noticed Lisbeth did not look at him but turned her head to face the window.

"Our mothers were indeed close friends for many years. That kind of friendship does not come often in a lifetime."

"Yes," I agreed. "It seems they were more sisters than friends."

The nurse came back into the room and there was a brief conversation between her and Wolfgang. He did not realise I understood what they were saying, and he did not hold back in his remonstrations that she had left his mother with a person no more than a stranger. Surprisingly *Krankenschwester* Helga did not seem intimidated at all. She replied that he could find another nurse if she was not satisfactory, and that seemed to shut Wolfgang up. How very odd?

"Come." He turned to me, all smiles again. "Let me escort you out as my mother needs her rest."

"Thank you. The palace is the size of a village, and I would get completely lost left to my own devices."

With a last glance at Lisbeth, who looked like she had suddenly shrunk in that massive bed, I followed Wolfgang out of the door.

He made polite conversation, mainly pointing out different artifacts as we walked along, offering up slices of history along the way. We started down the magnificent staircase and met Valentina who was ascending.

"*Bon giorno, Fräulein* Rutherford. What an unexpected pleasure it is to see you at the palace." Her black eyes flashed over to look at my escort. "I did not know you and the lovely *Fräulein* had a tête-à-tête this morning?"

I did not care for her tone, nor the insinuation, and I bristled immediately. Wolfgang, however, just gave her a lazy smile.

"*Fräulein* Rutherford came to see *Mutter*, dear sister. I am showing her the way out of the palace. I hope that is agreeable with you?" He raised an eyebrow.

"Do not concern yourself with my thoughts," Valentina said as she continued up the stairs. "Though Katja might have objections."

My intake of breath was audible. Wolfgang placed

a hand on my forearm and when I looked up at him he shook his head. He then led me down the remaining stairs and walked me to the door before he spoke again.

"Pay Valentina no mind," he soothed. "She is spiteful only because it pleases her."

"But why would she say such a thing?" I gasped. My anger was only equal to my embarrassment. Though I had done nothing to be ashamed of. "I barely know the woman."

"Valentina is a diva, on and off the stage. She can be quite nasty, especially to other women who she perceives as a threat."

"What are you talking about?" I was incredulous.

"My brother, Max."

"What? That is ridiculous."

"Yes," he said gently, staring into my eyes. "But you are an attractive young woman, and Valentina does not like any attention taken away from her. Do not give it another thought, *Fräulein*. My sister-in-law is a passionate Italian woman. But her sting is like a wasp, painful, but brief and does not penetrate deeply."

A footman appeared to open one of the large doors. I thanked Wolfgang and then left the palace at a walk, though I wanted to run.

"OOH, SHE'S A NASTY PIECE of work." Joan was quick to my defense when I recounted the exchange with the opera singer. "Now don't you go and get upset miss. Women like that will be wicked to anyone. If it hadn't been you 'twould have been somebody else."

I was up in the room, changing into another dress as I planned to go outside and work in the garden.

"Perhaps," I mused. Then I had another thought.

"Joan, was I a sickly child?"

She paused from hanging up my discarded gown. "Well now, I didn't know you as a baby. You were five when I come along. But you were seldom ill, and I don't recall Miss Marta sayin' otherwise. Why do you ask?" She hung the dress inside the wardrobe.

"No reason."

I finished dressing and went down for luncheon.

IT WAS ANOTHER FINE afternoon. Being Sunday, the workers were off today. I wanted to spend some time in the garden. The combination of fresh air and mindless work would give me time to empty my head and stop thinking for a while.

I was still rather put out by Valentina's rudeness, though if I were honest, there was a trace of guilt. I had done nothing wrong, nor behaved inappropriately with her husband, the baron. I was lonely, and Max had been kind to me. Wouldn't any woman react the same way to the attention of a considerate, handsome man?

I walked through the garden until I reached the little bench underneath the Willow. I sat down as though the weight of my thoughts were too heavy for me to stand. I glanced around, noting all the changes which had occurred since my last visit. There was much progress made, and I reminded myself to make a point of thanking the gardeners for their efforts when they were back tomorrow.

My fingers fumbled with my pendant as I pushed the exchange with Valentina to the back of my mind and revisited my conversation with the baroness. I understood she thought I was my mother. I was confused at her mention of my being a sickly baby, but the woman was hardly expected to remember things that far back. But what bothered me was her strong opinions of my father.

Thomas Rutherford had earned his reputation as a difficult man. The epitome of the British upper classes, he desired to live in what he considered perfection. A stickler for cleanliness, good behaviour and above all, flawless societal manners, he'd stepped outside his carefully tended boundaries by marrying a German.

Marta Bergman, young, beautiful and intelligent, was travelling through Europe and met my father in Paris. I fancied that free from the confines of his British entrapment, he had been an exciting and interesting fellow, for my mother often spoke of those days with warmth in her dark eyes.

But the father I knew was nothing of the sort. He was certainly handsome, cut a fashionable figure and was often remarked upon. But he was cold. If he loved me, he did not show it. I was another possession, as was Mother, one he kept a tight rein upon. Yet I knew he loved her. Though he designed her daily activities and oversaw most of her actions, she allowed him that power.

When my mother died, he was devastated. His abhorrence of being in my presence evident. Though it hurt me, I was not unused to his indifference. However, at the loss of my darling mother, I craved the affection of my only remaining parent.

"It's 'cos you look like her," Joan would remind me, after a particular experience might upset me. "Image of her, you are," she always said. "If it weren't for your father's ice-blue eyes, you could be the ghost of her come back." Joan insisted that was why Father stayed away from me except for the times he had no choice.

I toyed with my necklace and sat back against the bench staring up into a cloudless sky. Was it any wonder I found Max so appealing? For he was the first male to have shown an interest in me, and my opinions. At this revelation, a calm settled upon me, and I found it welcome.

Getting up, I walked around the hidden garden looking at the improvements and the foundation set for a small fountain, should I have one installed. I planned to have several flowerbeds dedicated to flowers I found particularly pleasing, and the beds would be in the shape of an actual flower. There would be five 'petals' planted with a variety of summer blooms, but the centrepiece of the design would be filled with my mother's favourite, and now mine. Cornflowers.

Though a simple name for such a lovely bloom, it had been symbolic of my life with her. Prussian blue in colour, considered a weed that grew wild among the fields of corn, it had become the favoured flower of the German nation. A relatively small flower, it was hardy. I liked to think that as a woman, I was like that flower. Not mighty, but strong and determined.

I wandered out of the garden and back onto the path, but I walked away from the lodge. Joan had told me there were bluebells growing in the nearby forest, and though it took me closer to the palace gardens, I was curious to see for myself.

The fir trees were thick and there was no marked place to walk, so I slipped between the trees and looked around. No sooner had I done this when the familiar scent of pine hit my senses and I stopped where I was.

Since realising I had been here before, I had begun noticing other small reminders and thankfully did not experience the strange feeling I had in the beginning. Now I stood stock still. I closed my eyes and inhaled the fresh, clean scent of pine.

"I shall tell her!"

The words were clear, the woman's voice distant, but loud enough to snap me from my reverie. Where had it come from? Deeper in the forest, I was sure. I took a few steps.

A low laugh, male. "You expect me to believe that?"

I moved farther, careful to be as quiet as possible.

"I don't care if you believe it or not. I tire playing this game with you. There are many others who would—"

A sudden gasp from the woman and then the man's voice. "Would what, Valentina? Would take my place?"

They spoke in German, hers accented, his harder to hear. I recognised the Italian woman before he spoke her name as her voice was so unusual. But the man? I stepped forward.

"You are a spoiled and greedy woman, my lovely songbird," he said softly. "You always desire that which you cannot have."

"That is not…" She stopped abruptly, and from the next sound I could tell they were perhaps locked in a kiss. I should go. I turned and my foot stepped heavily on a twig. It might just as well have been gunfire, so loud did it reverberate.

"What was that?" Valentina said in alarm.

"A deer, or perhaps a badger." Came his reply.

I slowly and carefully went back the way I had come, holding my breath until I was on the familiar path around the lodge. I felt guilty overhearing their private conversation. But I was also perplexed and annoyed that I did not know who Valentina spoke with, for he had kept his tone quiet. Yet as I remembered the woman's irritation at my being at the palace, and Wolfgang's advice about her jealousy, with a sinking heart I realised it had to be Max there with her in the forest. Though he proclaimed they were estranged it was not true. He still loved his wife, and what better reason did I now have to stop thinking about him?

THAT NIGHT, THE DREAM assaulted me with a vengeance. It took the same direction. My being chased by ferocious beasts, running to the hidden garden, and pounding upon the door. But this time it played out slowly, and at the vital moment where I saw myself on the other side of the door, I did not wake as I always had. The dream continued. I followed myself into the garden and saw the von Brandt family assembled in a group, staring at me. In the background I could hear Valentina singing an aria, which suddenly turned into my screaming.

"Wake up, miss. Wake up."

I opened my eyes to see Joan peering over me. She spoke softly until my breathing slowed to a normal rate. But after she had gone, I lay there unable to sleep until dawn.

A NOTE ARRIVED MONDAY morning from *Herr* Vogel. He had located an address for my aunt's former employees, *Herr* and *Frau* Krause. He wrote that the husband, Gustav had died, and the death certificate stated he had been buried in Dresden. *Herr* Vogel had sent a letter to his widow with a request to meet at her convenience.

I was delighted. It would be marvellous to speak with the woman- if she was inclined to help. Perhaps if I knew the story of my past I could get answers and banish the nightmare once and for all.

Other than taking a short walk to thank the gardeners, I stayed busy in the study. After two weeks in Germany, it was time for me to think about my future. Yet how to plan for that future when I was desperate to understand my past? The irony did not escape me—still, it must be done.

I dug through the account books and made notes to determine the cost of running the lodge. This was the same exercise I'd employed at the London house after Father died.

Our house in Mayfair held no pleasant memories for me, indeed quite the opposite. Mother had never been happy there, and ever sensitive to her, the discomfort had passed along to me. Should I sell the house? It would bring me a tidy sum, and I had ideas to use some of my fortune to do something good.

There was a building for sale near Teddington, in Middlesex, not far from London. I had instructed my family lawyer in London, Martin Francis, to make enquiries on my behalf. I was considering purchasing the property and converting it to an orphanage, in my mother's name. Caring for underprivileged and vulnerable children had been her passion.

The question was where I would live. I could remain in Germany and stay on at the lodge, making frequent visits to England, or I could sell this place, never to return.

Strangely, I did feel a connection to Lorelei. I wondered why when I had spent little time here. In fact, no one remembered me, except the baroness. It was a big decision, and I knew the von Brandt family would be happy to get Lorelei back.

I was interrupted before luncheon by an unexpected visit from Wolfgang. Taken aback by Fritz's announcement that Max's brother was calling upon me, I had only just risen from the desk when he marched into the study, his hair tousled from being outside.

"*Guten Tag, Fräulein*," he said as though it was natural for him to be in my study.

"Good morning, Wolfgang." I set down my pen and watched as he took a seat. "This is unexpected."

His eyes settled on my face for a moment, as though he was considering what he wanted to say.

"Is everything all right?" I was puzzled at his coming.

"*Ja*, of course. I was taking a stroll around the grounds, and I found myself near the lodge. I saw all the activity in the walled garden, and I could not help but take a look." He gave me his usual disarming smile which melted Susanna's heart and made mine cower. "What are you doing to the little place?"

Comfortable to be on an easy subject, I relaxed. "Mainly clearing everything up as it has been sadly neglected. It is a nice, secluded spot, and one which I have some memories of."

One eyebrow rose. "Memories? Of the garden?"

"Yes. Since my mother died, I have dreamt of that

very place for years. Not a nice dream," I added. "But a disturbing one, and it involves the garden. That, and a few other incidences has brought back memories I didn't know I had. I have remembered coming here as a child, spending time with my mother in the garden, the scent of the pine trees in the breeze. The longer I am here, the more my childhood experiences seem to return."

"How very strange, Ingrid. It must be quite unsettling?"

"Not at all. In fact, it helps shed light on questions I have from my past, or should I say my mother's secretive past."

Wolfgang sat forward, his expression serious, his eyes narrowed. "Marta Bergman had a secret past?" The grin slipped back upon his face. "Was she a spy, or something exciting as that?"

I chuckled. "Of course not. But she was very tight-lipped about our family here in *Linnenbrink,* which makes me all the more curious. Do you remember her, Wolfgang?"

His brows drew together, but it seemed to me as though it was a pretense. "I do remember your mother, for she was like a sister to my own *mutti*. But I don't recall spending time here very often as we had a tutor who kept us occupied at the palace."

"Did you ever meet me?"

His light brown eyes regarded me thoughtfully, and longer than appropriate. Wolfgang really did believe in his power over women. And although I could see how others fell under his charm, I was not impressed.

"Ingrid, I think had I known you, I should have found you hard to forget. So, my answer is *nein.* I do not recall seeing you as a child. Perhaps you are mistaken that you were here. Your mother could have recounted memories of her own which have stayed with you."

"I disagree. The garden is too familiar. The small iron bench, the Willow tree. I can remember sitting on a blanket under that very tree."

Something flickered across Wolfgang's face, but in an instant it was gone.

"What changes are you making in the garden?" he enquired. "It looks as though there is much being done."

"Replacing the paving stones, digging new flowerbeds and tending the lawn, mostly." I replied. "Although I am tempted to add a fountain since I saw the spectacular one in front of the palace."

"Ah, yes. That is a fine piece, and quite old. The plumbing causes headaches from time to time, but it is part of the history of the *Safranpalast*, so there it must remain. Although I can understand the idea, I would caution you to think carefully before you decide to install one. You will have to tear up all the ground to install the pipes to run the water."

"It does sound like a large project," I agreed, disliking the hint of condescension in his tone for it reminded me of my father, who considered all women to be less intelligent. "We shall see what happens."

"*Entschuldigen, Fräulein Ingrid, Fräulein Koppelman is here,*" I had not noticed Fritz in the doorway until he spoke. He had barely finished making the announcement when Susanna came up behind him.

"Good day to you both." She sailed past the butler and went to sit in the chair next to Wolfgang. Susanna was dressed in periwinkle blue and looked stunning. Her eyes sparkled, and her hair looked like spun gold under a jaunty hat. "I am so sorry if I am interrupting something, but I just had to get away from the hotel." Her eyes never left Wolfgang.

He politely got to his feet, and I watched the mask slip back onto his face as he bestowed the young American with a dashing smile and collected her slim hand in his to bring to his lips.

"*Fräulein* Koppelman. You are a ray of sunshine on a cloudy day. How charming you are in this delightful shade of blue. *Deine Augen sind so hell wie der Himmel über dir.* Your eyes are as bright as the skies above."

Susanna blushed, but she boldly met his appreciative assessment. "Why thank you, sir," she crooned. "Whatever brings you to visit Ingrid? Were you bored to tears like me?" She gave a little laugh.

"*Nein*. I was on a walk and came to chat with *Fräulein* Rutherford about her gardening project." His eyes glanced over at me. "But we are finished, and now I shall leave you lovely ladies to your conversation." He gave a curt nod in my direction, and with a smile to my guest, he left us alone.

"Well, I never." Susanna ungraciously flopped down in a chair. "I didn't expect to see him here. Why, it fairly took my breath away when I walked in."

I wanted to say it had done the same to me, but Susanna would misinterpret the connotation.

"I am on my way into town. My driver is outside waiting. I thought I might invite you to come along. I understand from a lady I recently met at our hotel, that she purchased a beautiful green silk last week from a

Prinzenstadt Dressmaker, and I have a mind to see for myself."

As Susanna launched into a long discussion comparing silk to satin, my mind had already wandered away. Though I heard the tone of her voice, I was far more interested in Wolfgang's sudden appearance at the lodge and his odd demeanour. The man had acted very strangely. Why was he against my updating the garden? Was it proprietary behaviour on his part and a belief that his family held dominion when it came to Lorelei?

"Ingrid, I do believe you are not listening to a thing I've said." Susanna pouted. "I'm going into town. Please say you'll go along with me."

I had no desire to accompany her. But I could not help feeling compassionate. I got to my feet and saw her face brighten with pleasure.

"I shall come. But I can only stand to shop for short increments of time, and you must promise me a rest in one of the coffee shops."

Chapter Ten

THE GUEST LIST FOR SUSANNA'S dinner-party was not a long list, due to the Koppelmans being visitors from the United States and not knowing many people. But most of the responses were acceptances.

Wednesday afternoon there was a flurry of activity at the lodge, and I kept out of the way after informing the staff earlier in the day to let me know if there was anything requiring my help. Joan and I collected fresh flowers and arranged several urns of Iris, Daffodils and a host of tallow and red Tulips in the drawing and dining rooms, which cheered the place up.

For Susanna's present, I purchased a leather-bound journal, and a pen engraved with her name. I thought it a good gift for a traveller, and I had a feeling she probably kept a diary.

The menu, one which had not pleased Cook, was a mix of traditional American dishes. There would be split pea soup, baked pork and beans, fried chicken, string green beans, baked yams, and for dessert, an apple and a pumpkin pie. The recipes were found in American magazines which Saul had taken from a stack his sister received from their mother.

I had informed the staff they would all receive an extra day off during the following month of June, in appreciation of their hard work. This was met with much pleasure and even Cook relented.

The Secret of Lorelei Lodge

It was almost time for me to change for dinner, but I decided to take another look at the garden to see the day's progress. I passed one of the workers leaving for home on the pathway and he bade me a friendly good evening. The door to the garden was open, and as I stepped inside my eyes were drawn to one of the corners where they had been working close to the Willow tree.

The plans were to keep the area there grassy, but due to the overgrowth and the soil's poor condition, the existing grass would be dug up and new turf lain. The little iron bench had been moved out of the way to enable this and now sat up against the wall. I headed straight for it and then took a seat to survey what had been done.

It was quite the transformation. New flag stones were in place and the foundation for the fountain awaited the plumbing installation. Flower beds were still being dug, but it was easy to visualise the shapes of each being petals. Though there was plenty left to do, the garden showed promise.

I leaned back against the bench and thought of Mother. I hoped she would have been pleased to see the improvement here, unlike Wolfgang, who was quite disdainful about the prospect. I considered asking Max if he would bring his mother to the garden when it was completed. Her long relationship with my mother kept the baroness ever near in my thoughts, and I felt sure she would enjoy such an outing.

The sun sank lower in the sky and sunlight shone directly into my face. I turned away from it and then spotted something glinting not ten feet away from me, up near the wall. I got up and wandered over. What was it? It must be metal, for the sun reflected brightly off its surface. I drew closer, watching where I stepped because all the dirt had been turned over and I did not want to get muddy before the party. It was easy enough to spot and I reached down expecting a broken piece from one of the gardener's tools, or perhaps even a coin. But it was neither. I picked it up, brushed off the dirt with my thumb and gasped.

It was a small gold pendant! A replica of the one I currently wore on a chain around my neck—the very pendant worn by my mother and taken to her grave. A sudden wave of unrest rocked my senses, along with a ripple of nausea, though I could not say why. My lungs struggled for a breath, and I was at once filled with the urge to bolt.

I left the garden as quickly as possible, hurrying towards the lodge, practically breaking into a run. I do not know why I felt so panicked, I only knew I had to get away.

I went straight up to my bedroom and immediately rinsed the dirt from the little circlet of gold in my hand. Examining the pendant, I told myself it was likely a common piece of jewellery found locally. The symbol of the flower held national importance and pride. It could be that a local jeweller had made several of these pieces and sold them in the area. But why would one be in the garden? Someone had to have been wearing the pendant when it had been lost there, but who? It was not my mother's, it was not mine. Could it have belonged to my aunt? Perhaps it was a family tradition that all the women in my family owned such a piece. That was a likely explanation. I would see if Joan could ask the servants if they remembered my aunt owning one.

This calmed my unexpected anxiety. I popped the little piece of gold into my jewellery box, and then set about getting dressed for the evening's entertainment.

"You and Saul are so very clever!" Susanna's excitement was evident in the radiance of her smile and her twinkling eyes. "I never in a moment suspected a thing when Saul told me to dress for dinner. I just knew he was taking me for a boring old evening in town. Imagine my surprise when we came down the driveway and I saw all the carriages here!"

I quietly extricated myself from the small group who were currently being entertained by the lovely American. She looked so pretty in her pale green silk. I made my way over to Dieter, the footman, and took a sherry from his tray with a thank-you.

"Susie's having such a wonderful time, Ingrid. Thank you so much for doing this." Saul joined me, looking dapper in a black dinner suit, gold waistcoat and gold cravat.

"It's my pleasure. Your sister is a delightful person." I looked around the room at the array of guests. The only noticeable absences were those invited from the palace.

"I assumed the von Brandts would be here. Max said as much yesterday," Saul observed.

He had read my thoughts. "Yes," I agreed. "He sent an acceptance as well. I am sure he will arrive in time for our meal."

We discussed other topics amiably until he was drawn away by another of the guests, whose name I had quite forgotten. It was a nice turn-out for Susanna. The table had been set for twelve. My fingers toyed with my pendant. I had decided not to wear anything special this evening.

"*Ciao a tutti!*" The room abruptly fell silent as the melodic voice filled the air. In the doorway of the drawing room, dressed in a magnificent flame-red gown, with her ebony hair artfully pinned in an array of curls, stood Valentina. My eyes flew to Susanna, who suddenly appeared insipid in her pretty green dress, a peacock in the presence of a phoenix.

Valentina came in with the palace entourage of Wolfgang, his wife Katja, and much to my shock, the baron. I automatically stepped forward to greet them in my role of hostess but gestured for Susanna to come with me.

"Good evening." I inclined my head. "It is wonderful to see you."

The gentlemen nodded curtly as did Katja. But Valentina disregarded me and stepped forward to clasp Susanna by her hands.

"*Sie ist so ein hübsches kind,*" she said in silky tones, kissing Susanna on both her flushed cheeks.

"Thank you." Susanna had no idea she had been told she was a pretty child, a veiled insult I thought.

The grand dame turned to me. "I hope you do not mind my coming with the others, *Signorina* Rutherford. I changed my mind and did not want to be alone." Her lips were painted the same intense colour of her gown. The woman was absolutely gorgeous.

"You are most welcome," I said politely, though I wondered at her propensity to constantly show up at dinners even after she had declined. I was convinced it was done for effect. She walked away to greet her delighted audience, who were only too happy to focus their attentions upon her.

I made a polite comment to Katja, looking wan in a pastel pink which did not suit her complexion, and then greeted Wolfgang, handsome as ever, though he had little to say, and I imagined it was because of the garden. He also barely had time for Susanna. She must have felt slighted, for she moved away, now an onlooker at her own party.

As Max stepped forward, I fought the tug in my chest when his dark eyes locked with mine. What was it in his expression which pierced the armour I placed between us so he could not affect me? He took my hand and raised it to his lips and the warmth of his skin sent pleasure rippling throughout my entire body.

"Ingrid, it is a pleasure to see you this evening."

"Likewise," I said as casually as I might.

He released my hand. "I sincerely hope Valentina's insistence upon coming tonight has not thrown your plans into chaos?"

"Of course not," I said politely. "We can easily set another place at the table." She may not have caused an issue with dinner, but she had with my heart. For it was obvious the Italian and Max had rekindled their relationship. Had I not overheard them in the forest only two days earlier? Now, she partnered him this evening for all to see. They were undoubtedly a couple once again. Thank goodness our friendship had been purely platonic. I stepped back and Max had no choice but to continue into the room and greet the others.

I found Susanna standing by the window, a solitary figure with dejection painted across her face. Quickly I went to her knowing the source of her unhappiness.

"Dearest Susanna, I was not expecting *Signora* Cavaletti. She declined the invitation, but I suppose as she is the baron's wife…"

"It is fine," Susanna said quietly, the catch in her voice belying her words. She was close to tears. I cast my eyes around the room and saw Saul already engaged in conversation with Max, while Katja stood alone near the piano, watching as both Wolfgang and Valentina held court in the centre of the room.

"To think I admired that woman," Susanna said softly. "Yet she is a viper."

"That is strong language," I said. "I understand you are angry that she is always trying to steal the spotlight, even when off the stage, but still."

Susanna turned to look at me. "If you knew the things I have learned about *Signora* Cavaletti, you would throw her out of your home." With that, Susanna walked off and went to speak with Katja, the wife of Susanna's unrequited love. How strange that the American's blatent admiration of the Italian soprano had changed so dramatically. What on earth had she found out about Valentina?

DINNER WAS A SUCCESS. I sat Susanna at the opposing head of the table to me, and there she was able to command some of the attention stolen away from her earlier. She was absolutely delighted with the menu and at each new course brought to the table, Susanna regaled us with a story of the food's history. It was fascinating.

Max sat several seats away from me, an intentional plan and a wise one, all things considered. He conversed with Saul, but occasionally I glanced up to find him looking at me. I did not meet his gaze but focused upon the people sat directly beside me.

Everyone seemed to enjoy the different cuisine, although Valentina declared American food to be "*Semplice e insapore*," which someone translated into German and Max translated to English. The songstress found the fare plain and tasteless.

But Susanna would not hear of it, and I commended her for standing her ground against so strong an adversary. "Just because it is unfamiliar, *Signora*, that does not make it tasteless. One could say Italian fare is repetitive and boring."

"How do you mean?" Valentina's voice was tight. She was unused to being challenged.

"Tomatoes, cheese, onions, peppers, olives, and pasta," boomed Wolfgang, joining the conversation.

Susanna beamed at his defense. Valentina scowled. Katja looked amused.

"Ridiculous," the diva argued. "The best cooks are from Italy. They are renowned around the world."

"And many of them have emigrated to the United States," said Susanna, barely concealing her smugness. "Where they cook meals similar to those you have eaten tonight."

"Touché!" Wolfgang laughed and applauded. "Valentina, you must admit defeat." He suddenly got to his feet, his wine glass in hand. He raised it into the air and gestured towards Susanna who sat at the head of the table looking radiant.

"A toast, to our dear Susanna on this her special day. *Alles Gute zum Geburtstag*! Happy birthday!"

Everyone raised their glasses for the toast, even Valentina though she looked sulky. It did my heart good seeing Susanna beaming with pleasure—her happiness restored. I looked around the table and my eyes met Saul's. He gave a slight nod in my direction, and I understood he was pleased to see his sister enjoying herself.

We dispensed with leaving the men to their cigars as it was Susanna's night, after all. Once the final course was complete, Dieter served coffee and cognac in the drawing room, and everyone migrated in there together.

Valentina was less effervescent, which was a welcome reprieve from her regular behaviour. Susanna, bolstered by her handling of the diva, shone like a little beacon. I made a weak attempt to mingle with the guests but found it awkward with two of the couples I had not met until this evening. They huddled together set apart from the others as though unsure how to mingle with people from the *Safranpalast*. I approached them and they immediately stopped speaking.

"*Guten Abend,*" I greeted them in their native tongue. The two gentlemen bowed, and the ladies inclined their heads.

"*Fräulein* Rutherford, it is a pleasure to meet you." The younger of the two men spoke in accented English. "I am *Doktor* Carl Engel, and this is my wife Birgit." he gestured to the woman at his side in a dark blue gown. Her face was plain, yet there was an intelligence about her eyes and a hearty colour to her complexion. Had she not been so well dressed and turned out, I would have easily cast her in the role of milkmaid or farm girl. She just emanated a capable spirit. She smiled and it seemed genuine.

"And I am not sure if you have been introduced to

Gottfried and Gertrude Ludendorff." Continued the good doctor. "The Ludendorff's manage the fine hotel you have visited in *Linnenbrink*. They have lived here far longer than us. We are relative newcomers."

Frau Ludendorff seemed at a loss how to act, she practically curtsied. Her husband cleared his throat which seemed to alert her, and she quickly recovered herself.

"*Fräulein* Rutherford, we are highly honoured being included in this evening's festivities," said *Herr* Ludendorff who in direct contrast to *Frau* Engel, looked as though one good gust of wind could blow him over. "It has been a delight having the Koppelman family stay at our prestigious hotel. We could not wish for nicer guests. Could we, my dear?" He addressed his wife, whose expression turned to one of utter shock as though he had asked the colour of her undergarments. I suspected the poor woman's opinion was seldom requested. I immediately warmed to her.

"*Frau* Ludendorff, I must tell you Susanna raves continually how much they enjoy staying at your hotel. I believe, as she does, that it is a woman's touch which brings the comforts of home to a strange place when you are a traveller. You have my compliments."

I admit to feeling some pleasure at the immediate change in the woman's demeanour. Even her husband stood a little taller. I often marvelled at the power of the spoken word. It could incite violence, lust, pleasure, and in the pallid *Frau* Ludendorff, dignity.

"Are you the only physician in the area?" I asked *Doktor* Engel. I estimated the doctor to be in his mid-forties, with thick brown hair and a bushy moustache which curled upwards either side of his nose.

"Yes. I am the only doctor in *Linnenbrink*, though there are two others in *Prinzenstadt*. We have a small hospital there also, and for the time being that suits our needs."

"Tell me," I asked. "Did you attend my aunt when she took her fall?"

His face grew serious, and he frowned. "Yes, I did come. But unfortunately, when Gisela fell, she landed in an unfortunate way, hitting her head severely. Had she lived, I fear there would have been repercussions to her mental state. So, as sad as the circumstances were, the outcome was likely a blessing in disguise. Though you have my commiserations for her loss."

The Ludendorffs hung upon his every word, but I noticed Frau Engle's demeanour had shifted.

"Thank you. I did not know my aunt, but I am sorry she is gone. I should have liked meeting her."

Raucous laughter spilled through the air, and everyone paused to direct their attention over to Wolfgang, who had his head tipped back and was trying to catch grapes being thrown by Valentina. The behaviour was inappropriate, and as I watched, Max approached his brother and said something stern, judging by the look of irritation that spread across Wolfgang's face. The moment was awkward, but surprisingly Katja came to the rescue and announced she would play piano for us, should anyone care to listen.

Within minutes, she was playing a jaunty tune with Susanna and Wolfgang standing either side to turn the pages and then eventually they sang along.

They sounded delightful. Susanna's voice as clear as a new bell, Wolfgang's a baritone, with less polish but still pleasant. I could not resist turning to watch Valentina's expression as two amateurs performed a popular song. I half expected her to look sardonic at their attempt to sing in the presence of a professional. What I did not expect to see however, was the hostility of her expression as she stared at the vocalists. Surely she could not still be cross about the wordplay at dinner? But there was no mistaking her thoughts. The beautiful Italian looked murderous.

"You must congratulate yourself on hosting a fine evening for Susanna." It was Max, who came to stand next to me. He leaned closer as he spoke into my ear and the warmth of his breath caressed my skin.

I pulled myself together. "I do not believe congratulations are necessary, yet I am beyond pleased Susanna is enjoying her evening. She is a dear person whose birthdays are still significantly important to her." I kept my eyes straight ahead.

"You speak as though you have never enjoyed a birthday celebration, Ingrid. Tell me that isn't true?"

At this, I turned and looked at him. His eyes were the soft colour of cinnamon, warmed no doubt from the cognac. "It is difficult to miss something one has never actually had," I replied. "My mother usually took me somewhere special on my birthdays, but it was only the two of us that celebrated. My father did not enjoy disruption and consequently other children were never invited to our home."

"How awful you were forced to spend so much time with adults. It's no wonder you are so mature. I cannot imagine you ever being childish or silly."

There was an undertone of pity in his voice which I took offence to. "That is a baseless opinion," I stated.

"You surmise much for someone who does not know me at all." Before he could see the heat I knew stained my face, I walked away to speak to Saul.

WHEN THE VON BRANDTS took their leave, everyone else began to depart. Except Saul and Susanna, who remained for a late cup of rich coffee, but even they looked weary.

"Oh, Ingrid," sighed Susanna, setting her empty cup onto the tray. "Thank you so much for making my birthday special. It has been such a wonderful evening."

"I am glad you have enjoyed yourself," I replied. "But you must thank your brother, for this was his idea."

I caught the look Saul threw me—part guilty, part pleasure. Then I watched him bask under the adulation of a very grateful sister.

"I cannot believe Valentina came after declining the invitation." Susanna said.

I stiffened. "It is her prerogative as Max's wife—"

"Nonsense," Susanna scoffed. "They are not a couple, everyone knows that. She just didn't want to be left out, and there's an end to it."

"Susie, we don't actually know their business. Max never talks about his personal affairs," her brother said sternly.

"Phooey," she replied. "That woman is a piece of work. Why, Wolfgang says—"

Saul got to his feet. "Come along, sister," he said, reaching out a hand. "Too much excitement and too much cognac makes for bad conversation."

Susanna gave a little laugh, unaffected by her brother's accusation. She allowed him to pull her up from the chair in a most unladylike manner. I realised she certainly had imbibed more than I had thought. Oh well. It was her birthday after all.

Eventually, the Koppelmans took their leave. I followed them out into the night and watched them get into their carriage. They waved a cheery farewell as the vehicle moved away.

I stood at the bottom of the steps and turned to Dieter, who waited at the open front door for me to return into the house. But I lingered.

"I shall bide here for a moment, Dieter. The air feels good this evening. Please go about your duties. I shall be in shortly."

The handsome footman gave me a brief nod and went back inside while I stepped further out onto the driveway.

The hour was late, close to eleven, I shouldn't wonder, but the air was still, and cool. There was no sound, not even an insect chirping or a small mammal foraging in the grass. After a room full of people chattering, it was pleasant just to stand and breathe.

"Ingrid?"

I started in surprise at the sound of my name, and then saw a figure drawing closer. Though it was dark I still recognised Max, and I took an involuntary step backwards. The door was open, and light spilled out onto the flagstones, yet he remained in the shadows of the night.

"What are you doing here?" I said, though my voice was barely more than a whisper.

"I wanted to speak to you. To apologise for upsetting you earlier. To explain about Valentina—"

I held up my hand. "No, Max. You owe me no

apology, nor any explanation about your ...wife."

He took a step closer. "You are wrong, Ingrid. On both counts. I did not mean to be unfeeling about your childhood, or judgmental. I only compared it to my own, which was far different, and I had no right to pass comment and upset you. As for Valentina. She would insist upon coming."

"Max," I said sternly. "Valentina is your wife and where you go so should she. Why do you feel the necessity to explain your actions? It is ridiculous."

"Is it?" He moved closer still.

I held my ground. I could see the firm set of his chin, the movement of a muscle in his cheek. His eyes searched mine and then settled upon my mouth. There was a weighty atmosphere in the space between us, something intangible that I did not understand. Though Max made no movement, just his observation of me was a caress.

My breath picked up speed, and when his hand lifted to touch my cheek I could not stop the sigh leaving my parted lips.

"Dearest Ingrid," he said softly. "If only..."

"What are you doin' out there in the dark? You'll catch your death." Joan barked from the doorway and Max's hand quickly fell away.

Without turning to look at her I called. "Just getting some fresh air. I shall be there directly." Then I watched as Max gave me one lingering look before he stepped back into the night.

I made my way towards the silhouette of my maid in the open doorway, Max's words burning into my soul....*if only.*

Chapter Eleven

I HAD ESCAPED THE DREAM for a night. My mood was elevated this morning as I contemplated the positive effects of uninterrupted sleep while eating a pastry and drinking coffee.

When Joan came into the dining room unannounced, I dropped my fork at her sudden entrance as she surprised me. I could tell immediately by her face that she was excited about something.

I held up my hand. "Before you speak, pour yourself a cup of coffee and sit down with me."

She went to the sideboard and did as I bid, then returned and pulled out the closest chair to where I sat.

Her little brown eyes were sharp with anticipation. "I've just heard somethin' from Dieter, who got it from one of them fancy footmen at the palace." She took a quick sip of her drink and then her face contorted with disgust. "You shouldn't be drinkin' this muck, miss. You need a decent cup of tea first thing in the mornin'."

"You were saying?"

"Oh yes. Well, you'll never guess, but it seems that the old baronesses' nurse has done a bunk in the middle o' the night."

"I beg your pardon?" Sometimes Joan's slang was a foreign language, even to my ears.

"Run off, she has. Disappeared without tellin' a soul she was goin'. Apparently, the family's livid, bein' left in the lurch, so to speak."

"Oh dear. I can see why. But surely they can replace her easily enough? A job at the palace would be most desirable, I should think."

"I s'ppose you're right. Still, it's strange to go off like that. Dieter said she left so quickly, she never picked up her week's wages neither."

Now that was odd. "No one usually walks away from money that is due." I mused. *Unless they disliked working there*, I thought, remembering the atmosphere in Lisbeth's room especially whenever Wolfgang was present. There had definitely been an undercurrent.

I had an idea. "I shall call on the baroness today. Perhaps I can help." My intentions were not all honourable. A few uninterrupted hours with Lisbeth might prove interesting.

Joan pushed her full cup away. "That's a fine notion, miss. While you do that, I think I'll go down an' teach Cook how to make a decent cuppa."

I WALKED THE BACK WAY TO the palace, down the long path through the forest, connecting its grounds to the rear of the lodge.

It was readily apparent all was not well at the *Safranpalast* when I was admitted by a harassed looking footman. I waited in a small anteroom off the magnificent hallway, where I was surprised to be met by Katja von Brandt, Wolfgang's wife.

"*Fräulein* Rutherford, how can I help you?" Her face was drawn, her manner harried. Katja's English was not as clear as her family's, but she was still quite fluent.

"I have been informed you are suddenly without a

nurse for the baroness. I wanted to offer some time with her this morning. I enjoy her company, and I thought it might help if you are short-handed."

I expected her instant refusal, so I was shocked when her face crumpled, and tears filled her eyes.

"It is *ein durcheinander*... a mess. Wolfgang is furious. He has asked other staff to care for her, but none of them have any experience of nursing. Lisbeth is beside herself and crying because she does not know the strange people in her bedchamber, and she will not let any of us near..."

"I can help you," I said quickly. "Lisbeth knows me. Actually, she thinks I am my mother, Marta, but she's at least calm with me. Please take me to her and let us see if she'll have me there."

Katja did not hesitate. She escorted me to the baroness's room which was now becoming a familiar journey.

We could hear the older woman before we reached her room as she was wailing and shouting at the top of her lungs. Katja pushed open the door to see pandemonium ensuing.

Lisbeth, clad in her night attire, stood in front of the hearth throwing anything she could get her hands upon at two terrified maids, no more than children themselves. Katja quickly ordered them to leave, and I rushed over to the Baroness, who had a small vase in her upheld hand.

"Lisbeth," I said quietly. "What are you doing?"

Her wild eyes shifted, blinked, and then stared into my face. "Marta?" she whispered.

Though it pained me to be dishonest, it was for the best. "Yes, dear friend. I have come to sit with you.

Please put down the vase. We must go to your wardrobe and choose something for you to wear today. It is time to wash and prepare for breakfast." I gently encouraged her to lower her hand and she eventually loosened her grip of the vase. We walked over to a grand piece of furniture, and together we looked at her assortment of gowns and selected one.

Lisbeth recognised her daughter-in-law, although she was not friendly. But she allowed us both to assist her into her clothes, brush her hair, and prepare her so that breakfast could be brought in.

A half hour later, after she had eaten a croissant, we helped the older woman onto her bed. She was exhausted, no doubt from her emotional outburst and confusion. When at last she was settled, Katja and I stepped outside into the hall.

"*Danke*, Ingrid," she said in earnest. "I could not have managed without you."

"It is fine," I said. "I shall go back in and sit with her a while. You can see to your business this morning and perhaps they can look for a replacement nurse today?"

"Oh, we cannot expect you to—"

I placed my hand upon her arm, "I insist. There is nothing urgent needing my attention. Allow me to help while you need it. Lisbeth is content with me while she believes I am her best friend. Let her think what she will so she can have peace."

Katja could not disguise her relief. "If you are certain?"

I nodded.

"Then I shall leave you to it and see what can be done. There are medications she must have, but we cannot administer them without being qualified to know what we are doing. I have sent for *Doktor* Engel to attend us, and we expect him by midday."

With that, Katja left me, and I returned to the bedroom.

Lisbeth slept peacefully, and for a moment I stood by the side of her bed watching her rest. Her face was smoother in slumber, and I could imagine how she would have looked at my own age. I thought of her and my mother and their wonderful friendship and envied them something I had never had.

I wandered around the large room, picking up items here and there to examine them. A trinket, a small painting. In one corner stood a wash basin, and a cupboard on the wall next to a mirror. This was a medicine cabinet. It was not locked, but there was a tricky mechanism to open it which would likely prove difficult for someone in the baronesses' condition.

I examined the contents. There was not much to be found. Two bottles, the smaller marked with the label 'Morphine', the other twice its size and labeled as 'Tonic'. I took off the lid of the larger bottle and held it to my nose. It was rose hip, quite pleasant in fact. I put it back and fastened the door shut. If these were the sum of medicines administered to Lisbeth, why did she seem so affected? Was it as Max said, a disease of senility?

Lisbeth slept for an hour or more, and when she woke, sat bolt upright in bed. I was in a chair next to her.

I addressed her in German, asking how she was feeling. "Wie fühlst du dich, Lisbeth?"

"Marta? What are you doing here?" she replied, smiling broadly at me, delight shining from her eyes.

I was a little taken aback. Her voice seemed sharper, as did the brown of her eyes.

"I have come to sit with you, Lisbeth. *Krankenschwester* Helga could not be here. Is that all right?"

Lisbeth swung her legs around and now sat on the side of the bed. She stared directly at my face. The cloud of confusion seemed thinner, and instinctively I could sense a subtle change in her demeanour. Why? I considered her medication. Katja said they had not dispensed anything, therefore Lisbeth was not sedated.

"I do not like *Krankenschwester* Helga. She is unkind and her skin smells like mothballs, but Wolfgang makes her stay. You never liked her either, Marta. Remember? You would laugh and say she looked like an angry bird. But Gisela insisted she was a good servant and paid her well, and the husband was a hard worker. Wolfgang tells me to stop complaining. That he likes the nurse. But he would say that, wouldn't he?"

Lisbeth got to her feet and strolled over to the window while I dissected what she had said. She was confusing her time frame with the past and the present, obviously. But I was interested in her comments about Gisela.

"I don't remember much about Gisela." I joined Lisbeth at the window.

She turned to me and gave a chuckle. "How could you forget? She was always so unhappy and worried about money. But you were good to her, Marta. You helped her. And look how she repaid you?" Lisbeth's hand came up to her mouth and she bit her knuckles, her eyes widening with horror.

"No, it is all fine now, Lisbeth. You must not fret." I had not intended to upset the poor woman. "Come," I said, "let us sit a while on the sofa and we can speak of happy times." I gently placed my hand on her arm and guided her towards the group of seats near the fireplace. I scrambled for something uplifting to say.

"Do you remember the picnics in the walled garden, Lisbeth?"

She beamed with delight. "Oh yes. My darling boys. Two away at school and two little ones who would always run and hide from us, didn't they, Marta? And your sweet girl, how they chased her!"

She was talking about me and the younger von Brandt boys. "Did you sit under the Willow tree and look at the pretty flowers?"

Her brown eyes settled on me as I spoke, and seeing so much of Max there gave me warmth, and I reached out to take Lisbeth's hand in my own. Her skin was soft, papery, and her fingers long and slender.

"Now she's dead," Lisbeth said flatly.

"Gisela?"

"All of them."

Before I could ask what she meant, the door opened and both Wolfgang and *Doktor* Engel stepped into the room.

In my grasp, I felt Lisbeth's hand stiffen and then it trembled like a little bird.

In English, the doctor greeted me. Then he switched to German and spoke firmly and directly to Lisbeth. "Come along, Baroness," he said as he went to the medicine cupboard. "Let us give you some of your tonic. You are late to take it today."

Lisbeth looked at me with pleading and my heart

lurched. "Do not let them give me the drink," she said in German. "I do not like it, I cannot think. Please, Marta. Stop them."

But Wolfgang came to her side, and still speaking in his native tongue, he encouraged her to her feet and led her to the bed. Lisbeth looked over her shoulder towards me several times, and I felt as though I betrayed her by my inaction. They were not going to harm her, but she looked so fearful, so very alone.

I remained where I sat. I knew the two men were unaware of my ability to understand their language, and I chose to keep it that way.

"Can you give her a stronger dose this morning? She has already missed the early tonic, and Katja said she was hysterical earlier," Wolfgang asked the doctor.

"She seems to be calm at the moment. I do not see any reason to—"

"I am not asking your opinion," Wolfgang said sternly, "I am telling you to do it. I need her sedated today until the replacement nurse comes later this afternoon."

The doctor reluctantly poured another measure into the small cup he held to Lisbeth's lips, and she meekly obeyed and swallowed the medicine. He replaced the cap and glared at Wolfgang who stood across the bed facing him. I think they had forgotten I was still there.

"This medication is already strong enough, *Herr* von Brandt. It is not ethical to drug your mother. She is no danger to anyone. She just suffers from the malady of age to her mind."

"I do not pay you to remonstrate with me," Wolfgang said unkindly. "If your conscience bothers you, I can send for another doctor."

Doktor Engel straightened up and went to put the medicine back in the cupboard. He did not meet my gaze, but I could see he was not pleased. He strode to the door, then as an afterthought remembered my being there. He wished me a good morning and left the room.

Lisbeth was already laying still when Wolfgang walked over to the sofa where I waited and took a seat facing me in one of the armchairs. His jaw was tight, his eyes harsh.

"Katja tells me you were a great help to us this morning, Ingrid," he said. "Thank you for your kindness. It was fortunate you called when you did." His words lacked sincerity, and there were undertones of subdued anger.

"It was nothing." I kept my voice level and strong. "I heard the nurse had left you unexpectedly, and as the baroness seems to gain great comfort believing me to be my mother, I thought it would help calm her for a spell."

He smiled, but it did not reach his eyes. "And again, we thank you for that." Abruptly he got to his feet. "But we have everything under control now, so allow me to see you out if I may?"

I acquiesced. As we reached the door I looked over at the bed to see his mother already in a light slumber. We went into the hall.

"Will the doctor help you find a replacement nurse?" I asked.

"Yes," Wolfgang said. "That is what we spoke about just now. He thinks mother needs to remain sedated for a while due to her hysteria. With the increase in her medication, we must have someone skilled to care for her, even though she would prefer the companionship of her friends."

I caught the barb, but more importantly, I caught his lie. He had no notion I'd understood their entire conversation. Why was he being so deceitful?

This time, Wolfgang only escorted me to the top of the stairs. I assured him I could find my way out. I reached the ground floor of the palace and wound my way through the corridors as I had the time before. I heard footsteps approaching, and as I rounded a corner I came face to face with Max.

"Ingrid?" He sounded surprised. "I did not know you were here."

I felt the warmth rush to my cheeks as I remembered his last words to me, not hours since. "It was not planned," I gushed. "I heard about the nurse leaving, and I came to sit with Lisbeth for a spell."

"What are you talking about?"

"Your mother, and the nurse. You do not know?"

"I have just returned from an early meeting in the village with Saul." His eyes showed alarm. "Has something happened to my mother?"

"No. But her nurse has walked out, consequently leaving no one to watch over the baroness. The servants who tried were not skilled at coping with a lady of her condition. Your mother became upset and frightened. I stayed with her because she thinks I am my mother and the subterfuge placates her. All is in hand now. The doctor has been to attend your mother and Wolfgang says a replacement nurse is being sent for."

Max frowned as I spoke of his brother. When I finished, he gave a questioning look. "Something troubles you about my brother. What has Wolfgang said to you?"

I did not meet his eye. "Nothing. I was only concerned for your mother's wellbeing. Sometimes a woman's touch is more pacifying than a son's. You should speak with Wolfgang and Katja. They can tell you what has occurred better than I." We stared at one another, and I recognised the energy which passed between us. I wished I could call it by name. The tension, the shift in atmosphere. I was unsure what to do or say next. But the concern dissipated, for as luck would have it, we were joined by another who ventured down the hall.

"Well, if it isn't *Signora* Rutherford," came the silky tone laced with an Italian accent. "To what do we owe the pleasure of your company here…again?"

I did not dignify her question with an answer. Nor did I linger to make conversation. I politely excused myself, brushed past the woman and left for home.

MY WALK WAS BRISK—I could not get away from the palace quickly enough. Although I wanted to think about Max, dwell upon his wife's appearance and her tone with me, I pushed them both from my mind for there were far more important facts for me to consider. I arrived back at the lodge and rang the bell for Fritz. He did not come to the study, but Dieter arrived in his place.

"Yes my lady?" he asked in his best British accent.

The term, my lady, sounded so strange having not heard it for so long. "Dieter, would you be willing to answer a few questions I have?"

The handsome young man bit his lower lip and took a deep breath.

I sought to reassure him. "It's nothing bad, so

please don't be nervous. There are just some items I need help clarifying."

He nodded.

"Did you ever meet the Krauses, a married couple who had been employed by my aunt for many years at Lorelei?"

"*Nein,* my lady. I did not, but I know who they are because the people in the village spoke of them for a time."

"I see. What did they say? Can you tell me?"

He shrugged. "Not much about the wife. I don't think she ever went into the village. But her husband was liked well enough, he often stopped at the inn. The gossips say everyone at the lodge kept to themselves. They shopped only in *Prinzenstadt* and were …zurückgezogen."

The word Dieter used translated into reclusive. Which explained the mystery surrounding my aunt. Secrecy must have been a family trait for had not my mother inherited it too?

"Did you ever wonder why my aunt hired all the new staff, including you, from other places instead of locals?"

He chuckled. "*Nein.* From what I understand there were no people willing to come here from the village. They were afraid *Fräulein* Bergman would restrict their movements as much as she had the Krauses. She was not an easy woman to work for."

"I see. When you came to work here, did my aunt make those kinds of rules for the new staff?"

"No. She was just like any other employer. I wondered if everyone was making her sound worse than she really was."

"Thank you, Dieter. You have been most helpful. When you return downstairs, would you please ask Cook to make some coffee?"

The young footman left to do my bidding.

My fingers itched with lack of occupation and my mind tied itself into knots. I tried to paint a picture of everything I had learned about my family in my head. My mother's childhood, her friendship with Lisbeth and then Mother's marriage to my father and subsequent move to London. It was no good. I could not keep my thoughts in order. It was time to write it all down.

I was a visual person. My grasp was considerably stronger when I could step back and look at a situation to gain perspective. Using the family information and then the accounting books, I noted the date the Krauses left Lorelei, and then I went through each servant's hire date after that. There was a discrepancy of almost one month where there were no house servants, including a coachman, working at the lodge. The gardeners were not included in this study.

I looked up as Dieter came in with my coffee, thanked him, and then I returned to my project.

Aunt Gisela would have been at least seventy-three when the Krauses left. She would not have remained here alone for so long a time, surely? How did she manage without help?

I retrieved more of the accounts and studied the entries. I backtracked through bills from the grocer's and other businesses. It took me some time, but eventually I could see that between the last two weeks of July, and the first three weeks of August, there were no regular bills remitted. I found no paper trail of any activity during that time frame. This argued that my aunt would have most likely gone somewhere else, and had her letters held at the post office. But where would she have gone?

Had she left the area in pursuit of new staff? I doubted it, as this was probably done through an agency I should have thought. Had Aunt Gisela taken a holiday somewhere, or visited friends? I got up from the desk and took my cup of coffee to the window where I stared out aimlessly. I heard the clock strike one o'clock. It was time for luncheon.

Dieter served my food. I did not ask the whereabouts of Fritz. But I did engage the footman in another conversation. This time I questioned him about the groundskeepers. Though I had communicated with them on several occasions, I did not know their history here. I was surprised to learn that even the external staff members were brought in after the Krauses. Prior to that, there were no full-time gardeners employed.

This made me more curious. Gisela Bergman had let her entire staff go, survived without help for over a month and then hired people from other areas. As I nibbled a particularly flaky piece of pastry, I realised that my aunt had most definitely been up to something. But what?

THAT AFTERNOON, JOAN AND I were discussing the fact we had already been in Germany for two weeks. She had kindly brought me a cup of tea, and was lamenting missing her shortbread and the London newspapers, when we heard frenzied barking coming from close by. Frowning, I set down the teacup and went to the drawing room window which looked out across the front of the house. The noise seemed to be coming from the forest.

"Something has happened," I stated. "The dogs don't normally bark like that. We should see what it is."

"Not me," said Joan. "I'm goin' nowhere near those bloodthirsty giants. An' if you had any sense you'd stay put too."

I rolled my eyes. "They are harmless, Joan. They just look frightening." But she was having none of it, and so I left her and headed for the door. Had something happened to Max? This concern quickened my step.

As I crossed the driveway in the direction of the forest, the dogs had quietened, but I could hear someone's voice. I followed the sound into the thickets of pines, and when I heard one of the dogs whimper I called out.

"Max? Max, are you out here?"

"Ingrid," he shouted back. "Don't come any closer. Stay exactly where you are and let me come to you." There was a note of urgency in his voice, so I stopped immediately. What on earth was going on?

"All right," I agreed, but wondered why. I knew he was close when the dogs cantered down the trail and bounded towards me. I greeted them, but they were agitated and excitable. Max arrived a moment later. His face ashen, his eyes bright, and his breathing irregular.

"You must go back to the lodge, immediately," he said firmly as his hand grabbed my forearm to turn me away.

"What are you doing?" I asked, shaking his grip from me. "What is going on, Max?"

A shudder seemed to pass through his body. "The dogs…they have found something in the forest. I must return to the palace and summon the authorities."

"What?" I was aghast. "What have they found, Max?"

He blew out a hard breath. "Ingrid, I think they have found my mother's nurse."

Chapter Twelve

JOAN ADMINISTERED MORE TEA. "That poor woman," she lamented. "She must have gone off on her own an' had a fall."

I remembered Herr Vogel's comments about my aunt. She had died from a fall as well. I shook the thought away.

More than two hours had passed since I met Max in the forest. From the window we saw little, but a while earlier, Dieter reported he heard voices, and it was apparent the authorities were out there.

The gardeners had stopped their work and curiosity brought them to the edge of the forest. At length, the sound of wheels on the driveway caught everyone's attention. Our worst fears were realised when the undertaker's cart drew alongside the trees. Three stout men leapt to the ground. Two lifted down a crude wooden coffin and disappeared into the thicket of pines while the other held the reins of the horses.

Joan and I stood transfixed at the window. At the perimeter of the forest, the workers waited as well. Eventually there was activity, and the men returned carrying the coffin, with Max and one of his servants assisting. The gardeners stepped forward to help lift the wooden box onto the back of the cart. Max spoke with the men, who then clambered back up on their vehicle, and made a turn to go down the driveway from whence they came.

We watched them leave, and after a few words with the baron, the workers dispersed. My eyes went to where Max stood alone, apparently taking a moment to contemplate the sombre event. Without another thought, I left Joan and hurried outside to see him before he walked away. I was almost too late.

"Max, please wait!" I called to his back as he headed around the side of the building.

He turned and walked towards me. He looked dreadful.

"You can't go without telling me what happened?"

He gave a heavy sigh. His face bore traces of dirt smudged on his skin, his eyes cloudy and worried. "I am sorry, Ingrid. I planned to come back and see you once I had cleaned myself up. All I can tell you is the dogs found Helga while we were out for our walk. At first, I thought she must have stumbled, for she was lying at the bottom of a steep hill. It is easy to lose your footing with the slippery ferns and such." His dark eyes met mine. "But unfortunately, *Krankenschwester* Helga had no accident."

"What do you mean?"

"The poor woman was garroted."

My hand involuntarily rose to touch my own throat. "Dear God," I whispered.

"I am sorry to distress you, but you should know the truth. *Doktor* Engel will need to examine her and confirm the finding, but it was not difficult to tell."

It took me a moment to catch my breath. Max's words were too surreal to absorb. Murder? Here? "Why would someone kill the poor woman?" I asked, unable to halt the quiver in my voice. "Do you think it a personal vendetta, or a random killing? Was she robbed?"

Max held up a hand. "Ingrid, I cannot answer any questions. We know nothing yet. But as soon as that changes I will tell you at once." He gestured to the lodge. "For now, you should go home. There is nothing to be done, and it would put my mind at ease knowing you were safe in the house. Under the circumstances it would be unadvisable to remain outside today." His dark eyes searched mine. "I must go, I shall return later in the day. Please excuse me."

I took his advice. As Max walked off I hastened indoors, where once in the drawing room I poured myself a small glass of brandy and sipped it quickly. The warmth of the drink melted the ice in my bones and pushed back the chill of fear.

The severity of Max's words was sobering. A ghastly crime had been committed practically at our door. A life had been ruthlessly taken while I had been safe in here doing what? Drinking tea? Reading a book? It was a horrible notion to contemplate.

I considered my walk to the palace and back that very day. Had the murderer watched me as well? The shudder that passed through me had me reaching for a second measure of brandy, and then I calmed myself, and took a seat in front of the unlit fire.

I thought about the nurse. I pictured her on the few occasions our paths had crossed. Her unfriendly demeanour, especially for someone in the employment of care and kindness. The way she had looked at me each time with that curious expression. That the baroness did not care for her was not surprising. Elderly patients were often antagonistic with those overseeing their wellbeing. Yet out of all my musings, the one factor which stood out above them all was plain. Helga's obvious disregard for Wolfgang's authority. Why did that concern me? I did not quite understand. But I certainly planned to figure it out.

MAX HAD NOT RETURNED that day. He sent a note to explain he was travelling to *Prinzenstadt*, to consult with the magistrate and the police. He instructed me to be cognisant of our safety.

I spent the evening with Joan. Though Dieter ensured the lodge was locked up securely, I do not believe any of us slept particularly well. I had my bad dream, which was becoming a nightly occurrence. I still dreamt of being in the walled garden with the others present. Yet in this version, I saw the body of Helga lying in the grass, a red slit across her throat, while Lisbeth laughed, held out my necklace and dropped it into the dirt. I woke in a sweat with my heart racing.

In the morning the building felt as if it were draped in a shroud. The mood was solemn. Even the maids were quiet as they went about their work, for who could not be preoccupied with what had transpired.

I had finished luncheon and was in the drawing room reading when I heard a carriage. I peered out of the window to see Susanna alight. And though I was not in the mood for her silliness, I welcomed the intrusion and some company.

Susanna blew into the drawing room in a flurry of peach silk and came straight to me, hands extended.

"Dearest Ingrid. I cannot believe what has happened. Is it not the most dreadful thing? That poor woman! How utterly terrifying." As if her legs could hold her no longer, she sank down into a chair in a puff of silk. "I told Saul it was time he concluded his business and we went home. I cannot stay in a place where a madman is butchering women."

Fritz came in to place a tray on the table. I thanked him and waited for him to leave.

"Susanna, we do not know what happened. There could be a madman as you say, but the killer could have also been known to Helga. A spurned lover? An enemy? We have to see what the magistrate can discover."

"It matters not to me," she said forcefully, accepting the proffered cup of coffee. "I see no reason to stay where there is a threat to my well-being."

"And what of Wolfgang? Will you not be saddened to tell him farewell?" I could not help myself, though I shouldn't have baited her.

Her pretty eyes narrowed. "What of him? As you kindly reminded me, he is a married man, Ingrid. I shall just call it a flirtation and leave it there."

I did not believe a word of it. Susanna was far too transparent. There was an agenda here and she was doing her level best to conceal it.

"Does Saul know you are here?"

"Goodness, no. He forbade me to leave the hotel as he believes the villain lurks around every corner. I waited for him to go and then came here. I had to do something and get outside, and you did say I could come any time."

"Yes, and I meant it. I just don't want your brother worrying about you."

"I left him a note at the front desk. Now," she said with a wicked gleam in her eye. "Who do you think could be the murderer?"

I took one look at her face and realised it was going to be a long visit.

MAX CALLED HOURS AFTER Susanna had gone back to *Linnenbrink*. He arrived as dinner was served, and I asked Fritz to set another place and invited Max to dine with me. His acceptance surprised me, but I was glad of the company.

As we ate, he talked about his day in town, his meetings, and many conversations with the authorities. There would be an inquiry, of course. The police would conduct interviews but were currently trying to locate Helga's next of kin.

"You look drained," I said, noting the dark smudges under his eyes. His face was drawn, and his brow furrowed. I imagined his position in the community would demand his involvement in the investigation of criminal activity. A Baronetcy was somewhat feudal after all. "I can see the day has taken a toll upon you. But how fares everyone at the palace? Did the new nurse arrive?"

He sighed. "Hiring a nurse is not straightforward, unfortunately. Katja is spending a great deal of time with my mother, and one of the older servants is assisting her. Apparently the Baroness responds better to someone of a mature age, and she is calmer than you witnessed yesterday." He paused as though a thought struck him. "It's odd, but my mother seems to be in better spirits today, of all days. She is still confused, but her mood is cheery, and she has been talkative."

I immediately thought about the morphine in the cabinet. I suspected Helga had been administering more than necessary, but I did not voice this—it could wait. Max had plenty to think about as it was.

"Let us speak of something else," Max announced as he set down his cutlery and dabbed his mouth with the linen serviette. "Tell me. How are your plans progressing? Have you given any more thought to your future at here?"

"Not really," I answered honestly. "I've been distracted with updating the garden and my growing curiosity about the past."

One dark brow raised. "The past? You refer to your ignorance of this side of your family?"

"I do. There are questions I have, but more compelling, I want to learn about my aunt, in particular. Her legacy is one of confusion. I know nothing of her life at Lorelei."

Max leaned back in his chair and his warm brown eyes leveled on my face. "Can you give me an example?"

I met his gaze, struck as always by his handsome features. I looked away quickly. So much for my plan to feel indifference. "It seems Aunt Gisela was paid rather well to live here during her later years. Yet she employed only two house-servants, a married couple by the name of Krause, who by all accounts, were relatively unknown. The husband was seen in the village periodically, but the wife was a mystery—a recluse."

Max frowned. "And this perplexes you? It is not so unusual. In the city, everyone lives on top of one another, and therefore it's unavoidable meeting people and seeing your neighbours. But here, we are a rural community, and the culture is vastly different.

Personally, I do not find it so strange."

I shrugged. "Perhaps you are right. Yet at some point, my aunt paid the couple a large sum of money and they left her employ. Then, Gisela went away for many weeks, and when she returned, had hired several new people, all with a common thread."

"Which was?"

"That none were local. It seems she specifically sought out servants from other cities."

Our eyes met.

"Do you not find that odd, Max? There are likely any number of people willing to work in this vicinity. Why go to such extremes?"

"I will grant you that is unconventional," Max agreed. "However, Gisela was a little eccentric. She was probably paranoid about people knowing her business. To the extreme in this case?"

"Yes. I have considered that. But all indications are to the contrary. She was private, yes, but she was clever."

"Then what do you suspect?"

It was a good question. For I didn't actually know. "It isn't that simple. All I can tell you is that since coming here, I have had the impression that something is amiss. More specifically, it feels like the place itself hides something from me, which Gisela wanted kept to herself."

Max chuckled. "That is a fanciful notion indeed. Do you expect to find buried treasure?"

He mocked me, although gently. I immediately thought of the pendant I'd found in the garden. Did that constitute as buried treasure? "All right," I challenged. "Listen, and then you can give me your opinion."

Max poured himself a glass of port from the decanter seated close to his place at the table. "I am all ears, Ingrid."

I took a breath. "I have inherited a hunting lodge I was unaware Mother still owned, only to discover it was occupied by an aunt I did not know I had."

"It sounds like a riddle." Max chuckled.

I ignored him, intent on staying focused. "After being here a few days, I realised I had been here before, but a long time ago. Unfortunately, There's no clear memory of it, but as certain things have occurred, bits and pieces are beginning to filter through my head."

"That is not so strange, Ingrid. Most of us can't recall events that happened at young ages."

"True. But I have not told you about the nightmares."

The smile disappeared from his lips. "What are you talking about?"

"I have long suffered with a recurring nightmare. Historically, it always visits whenever I am away from home, or in some state of anxiety." My fingers crept to touch the pendant at my neck. "It's the same thing which happens each time." I explained the details of my dream and Max did not interrupt.

"But since arriving at Lorelei Lodge, the dreams have started to change. When I found the walled garden, I was amazed to recognise the very place from my dream. And though I find the garden calming and peaceful, something about it disturbs me still."

"I can see why your imagination could easily get the better of you, Ingrid. Those experiences are unsettling, to say the least. Especially on the heels of two deaths in your family. But why are you so suspicious about your aunt?"

"Partly because Mother kept her existence from me *and* paid her a healthy stipend to remain here. But also because Gisela received an anonymous payment every month, going back almost two years. The amount is recorded, but not its source, and our family lawyer has no knowledge of it. The payments coincide with the departure of the Krause's and precedes the arrival of new staff. A staff who conveniently have no information they can tell me of Gisela's past.

"All right," said Max. "That explains your curiosity—all these events occurring close together would make you think they are linked. But it isn't justifiable. There is nothing to connect what you have told me as any type of conspiracy. What do you imagine is being kept from you?"

His tone implied that I was overreacting, letting my imagination run away. I concealed my irritation. I was disappointed. I'd hoped Max would appreciate I was not a woman easily led to fancy. Yet here we were, and he had not changed his opinion or recognised my urgency in understanding my heritage and filling in the missing gaps in my family history.

"I don't imagine anything specific," I answered his question. "But much as a clerk seeks to balance a ledger sheet, I shall continue to do the same." I changed the subject. Max was not in alignment with my thoughts tonight and we were both tired. "Tell me. Will they be able to have a funeral for poor *Krankenschwester* Helga?"

Max sighed. "Not yet. Family must be found so she can be officially identified. In the meantime, she will be autopsied tomorrow in *Prinzenstadt*."

I shivered. What a macabre thought. Again, I visualized the stern-faced nurse. No person deserved to die like that. To have suffered at the hands of a brutal murderer and now to bear the ignominy under the doctor's investigative instruments was more than I wanted to think about. I suppose my face must have conveyed my distress.

"That was indelicate of me, Ingrid. I am sorry. It was not a conversation to have at dinner."

"No, do not apologise, Max. I asked the question." I got to my feet, suddenly desiring fresh air. "Let us go into the drawing room. It is warm in here and I should like to stand by an open window.

THE NIGHT AIR WAFTING IN was sweet with the scent of pine, which seemed ever present. Max stood at my side, and we gazed out across the front lawns.

"I have always liked this place," he mused. "Although the palace is a beautiful piece of architecture, it is more of a museum than a home. Lorelei has a comfortable feel to it. It envelops a person as soon as you step through the door."

Fritz had already been in and left a tray bearing coffee. I poured two cups and passed one to Max, then settled into one of the armchairs.

"Ah," I said. "You state another reason to buy Lorelei. Does it really mean that much to you?"

He took a seat directly across from me. "Personally, I would not mind living in a small cottage somewhere. Or an apartment like they have in New York City."

"You don't expect me to believe that?" I laughed. "This from a man living in a palace filled with treasures and marvels. Goodness, your library alone could house twenty families. What on earth would you do in a cottage? Where would Valentina put her belongings?" No sooner had I said the barb than I regretted bringing the Italian into the conversation. Our companionable easiness evaporated and was instantly replaced with a veil of tension.

"You do not like Valentina, I take it?" Max stated, with no emotion in his voice so I could not tell why he posed the question, or if there was a right or wrong answer.

"I do not know her, so I may not judge whether I like her or not. What I do know is that your wife is a formidable woman, and unlike any person I have ever met. In life Valentina is as bold as she is on the stage and under a spotlight. She is a skein of silk to my being dull as a dishrag."

Max set his cup down and his brown eyes looked black as night as they pierced into my own. "Ingrid, you astound me. Do you never look in a mirror? Are you so unaware of your own beauty?"

I gasped, quickly evading his stare as warmth flooded my cheeks. Wolfgang had said I was attractive, but no man had ever called me a beauty. That the first should be from a gentleman I was already drawn to was more than I knew how to cope with. I set my coffee cup back on the tray, and my discomfort was evident as the saucer rattled under my trembling hands.

"I have spoken too plainly," he remonstrated, getting to his feet. "Forgive me, Ingrid. It seems my self-command is somewhat lacking this evening. Please accept my apologies and put it down to the unsettling events of the past two days."

I rose but did not step closer to where he stood, still staring at me intently. The tension was palpable between us since the mention of Valentina, but it had shifted from irritation to what? I could not name it for it was foreign, yet every fibre of my being was aware of the man standing not three feet from me.

Max's expression was troubled. He let out a long breath. "I am sorry, but I have to be truthful about my feelings for you. You have sensed this...this connection that we have?" He took a step nearer, and my heart sped up. My breath came a little faster as my eyes locked with his. I said nothing.

"My life is so complicated, Ingrid. In the eyes of everything but the law I am a single man—heart, and soul. Yet I am tied to Valentina, though there is no love between us anymore." He stepped closer still, and my mouth went dry. I wet my lips and his gaze grew bolder. Another step and he was barely inches away from me.

"Ingrid?"

I glanced up and saw his thick, sooty lashes, the dark beard shadowing his face. Max's eyes locked with mine, and I noticed tiny chips of amber flecked in the sultry brown of his irises. His breathing rose and fell in harmony with my own. And when his hand gently cupped my face, I did not flinch. I was utterly mesmerised, lost in the essence of him. He tipped up my chin, and without taking his gaze from my own, Max leaned forward and touched his mouth to mine.

I was unprepared for the sudden rush of heat which engulfed my body. The warmth of his lips, soft yet pliant, the intimacy of his skin against my own. He did not embrace me, nor did I him, yet the kiss in its solo aria filled every tiny pore of my being. The pressure intensified, until our mouths were one, joined together in a moment of complete abandon, with no regard for anything or anyone. The world had stopped turning, and I ached for him to encircle me in his arms and pull me close against his body.

"Miss, has your company—" Joan burst into the room and Max broke away quickly. Had she seen us? I turned my back to the door and quickly covered my mouth.

"Oh. 'Scuse me, Baron. I didn't know you were still here." Joan did not sound in the least apologetic. I took a deep breath and faced her.

"Max was just leaving," I said, hoping my voice sounded calmer that I felt. "Would you mind seeing him to the door, Joan?"

But he held up a hand. "No, that is unnecessary. I can see myself out."

We looked at one another and I saw his eyes were still dark with emotion. I expected mine were as well. I swallowed.

"Then good night, Max."

He gave me a curt nod and left the room.

Joan did not speak for a few moments, and I knew she was allowing enough time for Max to be well clear of the lodge. She walked over to the open window and watched him walking away. Then she glanced over one shoulder to look at me. "Well now, miss. If I was a bettin' woman, I'd say you'd come out a lot more ahead if you was to take on those great, nasty dogs o' his, rather than their master."

She was probably right.

Chapter Thirteen

After two days of staying within the safety of the lodge, I could stand it no longer. Trapped inside, I had spent hours ruminating over my current situation and the choices I must decide upon. It surprised me that I was in no hurry to return to London, though I speculated how much of that was due to my attraction to Max and not researching my past.

My relationship with Max pleased and troubled me simultaneously. I liked him a great deal, and his company was desirous, yet everything else about the man confounded me. The memory of his kiss still lingered, and my mind tormented me each time I thought about that evening. For as much pleasure as his passion had brought, I was consumed with the guilt of betrayal.

I needed to stretch my legs. A short walk to the walled garden sounded just the thing. I'd be safe there in the company of the gardeners. The day was pleasant, still cool as it was barely ten in the morning, but it was a welcome relief to be outside, hearing birdsong and smelling the hint of summer on the breeze.

As I came into the garden, I noticed the three gardeners usually working very hard, were stood together, clustered in front of the Willow tree staring at the ground. I quickened my step and went to join them.

Wilhelm, the younger of the three fellows,

somewhere in his twenties, spoke passable broken English. When he caught sight of me, he quickly removed his hat, and the others followed suit.

"*Guten Tag meine Dame,*" they chorused.

"*Guten Tag.*" I looked at Wilhelm. "Is something wrong? What have you found?"

The gardener pointed to a small bunch of blue cornflowers tied with a blue ribbon laying at the bottom of the tree trunk. "Someone being here, *Fräulein* Rutherford, they leaving this."

I frowned. How odd. Why would they place a bunch of flowers by the tree? "Have you seen anyone?"

"*Nein, Fräulein,*" said Wilhelm, who then translated my question, to which the other two men shook their heads.

"*Es ist eine Hommage,*" said one of the gardeners, a middle-aged man with protruding ears and a bald pate. Wilhelm did not translate as he probably was not fluent enough, but I knew what he meant. A tribute. Someone had left a tribute to mark a spot. But who? And why? Another minute passed and the men finally dispersed to resume their work. I went to sit on the little bench, where I contemplated the cornflowers.

Every day I remained here I became more convinced that there was something I was overlooking. I had no inkling what it might be, but it was like the missing page of the family book in the study. No irrefutable proof, but the knowledge that just beyond my fingertips was an answer which would put me out of my misery.

Perhaps it was time to visit Lisbeth once again, for she, more than any other, seemed to have some answers. But what if I saw Max? Well, what if I did?

The man had kissed me, and I had allowed it to happen. No matter my feelings, or his, he was married and that was an end to it. I would not let a man get in the way of discovering my past. And the sooner I did just that, the quicker I could return to London.

WITH THAT AMBITION, I set off for the palace that very afternoon. I went in the carriage as I had no intention of walking alone near the forest with a murderer at large. Upon my arrival, I asked to see the baroness, and was collected by a grey-haired woman who spoke no English but escorted me to Lisbeth's apartments. We did not encounter Max or any of the family on the way, for which I was most grateful.

When we entered the baroness's room, I almost did not recognise the lady sitting poised in her chair. Her dark hair was swept up in a tidy arrangement and she was dressed in a fetching beige gown. As I approached Lisbeth, she got to her feet, held out her hand and smiled.

I could not help but return the gesture, and my pleasure in seeing her was genuine. For though I beheld a woman who might not have all her faculties, there was a light in her eyes I had not seen before. She gestured for me to sit, and I waited for her to initiate the conversation.

"Dear girl," she said in English. "I do not remember you for I believe I have mistaken you for Marta. Are you her child?"

I was elated. "Yes," I exclaimed. "I am!"

"Which one?"

The question took me aback. "I am Ingrid. Mother only had one child."

It was Lisbeth's turn to frown. "Oh dear," she said softly. "Sometimes I get very confused. Please forgive me. Tell me, how is your mother?"

This was becoming awkward. "I am sorry, Baroness. But my mother died several years ago."

Her brown eyes, so like Max's, filled with tears.

"Please don't be sad," I soothed. "I wanted to visit you and chat about your friendship with my mother. I did not intend to distress you."

"You do not. And I am better for your coming. I am old and my mind plays tricks with me and sometimes I forget who has already gone before me. We shall have coffee and you must tell me all about yourself, Ingrid."

The servant who had escorted me left to get our refreshment.

"You appear in much better spirits since I saw you last, Baroness." I saw something flicker across her expression, but it was too quick for me to interpret.

"I did not care for my nurse. She was not a kind person, yet Wolfgang allowed her to remain. He is not my favourite child. Do you know I have four sons? I believe my husband is dead, though I did not love him much because he used me as a brood mare."

Her conversation startled me. It was unfiltered and I realised it was purely the effects of her illness. Better her frankness than her confusion under the influence of morphine.

"Your sister, Marta, was like a sister to me also."

"Marta was my mother," I corrected gently.

"Yes. You see, I have already become confused. Marta and I were the best of friends. It was marvellous living so close to one another that we could meet every day." Her expression grew wistful, and I knew she revisited her past.

"I should love to hear about your time with her growing up. I miss her terribly, and it would bring me joy to hear her spoken of with such love."

Lisbeth smiled, and I saw warmth in her lovely face. And then she began to speak.

ONE HOUR AND TWO cups of coffee later, I had already learned more about my mother than I knew after living with her for twelve years.

Lisbeth painted a picture of a person I should have enjoyed being friends with as a child myself. I could easily imagine the vivid stories she shared. I visualised what they both looked like as young girls and even felt their spirit in the choice of her words. Every so often she would get a little confused, and the tales were not chronologically sequential, but I thoroughly enjoyed them all.

Periodically, I noticed her eyes strayed to the pendant I wore, and finally I asked if she recognised it.

"Yes." She smiled. "Marta wore that same necklace. Was that hers?"

"No. She had a matching one made for me as a birthday gift." My fingers automatically touched it. "I try never to take it off." I had a thought. "Did you ever wear one, Baroness?"

The older lady blinked a few times, and I could tell she was trying very hard to reach into the corners of her memories. "I do not think so. It is a familiar piece because of Marta." She gave a deep sigh. "You know, the nurse has gone now. I didn't like her, so good riddance I say."

She was slipping back into her fugue right before my eyes. Though even in this state she was far more lucid than she had been on my previous visits.

"Why didn't you like the nurse?" I would follow the conversation wherever she led it.

"Scheming and sly, she was. Plotting with my son at every turn. She thought I didn't know her," Lisbeth grinned, and she looked a little mad. "But I did. That's why she gave me all the medicine so I wouldn't tell." The baroness tapped her nose. "I still knew. I never spoke a word, but I wrote it down." Her eyes gleamed and she got to her feet. She walked over to her bedside table, but instead of opening a drawer, she reached underneath and retrieved an item. She returned to sit back down.

"Look," she said, opening her hands to reveal a small notebook. "It's all in here, though you mustn't tell them, Marta's girl."

I accepted the proffered book, which was no larger than my palm, and gingerly opened it up. The pages were covered in tiny, spider-like scrawls, most of which was unintelligible to me. Disappointment engulfed me, what had I expected to read here anyway?

"See," Lisbeth smiled once more. "It's all there. All the secrets, even my boy's."

I could not follow her writing, nor her conversation. What was she talking about? And what boy? She had four of them. The baroness got up and came to where I sat. I held out the notebook which she took, but instead of putting it away she flicked through more of the pages.

"Here," she said. "Here is one secret." She held out the book and I squinted to read it.

There was a drawing, it was crudely done and not very big, but I could tell it was a woman wearing a uniform of sorts with a large cross on her breast. I understood it must be the nurse. Why was Lisbeth showing me this?

"Do you see the secret?" she whispered.

Frowning I leaned closer. There was a small inscription underneath the picture. I glanced at the words and then read them once again for I was sure my eyes deceived me.

The picture of the nurse bore the name—Klara Krause.

I LEFT FOR HOME in time for tea, only to find I had company. Susanna had arrived in my absence, but was quite happily relaxing in the drawing room, sharing a pot of the brew with Joan. They made quite a singular pair. The American was in a froth of lemon silk, and currently enjoying a slice of cake, while Joan was in plain grey serge, expounding upon her dislike of German cuisine.

"An' who wants to eat blasted cabbage with every meal?" she complained. "If it isn't boiled, it's pickled or covered in some strange sauce. I'd give anythin' for a bit of normal bubble an' squeak."

"But isn't that fried cabbage and potatoes?" asked Susanna.

"May I join in this culinary conversation?" I said, removing my gloves as I entered the room.

"Hello, Ingrid," Susanna said cheerily. "I was chomping at the bit to get out of the hotel, so I thought I would visit you and bring you an invitation. Obviously you weren't here, so Joan has been kind enough to keep me company."

Joan looked sheepish. I knew in one glance that she had been chatty, and I was likely the main subject of that conversation. This did not concern me in the least for I had more important issues to think about, especially after what Lisbeth had disclosed. I considered sharing what I had learned with the two of them, and then changed my mind. It would be prudent to follow up on it and go from there.

Joan rose and collected the empty cups to put on the tray. "I'll be leavin' you ladies to carry on then," she said with a cheeky grin to Susanna.

"Joan said you went to the palace to visit the baroness?"

"Yes," I said as I sat down. "She was looking rather well."

"Considering what has happened, that is fortunate." Susanna gave a sigh. "This is a strange country, Ingrid. The people are distant and the customs severe. I do miss New York."

I felt sorry for her. After all, Susanna was a lively young woman, trapped in a dull little village. "When will Saul finish his business with Max?"

"He says another week. I really don't know what is taking so long. I guess there are all kinds of paperwork and legal agreements. But mostly, I think Saul's just having fun going to the steel works and seeing how everything is run."

I wanted to ask if she had seen anything of Wolfgang. But though we were friends, our relationship was not that intimate. "What were you saying about an invitation?"

"Oh, it is to our farewell party. Actually, more of a

small dinner we're hosting at the hotel. I believe Saul humours me because I have been so sulky lately and it gives me something to dress up for. But regardless, it shall be on Friday at seven, if you can come along?"

"Of course, I shall come. I wouldn't miss it. Thank you for asking. It shall be strange your not being in Linnenbrink."

"I'll say," she said. "I feel as though I've been here for years! But I'm glad you'll come to the dinner. The von Brandts will be there also, and Doctor Engel and his wife, Birgit. She has been very kind to me. Their home is in the village, so I often stop in and see her."

I remembered meeting the woman on Susanna's birthday. She seemed a good sort and I was glad for their friendship. Yet as the young American chattered, I had an ominous feeling. I hoped Mrs Engel was not welcoming Wolfgang into her home at the same time as Susanna and facilitating clandestine meetings.

THE NEXT MORNING, I called for the carriage. *Herr* Metzger seemed surprised to be driving me out twice in two days. As he helped me into the cab, I noticed he smelled of soap, and his thin hair was combed. He looked quite well put together. What had brought this change about?

I arrived unannounced at the lawyer's office, as was my wont. *Herr* Vogel was welcoming and polite as always—though I am sure I interrupted his work.

"What an unexpected pleasure," he said kindly. "What brings you here today?"

"Information," I said. "You have of course, heard of the horrific murder which took place near the lodge."

"Yes. It has been the main topic of conversation for

the past two days. What a terrible tragedy. They have not apprehended the killer yet, and I do hope you are taking precautions and not venturing out alone or on foot, *Fräulein*?"

"Everyone is being vigilant. Now, *Herr* Vogel, I have some important news."

He gestured for me to take a seat in the usual spot, and once I was settled, joined me. He leaned upon his desk, steepled his long fingers together and stared at me through his little spectacles.

Quickly, I recounted my visit with the Baroness, concluding with the disclosure of *Krankenschwester* Helga's potential real identity. I could see his misgivings immediately as he sighed, and his mouth became a thin line.

Before he could say anything, I added. "*Herr* Vogel, I understand your being sceptical as it does sound far-fetched. But there are other factors which make this credible. I know for a fact the Baroness has been kept heavily sedated at all times by this particular nurse. I also recall the woman's strange reaction upon seeing me for the first time, and I witnessed her blatant disregard of Wolfgang's authority."

"These are noteworthy observations, *Fräulein*, yet they do not point to a false identity."

"But what if Klara Krause was in league with someone at the palace? The entire time she lived at Lorelei Lodge, she was an unknown by all accounts. Who is to say she could easily have used another name to gain employment with the von Brandts?"

"But why use a different name?"

"For the same reason she was paid a large sum by my aunt to go away. With her husband dead, perhaps the woman needed more money, and came back only to find my aunt had died as well. She might have had limited options."

"But again, I ask you, why the subterfuge?"

"She must have had something to hide." And so did someone else at the palace. No servant spoke to their employer in the manner the nurse had with Wolfgang. "Look. If you can discover any living relative of the Krauses, then you will know if I am right. I beg you contact the authorities here and see what they can do."

His wiry eyebrows shot up to almost touch his forehead. "There is no need for me to do that when you can report these findings to the baron. It is within his family's jurisdiction after all."

"Yes, but it is a conflict of interest," I stated. "I would encourage you to speak with the authorities here in the city instead. Klara Krause was well-known to my aunt, but perhaps she had been seen by the baroness also? If the woman was up to no good, whatever it might have been, then she would want to remain anonymous. With the baroness's mental health in decline, it would not be difficult to over-medicate her and keep her confused."

Herr Vogel sat back in his chair. "*Fräulein* Rutherford, I know you mean well, but this entire story you recount sounds very melodramatic. These musings from the baroness are likely just that. I am sure the *Krankenschwester* was a reputable person under the employ of an agency. Let me make some inquiries in that direction first, if you please."

I was disappointed, and rather annoyed. Had I been a man, I am sure the lawyer would have listened with an open mind and respected my concerns. But I was merely a woman. Society dictated that I was, therefore, prone to hysteria and a vivid imagination—no doubt attributed to the books I read.

My chair scraped the floor as I abruptly got to my feet. *Herr* Vogel did the same, his face a picture of concern that he had offended me.

"*Fräulein* Rutherford—"

"I am sorry to have inconvenienced you, *Herr* Vogel. I had hoped you would take my concerns far more seriously than you have done. If you choose not to help me, then I shall find another who will." I turned away and strode to the door.

"Wait!"

I paused with my hand on the doorknob and looked back over my shoulder.

"*Entschuldigen, fräulein.* I am sorry. Will you please sit down a moment longer?"

I was still angry, but I did like the man and would rather deal with him than someone else. I returned to my seat.

"Let us start again, shall we?" he said.

"It is not complicated," I said plainly. "I believe my aunt Gisela was involved in something she chose to keep secret. It seems likely the Krauses were complicit, hence their being paid money and ultimately being sent away. Klara came back, took a job using a false name, and the baroness recognised her. Whoever Klara was hiding from must have found her, and now she is dead.

I wish to know if the woman was killed because of something that happened while she was away, or if it had anything to do with her time at Lorelei. Because, *Herr* Vogel, if it was connected to my aunt, and my home, I might be in danger as well."

WHEN MAX STOPPED BY unexpectedly the following afternoon, I was as awkward as a foal standing on its legs for the first time. My only consolation was that he too seemed less confident. But I invited him to sit, and we made polite conversation after dismissing Fritz and turning down his offer of refreshment.

My cheeks felt warm. Ridiculous to be so uncomfortable with him sitting several feet away from me when not three days earlier his lips had been pressed upon mine.

"Ingrid, you look as ill at ease as I feel. Can we please put what happened the other evening behind us? I am sorry for my behaviour. I got carried away in the moment and it was wrong of me. Will you forgive me so we can resume our friendship? The atmosphere in here is making it hard to breathe."

I chuckled and saw the relief on his face. "You are forgiven, Max. Let us just accept we had a stressful few days. I think all of us were in shock after the nurse's murder."

"Actually, I came to talk to you about her replacement, though it seems callous when I put it that way. But I know you are fond of my mother and care about her welfare."

"Yes, I like her very much."

"Then you will be pleased to hear I have secured a new nurse, and the baroness is thrilled with the lady. Her name is *Krankenschwester* Magda, and she is about ten years younger than my mother. So far, Mother has told me she likes the nurse's hair much better than Helga's, and that Magda smells like violets."

"Well, those are important traits to have as a nurse."

"Indeed. But I am relieved to have her settled."

Something occurred to me. "Were you the person who originally hired Helga?"

His dark eyes grew puzzled. "That's an odd question. But to answer it, no. Wolfgang brought her on. She was recommended to him by someone he knew."

"I see. I do not wish to speak ill of the dead, but *Krankenschwester* Helga was not the right nurse for your mother."

Max's eyes narrowed. "Why do you say that?"

"Apart from your mother's obvious dislike of the woman, I think she was over sedating Lisbeth regularly."

"What?"

"I understand your mother has the aging disease, but I have been around people who suffer that way. Lisbeth seemed lethargic, confused, not just by memories but even normal actions, and her physical strength seemed constantly sluggish, regardless of rest." I paused, reluctant to offend the man.

"Well don't stop there," Max said, with a note of irritation.

"Surely you must have noticed she seems improved in the past few days? I could tell immediately when I visited her. I know she still has problems with her mind, yet her clarity is significantly better. Do you not agree?"

Max nodded slowly. "Now you mention it, you are right. Mother is more communicative and energetic. You really believe the nurse was drugging her?"

"I do."

"Why? Was it to make her work easier keeping my mother calmer?"

I longed to tell Max my suspicions, that Helga had really been Klara, likely in cahoots with someone at the palace. Yet I held back. "It would appear to be the case. I think it is not uncommon for patients to be kept in a state of apathy, more's the pity."

"You should have mentioned this to me at the time. What stopped you?" Max posed the question, and I did not care for the accusatory tone in his voice.

"I did comment on her being sleepy, and you told me that was her normal condition due to her medication. Perhaps you should have conferred with the doctor—"

"Ingrid, I do not think it your place to criticise my judgement of my mother's welfare."

"Criticise? That's not my intention, Max. I only speak of it to avoid the same thing from recurring."

"The inference is still offensive."

"And your tone is rather defensive." I replied, realising we were sparring. Yes, it was about his mother, but it went beyond that. We had an agenda between us that had not been addressed and instead swept under the proverbial rug.

Why did everything have to be so complicated? I looked at Max and remembered the feel of his lips against my own. How I had desired so much more. At once I felt a surge of humiliation rush through me. What was the matter with me? Did I think so little of myself that I was only fit for the attentions of a married man? I was as bad as Susanna. I quickly got to my feet. "I think you should go," I said tersely.

He stood up. "Yes, I think it wise. But please know I did not come here to antagonise you, Ingrid."

Our eyes met. My heart weighed heavy in my chest as I said what needed to be said. "Perhaps not. But Max, I do not understand why you come here at all. You should go home to your wife."

His expression grew dark, his jaw clenched, and I half expected him to speak for he looked as though he had much he wanted to say. But he remained silent and brushed past me as though I was not even there.

THE REMAINDER OF THE day was a blur, for I spent most of it sulking. My mood was so bleak that even Joan left me to wallow in self-pity. I felt like the baroness, as though I had emerged from some sort of fugue and could finally see clearly.

I was a fool. My head turned by the first handsome man who had shown me attention. A married man, no less. It did not matter whether Max's relationship with the beautiful Valentina was happy or not. They were bound as one in the eyes of the law and that was that. Yet, naïve as I was, I'd allowed myself to be caught up in the tide of my imagination and whisked away on a voyage of clandestine glances and smiles. The culmination of it being that kiss—one which had stayed with me and caused my heart to swell at its memory. But that had stopped today. There was an entire world between Baron Maximillian von Brandt and myself, and no path to bridge the gap.

I took my dinner on a tray in my room that evening, and then dismissed Joan early and told her I wanted to stay in my bedroom and read. She did not question my reasons, nor did she make a fuss. Joan could be surprisingly intuitive at times. She knew my dilemma, and I could tell by her manner she approved of my change of heart.

I lost myself in my book, and I fell asleep before it was even dark outside.

I AWOKE WITH A START, breathing like I had run miles. Sweat beaded upon my brow and my nightgown was damp. The blasted dream was growing more vivid with each telling, as did the knot of apprehension in my belly. What did it mean? Why were all the new people in my life present in the garden with me? Tonight, Helga walked among us once again, with a bloody slit across her throat.

I shuddered at the memory and sat upright to take a drink of water. My water jug was empty. With a sigh, I got to my feet and walked to the open window. It must be quite late, for the lodge was quiet and the night sky black as pitch.

My mouth was dry. There was nothing for it but to go down to the kitchen. I crept down the stairs using just a candle to see my way as I was unwilling to disturb a soul. I reached the kitchen and headed towards the sink where I knew a large container of water was kept. I filled the glass and took a welcome hearty measure. I set it down and turned to go back to my room when something caught my eye.

Through one of the kitchen windows a small yellow dot moved down the path in the direction of the palace. It had already travelled some distance, so I could not see anything else, but of course it was a person. I watched for a few moments, the urge to follow was great, but the fear of being murdered greater. I left the kitchen to seek out the hall clock, it was just past three in the morning. Far too late for anyone to be out. Who could it have been?

A shudder ran through me and I hastened back upstairs to my room, where I closed and locked the door. I did not blow out my candle, but let it burn as I lay under the covers, wide-awake with my thoughts afire. There was something underhand at play, here at the lodge *or* the palace. but which was it? A woman had been brutally murdered, and there were too many unanswered questions about the past which I believed were somehow connected. Tomorrow was a new day. And I intended to start a fresh chapter in this journey of mine. I would solve this puzzle once and for all, and then I would go home to London.

Chapter Fourteen

AT BREAKFAST I WAS TIRED from my disrupted night. I picked at my food with little interest and drank two cups of coffee in the hope it would clear my head. Tonight was Susanna's dinner party, and I had little desire to go and be in the company of the von Brandts. It would be easy to feign a headache and send my regrets, but I didn't want to be deceitful to either Susanna or Saul. I was a hypocrite. For had I not been deceitful kissing another woman's husband?

I turned my attention to the silver platter Fritz placed on the table which contained this morning's early post. There was a note from the village vicar regarding a fund-raising event which I made a mental note to speak to Fritz about. There was also a small white envelope without a stamp, apparently hand-delivered. I took my knife and slit it open, drawing out the single sheaf of paper.

As my eyes scoured the words, their meaning penetrated into my mind. My stomach churned and my hands began to shake. Two simple words with such ominous promise—

"You're next."

THOUGH I DID NOT want him there I had little choice. Joan had sent Herr Metzger to the palace with a request the baron come immediately. Now the initial shock had worn off, I was livid.

"You've had a nasty scare," Joan insisted. "Someone has threatened you, an' you need help."

I paced back and forth in the drawing room. "I need a weapon," I said angrily. "How dare anyone say that to me. And what good will it do telling the baron?" I scolded. "He's probably the one who sent it!"

"You don't mean that, miss," Joan placated. "He may have taken advantage of your kindness, but he's no killer."

"You're defending him?" The world was going mad.

We both turned as the front door slammed and footsteps approached. Max stormed into the drawing room, his face tense with anger.

"Who has threatened you?" he demanded. "Show me the note!"

I said nothing but pointed to the sideboard where it lay like a discarded glove. He swiped it up, looked over it and then set it back down. He glowered at me.

"Pack your things. You are not staying here another moment longer."

"What?" I said in disbelief.

Max looked at Joan. 'Your mistress is not safe here. She must come to the palace where it is more secure, and I know she can be protected."

"I am in the room, you know," I interrupted.

"Miss," Joan placated. "The baron's right. You don't know who wrote that nasty note. It could be anybody. You've only me and a couple of servants to look out for you. You must go, like he says. That, or go home to London. But don't stay here another night if you can help it."

Through my irritation, I saw the sense of her argument. It was true. Like it or not, I had to take the threat seriously, and short of hiring armed guards, I was in no position to protect myself. I nodded, and Joan left the room to pack some of my things.

The weight of my emotion grew heavy. I took a seat.

With his back to the window, Max watched me.

"What are you thinking?" I asked. For I knew like me, he would be trying to unravel the scheme behind the note.

"That there is no reason someone would have a grievance against both you and the nurse, supposing it is the same villain."

"I agree. I barely knew the woman, so unless the person takes issue with my gender, it is doubtful it is from the killer, more like someone who wants me gone from here." I stated. "And who might that be?" I posed the question and our eyes met. Did he read my thoughts? Was it Valentina? Was she horrid enough to send a missive which would strike fear into the heart of any woman? I pictured the Italian and her commanding, assertive presence. I spoke up.

"Consider this, Max. What if the person who sent this resides in your home? You will be taking me into the lion's den."

He acknowledged the point. "There is that possibility, Ingrid. But they do say keep your friends near and your enemies closer." He came over to where I sat and took the seat across from me. He looked weary. It had been a grueling few days one way or another. As Baron, there were likely many responsibilities Max endured, of which I had no knowledge.

I softened a little. "Thank you for watching over me," I tried to sound sincere.

His dark eyes fastened upon me, and for a moment, something glimmered there briefly and then disappeared.

"Ingrid. Regardless of what you think of me, my strange situation, hell even my actions, please remember, no matter what, I care about you and do not want to see you harmed. I only wish we had met at another time, when I was still…" He broke off abruptly as Joan's voice could be heard outside the room as she called for Dieter's help. He waited a moment until it grew quiet again and continued with a less personal statement.

"You may be half English, and you might not stay in Germany much longer. But while you are in this part of the world, you are always under my protection."

"Are you assuming I don't know how to take care of myself?" I couldn't help responding. I was no shrinking ninny, nor would I have him think it.

He chuckled. "Not at all. For a more competent and resilient woman I have yet to meet. But even the best generals need their majors, and their colonels, Ingrid. Why fight alone when you can have a battalion?"

"Point taken," I admitted.

MAX ACCOMPANIED ME TO the palace, along with Joan, my trunk and her bags. We were not put in the guest wing of the palace but placed in apartments close to the family. This, Max advised, was better to concentrate security.

A trundle bed was brought in so that Joan could share my room. We both found great comfort in this.

The Secret of Lorelei Lodge

Max also indicated the door could be locked from the inside, and we would be safe. He left us to attend some business but urged me to make myself at home as much as possible, hinting that it would be a good opportunity to look at the library. Joan shooed me away while she unpacked our belongings, so I took Max's suggestion and found my way to the ground floor.

I half expected to run into Valentina, for it seemed she was always aware when I was in the palace. But I only saw a few of the servants on my way downstairs. I stopped a young red-haired woman and asked if she could direct me to the library, and this she did. Once I stepped into the room, I felt my troubles lift from my shoulders for the first time that day.

It was a glorious place, with such light, such ambiance, that being inside was almost a spiritual experience. The colours were so bright, enhanced by sunlight streaming through the multitude of glass panes, illuminating each book, each piece of furniture, as though everything it touched was magical. I sighed with pleasure and walked towards a row of books. I needed to get lost in something other than my thoughts.

Most of the books were German, but eventually, I found the bookcases containing English titles. There were many fine first edition prints of some of my favourites, and I was glancing through Elizabeth Gaskell's *North and South*, when I heard footsteps. I placed the book back and was about to say something when I heard Wolfgang speak.

"*Was ist das für? Du bist heute früh aus deinem Nest.*" I translated it in my head. He was asking her a question. 'What is it? You are out of your nest early today."

"*Per favore*," came the unmistakable voice of Valentina. She switched to German. "I was awakened by all the noise. Do you see who has come to the palace?"

"*Ja*. My brother rescues a damsel in distress."

I flinched, instantly annoyed by the inference of my being weak. But I stayed quiet.

"Why? What has happened?"

"Something about her life being in danger," Wolfgang said sarcastically. "Though knowing Max, it is so he can have her under his watchful eye."

"Wolfgang, I do not think I can stand this much longer."

There came the sudden sound of a child calling his father. There were footsteps and I assumed Wolfgang and Valentina must have left the room. Cautiously I peered around the end of the bookcase. I was alone. I contemplated what I had overheard. I was not very popular with either of the two. Valentina disliked me because of her husband. But Wolfgang? Had I offended the man? I did not think so, but perhaps Susanna had shared my disapproval of his attentions towards her. No matter. Now I was aware, I would be on my guard.

TONIGHT WAS THE KOPPELMANS' farewell dinner, and I'd insisted upon being driven by *Herr* Metzger instead of being in the entourage of the von Brandts. I had no desire to be in close quarters and share a carriage with Valentina and Wolfgang. Max had shown concern for my safety, but Joan had volunteered to accompany me on the journey. We departed a full ten minutes earlier than the others and I was the first guest to arrive and be shown to the private dining room.

Susanna was stunning in a satin blue gown which matched her eyes. Her face was bright with anticipation of the evening as she came straight over to greet me when I arrived. I was cocooned in her lilac scented embrace.

"Ingrid, I am so happy to see you. Is it not exciting that we are to leave here, finally! I cannot wait to see Vienna. Did I tell you that is where we go first before Paris, and then home? I am practically packed, though we do not leave until Tuesday."

Susanna was certainly in good spirits. If her speech was a racehorse, she would win the Derby every year. I shook my head and smiled at the young woman, though I did wonder at her good mood. Perhaps she had stopped thinking about Wolfgang von Brandt now she was going home. I certainly hoped so.

"Ingrid, it is good to see you." Saul joined us and I shook his hand companionably. I had spent little time with the man but I liked him very well. Though attractive, Saul's scholarly personality defined him. Serious, and intelligent, I believed we could have been good friends given the opportunity.

"I am glad to see you and Susanna," I replied. "Though I shall be sad to see you go. You will both be missed."

"I doubt that," Susanna said. "Though the shops owners will miss our coin, no doubt. I cannot wait to go into a department store once more! I shall never complain about Macy's again."

Saul rolled his eyes. "I should like that in writing." We laughed, and then there was a commotion at the door as the palace contingency arrived.

As expected, Valentina's appearance was a

spectacle. Tonight, she wore a purple gown befitting a queen. The satin shimmered in the gas light, the decolletage cut deep to expose her olive skin and the swell of her generous bosom. Her magnificent black tresses were swept up in an elaborate arrangement of coils and braids, and she wore amethyst drops the size of grapes in her ears.

"*Buonasera cari*," she announced, entering the room. "Ah, Susanna! Look how lovely you are in your pretty blue dress." Her compliments never stuck but slid away in their ingenuity. She had a way of mocking you with kindness. Yet Susanna did not seem to care. She welcomed all the guests pleasantly, but I saw the way her expression changed when her eyes landed upon Wolfgang.

At first glance, one could not help but admire the handsome German. He drew the eye immediately. His dark good looks, his groomed appearance, his commanding physique were that of the hero in a novel. Yet in him I saw arrogance, a weakness of the chin, a callous glint in his eyes, or perhaps it was my pride now I knew for certain he did not like me.

And then there was Max. He hung back to accompany Katja who had been abandoned instantly by her husband, standing instead next to Valentina. Max and his brother were very alike at first glance. The same colouring, similar features. But where Wolfgang exuded a propensity to be seen and admired, Max was the opposite. He was quiet, observant, and there was about him the kind of strength that emanates from an individual born to lead. Would I call it magnetism? I was unsure. Either way I should not be thinking of him at all. My thoughts were better suited to remain on my hosts.

Valentina greeted me with a nod as I passed her while she spoke with Saul, who stood entranced by her every word. I walked over to Katja. Max had gone to get her some refreshment.

"Good evening, Katja," I said. "You look very lovely tonight." I envied her the pale lemon gown, for I was so sick of wearing nothing but black.

"*Danke*," she replied. Her brown hair was captured in a pretty clasp and fell in ringlets about her face. She was not an unattractive woman, but in the bright light that was Valentina, we were all moths to her butterfly.

"You have come to stay at the palace I am told?" she said.

"Yes. Although I am not sure that was the right thing to do."

"I understand you were threatened by the person responsible for killing Helga?"

"That is not certain. I received a note which because of the recent circumstances we've had to make that assumption. But I believe it is something else entirely. The police have it now, and we shall see what they come up with."

Katja's pale blue eyes were interested. "Why do you think the note is about something else? What do you mean?"

I sighed. "There have been many things which have occurred since I arrived here. In of themselves, they sound like nothing. Yet together, they form a string of events which makes me question—"

"Everyone, may I have your attention, please." Saul said loudly, as Max returned with a glass of sherry which he handed to his sister-in-law. His glance grazed over my face, and I quickly looked away.

"I want to thank you for coming tonight," Saul continued, with a nod to Doctor and Mrs Engel who had just walked into the room. "You have made Susanna and I welcome during our stay in *Linnenbrink*, and for that I shall be forever in your debt. Now then, let us go into dinner."

A footman opened adjoining double doors. Saul and Susanna linked arms and led the way, followed by Wolfgang and Valentina, the Engels, Max and Katja, and finally me, unescorted.

THE MEAL WAS DELICIOUS. A spicy soup, roast pork, apple compote, and a variety of roasted vegetables. The dessert was another cherry concoction, laced with brandy which I found almost too rich to eat. By the time our plates were cleared I was as full as a tick.

I had been seated between Doctor Carl Engel and Katja, and across from Max, who I avoided looking at the entire time. Katja was not particularly entertaining company, but the doctor was most interesting. We discussed new trends in medicine—in particular, the work being done by Louis Pasteur, a man the doctor held in great esteem. As he explained the many vaccines Mr Pasteur was responsible for introducing, I was enthralled.

"I am astounded I know so little about such brilliant scientists," I commented. "I wish there were more publications available to the everyday person so we could be better educated about these amazing contributions."

"Is that not what a library is for?" Katja commented. I hadn't realised she was listening.

The Secret of Lorelei Lodge

"Perhaps," answered the doctor. But usually, public libraries and university libraries are situated in larger towns. I think what *Fräulein* Rutherford means is the information of these discoveries should be easier to find, such as in local newspapers or periodicals."

I nodded. "Yes, that's right. But not just a headline, but ongoing information to make the general population aware. How can a young girl or boy amount to something without a role model. Not every child needs to emulate their parents' position in life."

"I do not understand, *fräulein*," Katja said.

"In England, if a man is a butcher, then his son will assuredly follow in that role."

"*Ja*, that is how it is in *Deutschland* also."

"But what if that son has the talent to become a surgeon. Perhaps he has taken his father's skill of sectioning up a cow and improved upon it to such a degree that he can lance an abscess, set a broken bone. A child should see beyond the confinement of their home, their own town, indeed their own country. And education is the key to it all." I suddenly realised everyone at the table was listening to our conversation. My face warmed.

"If all bambinos had an education, Signorina, then who would milk the cows? Turn down my bed? Wash my clothes?" Valentina's black eyes regarded me, and the malevolence held there was obvious.

I met her stare and did not flinch. "Everyone has different strengths, *Signora*. There are those who are content tending farms, or working as housemaids," I gestured to the footman in attendance, "even taking care of people at table. You miss my point. I am saying that before the die is cast and we choose a path for our future, it should be a future with endless possibilities no matter the class or wealth of the individual."

"You are an idealist," muttered Wolfgang.

"A communist," laughed Valentina. "Those who deserve success must fight for it. Rise up through whatever obstacles present themselves and overcome all to deserve what they get."

"Survival of the fittest," Max said, joining the conversation. "A standard well employed in the animal kingdom, according to Mr Darwin, yet hardly applicable among people."

"I disagree," snapped Valentina. "My fame was not given to me. I had to earn it and work hard."

"You miss my point," I said, earning a harsh glare from the diva. "Of course, a person must work hard to climb to the top of their desired ambition. I speak of another subject entirely. Exposure. Take Charles Darwin. Had he been born to a family of paupers would he have become the famed naturalist? Or could Lord Tennyson become the Poet Laureate were he illiterate? I state that with exposure to information and education, an individual has choices and can contribute to society in ways they cannot when kept poor and ignorant."

The room was quiet, and I realised I had raised my voice. I fell silent.

"Well said," Max broke the peace.

"Indeed," Saul agreed. Rising from his seat he cleared his throat. "Let us enjoy our coffee in the adjoining room where we can be more comfortable."

We followed Saul's lead out of the small dining room and into a drawing room, replete with several chairs and two sofas. There was little decoration in here, and it was obviously used for informal meetings, judging by the arrangement of the furniture. I noticed the French windows were open to what looked like quite a sizeable balcony overlooking the front of the hotel, facing the street.

Our coffee was served. A rich dark brew which was so popular with the Germans, though I found it somewhat bitter. I wandered the perimeter of the room, not ready to sit, but wanting to observe instead. Saul and Max were already deep in conversation. Wolfgang held court with both Susanna and Valentina, while Doctor Engel and his wife chatted amiably in German with Katja.

What an odd group we made. Though I was not close to any of them I would be sorry to see the Koppelmans leave. I did feel a kinship with Susanna, as if she were a younger sister. Though not many years separated us, it seemed a decade to me, based upon her maturity and the lifestyle she had endured thus far.

I was not paying attention to the ongoing conversations, but soon was engaged in a brief recap with Doctor Engel. After a while, I excused myself to attend to my toilette. I returned and noticed there were fewer people present. Susanna was nowhere to be seen. I caught a sudden flash of blue out on the balcony. I scanned the room and realised Wolfgang was also missing. My heart sank. I hoped the girl was not being foolish.

I observed Valentina looking bored while Saul spoke to her, and the Engles were engaged in conversation with Max, while Katja sat by herself on one of the velvet sofas. I hesitated. Should I join Wolfgang's abandoned wife, or search for my friend before she embarrassed herself? My feet automatically moved towards the open windows before I could answer that question.

I stepped out into the night and felt the welcome cool air engulf me. The balcony was surprisingly large, several feet deep and the length of the room. It was dark, the only light coming from our room.

I listened. I could hear the murmur of voices to my right, and I turned in their direction. I told myself it was not my business to morally patrol the young American. But Susanna was my friend, and I did not want to see her tarnished by a scandal which would devastate her family. Wolfgang von Brandt was not unlike his name. He was a predator, and I did not trust him whatsoever.

They were in a corner, tight against the wall of the building where it was the darkest. Their bodies were moulded as one, and it was obvious they were in a passionate embrace. I took a breath, but before any sound came out of my mouth, someone else beat me to it.

"*Tua moglie tis ta cercando,*" the Italian words were delivered in a low, menacing voice.

Instantly, the two figures broke away from each other. Their faces mere shadows.

"Sorry," Valentina said in English. "I forget you do not speak my language. I was telling Wolfgang that his wife is looking for him."

I spun around to see her walk away and back into the drawing room. Wolfgang quickly brushed past me, leaving Susanna and I alone.

"Don't say anything, Ingrid," she said quietly and walked to lean against the rail overlooking the street. "I need no lecture, least of all, from you."

I went to stand beside her. "Then you will get

none. The fact you expect it should tell you that your conscience is your guide." With that, I abandoned her and returned to the others.

Back inside, the group seemed much as I had left them, although Valentina and Wolfgang stood near the door in a heated discussion, I glanced at Max, who watched them, a frown on his face. Katja studied them too, but her expression was blank. I went to sit by her on the sofa.

"Did you enjoy the dinner, Katja?" It was an inane question, but I was struggling.

"It was pleasant enough." She turned and looked at me thoughtfully. "You must miss being in London. Dinner in a small village hotel must seem very provincial in comparison. I am from Berlin, and at times I feel living in a place like this will drive me mad."

I had never thought about Katja's background. I grasped the subject, grateful to have something to talk about. "Berlin is not much different in size than London, I imagine. It must have been a great change for you when you moved here."

Her gaze flickered to her husband, and then came back to regard me.

"It was. But when I saw das *Safranpalast,* I fell in love with it. It is, after all, exquisite. Wolfgang made me happy, and though I missed my family, I was ready to start a new life with him. And then Jakob came along."

I remembered the boy with the sailboat in the park. "What a wonderful place for your son to grow up. There is so much to do and see in the country."

She looked at me and a small smile played at the

corner of her mouth. "*Fräulein* Rutherford, I do not know you well, nor shall I. But I thank you for your kindness in spending time with me this evening."

I could not look away, though I wanted to. I felt ashamed of Wolfgang, and angry too.

"All women, once married, become aware of their husband's full personality. Once the shine of passion dulls, the conversation lags and the attraction dims, it is difficult to ignore. Please do not waste your time being concerned about me, *Fräulein* Rutherford. I am both wiser, and stronger than you realise."

Before I could formulate a response, Katja got to her feet and walked over to her husband, who instantly turned his attention from the Italian to his wife while Valentina walked away.

I rose from my seat and looked towards the balcony. Susanna must still be outside, and Saul was gone. Perhaps he had joined his sister. Should I venture out there?

"You look troubled, Ingrid." It was Max, coming to stand at my side.

"And you spend too much time being concerned about my thoughts, Max," I said unkindly. "I am quite well, thank you. A little tired and out of sorts due to my circumstances, but nothing I cannot manage." I would not look him in the eye, for it took all my strength to keep a distance between us. I yearned to talk to him, tell him all my concerns—especially about his brother. Yet we could not be friends—not anymore. My doing so would make me no different than Wolfgang.

"For a woman with your compassion, Ingrid, sometimes you are extraordinarily harsh. You judge me without being aware of the facts, and group me in the same classification as my brother." He glared at me.

I could not help but look at his face. The strong lines of his cheekbones, the deep depths of his dark eyes.

He continued. "I am not Wolfgang. But I am human. And human beings make mistakes. Young men and women who have not learned the first thing about life and love can join together in haste, only to repent later. Does that make them bad? Evil?"

"No," I said sharply. "Not by embarking upon something they were not ready for." I steeled myself and stared harshly at him. "It is their actions afterwards which count. Their treatment of one another, their loyalty and honesty."

"Your verbal talons are sharp," he said, raising a glass of what looked like brandy to his lips. "Would that I was a free man. One who elicited admiration and interest from you, not your apparent abhorrence." He set the empty glass down on a nearby table. Then his expression changed, and I almost caught my breath, for he looked fierce.

"You are quick to reprimand, Ingrid," he said quietly, for my ears only. "Yet you knew my situation from the beginning. And though I instigated our kiss, you did not resist, not for one second." His eyes were black with emotion, and he tore his gaze from me and strode away.

IT WAS STRANGE SLEEPING at the palace. I did not have the nightmare, but still woke early in the morning before the sun had risen. Joan slept soundly, and I wondered if her presence had eased my own rest. I lay under the covers, my mind drifting over the previous evening and what had happened between Susanna and Wolfgang. I replayed my conversation with Max, and though I tried not to care about his opinion, his words had bruised my feelings.

I closed my eyes, and for a moment allowed myself the luxury of revisiting our kiss, the only action where we had crossed the line of friendship. I grew sleepy.

Suddenly, a shrill scream ripped through the palace, loud enough to penetrate the walls of my room.

Joan sat bolt upright in bed. "Good lord! What's amiss?"

I did not answer but leapt out of my bed and grabbed my dressing gown, tugging it on as I ran to the door and pulled it open. The screams grew louder as I raced down the corridor, and when I reached the top of the marble staircase, I saw others had beaten me there. Katja, who had covered Jakob's small face with her hand, and a woman in a nurse's uniform stared down the winding stairs to the first landing, where a young maid stood rigid, clutching her duster against her breast with one hand, while the other pointed below in horror.

I pushed past the two women and ran down the stairs until I was level with the maid. I looked to where she pointed and covered my own mouth to staunch the scream rising from my throat. For there at the bottom of the stairs, her head at an unnatural angle and one leg bent underneath her body, lay Valentina von Brandt.

Chapter Fifteen

THE PALACE WAS IN complete uproar. Max and Wolfgang had flown down the stairs to attend to the poor woman, but it was to no avail. A footman was dispatched to telephone Doctor Engel, and the servants were told to remain below stairs and bring refreshments to the family drawing room. There we congregated and waited for Max and the doctor to come and talk to us.

I cradled a small glass of brandy between my trembling hands, trying in vain to push away the image I had seen of the beautiful woman laying broken on the cold marble floor—her body encased in a white silk nightgown, her jet-black hair fanned out, while a small trickle of crimson blood ran from her mouth down her chin. It was a macabre picture, and one I would never forget.

Katja sat as stunned as I was. Wolfgang had left the room and we knew nothing of his destination. I had seen the wild look in his eyes, bright with unshed tears. He was a man who looked broken, devastated, while Max had remained calm the entire time. The baroness was being confined to her apartments, and Jakob was with his tutor in the schoolroom.

It seemed an age until the door opened and the doctor entered with Max at his side. I got to my feet and went to pour them both a cup of coffee from the tureen brought in by the footmen earlier.

I sat down next to Katja and reached for her hand. It was ice cold.

The doctor took a seat, while Max stood in front of the fireplace where he could see us all. He took a sip of his hot drink and then set the cup and saucer on the mantelpiece.

"Doctor Engel has examined Valentina and I would like him to tell you his findings."

I paid close attention to his voice. He sounded so formal, there was little emotion there.

The door suddenly opened, and Wolfgang strode in. His hair was tousled and there was the stain of the outdoors flushing his cheeks. By the state of him, he must have been riding, and I imagined his horse was probably put through it judging by his demeanour.

"Wolfgang," said Max. "Please take a seat so that the doctor can speak with us all."

His younger brother threw Max an angry glare and went to stand by the window.

"First," the doctor said in German. "Let me start by telling you how sorry I am for the tragic loss of someone as young and talented as *Signora* Cavaletti. I know you are devastated, and certainly in shock. So please, forgive me if I sound clinical in my delivery, but I want to tell you the facts." He took a sip of coffee and then set it down on the table before him. He retrieved a small notebook from his breast pocket.

"From my first observation, *Signora* Valentina appears to have taken a steep fall down the stairs, resulting in a broken neck, broken leg and various other injuries. The cause of death is from a broken neck. As to the reason she fell, that is not for me to speculate. I did notice however, that she was wearing long night attire, and it would not be surprising if her slipper had caught in the fabric resulting in her losing her balance. The stairs are marble, therefore the impact of the stone against her would certainly cause serious harm."

"Are you saying it was an accident?" Wolfgang asked, his voice strangely unsteady.

"At this juncture, yes. It is for the authorities to determine another outcome."

"As in?" asked Max.

"That she was pushed," answered Wolfgang. "It's the logical answer to me. After all, the woman lived here. She traversed the same stairs frequently. It makes no sense that on this one occasion she would trip."

Though I could not comment as they thought me ignorant of their language, I found myself silently agreeing with Wolfgang. Accidents did happen, of that there was no doubt. Yet it seemed a hard verdict to accept in this particular case. Especially in light of one murder already occurring and my receipt of a threatening note.

The doctor got to his feet. He turned to look at me and recounted the gist of his conversation in English for my benefit. Then he picked up his bag and addressed the group in German. "That is all I can tell you for now. The *polizei* from *Prinzenstadt* are here and the funeral home has already collected the *Signora*. Again, please accept my condolences, and let me know if there is anything I can do to help." He gave a curt nod, told Max he could find his way out and left us alone.

A few moments passed. Max poured everyone a small drink from a cabinet in the corner of the room. He brought around four brandy glasses on a tray, and we each took one.

Katja took a sip and then promptly burst into tears. I looked at Wolfgang, expecting him to come to his wife's aid, but he stared out of the window sipping his drink. I placed my arm about the woman's shoulders.

"It is a terrible shock," I soothed. "But she is at peace. You must be strong, Katja. For Jakob's sake."

"Strong?" Wolfgang said derisively setting his empty glass down on a nearby table. "That has never been one of her traits." He threw a dismissive glance at his wife, then walked out of the door.

Katja, seemingly used to his tone did not display a change in demeanour. But I looked up sharply at Max, my brows drawn together.

"He should not speak to her like that, Max. You should take him in hand. Everyone is shocked and there is no excuse for him to be cruel."

"It is all right," Katja answered. "Wolfgang is hot-headed. He and Valentina have been great friends for many years. He is overwrought. He will apologise to me later." She slowly got to her feet. "For now, I must talk to my son and explain what has happened. Then I think I shall rest for a while." Katja left the room and I found myself alone with Max. What should I say, what *could* I say?

"I am so very sorry about Valentina, Max. If there is anything I can—"

"Please," he interrupted. "I can assure you I am perfectly fine. You are well aware there was no love lost between us. I am deeply saddened and disturbed by her death, but I am not overcome and despondent, and I would rather not pretend otherwise."

The coolness of his tone took me aback. Was he so callous and unfeeling then? I did not care for his lack of emotion. Did he feel so little for the woman that seeing her lying at the foot of the stairs like a broken doll had not moved him? Suddenly I felt I did not know this man, and I wanted to leave as quickly as possible. I got to my feet.

"If you will excuse me," I said, and made towards the door. I left the room without him saying a word. I hastened up the very steps Valentina had fallen down, practically running to my room. I burst open the door and Joan started in surprise, dropping her sewing.

"Please get our things together, Joan. We are leaving here at once. I cannot spend another moment in the company of these people."

Joan's little eyes studied me for a moment. Then she gave a small grin. "Thank gawd for that, miss. I'd rather take my chances at the lodge any day. This place is like sleepin' in a bloody mausoleum."

JOAN PACKED OUR BELONGINGS and left them in our room. I wrote a quick note to Katja, thanking the family for their hospitality. Then Joan and I walked back to the lodge feeling safe enough as there were the two of us. I doubted anyone would get the better of Joan McCullum. Once we arrived, she would ask Herr Metzger to collect our things in the carriage.

When Fritz opened the door to the lodge I did not expect to feel I was home—yet I did. As I walked down the hallway to the drawing room, I absorbed the welcome sensation. The warmth of the building seemed to wrap itself about me, a far cry from the cool, palatial *Safranpalast*. Within ten minutes, I was in my favourite armchair, with a cup of tea and a piece of toast, eating a late breakfast.

I spoke with Fritz briefly. The servants had already heard about *Signora* Cavaletti, and I told him all that I knew. He expressed his commiserations and returned downstairs. I drank my tea, imagining the public outcry of despair which would follow the announcement of her death. For Valentina was the darling of her audience. With her beautiful voice and her fabulous stage presence, she was larger than life. How anyone so famous, so talented could be wiped out in a stupid fall was tragic.

A fall. I considered this momentarily. How long had I been at Lorelei Lodge? A day or two shy of one month. Yet in the space of that time a woman had been murdered, I had been threatened, and now this. Was I being fanciful, or was it strange that three unusual and frightening events had occurred? I sighed. I must not allow my imagination to run away with itself. The doctor had explained how easily Valentina could have fallen. Yet Wolfgang was right. Why now, after her years of living there?

My train of thought disappeared at the sound of carriage wheels outside the window. I knew who my guest would be, and I was correct.

"Dear God," Susanna exclaimed, marching into the room, while simultaneously removing her gloves. "Can it really be true? Were you there? I went to the palace, but they would not admit me. The footman told me you had returned home. Oh my, Ingrid. The world is going mad!" She sank onto the sofa, her eyes wide with disbelief.

I looked at her pretty face. She was genuinely upset. Then I remembered the previous evening when Valentina and I had seen her in Wolfgang's passionate embrace. Susanna watched me intently, and her expression shifted as if she read my thoughts.

"Ingrid, please don't say anything to me about last night. I made a complete fool of myself, and I don't need reminding."

"All right. It is history now."

"You were at the palace when it happened, were you not? It must have been a frightful shock."

"I shan't forget it," I said with a shudder. "Such a horrible accident. Someone full of life, so talented, and then in a wicked instance, she is gone."

"I can't imagine. The family must be devastated."

I nodded and then got to my feet. "Come. Let us take a walk to the garden. I could use the fresh air. Talking about death is depressing."

"Are you sure we should be out walking?"

"Yes," I assured her. "We will be safe enough together this close to the lodge."

Susanna obliged, and we went out into the sunshine and turned down the path. She absent-mindedly linked her arm through mine as we strolled leisurely. The desire to walk slowly, absorb nature's beauty around us and be thankful we were still young and healthy, was forefront in my mind. We still had our lives ahead of us, unlike poor Valentina. Guilt assailed me as I mulled over my ill-thoughts of the woman.

"Max must be a wreck," Susanna said. "First a son, and now a wife. How sad to lose them both."

I said nothing but considered Max's unemotional behaviour. It still bothered me, more than I cared to admit.

"Saul thinks we may have to stay on another week. He says there will be an inquest, and Max will be too preoccupied with his private affairs to conclude their business. I told him I didn't mind."

I looked at her quickly.

"No," she said reassuringly. "I am not planning to see Wolfgang again. I said I didn't mind because I know I am going soon. Perhaps I can spend a little time with you instead? Oh, is this the garden?"

We approached the wall, and I led Susanna down to the open wooden door. The regular gardeners were working, and each glanced up and tipped their caps as they saw us.

"My," Susanna said. "This looks lovely!"

It really was quite something. The flowerbeds were finally complete, and the clever designs of the flower and petal shaped beds were striking.

The men had planted masses of Cornflowers. Their violet Prussian blue hues so beautiful, the ground was awash with colour. Mother would have loved it. The courtyard was finished and looked so inviting, while the fountain set in its centre awaiting completion.

"The fountain itself is still being designed. We have yet to do all the plumbing required, but hopefully we shall start that in a day or so." I pointed over to the corner where a small patch of grass lay beneath the Willow tree. "Over there, where the bench stands, was a favourite spot of my mother's, and I too have some memory of it, though I was very young. But it is a wonderful place to sit and relax, and I come here often."

"I can see why. There is a calm atmosphere within these walls. It is very inviting. What are those flowers there by the tree?"

I looked again at the Willow as we walked in that

direction, and there at the base of the trunk lay a fresh posy of Cornflowers. Once we reached them, I picked them up to look at them closer. They looked much the same as before. A small bunch of freshly cut flowers, bound together with string.

"Someone keeps leaving them here," I said to Susanna. "And we don't know why." She had walked on and taken a seat upon the little iron bench.

I placed the flowers back where I found them and joined her.

"Don't you think it's rather strange?" she said. "That someone mysteriously sneaks in here to do that. Doesn't it bother you?"

I considered the question. "I suppose it is odd, but no, it doesn't really bother me. It isn't hurting anything."

Her blue eyes settled upon my face. "Honestly, Ingrid. Sometimes, I think you are as unexcitable as these German people. You casually mention something which even you agree is bizarre, while at the same time there's been a murder on your property, and let's not forget the letter you recently received which was terrifying." Her brow furrowed. "Do you honestly not want to figure it out? What if the flowers are connected?"

I frowned at her. "What do you mean? Why should they be?" Something ran cold in my blood.

"You are silly," she chuckled, though her subject was chilling. "It's pretty obvious to me what the flowers are for."

"What?"

"For someone who has died. It's no different than leaving them on a grave. They are being put here in remembrance, and I doubt very much it is for a bird or a squirrel. Why else would you leave flowers at the base of a tree?"

At her words, a veil lifted inside my mind. I was amazed I had not reached the same conclusion. Of course. Susanna was right! The flowers were indeed an actual tribute to the memory of a person. But who?

Chapter Sixteen

THAT NIGHT, I ASKED Joan to sleep in my room. In truth, I believe we were both still scared, especially after the death of Valentina. Dieter set up a trundle bed and reassured me the building was safe and secure. At my request, he had enlisted two more staff—burly young men from the village, who were to watch the outside perimeter of the lodge during the night. This eased my mind considerably. But my sleep was still restless, for though I did not have the nightmare, I tossed and turned—the image of Valentina lying at the foot of the stairs never far from my mind.

I ate an early breakfast and looked out of the windows noting it had rained during the night. According to Dieter, the workers hoped for rain. If they were to begin the installation of plumbing for the fountain, the ground would be softer and more malleable to work with.

After my meal I went into the study in search of an occupation. My mind needed something to engage with to prevent my dwelling upon the previous morning's awful events.

I sat at the desk, and as usual, my eyes fell upon the photograph of my mother as a young woman. It really was like looking in a mirror, apart from our eye colour. Hers were as dark as her hair. I touched her face and wished so much that she were still here.

Marta Rutherford had been a good woman and given so much of herself. It was cruel that those who had much to share were taken so young. This brought me back to Valentina, and I pushed the thoughts away.

I picked up the ledgers I had studied earlier, showing Lorelei's income from its farming tenants, and the expenditures to maintain the staff and run the place. There was not a great difference between the two, yet it was sufficient. Aunt Gisela had been well taken care of with Father's and Mother's stipends.

The extra income which had materialised two years prior to Gisela's death still niggled at me. I did not care for puzzles, nor did I like to be outwitted. Surely there was something here which could help reveal where it had come from?

This time, instead of looking at the books, I started to dig through all the drawers. I pulled every scrap of paper I could find, laying them in a pile before me. I also went to the locked cabinet and garnered anything I had overlooked. Then I rang for Fritz and asked him to bring me tea. I planned to immerse myself for the duration of the morning.

Most of the papers were notes, lists of reminders, calling cards and things of that nature. There were recipes, invitations and such. I discarded them all and placed them into the rubbish bin.

Fritz came and went, refreshing my pot of tea twice, and bringing me a small pastry. I had just finished eating it when something caught my eye.

It was a receipt from a shop named Meyer's. I scanned the piece of paper. It was for a significant amount of clothing. The date was May of eighteen-ninety-three, two years ago. Where was this shop?

Perhaps *Prinzenstadt*? I had never heard of it, but then I wouldn't have unless I'd accidentally seen it in passing.

I scribbled down a note. I would ask Fritz and Dieter. I continued my search but yielded nothing of interest. As I finished up, I heard the front door being opened and the low rumble of male voices. I hoped it was not Max. I was in no state of mind to see the man.

Fritz knocked on the study door.

"*Fräulein* Rutherford. There is an *Inspektor* Schinkel here to speak with you. I have put him in the drawing room."

A little shiver of dread trickled through my veins. A policeman? Max had contacted the authorities about the note, but I wondered what they wanted with me? Well, there was only one way to find out, and that was to go and meet him.

As I entered the room I saw a giant of a man staring out of the window. I would guess him to be in his mid-years. He wore a tweed suit which stretched across broad shoulders. When he saw me, he swept off his Fedora, revealing a thick crop of clipped grey hair.

"*Entschuldigen, fräulein*," he apologised, smiling beneath a trimmed grey moustache. "I am sorry to arrive without forewarning, but I needed to speak with you as soon as possible." His English was excellent, and again I was impressed how many people spoke a second language. The English should strive to be as competent, I thought to myself.

"Please," I gestured to the sofa. "Have a seat, *Inspektor* Schinkel. Your command of my language is impressive. Since my coming here, I have been astounded how many people speak English."

"Many of us learn in school, *Fräulein*. But I also

spent some time in your country working with Scotland Yard."

He took a seat, as did I. We faced one another.

"Tell me, what may I help you with?"

"I have in my possession a note given to me by Baron Maximillian von Brandt. It was sent to you last Friday if I am correct?"

"Yes. It was left sometime in the early hours of the morning."

"How do you know this?"

"I was in the kitchen getting a glass of water. I saw a light moving away from the lodge towards the palace. The note was hand-delivered."

"I see." His bushy grew brows drew together. "*Fräulein*, I understand you are new to the area, that you have come to claim an inheritance."

"I have."

"Do you know of any reason someone would want to harm you, perhaps stop you from inheriting?"

"No," I answered honestly. "Both my mother and father had no remaining family. There is no one to contest my claim. Other than when I was a young child, I never visited here, therefore I do not even know many people."

"Why then, do you think you were targeted by this person? Do you have any ideas yourself?"

I pondered the question, just as I had several times already since getting the blasted note.

"I have absolutely no clue. Nothing has changed since I arrived. The staff are the same as before. I have not had a falling out with anyone. If it is linked to what happened to the nurse from the palace, then I am oblivious of it. I had never laid eyes upon her until recently, and even then we barely spoke but a few words in passing. In truth, *Inspektor,* had my name not been on the note, I would have guessed it was intended for another."

"Hmm. It is very odd, very odd indeed." He chewed his lower lip contemplating his next question. "I understand you were at the palace when Signora Cavaletti had her accident?"

I nodded.

"A very disturbing thing to see, and a great loss to the world of opera," he said solemnly.

"Yes. I cannot begin to imagine how everyone at the palace is coping. Two deaths so close together seems—"

"Unusual," he chimed in. "Yes, it is. What concerns me is the addition of this nasty note as well. This is a peaceful community, yet there is something malevolent at work. Can you tell me, have there been any other strange occurrences lately?" His pale eyes stared at me, and I thought he would be an intimidating foe should he be crossed.

I gave it some thought. "Flowers," I said. "We have a small walled garden here which my gardeners have been renovating. Someone has started placing a posy of flowers at the base of the only tree there."

"When did this begin?"

"Perhaps a week or so ago. The second posy was left yesterday."

"If you were to hazard a guess why, what would you think?" he asked.

"Initially I thought little of it, only that it was strange. The gardeners called it a tribute. But then a friend pointed out that it was like leaving flowers on a grave." I shuddered.

"May I take a look at this garden?" he asked.

"Of course. I shall ring for my footman and have him escort you there."

The giant got up. He gave me a nod. "I thank you for your time today. I shall be staying at the palace for a few days. I expect I shall call upon you again."

"Certainly. Good day, *Inspektor*."

I stood at the window and watched as he and Dieter passed by on their way to the garden. In truth, I was relieved an official was finally here to conduct an enquiry. It had been a full ten days since Helga, or Klara had been killed. As I stared out of the window at the row of thick green pine trees I wondered about Klara Krause. What was she doing working up at the palace? Why had no one recognised her?

A flash of movement caught my attention, and I could not help but smile. For though my thoughts were sombre, it was a welcome break to see the lithe bodies of Frido and Sascha, who bounded in and out of the forest border like they were sewing thread. I could hear their distant barking as they chased one another. And then suddenly I saw their master.

Max emerged from the dense copse, dressed in walking attire. He was quite a distance from where I stood looking out the window. But as I watched he paused and seemed to look right at me, though I doubted he could see me behind the glass. He did not move but stared in my direction for what seemed a while. Then he turned and the forest swallowed him up.

I went back and sat down. Seeing Max brought everything to the front of my mind again. Each event with him was a like a picture in a book, and I was fanning through the pages in a rush of memory.

I remembered our first encounter in the forest out there, and my fear of his animals. How his strengths which I found so attractive were only enhanced by the streak of sadness he carried with him, adding to the element of mystery. I admired his strong character, his ability to lead. But there was something he kept from us all. His heart-breaking loss. Losing a child would cause such pain that he would have buried it deep inside so as not to crumble. Was that it? What about Valentina? His relationship with her had seemed unusual, complex and mystifying.

The words he spoke at the Koppelmans' party came back to me in a rush.

"For a woman with your compassion, sometimes you are extraordinarily harsh, Ingrid."

"I am human. And human beings make mistakes. Young men and women who have not learned the first thing about life and love can join in haste and repent later. Does that make them bad? Evil?"

"Would that I was a free man. One who elicited admiration and interest from you, not your apparent abhorrence."

The concoction of emotion Max elicited from me was a tangle I found hard to separate. Yet as I mulled over his words, the outcome of each thought was that the morning after he'd shared his feelings with me, his wife, the one person who kept him from freedom, was found dead at the bottom of the palace stairs. Finally, I allowed the seed of ugliness to sprout within my heart. For I had been too frightened to admit it until this moment. Had Max pushed his wife down the stairs?

JOAN AND I WENT into the village after luncheon. We were both feeling claustrophobic trapped inside the lodge, and the atmosphere was still morose. It was a cloudy afternoon, much like our spirits, but it was a welcome relief being out. I teased her about the friendly way *Herr* Metzger spoke to her as we got into the carriage, and his valiant effort using English when addressing her. Her response was most unlike the Joan I knew—she blushed furiously.

"My goodness, Joan. Do I detect an attraction to our driver?"

"Don't be silly," she snapped, guilt written all over her face. "What would I want with the likes of a man like that? An' a German to boot."

So, Joan had feelings for him! It certainly explained the changes I had noticed in the man over the past few weeks. When we first came to the lodge, *Herr* Metzger had been foul smelling and dishevelled. Now his moustaches were trimmed, his hair and clothing clean, and if I wasn't mistaken, when I passed by him I caught the distinct and not so pleasant fragrance of cloves.

Joan and I perused the handful of shops in the village. We did not go into the hotel, though I felt a twinge of guilt. But I was in no frame of mind for Susanna. After a while we returned home with a few small purchases, and a mouthful of delicious toffee we had bought for a special treat. This made it difficult to talk, and we giggled several times while trying to form words with our teeth stuck together.

"Ooh, that did me the world of good," Joan said as the carriage drew down the driveway. We came to a halt, and I kept a keen eye out to observe *Herr*

Metzger's behaviour as he managed to beat Dieter and swing open the cab door in time to assist us down the steps. I went first, and then stood and watched as he offered a hand to my maid. Oh my, how had I not noticed before? The older man's face was suffused in adoration as Joan took his arm. Her normally pale London skin flushed to an attractive shade of pink, and I could tell she was torn between looking at the man or seeing if I was staring. I quickly turned away and headed inside so they could have their moment.

I settled into the study and put away my new bottle of ink and some stamps into the top drawer of my desk. I planned to write a letter to Herr Vogel and ask him to pay me a call. I had heard little from him since my visit three days ago. I remembered our disagreement, and my final words to him about my being in danger.

Goodness! I was such a fool! I had stated it was imperative to discover the true identity of Helga, or Klara, as I preferred to call the nurse. Yet I had overlooked the most obvious reason I'd been sent that note. How had I missed it? That letter was not sent to me in error, far from it. Someone had discovered I had learned Helga's real identity and that knowledge was apparently dangerous.

The realisation hit me so boldly, I could not sit any longer. I got to my feet and began pacing the room. Of course! It all made better sense. Helga was murdered because she knew something that had to be kept secret. But Lisbeth had told me the nurse was not who she claimed to be, that she was really Klara Krause. Somebody found out I knew the truth.

I had to sit once again for my legs suddenly felt too weak to hold me. Though the letter had unnerved me from the beginning, part of me still thought it sent in error because I was a stranger here. But now?

Everything had instantly changed. For I finally understood that there was something sinister going on in this sleepy little German village. And for the first time in my life, I was truly afraid.

Someone wanted me dead.

Chapter Seventeen

MONDAY MORNING, I RECEIVED a letter from *Herr* Vogel. In the missive, he said he'd confirmed the identity of the von Brandts' nurse was indeed Klara Krause. This information had been obtained by the lawyer contacting the authorities and advising them there could be identity fraud at hand. The nurse's belongings had been confiscated, and paperwork, including a marriage license, had been discovered.

I read the letter and realised *Inspektor* Schinkel must have known about this when he spoke with me the previous day. Why had he not mentioned it? I suppose it was not my business. But it confirmed everything I had suspected, and proved Lisbeth was not imagining anything. That said, it would be prudent for me to pay her another visit. Perhaps I would discover more information to help me unravel the conundrum I felt immersed within.

LISBETH WAS HAPPY TO see me, and I felt the same, especially when I saw she still looked more alert.

"Marta's girl," she informed *Krankenschwester* Magda in German. "You must bring us a cup of tea. That is what they like to drink you know, in England. Go on, off you go."

The nurse gave me a smile and went out of the door. Lisbeth now spoke in English.

"I am so happy to see you. Did you know about Valentina? Broke her neck." She put her fisted hands together and twisted her wrists in the same motion you would use to kill a chicken. I flinched. It seemed rather macabre.

"I did know," I replied. "And it is very sad."

"Sad? I suppose it is sad when anything dies. But I don't miss her. She never came to see me, only in the beginning because she wanted my Max. And she got him too!" Lisbeth sat in her usual armchair, but she was becoming quite animated with a topic she obviously felt strongly about.

"Poor Nikolai," her dark eyes suddenly filled with tears as she gazed at me. "He was a good boy, just like his father. But he took the horse out on his own. Max was too late to save him…" she stopped. I badly wanted her to continue, for I hungered for the story, to understand what had happened to Max's son. But I could not say a word. It was not my place, nor should I upset the sweet older lady, my mother's dearest friend.

"Do you remember the walled garden?" I asked. Though we had spoken of it before, I was unsure how much the baroness's memory retained from day to day.

She gave a broad smile. "Yes! I loved to go with you and Marta and my smallest boys. We would have a picnic there."

She turned her head as the door opened. Wolfgang came into the room, and just as before, I felt Lisbeth stiffen.

"*Guten tag*, *Fräulein* Rutherford," he said blandly. "Am I interrupting?" He came over to where his mother sat and perfunctorily kissed her on the top of her head. She flinched.

"Not at all," I answered, forcing a weak smile. Wolfgang looked terrible. His face was drawn, his skin sallow and he was unkempt. "I was just talking to your mother about the walled garden. She remembers it well."

"I am sure she does," he said.

The door opened once again. This time it was Magda carrying a tray with tea things. She greeted Wolfgang politely and then placed the tray on a table next to me. I smiled at the woman. Magda was plump with a round, jolly face and a good deal friendlier than Klara. I told her I would pour the tea.

"*Ich habe nur zwei Tassen mitgebracht,*" she said, casting a worried glance at Wolfgang. I understood her but said nothing. She was concerned she had only brought two cups and now Wolfgang was here.

He waved his hand dismissively. "*Ich trinke diesen Mist nicht. Lass sie nicht allein und lass mich Wissen, wovon sie sprechen.*"

I tried to keep my expression neutral. For he had just instructed the nurse not to leave me alone with his mother, and to report our conversation to him. Why was Wolfgang so concerned? Could he have written the note to me? Dear God, had he killed Klara?

Still standing, he turned his charming smile in my direction, but it left me cold. What was it about this handsome man which had consistently given me concern?

"It is good of you to visit my mutti."

"I enjoy speaking with the baroness. She has such fond memories of my mother, and I enjoy hearing about their times together all those years ago."

"Then I shall leave you to it," he said. "I have

promised to watch Jakob take a turn on his pony. So, if you will excuse me?"

"Of course," I replied, and watched him head to the door with a last look at the nurse, who sat in a chair next to the bed sewing.

Once he was gone, I addressed Lisbeth who still stared away from me.

"The tea is very good," I said. "Have you tried it?"

She snapped out of her trance. I saw the light leap back in her eyes and she collected her cup and lifted it to her lips. She took a sip and replaced it in the saucer then looked at me. "That one's always been difficult," she said in English, gesturing with a nod of her head towards the door. "Like my brother, he is. Too much time admiring himself and chasing skirts. He's been trouble from the start, not like his brothers. Now they were good boys." She flashed a glance over to her nurse. "She only understands a little of what we say, you know. Wolfgang assumes she speaks English. She can't tell him what we talk about."

I almost chuckled, for the baroness was right. Our conversation was still private. How canny of her to figure that out.

"And she doesn't make me take so much medicine. Though she tells *him* she has." A grin played at the corners of her mouth.

"That is a good thing," I replied with relief. "She seems a nice nurse, and a great deal friendlier than your last." I hesitated bringing Klara up after her awful demise, but I didn't think it would bother Lisbeth terribly. And judging by her face I was right.

"You remember what she was like, Marta." Lisbeth had forgotten who I was again and slipped back into thinking I was my mother.

"Yes," I played along.

"Gisela liked her, though I don't know why. Tight-lipped that nurse. But no nurse really, we knew that didn't we?"

I nodded, hesitant to stop the flow of information.

"I recognised it was her when he brought her in. Told him to take her away. But he wouldn't have it—arrogant child. He paid her you know."

I assumed she spoke of Wolfgang, for he had been the one to hire Klara. "Of course, he paid her, Lisbeth. She worked here."

She waved a bony hand. "Not wages. He paid to keep her quiet. I heard them talking about it. She was angry." Her dark eyes fastened upon mine. "But he doesn't pay me. No one does, and I say whatever I please."

And something else clicked into place, thanks to Lisbeth. The connection between Klara and Wolfgang confirmed, and the reason the woman was not intimidated by the man. I decided to press her, but gently.

"Do you know if she kept a secret?" I asked as nonchalantly as I could and took a sip of tea.

Lisbeth gave a grin. "Marta, you know she did." I watched her eyes cloud a little. "I want to see the garden." She sounded suddenly petulant. "Will you take me to see the Willow tree, like we used to? Can we have a picnic?"

The conversation was over. Lisbeth had retreated back into her safe place, and I would not force her out. She had helped me so much already. So, I spoke of the walled garden, and the Cornflowers planted everywhere, and this brought a sweet smile to the old woman's face. I was explaining about the fountain when the door opened yet again, this time to admit Max.

He came into the room and stopped when he saw me there. I automatically got to my feet, the urge to leave pounding in my temples. He glanced at the nurse to dismiss her, and as she left the room he walked over to join us, going to his mother to bend down and kiss her on the cheek first.

He looked directly at me. "Good day to you, Ingrid. I hope you do not leave on my account?"

I wet my lips which had suddenly become dry. "No. I have been here for some time and had tea with the baroness. She is likely tired."

He glanced at his mother who gave him a wide smile. "Mutti looks very happy. I believe these visits from you do her the world of good. Thank you for taking the time to see her."

"Marta is my best friend, Maximillian," his mother remonstrated. "Don't thank her for coming to see me. She's a sister to me. Just try and stop her from coming here," she warned. "Her husband did, but she took no notice."

"My father?" I asked. "He forbade your friendship?"

"Big bully, that Rutherford. Handsome, I'll give you that. With eyes as blue as a cold winter sky." She looked at my face and pointed. "Like yours, Marta." She stopped. "Wait. Marta, your eyes are different? Why are they like his?" She frowned. "Where is she? I can't remember." She became tearful and Max went to console her. I got up to fetch Magda back in the room, and within a few minutes she had comforted the baroness and led her to lay down and rest on her bed.

Max followed me out of the room. I wanted to run from him. My feelings were tied in an intricate knot. One thread full of admiration and desire, the other mistrust, suspicion and uncertainty. Now, when I looked at him, I envisaged his hands pushing against Valentina's back and him watching her tumble down the stairs.

"Ingrid, please wait a moment." I began walking faster. He reached for my arm to stop me. "I need to speak to you—it won't take but a minute."

I stopped and turned to look at him. He was but two steps from me. I saw the shadows underneath his dark eyes. Though he was well groomed as usual, there was no spark to him, no energy. He looked defeated—a sailboat with no wind. At this moment in time his was not the face of an evil murderer, but a person consumed with bereavement.

"What do you want to talk to me about?"

"I wanted to make sure you are well. I wish you would have stayed here for your safety. I worry about your being there at the lodge."

"My safety? Your wife fell to her death the night I stayed here. I feel more secure where I am. Though I thank you for your concern."

His face darkened. I had been too blunt.

"Max, I am sorry, that sounded tactless."

"Valentina fell, Ingrid. She had a terrible accident."

I stared at him. "Are you certain that is what happened?"

He looked aghast. "What are you implying? That it was intentional? You think someone had a hand in her death?"

I could not hide my feelings and I knew he read my face as though it were a page in a book.

Realisation dawned and he took a step back. "*Mein Gott*," he said with a shudder. "You think I had something to do with it?" He was incredulous. "You think I killed my wife?"

I said nothing. My emotions battled for me to apologise and tell him I would never believe him to be so wicked. Yet there was that other part of me who knew there were secrets kept here—things I was not yet able to understand. My silence was an answer. He looked at me and I saw pain in his eyes, enough that I felt a pang of guilt. Then he straightened, his expression taut, his chin tilted up.

"I thought better of you, Ingrid," he said flatly, and then brushed past me leaving me standing in the corridor alone and bewildered.

UPON MY RETURN HOME, the first thing I did was take a measure of brandy. I could not settle my mood. The elation of discovering more information from Lisbeth had been supplanted by a mass of contradictions in what I thought Max capable of. My head was a jumble.

But was Max a murderer? What about Wolfgang? The peacock of the family, why was he paying Klara for her silence? What was the damnable secret that was slipping through my fingers? Why was my aunt getting paid by a mysterious benefactor? Was it for the same reason Klara was paid?

I flopped down on the sofa, pulled my legs up and stretched them out before me. If Fritz came in and saw me lying like a limp rag doll, I cared not. I was tired.

Tired and fed up.

Coming to Germany to see my mother's home seemed like such a wonderful adventure after my gloomy, morose year. But now? Part of me wanted to pack up and go home, leave these strange people to their odd lives and lies. Yet how could I? A woman had been brutally killed, I had been threatened, and there were still so many questions I had about the past.

Who owned the pendant I found? Who wanted me gone because I knew about Klara's pretense? Why did it all matter? I closed my eyes.

I HEARD JOAN CALLING before she came into the room and my eyes opened, disorientated. I was in the drawing room and must have fallen asleep. I swung my legs off the sofa, and sat up, rubbing the sleep from my eyes as the door flew open.

"Gawd, there you are!" Joan said with relief. "You'd better come quick, there's such a to do goin' on out there. The gardeners are in a flap. Dieter's tryin' to get them settled…"

"Wait," I said loudly, holding up a hand to quieten her. "Slow down, Joan. What is amiss? Why are you in such a panic?"

I got to my feet and smoothed out my skirts, then I looked at my maid's face. White as a sheet, only Joan's eyes held any colour.

"It's the gardeners, miss. They've been diggin' up the grass to lay the pipes for the plumbin', an' they've only gone an' dug up a body."

Chapter Eighteen

THE SMALL GROUP STOOD a few feet away from the base of the Willow tree. Joan indicated she was not going any nearer, and I went on alone. They heard me approach and turned around in unison.

"*Guten Tag meine Dame. Das ist sehr schockierend,*" said the oldest of the three, a grey-haired man in his sixties with deep wrinkles across his brow. I understood he was telling me I would be shocked, but I came closer still.

They stood next to a trench which had been dug, leading from the fountain's foundation in the direction of the lodge towards the water source. The trench was about one foot in width, but once something had been spotted, the men had carefully dug a larger area and exposed bones wrapped in the remains of a sheet or blanket.

Though I was certainly taken aback, the sight did not have quite the same impact upon me as seeing Valentina lying at the foot of the palace stairs. Yet at the same time, a strange feeling passed through me. I cannot describe it, for it was not fear, nor revulsion. It was recognition, much like the other sensations I had felt since coming here to Lorelei Lodge.

I turned to look over my shoulder. "Joan, please have Herr Metzger go to the *Safranpalast* and ask for an *Inspektor* Schinkel who is staying there. He must come at once."

She took off at a brisk pace and I returned my attention to the remains, while the gardeners moved off to one side, one of them lighting their pipe while they spoke quietly. The men had exposed most of the skeleton, which was quite intact, and very straight, likely due to whatever had been wrapped around it to begin with. My fingers automatically reached for my pendant and began to worry it. My throat became dry, and I was a little lightheaded. Perhaps I should step away and take a seat on the bench.

I sat down, and the dizziness abated. I let go of the pendant and, as I did, recalled when I had found its double. I sat forward, my eyes scouring the ground. Yes, the pendant had been very close to where the remains were laying. Could the necklace have belonged to whoever was buried here?

My mind raced. The flowers! Of course! That is why they had been left here, in memory of the person buried underneath the Willow tree. Someone obviously knew about the body, yet the flowers had only been left since I'd arrived. But then the garden had been untouched for a while, and inaccessible. What a tangle.

Above, the skies grew cloudier. I approached the men and asked Wilhelm to find something to cover the excavated area to protect the poor body lying there. He translated to the other two, and I left to go back to the lodge. It was no use just sitting there. I would wait for the *inspektor* inside.

I POURED MY SECOND brandy of the day and did not care. Goodness, how ordinary my life had been in London. Who would have thought all these events would happen on a dutiful trip to claim my inheritance?

Joan stuck her head around the door. "You all right, miss? Need smellin' salts or anythin'?"

I lifted my glass in her direction. "This is doing just the job, thank you, Joan."

"Good. Well, I'm off into the village in the carriage. *Herr* Metzger says to tell you the *inspektor* will be here within the hour. He's with the Koppelmans apparently, so he'll not be long."

"Thank you, Joan."

After she had gone, I went into the study and sat behind the desk. I drew out a piece of paper and started to map out my thoughts. In the centre, I put Klara's name, for she seemed to be connected to many people and it was her disappearance which started things off.

I would have to speculate. What if something happened which Klara and her husband were privy to? Is that why my aunt Gisela paid them money and they went away? Perhaps. Could that something be the body that had just been discovered? It certainly could. Had Klara been killed because of that knowledge? I thought it very possible.

Another piece of paper. This time, I wrote Wolfgang's name in the middle of the page. He had a connection to Klara. But did he know about the body in the garden? A memory sparked in my head. It was the day Wolfgang had come to call and questioned me about the garden. What is it he had said? He'd cautioned me against installing a fountain and explicitly said the plumbing would be a concern and tear up all the lawn. He must have known about the body, or why would he have tried to put me off?

I could not help the rush of excitement building. I

drew another page. This time I wrote Max's name in the centre. Where could I connect him? To the garden? No, he had encouraged me to pursue my plans. To Klara? Unlikely, and Wolfgang had been the one to hire her anyway. The only connection Max had to anything, was the discovery of the nurse's body. No, that was not entirely true. I distinctly remembered the morning the nurse was found missing, Max had been out riding, for I had been the one to tell him she was gone. Could he have had something to do with her disappearance? I scribbled it down and drew an arrow towards the discovery of her body. I then wrote Valentina's death on the paper and drew another line to Max's name.

What about the note I was sent? Was that connected to Wolfgang because I suspected Helga was Klara, and Klara knew the secret of the garden?

My head spun, both from thinking too hard and the glass of brandy. A loud knock on the door made me start.

"Come in," I said and quickly placed my papers in the drawer. The door swung open and *Inspektor* Schinkel filled the doorframe. The man was the size of a bear.

I got to my feet. "Good day, *Inspektor*. Thank you for coming so quickly.

"*Guten Tag meine Dame.* I was still in the village. Now, what is this I have been told about a body?"

"Let me show you. Please follow me." I led him outside and down the path, explaining what had been found as well as the garden's history, though I did not share any of my thoughts or suspicions. He was complimentary on the design of the garden as we passed through on our way to the Willow tree and its treasure.

Though it had rained a little, the tarpaulin cover had held, and when the gardeners lifted the oil-soaked cloth, the soil beneath was still dry. I watched the *Inspektor* draw close to the trench, squat down and study it carefully. I stood behind him and said nothing. He rose and walked around to squat again, here and there, looking at the remains from many different angles and positions.

"Do you think it has been here for a long time?" I asked.

"Difficult to tell," he said. "*Zersetzung*...that is decomposition varies dependent upon the environment. In this case, the body has been exposed to soil and therefore would decompose much faster than if it were inside a coffin. I shall have the doctor come immediately and look at the body. He will be able to give us a better idea." He called over to Wilhelm and the others, and together they spread the tarpaulin back to protect the site. He spoke to them in German, but I listened. He asked that someone stay and guard the area until he could call the headquarters in *Prinzenstadt* for help. Wilhelm offered immediately. I made a mental note to see how much the young gardener earned, for he was a good, dependable person.

Inspektor Schinkel escorted me back to the lodge, and I insisted he allow *Herr* Metzger to take him to the palace as he had just returned with Joan. Schinkel resisted at first, but I reminded him he would save a great deal of time. He finally accepted, with my driver looking pleased to be involved in something as important as a murder case.

The rest of the afternoon dragged along. I saw the

The Secret of Lorelei Lodge

return of my carriage, and the subsequent arrival of another, presumably Doctor Engel's, but I stayed away so they could work without being bothered. I told Fritz to ask Cook to prepare sandwiches for the gardeners, and then I sent Dieter to deliver them to the men and invite the doctor and *inspektor* to the lodge for refreshment when they were finished.

I was uncertain they would come. But having spent a great deal of time outside overseeing the removal of the body, both men did stop in before taking their leave. I asked Dieter to show them to a washroom where they might clean up, for they had both been kneeling in the dirt. After a short time, Fritz brought the men to the drawing room, where I awaited with a pot of coffee, sandwiches, and some pastries.

"Please." I gestured to the sofa with the laden table in front of it. "Have a seat and help yourselves to the food." They took little encouragement, and I watched as they ate. I struggled to come up with a topic of conversation. After all, what did one say about digging up a body? The thought made me shudder. The day had been so very strange and the reality and horror of what had been uncovered was only now beginning to sink in.

"*Dankeschön, Fräulein* Rutherford." Doctor Engel wiped his mouth with a serviette. "I did not even realise I was hungry." He took a sip of coffee, then looked directly at me. His small brown eyes were bright with intelligence. "You are shocked by the discovery today, I am sure. But if you are willing, I can tell you what I think."

"Yes," I sat forward, my hands pressed together. "I should like to know."

"You must understand this is police business," the

inspektor interrupted, his tone intimidating. "Whatever you are told is not to be shared or spoken of. As this occurred on your property, you have the right to know certain details. But if you discuss the case with another, you could be charged with disclosure of confidential information."

"I understand," I said meekly.

Doctor Engle continued. "The subject is delicate, but I shall speak from a medical point of view. I hope you will not be inclined to faint. If you are uncomfortable, then please tell me and I shall stop."

"Thank you. But I am most interested and also fascinated by science. I am not prone to swooning, Doctor."

He nodded. "The skeleton is of a woman. This I know from the shape of her pelvic bone and also her bone structure and size. I will need time to estimate her age, but my first guess would be she is an adult, but young in age, perhaps in her twenties. Her teeth are still intact, which indicates youth and also a healthy diet. At my examination, without the correct instruments and lighting, I cannot tell you much more."

"Do you have any idea how long she has been there?" At once, I felt strange. Not ill, or lightheaded from his topic of conversation, but as though I was outside of my body, watching myself converse with these gentlemen. I took a sip of coffee. The hot liquid brought me back to normalcy.

"More than one year, but less than five. That will be difficult to come up with, so I shall have a forensic scientist come and look at her. Those fellows can tell so much from bones."

"It is an odd place to bury someone, don't you

think?" I said to the men.

"It is, if the place was being used." The *inspektor* agreed. "But you said the garden had been left to grow wild before you arrived and decided to clear it out. Do you know how long it was left in disarray?"

I considered the question. "No, I do not. I understand from the servants that they were all brought here in the past eighteen months, and none of them local. Consequently, finding out any history here has been challenging. The gardeners might know. Even if they are new, they can estimate how long it took for everything to grow wild the way it did." I pondered for a moment. "You think the garden was ignored because of the body being buried here?"

"Or it was already overgrown and a good place to hide a grave," the burly man replied.

"Well, whatever the outcome," I said to them both. "I should like to purchase a coffin and have the poor thing buried properly."

"That is a generous offer," Doctor Engel said, getting to his feet. Both the policeman and I did likewise.

"I shall take the good *inspektor* here along with me. He is staying with us tonight as we have more work to do."

"Please do not hesitate to call back here if I can help with anything. And of course, we will stop all work in the garden until you tell me we can recommence."

The men were already walking to the door. *Inspektor* Schinkel turned to look at me. "No one is to go into that garden. I have a guard posted there to ensure they don't. Thank you, *Fräulein* Rutherford."

THE LODGE WAS BUZZING with the news. Joan had flown into the drawing room as soon as the doctor's carriage had departed. Though I wanted to tell her what I knew, I kept my promise and remained quiet. I told her I knew very little, but that eventually we would be told their findings.

"Gawd, I won't get any sleep tonight," she moaned, collapsing on the sofa. "I'm right glad I'm in your room, else I'd be terrified to shut my eyes."

"Joan, those bones have lain out there for a long time. We have been here weeks without even knowing."

"Maybe so, miss. But with a skeleton buried on one side of the place, an' a woman killed on t'other, an' if you count the Italian missus tripping down the stairs, it doesn't make for a nice tale now, does it?" She gave a little shudder. "Cor, I'll be glad to be back in London."

"I don't believe you," I said. "Because then you won't get to see Metzger, will you?"

Joan's lips formed a tight line as she searched for a clever response. And then she gave a broad, toothy grin.

I sat across from her. "We've been in Germany a month already, Joan. It hardly seems possible. We've adapted well to all the differences, all things considered."

She chuckled. "Differences? I'll say. All them years I've been at your London house an' never had a murder there, unless you count the mice." Her expression grew serious. "Are you goin' to stay put here do you think, or go back to London?"

I sighed. "Going back seems the natural thing to do, I suppose. *Linnenbrink,* and the lodge, are a far cry from our life in the capital. Yet there is no one back there to return to, nor anyone to miss either." I looked at my maid, her cheeks rosy and so familiar. "You are the only family I have now, Joan, and your being here with me makes all the difference in the world."

Joan's eyes grew teary, and she quickly wiped them with the back of a hand. "The food's bloody awful here," She got up. "Speakin' of food, I'd better go downstairs and see what kind of cabbage is on the menu for dinner." She went to pass me where I sat but stopped. In a rare show of affection, Joan placed a rough hand on my shoulder.

"You mum was a goodun'. She'd be so proud of the woman you've grown into." Her fingers gave me a brief squeeze, then the moment passed. "I promised her I'd keep an eye on you after she was gone." Joan added. "Though what she'd think about all this nonsense, I don't know."

I looked up at her. "She would be right in the middle of it all," I said.

Joan shook her head. "Well this bloomin' apple didn't fall far from the tree then, did it?"

Chapter Nineteen

THE NEXT MORNING PROVED a noisy one as a succession of carts came and went from the lodge. It seemed the *inspektor* was being thorough, and not only examining the walled garden, but also the location in the forest where Klara's body had been found. There were many uniformed policemen, some with dogs, and they appeared to be combing the ground, though I do not know what they searched for.

At length, I grew tired of the distraction, and called for Metzger to bring the carriage around. This time, Joan was busy, so I decided to pay a visit to the village and call on Susanna. I was surprised I hadn't seen her yet, for she was usually the first to arrive when there was anything newsworthy going on.

Metzger dropped me outside the hotel, and I asked him to return for me in two hours. That would be sufficient time to have coffee with my friend. This would be her last week with us, for they were to leave by the end of the week.

The lobby of the hotel was busy. With so few businesses in *Linnenbrink,* I think the place served as a social hub for all and sundry. Their restaurant was popular, and there always seemed to be people in there. This morning was no different.

I asked for Susanna at the front desk, but the portly attendant, a man with a nose which seemed to take up half of his face, poor fellow, told me she had already gone out. I hadn't expected that and did not have an alternative plan. But it was a pleasant morning and I had two hours on my hands, so I decided to walk through the village as I had done so recently with Joan.

I was aware of the attention directed at me. It was hardly surprising with the current situation at Lorelei. I wondered what the locals thought of people like me, those fortunate enough not to struggle for every penny, or in this case pfennig, that they earned.

Linnenbrink Village was not large. It consisted of one main road, culminating with the impressive hotel. There were the usual businesses one would expect in a small community like this, offering the basic necessities, but little else to occupy my time.

But passing the post office, I spotted the blonde hair of Susanna across the street. She had her back to me, but there was no mistaking the cut of her fine clothing. I started to call out, until I realised she was in conversation with someone.

I crossed the road and having done so, saw she was with Wolfgang. My heart grew heavy, and I stopped where I was. Judging by their appearance, the conversation was animated. I was rather surprised to see them together in full view of everyone.

At length, she moved away from him, walking in the opposite direction from me quite briskly. I remained where I was and watched Wolfgang. He pulled a timepiece from his upper pocket, glanced at it and then turned in my direction. I ducked into a small alleyway between the buildings where I stood, and he passed by without realising I was there. I don't know what came over me, but I felt compelled to follow him.

He walked in the direction of the hotel, and it was easy to keep my eye on him initially. But a young lad bumped into me, and I took my eyes off Wolfgang for one moment only to find him gone when I looked up. Where had he disappeared to? There were several shops separating where I stood and the hotel entrance. Perhaps Wolfgang had gone inside one of them. I glanced through each shop window but did not see the man.

It was then I noticed another alleyway separating two of the buildings, not unlike the one I had concealed myself within just moments ago. It seemed the obvious choice. I quickly turned the corner and headed down the alley, though I could not see Wolfgang ahead of me. It was dim here, sunlight being unable to penetrate such a tight space tucked between the buildings. The air was musty, and the ground was littered with old papers and rubbish.

Either side of the alley was bricked, and as I ventured along I began to feel a sense of unease. What on earth was I doing? I had no business wandering down a darkened alley alone. I must be mad. Wherever Wolfgang had gone was not important enough to place myself in danger, especially under the circumstances.

Abruptly I turned around, my blood up, my heart racing. My breathing quickened as I walked faster, suddenly panicked. I had come further down this blasted place than I realised.

Suddenly a blinding pain exploded in the back of my head. As my knees buckled, my mind whirled into confusion. What was going on? What had happened? Falling to the ground, I registered something had hit me hard enough to knock me down and that I was in imminent danger. My hands broke my fall, and I pressed one against the wall of the alley to help pull myself back up. My head spun and I felt sick as I turned to look each way for my attacker. I saw no one but heard the sound of running feet somewhere in the distance.

It had all happened so quickly that my thoughts were far behind and for a moment I stood there stupefied. Then I felt something warm and wet on my neck, and I reached back there to touch it. Pulling my hand back I looked down at my glove to see the white fabric soaked in blood. A cold sweat rushed over me, my ears rang and I became extremely dizzy.

"*Frau, geht es Ihnen gut?*" Came a strange voice. I opened my mouth to speak and was violently sick. Then everything went black.

"SHE'S COMING AROUND NOW," the man's voice filtered through my slumber. I opened my eyes—where was I? I blinked several times, and eventually the blurriness faded to reveal the concerned face of Doctor Engel close to mine. He held a small light which he now shone into my eyes, and I moved my head to escape the brightness. I tried to sit up.

"*Nein, fräulein.* Not so fast. You have received a very nasty blow to your head. I want you to lie still for a while longer please."

I closed my eyes once more, and the memory flooded back. Wolfgang…the alley…the assault. Nausea ripped through my stomach.

"She is going to be sick." This, a woman's voice in German. The doctor gently pulled me onto my side, I felt the cold metal of a bowl beneath my chin and then a release. After a time, I rolled back and closed my eyes as something cold was lain across my forehead while a blanket was spread over my body. Then nothing.

BY THE TIME JOAN and Metzger arrived at the doctor's house, I was sitting up and drinking a cup of hot chocolate. My head throbbed like it had been hit by a cricket bat, and I kept shivering, but other than that I was doing much better—at least the vomiting had stopped.

"Oh my gawd!" cried Joan, swooping into the room and flapping about me like an agitated ostrich. "Will she be all right, Doctor?" she asked, her face pale as milk.

"It was a close call," he replied. "Had the blow been higher, Ingrid would have certainly sustained damaging injuries which could have been life-threatening." This he automatically answered in German, which Joan knew little of. He realised his error and then rephrased the entire answer by saying, "Yes. It was a terrible blow to the head, but Ingrid will recover well. A headache for a few days, and then she will be fine."

Joan grasped my hands, hers shaking. "If anythin' had happened to you...why—"

I squeezed hers. "I am well. You heard the doctor. Now please go and fetch Metzger so we can go home."

Always better with an occupation, Joan left to do my bidding while I thanked Doctor Engel for his ministrations.

"It was my pleasure," he said, helping me slowly to my feet. I wobbled momentarily but recovered with the support of his arm under mine. We moved towards the

The Secret of Lorelei Lodge

door to his surgery.

"I have sent word to the *inspektor* about what has taken place. It is imperative you speak with him about this once you feel well enough to see him. I don't want to worry you, *fräulein,* but you must face the gravity of what has happened."

"Yes. You are right. I will talk to *Inspektor* Schinkel whenever he comes to call, you can count upon it."

AS IT HAPPENED, THE *inspektor* wasted not a moment. He was already overseeing the investigation in the grounds of the lodge and called to see me directly he heard our carriage arrive. There followed a heated exchange between the policeman and Joan, who thought I needed rest and sleep and 'not bein' bloody harassed by a copper.'

I intervened. "Joan. My head already pounds, and your shouting isn't helping. Be a dear and get me settled on the sofa. I'd rather lay there and be closer to everyone than stuck up in the bedroom alone. *Inspektor* Schinkel needs to talk to me while everything that happened is fresh in my mind. A pot of tea and a nice biscuit would set me to rights as well."

Reluctantly, Joan did as she was told. She clucked about until I was surrounded by cushions and swaddled in a warm blanket. Then with a warning glare at the *inspektor,* she departed to fetch us tea.

He settled down in a nearby armchair. "It is most distressing to see you in this condition," he said kindly.

"I won't argue with that," I said, giving him a weak smile. It was the best I could do. My head ached terribly, but the powders from Doctor Engel had eased it considerably.

"I do not want to upset you, *fräulein*, but as you pointed out to your maid, the time to talk is now. So, please tell me what happened as well as you can remember."

I related everything as it had occurred, omitting seeing Wolfgang with Susanna or that I had followed *Herr* von Brandt. When I spoke of the attack, my voice trembled unexpectedly. I had not been prepared for that. I blinked back threatening tears as the door opened to admit Joan, and close upon her heels was Max.

Joan came in and set the tea tray in front of the *inspektor* and gestured over a shoulder. "This one wouldn't take no for an answer," she tutted disapprovingly. "I'd like to know where they all were when someone was tryin' to kill you!" Her hands crept to her small hips. "Now I'm warnin' you lot. Don't tire her out. She might look strong, but she's had a nasty shock and bin frightened out o' her wits. I'm comin' back in fifteen minutes an' chasin' you all out." She glared at the mountain of a policeman and straightened herself to every bit of her four feet eleven. "An' I won't hear no—even from the law. Understood?"

Inspektor Schinkel nodded assent, and I couldn't help but smile. Talk about David and Goliath.

Max came to stand by me. "Ingrid, I came as soon as I heard what had happened."

I waved towards the chair next to the *inspektor's*. "You'll have to sit, Max. If I look up, it makes me dizzy."

He remedied that quickly. "How do you feel?"

"Like someone tried to knock my head off my shoulders." I looked away from him to the policeman.

"Would you mind pouring the tea?"

Even in my current state, I have to admit I took great delight watching the beefy *inspektor* diligently trying to lace his very large fingers through the handle of the teapot. But he succeeded and handed me a cup of strong tea with two lumps of sugar added. I sipped it with relish.

"I shall recover," I told Max, whose dark eyes stared intently at me. "I have a goose egg on the back of my head, and it aches like the dickens, but Doctor Engel assures me there is no permanent damage as far as he can tell."

"Thank God for that," Max said. "This happened in the village?"

"Yes," I answered, "but I don't want to re-hash the entire story. Perhaps *Inspektor* Schinkel will fill you in on the details, if he wouldn't mind?"

The policeman recounted the tale in German, neither man realising I understood every word. In addition to the telling, he also added several other comments showing concern for my safety, and that I should consider returning to London. He told Max he was worried there was a connection between Klara's death and the body in the garden. That he had not taken the threatening note as seriously as he should, but now felt my life was in imminent danger.

"She will not leave," Max replied, still speaking German and convinced I was ignorant of their conversation. "Ingrid is a brave but stubborn woman. I tried to make her stay with us at the palace, but then my wife had the accident, and everything has been a mess since." He glanced in my direction and then back at Schinkel. "I hope you find the bastard who did this to her before I do, because I will rip his heart out." Max's face was dark with anger. He would be a formidable opponent I shouldn't wonder.

"That will not be necessary, Baron," Schinkel replied. "And I will thank you to remember it is my job to carry out the law, not yours. You would do better allowing me to hunt down this man, while you focus on protecting this woman's safety. I believe she is better off remaining here at the lodge as the place is smaller and easier to watch. I intend to leave a guard here around the clock. If you have more time, you could spend it here also. The killer will feel less bold if there is constant activity, But I think it imperative she goes nowhere for the time being."

Without showing I understood the conversation, inwardly I groaned. So I was to be a prisoner then. Although in truth, I was not too bothered. I didn't want to go anywhere for a while. I set my cup down and found my head suddenly felt very heavy. I rested it against the cushions while the men continued their discussion, and I faded into sleep.

Chapter Twenty

THE NEXT DAY MY headache still plagued me. I took the medicine given by Doctor Engel and decided to have a quiet day. Joan was taking very good care of me, and for a change I allowed her to fuss and coddle. I think the past month had caught up with me and I finally gave myself permission to stop pushing back and rest.

I stayed in the drawing room, for my eyes were sensitive and in the study I would be too tempted to read. Dieter dragged an armchair over to face the large window overlooking the front of the house, and it was here I sat, guarding the lodge like a living gargoyle.

Gazing out was pleasant. My vast landscape encompassed the driveway, the main lawn, and off to one side the dense forest. The policemen were still quite visible, but under the circumstances I found this most reassuring. I was pondering this very topic when I saw a carriage coming towards the house. It did not look familiar, but as it turned parallel to where I sat, I saw the von Brandt emblem emblazoned on the door.

The coachman leapt down to assist the occupants from the cab. I was surprised to see Katja alight from the vehicle but astonished to see none other than the baroness. Her nurse, Magda, followed close behind as the ladies made their way inside the front door. I could hear Fritz's excitable voice at their company, and I quickly removed myself to a chair in its usual position so I could welcome them in.

As Fritz made his announcement, I rose to my feet.

Katja came over, her face full of concern. "Dear Ingrid," she gushed. "What a terrible thing to have happened to you. Are you recovered?"

"Let me see her," barked Lisbeth to her daughter-in-law. She approached, leaning heavily upon Magda's arm, a cane clutched in her other hand. She came close, so close I could almost count the lines on her face.

"Are you hurt, Marta?" she asked.

Over her shoulder I saw Katja frown, and I gave a shake of my head so she would not correct the baroness.

I smiled at the elderly lady. "All things considered, I am doing very well. Just a bit of a sore head actually." I gestured to the sofa. "Please take a seat and I shall ring for refreshment."

"No," Lisbeth snapped. "No need. I just wanted to see the place. It has been too long, Marta. I never liked coming here when that woman was around. Miserable face, and not too kind."

I assumed she referred to Klara, but I said nothing.

"Your husband," she raised a brow directed towards Katja. "He dressed her up like a nurse, yes, the nerve of it." She tuned to look at me again. "She was a fraud. Not like Magda. This one is a real nurse. The other, well she got what she deserved."

Katja's gasp was audible. We exchanged glances.

"Where's the girl?" Lisbeth asked. I knew she meant me, but she also thought I was my mother. What to say?

"She's gone for a walk," I replied quickly.

"Then get her back here. It's too dangerous for her

being out there now. I insist!"

Though the nurse did not speak English, she heard the tone in Lisbeth's voice. Our eyes met, and somehow we managed to convey our mutual concern.

"*Baronin*," Magda said kindly. "*Komm und schau mit mir aus dem Fenster*." She asked Lisbeth to come and look out of the window. Magda slowly guided her, talking softly as you might to a child.

"Poor Mutti is easily confused," said Katja with a sigh.

"Yes. She often thinks I am my mother, Marta, as I resemble her greatly. But it doesn't bother me at all, and I think it pleases the baroness to think her friend still lives."

"She was adamant about coming to see you today when she heard you had been attacked. Tell me, how are you? It must have been terrifying for you, I am so sorry."

"I feel rather dreadful, but mainly because the pain in my head will not cease. Fortunately, that is the worst of my injuries, it could have been worse."

"Were you robbed?"

"No," I replied. "That is what is so strange. I had my coin purse in my bag, yet the assailant didn't take it."

"She's in the ground now, you know." Lisbeth's voice came across loudly. She made her way back to where Katja and I waited.

"I miss her." Lisbeth's brown eyes filled with tears as they met mine. "She was so sickly. Right from the beginning." A tear rolled down her face. "Poor Marta. The things you do for love." The baroness turned to her nurse. "I want to go home," she said in a reedy voice.

"Please take me home."

The nurse looked at Katja, who translated. "*Sie will nach Hause*," she explained, telling the nurse to make her way to the front door and their carriage. As the two left the drawing room, Katja lingered behind.

"I am truly glad you will be all right, *Fräulein* Rutherford. I wanted to talk to you about what is happening in the walled garden, but perhaps it should wait for another time. I must get the baroness home."

"Of course." I rose. "But please come back any time you wish to visit. You are always welcome."

With a nod, Katja left after the others. I walked to the window and resumed sitting in my chair, watching as the three women stepped into the carriage and then were driven away.

I reflected upon their visit for some time. What had Lisbeth said? She had acknowledged Klara being employed at the lodge and as her nurse, and Wolfgang's having a hand in it. She had fretted over my safety when she thought I was out alone. But the most interesting comment had been about someone being in the ground. Who? My mother? Klara? Valentina? Yet whoever it was she said was sickly. And what about my mother and the things she did for love? What was she talking about?

My head ached, and the back of my neck throbbed. It hurt too much to think. I closed my eyes and rested.

THURSDAY I FINALLY BEGAN to improve. Joan informed me Max had called in the morning, but I had slept late, and she would not wake me. He had asked to come back in the afternoon. It was odd, since sharing my room with Joan I had not had the nightmare at all. This was a welcome reprieve, especially considering my current situation.

Susanna sent a note asking if she could call later that day. And though I was unsure if I was really ready for that, I could not in good conscience tell her no, for her departure was imminent. I sent a message back to the hotel and then set about my day.

I ate a good breakfast, took my powders from the doctor, which had worked wonders thus far. Fritz had left a small pile of post on the table, and I leisurely slit open the envelopes, none which were of much interest. Until I reached one near the bottom of the stack. I recognised it immediately, and without touching the thing, I rang for Fritz.

In less than a quarter hour the *inspektor* was in my study with the envelope in his possession. He picked it up with a set of tweezers and examined it carefully before opening it with a knife and drawing out the single sheet of paper within. His eyes flickered over it.

"I wish to see it," I said firmly.

He held it closer for me to look. The handwriting was the same.

'That was your warning. Go back to England while you still can.'

Schinkel's capable hands placed the note back inside the envelope and into a small paper bag retrieved from his pocket. He turned his grey eyes to look at me, and I was surprised to see a dash of concern in them, "*Fräulein* Rutherford, are you well?"

I nodded, though I was unsure how I really felt. Scared? Numb?

He got up and left the room for a moment. I heard the rumble of his deep voice and then he returned. "I took the liberty of ordering coffee from your butler," he said, sitting back down across the desk from me. "*Fräulein*, I wish to commend you. I admire a woman who does not run to hysterics, such as yourself. Your resilience during this troubling time is admirable."

"Thank you. Coming from you I believe that is quite the compliment. But I'd be dishonest if I didn't admit I'm actually quite terrified by the entire situation."

"Fear is what keeps us safe, *Fräulein*. How we respond to it is what makes us brave..." He trailed off at the sound of the front door opening and then footsteps against the tiled floor.

After one knock, Max entered the study. He took one look at my face. "What has happened?" he asked the *inspektor* gruffly.

The policeman told him the gist of it, and I watched Max's expression grow darker. He looked livid and anxious at the same time.

"This will not do, Ingrid." He approached my desk. "I cannot rest leaving you here so, so vulnerable." His brown eyes were almost black. "You must come and stay at *das Safranpalast*. There we at least have the staff to protect you."

"Like they did Valentina, or *Krankenschwester* Helga?" I responded, harsher than I meant.

But Max was undaunted. "That has nothing to do with this. Valentina fell down the stairs and—"

"Did she?" My question pierced the air, and I felt the eyes of both men bore into my face.

"What is that supposed to mean?" Max said, his voice low.

"I don't believe she fell." I took a deep breath. "I

think someone pushed her down those stairs to get her out of the way." There, I had voiced my fear to the one person who would feel it the worst, and in front of a policeman too. Dear God, what was I doing?

"*Fräulein* Rutherford," began the *inspektor*. "I believe you overstep—"

"No, wait!" Max commanded the large man. "Let Ingrid have her say. I have nothing to hide." He glared at me. "Well go on. You seem to have all the answers."

But the fight was out of me. My head throbbed once again, and the weight of that damnable note was wearing me down. "I know you have been unhappy. Valentina would not grant you a divorce, and although I thought you'd repaired your relationship lately, it seems you had much to gain by her death."

His face blanched. "You think so little of me? That I would sink to the depths of becoming a murderer and callously kill my wife in cold-blood?"

Why was it that when he repeated my accusations, my thoughts sounded unfounded, those of an overwrought woman. I looked at Max, who stared at me as though I was the most appalling item he had lain eyes upon, then I saw the *inspektor's* expression, one that had been of such respect not a moment earlier and had now slipped into something like disappointment.

Fritz chose that time to enter with the coffee tray. Seemingly oblivious or uncaring of the atmosphere in the room, he deposited the tray on my desk and left. No one stirred.

"Ingrid," Max said firmly, and I forced myself to meet his eyes. They were cold. "I considered you a friend. That you so casually cast me in the role of the villain here goes beyond the pale. You disappoint me.

More than you will ever understand." Before I could respond, he walked away.

After a moment, the *inspektor* poured a cup of coffee and handed it to me. "I think, *Fräulein* Rutherford, that you have made a grave error when it comes to the character of the baron."

I took a sip of the drink. It helped thaw the numbness of my face, still set in the shock of what I had said to Max.

"First, let me ask how you know his history?"

I recounted what little I knew from Susanna. The loss of a child, his unhappy relationship, Valentina's Catholic faith and refusal to divorce. Then, nervously I added that he had shown an interest in me, that of a romantic nature. I did not look at Schinkel until I had finished my little speech. But when I did, I was surprised to see him shaking his head.

"Forgive me," he said. "But I would question your source of information. All these findings you have made are based on hearsay. If you'll allow me, I should like to set the record straight?"

I nodded and sipped my coffee, while my pulse picked up speed.

"Baron Maximillian von Brandt is no murderer, *Fräulein*—far from it. Though he is guilty of falling in love with a woman who was not as she appeared.

Valentina Cavaletti was an up-and-coming opera star when they met. And after a whirlwind affair, the two were married, but only because Valentina was pregnant. When Nikolai was born, she wanted little to do with the baby. She became depressed and listless, until she admitted wanting to resume her singing career.

The baron supported her choice and was

comfortable with the arrangement, for their relationship had become strained. He focused upon his son and encouraged Valentina to spend as much time as she wanted at the palace and with Nikolai, which she seldom did." He paused to take a drink. "When Valentina began having affairs, the baron turned a blind eye. But on one particular evening, the two of them had a terrible argument. Maximillian was unaware his son had been listening. The boy ran away and took a horse from the stables. Nikolai was too young to ride without supervision. The horse bolted, he was thrown, and dead by the time he was discovered."

I did not utter a sound.

"Afterwards, Valentina blamed the baron, though it was he who suffered the loss, for he had been the real parent. The man has carried that weight for three years, yet never retaliated against her words or reminded Valentina of her indifference to both her son and her husband."

"Then why did they not divorce?" I asked, unable to keep the accusation from my voice.

He shrugged. "The scandal would have ruined her career. The woman was of frail mind as it was, another blow and she might have fallen apart. Perhaps, in time it would have happened, but Max was insistent she receive the emotional support she needed, even though Valentina let him know in no uncertain terms she was finished with him."

"With respect, *Inspektor*. This doesn't make sense. I myself witnessed several occasions where they appeared as a couple and behaved as such too."

The bear of a man shrugged. "I do not argue any point, *Fräulein*. I simply tell you the facts which I have known for some time." He got to his feet. "I must go. Do not leave this house for any reason. I shall return later today and appraise you if any new information is brought to light." He strode to the door and pulled it open, then as an afterthought turned back to look at me. "If Valentina Cavaletti was pushed down those stairs, it was not by her husband."

I DO NOT KNOW HOW long I sat at my desk thinking after the *inspektor* had gone. His disclosures about Max had amplified the guilt I already struggled with from my accusations. The look on Max's face when I said those things to him. How he must hate me for it.

And what of his relationship with Valentina? Susanna had been correct in some of her information yet had misunderstood it as well. Oh, why had I listened to her and not corroborated any of it with someone other than a young woman with more interest in fashion and flirtation than reality?

The back of my neck ached. I would go and lie down. This morning's events had all been far too much. But as I got up, my hand hit my coffee cup, and in my bid to stop it tipping over, I accidentally knocked my mother's framed picture off the desk. It bounced from the thick rug laying under the desk and finally landed on the wooden floor with a resounding crack.

I bent down to retrieve it and watched helplessly as the frame fell apart in my hands. The glass was cracked, and the thin metal of the frame had come undone. The picture had already started to fall from its mooring. I grasped it, allowing the small shards of glass to fall to the ground where they could be swept, and placed the picture on my desk face down. I noticed some writing on the back, and I picked it up, hoping it might show the date it was taken and then I could determine my mother's age.

There was a date on it, but not what I would have expected, for it read 'eighteen hundred and eighty-four', eleven years earlier. The girl in this photograph could not have been older than thirteen or fourteen. My mother had died a year after this picture was dated, at the age of fifty. I did not understand.

Then I saw the other writing, written in a tiny, childish hand in one corner. It was just one word by itself.

'Astrid.'

Chapter Twenty-One

I BLINKED. MY HEAD spun. The strange sensation I had experienced since arriving at the lodge pulsed through my blood and my heart slowed to a dull thud. My legs shook, and I quickly sat back down at the desk. I rested my arms on the desktop and leaned over, laying my head there while I focused on breathing deeply. I did not want to faint, and for some reason I thought I might.

I sat that way for several minutes, keeping my eyes closed while I breathed in and out slowly. The dizziness abated, my head began to clear, and slowly I was able to sit upright again without feeling queasy.

I picked up the picture once again and re-read the back of it. I had read it correctly the first time. The picture was my mother, the date and name on it were wrong. What did it mean?

It was no good. I would have to get to the bottom of this, and immediately. I rang the bell for Fritz and asked him to call for the carriage. He fidgeted.

"This I cannot do, *meine Dame*. *Inspektor* Schinkel left orders that on no account were you to travel anywhere."

I bit my tongue. Fritz did not deserve my ire. "Fritz, I appreciate your doing your duty to the policeman, but may I remind you that you work for me."

His eyes seemed to shrink into his face. He was

The Secret of Lorelei Lodge

unsure what to say next when the sound of carriage wheels came to a stop outside. Fritz moved away from me before I could say another word, pulling the door open before anyone had time to even knock. I followed behind, and saw that Susanna was about to alight from a cab.

"Wait!" I cried out, halting her in mid-step. "You must take me to the palace." I brushed past Fritz who stood, mouth agape, and ran to the carriage. I climbed in after Susanna and shouted to the driver to take us to the *Safranpalast*.

As soon as the horses moved, Susanna was on me like an ant on syrup. "What on earth is happening? I thought you were at death's door. You're supposed to be—"

"Hush for one moment and I'll explain," I said harsher than I intended. "Since my head got bashed in, I have been kept at the lodge and I'm not allowed to go anywhere in case someone tries to kill me."

"Good grief!" Susanna gasped. "I thought you'd been robbed and that's why you were hurt."

"No. They took nothing. *I* was the target."

"But Ingrid, that's awful!" Susanna's eyes were bright with trepidation. "Why on earth would anyone want to hurt you? You only just got here and haven't had a chance to make many friends, let alone enemies."

"It would appear that you are wrong." I waved my hand in a frustrated gesture. "That's beside the point right now. I must see Lisbeth von Brandt, and you fortuitously arrived just in time to help me!"

"Well, I'll be damned," Susanna swore. "This is quite exciting. What is our adventure about?"

I held up the picture. "We are going to find out

who this really is."

KRANKENSCHWESTER MAGDA WAS WELCOMING when she saw me waiting in the foyer, though she gave Susanna a curious and interested second look. We were led upstairs to see the baroness, who much to my delight looked hale and hearty as I had ever seen her.

"Marta!" she said happily as we went in. I shot Susanna a warning glance not to comment on her use of the wrong name. We went to join her in her seating area, and the baroness instructed Magda to bring us all a cool drink of lemonade. Then she switched to English. "Marta, why have you brought your maid?"

I stifled the laugh rising to my lips as Susanna bristled with indignation. "No, Lisbeth. This is my good friend Susanna. She is from America, you know."

"That place?" She scowled. My Max spent too long there with that ugly man. What was his name?"

"Carnegie," answered Susanna. "He's a good friend of my father."

The baroness raised a brow and then turned back to me. "I am happy you came today as I am bored. Magda is nice, but she doesn't have much to talk about."

"I am pleased you like her, Baroness." I retrieved the folded picture in my pocket. "Now, may I show you something? I would like you to tell me if you know this person."

I held out the picture and her pale thin hands took it from me. I watched her intently. Her dark eyes stared at the face for a long time. Then she turned it over and looked at the writing. Slowly, she held the picture out for me to take back. I prayed she would stay in the present, that her eyes would not mist over into that place where only she could go.

"Marta," she said quietly. "I do not know if this is a game, but you know perfectly well it is Astrid."

"Who is Astrid?" I asked.

"That is a ridiculous question," she said, and then suddenly her brows knotted, and she frowned at me. "Wait. Which one are you?" She stared hard at me. Then something like recognition sparked in her eyes. "You are the one with his eyes. Blue like little pieces of ice." She pointed to the photo I still held in my hands. "That one, she was like my Marta. The same as you but with her pretty brown eyes." A long finger touched the corner of her mouth. "You all had the little mole, right there."

"But who is Astrid?" I said again. And with horror felt the strange sensation take hold of my body. I willed it to stop. I wanted my head to be clear, to understand what was happening.

Baroness Lisbeth von Brandt lifted her head up, her posture as regal as a queen. Her eyes were clear, her expression determined. "Astrid was your sister. She was your twin."

Chapter Twenty-Two

"WHAT?" THE BUZZING IN my ears began to die down but I felt my heart racing in my chest. "I have no sister."

Lisbeth gave a derisive cackle. "Of course, you did. But your father, he wouldn't have it. Only the perfect ones, that's all he ever wanted."

"What do you mean?" This was all too much to comprehend. The baroness was an old lady. She must be confused. Hadn't she thought I was my mother every time I came to see her? It was nonsense, it had to be. My intellect told me it was the musings of an old woman. My emotional and physical response was something entirely different.

"Marta is my dear friend," Lisbeth addressed Susanna. "We played together in the gardens when we were children, didn't we dear?" she asked me, her eyes beginning to cloud over.

By the time Magda returned with our lemonades, Lisbeth was back in her private world. There would be no more information forthcoming from her, and I wasn't sure I wanted there to be. My head ached again, and the exertion of the visit, and the explosive suggestion about the photograph were all I could cope with. So it was with great relief that we took our leave and made our way to Susanna's carriage.

Once we were underway, she leaned forward

where I sat across from her and grasped my free hand, the other still clutching the picture.

"Ingrid. Are you all right? You look pale and I am frightened you are unwell."

"I will be fine," I said. "It is my head. It still aches from what happened, and I think I just grew too warm in that room."

"You poor mite," she cooed. "What a crazy old lady that woman is. She really thinks you are your mother. And that nonsense about your having a sister?" She gave a little chuckle. "It's rather melodramatic, don't you think?"

I said nothing.

"Oh Ingrid, surely you didn't believe her?" Susanna took the picture from my hand and studied it. "Of course, it's your mother, Ingrid. Everyone says how much you resemble her. Your eyes are a different colour, but that is all."

"The words on the back—" I muttered.

"Could have been written by anyone. Perhaps this date is when the picture was framed. The old lady just read the name on the back. Your aunt likely had it framed, and the photographer's name is written here—see?"

She pointed to the word Astrid. I felt the now familiar ripple of nausea pass through me. "Stop the carriage," I said. "Quickly."

Susanna banged on the roof of the cab and the driver pulled the horses to a halt. I hastily pushed open the door, got out and went to the side of the road where I was violently sick.

Susanna was beside me in an instant. "Come," she said softly. "This has all been too much for you in a day. I should never have agreed to take you anywhere. Let us get you home and to bed." Susanna helped me back into the carriage.

THE HORRID FEELINGS FINALLY passed, and after being fussed over by Joan, she left me to lay on the sofa, Susanna sitting at my feet.

"How are you feeling?" she asked kindly.

"Much better now. I'm so sorry about that. It is unlike me to feel ill."

"Dearest Ingrid," Susanna exclaimed. "You are a warrior in comparison to me. I should have run a mile after that poor woman was found dead so close to this place. But you have stayed on regardless. Don't sell yourself short. You are tougher than most."

At that moment a part of me longed to tell Susanna all I had learned since coming here and explain why I was determined to stay. But instead, I held back. I knew the Koppelmans planned to remain in *Linnenbrink* an extra week, in deference to the death of Valentina. They would leave the day after her funeral, set for the following Tuesday. Why involve Susanna now?

She stayed for luncheon, and took her leave with a promise to return the next day. After the place was quiet once again, I returned to the couch and lay back down. Exhaustion plagued me, but I knew it was partially from the nasty hit to my head, and the subsequent problems resulting from it. I lay back, closed my eyes and felt myself drifting away.

I woke with a start, my heart hammering, sweat beading on my forehead. The nightmare! I sat up, my breathing ragged and fast. I must calm down. I took in great gulps of air, and eventually my pounding pulse began to ease and I cooled off. I got to my feet, took a sip from a glass of water, and carried it to the window where I stared out into the distance.

The sun shone brightly in the June sky, but my thoughts were dark as pitch. Still shaken, for I had not dreamt the dream in the daytime before, I kept breathing in a slow rhythmic pattern to see if it would help. Then little by little, I tried to recapture what had plagued my sleep.

The nightmare had started just as it always did. Hounds chasing me, but this time, when I looked at them, they bore the faces of Max and Wolfgang von Brandt. The walled garden was there, the door flung open. Klara stood just inside waiting with a smile, her throat slit with a ghastly bloody gash. Valentina, next to her, laughed at me, her head at a crooked angle. I passed them by, determined to get to the Willow tree where in the distance I could see my mother standing beneath it, the willow branches like a curtain around her still form.

I ran towards her, calling her name, but just as I reached her, the ground split open between us and a figure within the earth sat up and stared at me. The face that looked into mine, a mirror of my own.

Now, a shudder passed through my body as I stood at the window. I pressed my fingers against the sun-warmed glass, finding the sensation reassuring. I was safe and awake.

I returned to the memory of my dream, to the face that was my own...What did it mean? How many years had I dreamt about seeing two of me in that nightmare? Too many to count.

Lisbeth said I had a twin. But I had no siblings, no memory nor record of one. Mother had kept so much from me regarding her family. But the existence of a sister? Surely she would not be so cruel? I walked back to the sofa and sat down. The photograph lay on the side table, and I picked it up and examined it. Was this my mother? I scoured the details of her face—one I knew so well. But did I?

It had been ten years since I'd lost my mother, and me, not yet an adult. Was my memory so exact? After all, my reminiscence was of a woman in her late forties, not her youth, so how could I be certain?

I got back on my feet and paced the length of the room. It was incredibly frustrating. There was not a soul alive to help me get to the truth of the matter except the baroness, and she was as helpful as she was confusing. I needed answers to resolve this once and for all.

But what if I really did have a sister? Or was it *had* a sister, for couldn't it be her bones buried in the garden? They were in my dream. I touched the pendant hanging from my neck. Was it hers I'd found in the dirt? Had my mother given us both a necklace?

Yet how could it be? The body in the garden was not that of a child. If Mother had given birth to two of us, she would never have abandoned her baby. She was a natural parent, a loving parent, an advocate for those with no voice, which is why she'd dedicated so much time and effort helping the children at the orphanage. No. If there had been another child in my family, I would have known. Seen something, heard something. No one was invisible, were they?

But for argument's sake, what if it were true? What

if there was another Rutherford that I was unaware of, just like my aunt and uncle whose existence was unknown to me? I sat back down. Closing my eyes, I tried to let my thoughts flow openly and allow anything to come into my mind.

I sighed deeply. Loneliness. It was no stranger to me. Even when Mother was alive, there had been that constant sense of isolation. I lived in a large home, governed by a controlling, forceful man. Mother compensated wherever she could, her warmth and love an antidote for Father's indifference and cruelty. Even so, something had always been missing.

I'd believed the source of my feeling alone was because I was essentially friendless. I made some acquaintances to be sure, yet there was always a distance between them, and me. I'd never been able to name it, but I could equate the feeling to how a child felt when a favoured toy was taken away, or any item which brought comfort. It was always the sense of losing something I had never had, nor could name.

A vague stirring of memory flitted across my thoughts. I had read much in my short life, and I recalled a piece in the paper regarding the subject of twins. What was it? Something about their connection. Especially identical twins, whose lives were conjoined starting in the womb and continued throughout their years.

I baulked at the very thought of it. I was being ridiculous. The bang on my head was turning my musings into histrionics. Then suddenly another thought dropped into place. Laughter. Sitting atop a tall rocking horse, hanging onto its mane, while another sat behind me with their arms wrapped about my waist. I recalled the strange sensation I had felt seeing the rocking horse in the schoolroom. What did this all mean?

"*Meine Dame*, you have a visitor." I had not heard Fritz come into the room. My eyes snapped open.

A figure brushed past the butler. "*Guten Tag, Fräulein* Rutherford."

It was Wolfgang. What on earth was he doing here? I gathered myself and managed a weak smile. "Hello, *Herr* von Brandt. What brings you here?"

Wolfgang approached and took a seat in the armchair across from me. He looked better than I remembered, yet there were still smudges of darkness under his eyes, and though he smiled it seemed staged.

"I come only to see how you are. I have heard about the terrible thing that happened to you. I wanted to tell you how very sorry I am that you were hurt."

"Thank you," I said demurely. "But I am feeling much better. I appreciate your concern. It is most kind of you. Can I offer you some refreshment?"

Much to my surprise he accepted, so I rang the bell for Fritz and asked him to bring us coffee. Then I turned my attention back to my guest and immediately thought of when I saw him last, right before the attack in the alleyway.

"You must think living here is much less safe than London." he remarked, as though he read my thoughts. "*Linnenbrink* is such a sleepy little village, yet since your arrival, there has been nothing but one drama after another."

"You are right. Although I hope you don't think I am the harbinger of that."

"Harbinger? *Was ist das*?"

"It means the person who has caused these events to unfold. A bringer, if you like."

His eyes settled on my face—his expression difficult to fathom. "Ah, I see." He paused as Fritz came in with our coffee. The butler set down the tray as he always did and quietly left the room.

I leaned forward and poured our drinks.

"Life is strange, Ingrid," Wolfgang picked up the thread of his thought once again. "I believe that sometimes we are not aware of what can happen because of one single event."

"That can be called the domino effect."

He looked puzzled, so I explained. "When you stand a domino up and then place many in a long row, close together, all you have to do is tip one over and the rest fall down as well."

"I like this term. I shall remember it," he said, then sipped his drink. "Do you think you are the domino here at Lorelei Lodge?"

I frowned. "Not at all. Why would you say that?" A small tingle of apprehension ran up my spine. I maintained my expression, but I was on my guard at once.

He shrugged. This time a smile played about his handsome face. Such fine looks spoiled by the personality behind them.

"I mean no insult, Ingrid, *entschuldigen*—sorry. But since you took residence here at the lodge, it has triggered the beginning of many things."

I would not let him intimidate me. I returned his smile. "Perhaps. Yet none were of my making. Everything that's happened since my coming was already in motion before I'd even heard of Lorelei or your family. Another way to look at it is that whoever killed *Krankenschwester* Helga, intentionally waited for my being here before committing the crime."

"That was a terrible business." Wolfgang shook his head. "The *polizei* are no closer to solving it than your Englishmen are finding your Jack of the Ripper."

I chose not to correct him. "True," I agreed. "But they have at least discovered something about Helga which was interesting." I was treading on shaky ground, but I wanted to wipe the confidence from his face.

"What?" He tried to sound nonchalant, but I could hear the tightness in his voice.

"That she was not who she claimed to be. Apparently she used a false name. Didn't the police tell you? Wasn't it you who hired her at the palace, or perhaps I misunderstood?" I watched him carefully. Wolfgang was trying to formulate an answer. Had he been aware I knew Helga's real identity? For that knowledge may have placed me in danger, and someone who felt threatened had sent me those notes.

He shrugged. "They mentioned something about it, but to be truthful, I did not give it much thought. I was more concerned about finding her replacement to care for my mother."

More like keeping the poor woman drugged, I wanted to say. I didn't know what the man was capable of, but that day had made a lasting impression of my opinion of him.

Wolfgang finished his coffee and set down the cup. "We must face one hurdle at a time. Next Valentina must be laid to rest." His eyes became sad. "Such a great loss to my brother, and to the world. She was *ein schöner Singvogel*." His swallowed hard and then got to his feet as though to distract me from seeing his obvious emotion. "Thank you for the coffee. I am pleased you are making a good recovery. *Guten tag.*"

He was off to the door before I could respond. I heard his footfall and then the door open and close behind him. As I watched him walk down the pathway, I had a sudden moment of remembrance. Wolfgang had just called Valentina a lovely songbird, *ein schöner Singvogel*.

I thought back to the day when I'd overheard Valentina in the forest with Max. Their conversation, their kiss. That person had called Valentina the same endearment Wolfgang had just said. I had automatically assumed it was Max with the Italian woman, together in a romantic tryst. But I was wrong. It was Wolfgang I had heard that night. Of course! That would explain his emotion when speaking of her death. Had Wolfgang von Brandt been in love with his brother's wife?

Chapter Twenty-Three

I DISPATCHED A MESSAGE to *Inspektor* Schinkel and requested he visit me first thing the next morning. I could not continue keeping everything straight in my mind. While in my study, I retrieved the pages I had scribbled on previously, where I'd connected everyone together to discover the truth of my past and threw them away.

I started again now so many things had changed. I would work backwards. Why had I been attacked? Because I knew the truth about Helga being Klara. Why did that matter? Because Klara must have known about the body in the walled garden—I refused to think of it as my sister, for then I would not be able to go any further. Who would be concerned about the body being found? The killer. Did that mean Wolfgang was a murderer? Had he hired someone to attack me in the village?

And what of Max? I had accused him of betraying his wife based on my supposition they were a couple once again. What an idiot I was. I'd overheard Valentina with her lover and pushed Max away. To make it even worse, I accused Max of shoving his wife down the stairs so he could be free, when the entire time it was he who'd maintained the marriage.

A murder, an accident, an attempted murder, and a mysterious body. All somehow linked. Tomorrow, I would speak with the *inspektor* and tell him everything, even what the baroness had said about my having a twin. If that was actually true and Astrid was a real person, where was she? And if it was not my own sister buried in that sad little grave, then who was it?

TONIGHT IT WAS WARM. We opened all the windows in my room so what little breeze there was would cool us. Joan, as usual, fell fast asleep. She did not snore. In fact, her breathing was so quiet I often wondered if she had stopped altogether.

I lay on my back with my eyes wide open. My mind was too fretful to relax. I feared I might have the nightmare as I had done earlier in the day, and I did not want to go through that again.

Outside, the wind picked up, enough to hear the rustle of leaves on the large oak outside my window. I closed my eyes and contemplated Wolfgang's comment about my being safer in London. He was correct. So why did I remain? What reason had I to stay when my life was in danger? I knew part of the answer to that question. My past.

Coming to Lorelei Lodge had ensnared me from the start. What began as curiosity had morphed into an urgent desire to discover the secrets tucked away over the years. What compelled this fascination? A bloody-mindedness? Or had it always been some deep unconscious knowledge that there was another part of me missing—a sister.

I turned onto my side and faced the door. My neck was still so uncomfortable since I had been attacked and I had to move into different positions frequently. With a discontented sigh, I moved my thoughts and considered my meeting in the morning with the *inspektor*. I liked the man, though I could not explain why, especially since…

Suddenly a hand reached across my mouth and pulled my head back. I screamed into a dirty palm and thrashed my arms and legs, kicking the covers off me. I felt another arm go around my waist and then a strong heave as I was pulled from my bed. I fought frantically, using my body to squirm and move, until the hand loosened slightly, and I sank my teeth into its puffy flesh.

"Agghh!" Came a ferocious bellow of pain from my attacker, while simultaneously there came another shout, this one with a strong female London accent. Something smashed as it was cracked against a hard inanimate object and there came the sound of glass splintering to the ground.

I took a deep breath and screamed at the top of my lungs. "Help!"

WHEN THE MAN CAME around, his mouth was stuffed with a rag, his hands and legs bound together and tied to the foot of my bed. Dieter had been the first to burst through the door and had immediately rendered the stranger immobile. Then he and Fritz lit several gas lamps, while Metzger rode to the palace for assistance, and for them to get the *inspektor*.

Joan and I were led downstairs by Ursula the cook, Fritz's wife, who took us into the kitchen and made us a hot drink as we were still shaking. This is where Max found us once he had been upstairs to assess the situation.

"Ingrid, Joan, I am so glad you are both safe." We

sat at the table with Ursula, each of us nursing a warm drink in our cold hands.

"Where is the man?" I asked Max, unable to keep the tremble from my voice.

"The *inspektor* has taken him away, so you are safe now."

"Wish I'd bloody killed him," Joan said in a low voice.

"You saved my life," I told her, then turned to Max who'd sat down across from me. "Joan has been sleeping in my room on a cot since we came back from the palace. She broke a vase over his head and knocked him out."

"It weren't the vase that did it, miss. 'Twere his head hittin' the brass knob on your bed."

"No matter," interrupted Max. "Your quick actions stopped him from harming either one of you. Well done, Joan."

She gave him a quick nod, and then sipped at her drink. I knew Joan wasn't letting on how frightened she was. Her hands still shook.

"He was coming for me, wasn't he?" I said to Max, already knowing the answer.

"I'm afraid so. At least, that's what we have to assume. I am sure the *inspektor* will learn much more by morning." He turned his head as there came a strange whining sound from outside the back door.

"Excuse me a moment," Max said, getting to his feet. He opened the door and two massive hounds dashed inside the kitchen. One came straight to me, the other to Joan, who let out a cry of anguish.

"Be still, Joan," Max said sharply. "Sascha senses you are scared, and she has come to reassure you."

Dear Joan's face looked terrified. Yet after a moment, the large hound laid its massive head on her lap, and slowly she placed her fingers on its snout and began to stroke it.

"Well done," Max said encouragingly. "They are intimidating to look at, Joan, but they know when you are a friend." He glanced back at me. "And therefore, both the dogs and I will remain here with you at the lodge until this damned mess is sorted out once and for all."

I didn't know what to say. Perhaps even one day ago, I might have protested. But not now. Relief flooded my senses. I had not realised how utterly afraid I was.

"Thank you, Max," I said quietly, and hastily looked away before he saw the tears in my eyes.

URSULA SERVED BREAKFAST TO us later that morning. The outside guard had been replaced, the former having been hit over the head by the intruder was resting at home. *Inspektor* Schinkel returned from the gaol in *Prinzenstadt* as the food was put on the table.

"Before you ask me any questions," the policeman announced taking a seat and helping himself to a hefty forkful of bacon, "the man in custody refuses to tell us anything—including his name."

Max gave a deep sigh. "That is disappointing. I had hoped we might have a starting point."

"Don't worry," *Inspektor* Schinkel said, switching to German. "We will get it out of the man before the day is finished. There is more to this situation than I first understood. I will have him hung up by his feet if he does not comply and answer my questions. For now, he is locked up, no food nor water. The bastard can sweat it out until later today." He took another bite of his food and then gave me a calm smile. I was sorely tempted to say something in German, just to see his reaction, but I resisted.

"Now, *Fräulein* Rutherford," He cast his eyes on my face. "Are you recovered enough from the events of last night to speak with me after breakfast? You did send for me yesterday, did you not?"

"I did," I replied, feeling Max glance my way. I had not yet told him any of the things which had happened the day before. "Max," I said. "You are invited to meet with us also. I should like for both of you to hear what I have to say."

It was settled, and we finished our breakfast without much discussion.

"A TWIN SISTER?" MAX said in bewilderment. "Impossible! Marta Bergman could never have kept such a secret from anyone. Where would the girl have stayed?"

"I don't know," I said. "But there is a distinct possibility that if she did exist, she could well be the person buried in the garden."

"That is outrageous," Max said in disgust.

"Do you believe it could be true?" Schinkel asked me.

I nodded. "I didn't at first, I thought the baroness was confused. But then once I started thinking about all the odd coincidences, I began to wonder."

"Such as?" said Schinkel.

"First of all, the omissions. That my mother had come here regularly for many years, initially with me while I was very young, and then later without my knowledge, up until her death ten years ago. There were also my terrible nightmares, where I was being chased, and running to the walled garden for safety. Once there I would pound on its door to be let in. Whenever the door opened to allow me in, I would come face to face with myself."

"Freud would have a field day with this, Ingrid," Max commented.

"Please," said the *inspektor*. "Let her finish."

I got up and went to stand by the window. We were all in the drawing room. I turned to face both men sitting in the armchairs. "When I arrived here, the nightmares became worse, and increasingly more vivid. In addition, I started finding things familiar, though when I asked Joan, she said she had no idea of my ever coming to Germany. Max's family, other than Lisbeth, had no memory of meeting me either, which was strange. But *Herr* Vogel, Mother's lawyer confirmed I had visited as a child.

Then I discovered my father had sent money to Aunt Gisela over the years for the upkeep of this place and while Mother was living, she supplemented it also. Could it have been to help support the welfare of my sister?" It was strange, but the more I spoke of her, the more real it became that I had not been an only child.

I continued. "If my aunt cared for my sibling, others must have known, at the very least the people working at the lodge. But strangely, all the servants were released at one time, and their replacements brought in from other towns, as though there was something to hide."

"Like a body buried in the garden?" Max said. This

time his tone was not mocking.

"Yes, exactly. When I started asking questions, *Herr* Vogel told me about the original servants, and that they were paid a substantial amount of money when they left my aunt's service. Their names were Gustav and Klara Krause and I asked him to track them down. Max, when I spoke with your mother, she believed *Krankenschwester* Helga was actually Klara Krause, come back to the village once again." I looked at Max not relishing my next comment. "She also said that Wolfgang was aware of her true identity."

"What?" Max sat bolt upright in his chair. "Are you certain?"

"Yes. You can ask her. She insinuated the two of them had some type of an understanding. But that Klara had the upper hand."

"Yet you did not share this information?" Schinkel stated.

"No. I am sorry. But at the time it was not relevant to anything other than me searching for my family's past. The nurse had already been murdered."

"And you did not consider the possibility of the two being connected?" His tone was irritable.

"Actually, *Inspektor* I cannot tell you what I thought. When the baroness said things, it took me a while to pick through and determine what I believed and what I did not. Besides, the police had yet to be involved. Everything was becoming overwhelming. The walled garden was being worked upon, when I discovered a pendant in the dirt, one identical to my own. Mine was given to me by my mother, who also wore the same necklace. I assumed it could be my aunt's. And then someone started leaving flowers under the Willow tree, and the gardeners called it a tribute. After that, I received the first note, and then Valentina had her accident, and you know the rest." I went and took a seat on the sofa, suddenly spent.

"Someone was aware there was a body buried in the garden, and they were intent on drawing attention to that fact. The key is to identify whose remains we found, and that will open this case up completely." Schinkel cast an eye on Max. "I shall need to have a conversation with your brother."

"Of course," Max sounded compliant, but I could see how troubled he was. I wondered what his real opinion was of Wolfgang, and what Max thought him capable of. I immediately thought of Valentina, and also Susanna. Did Max know his brother had betrayed him? Perhaps Katja did? She seemed to take her husband's flirtations in her stride.

What should I say? Was it my place to humiliate Max in front of the *inspektor*? Or was it more important he was made aware of all the facts? Did Valentina and Wolfgang's affair have any bearing on the murder of Klara and the attacks made upon me? I doubted it. I made the decision to remain quiet. This part of the situation was between Schinkel and Max.

It was already early afternoon and we had talked through the lunch hour. I told Fritz we'd take coffee and some pastries in lieu of the meal, and he obliged. After which, the *inspektor* announced he was returning to *Prinzenstadt* to check on his prisoner. He switched to German, asking Max to bring Wolfgang to the lodge that evening.

"Here?" Max frowned. "Why not at the palace?"

The large man settled his gaze on Max. "Because

everything that has occurred is tied to Lorelei." He gestured a big beefy hand to emphasise the point. "Therefore, there is an emotional component which will elicit a better response from your brother."

Max raised an eyebrow. "You mean it will be easier to tell if he is lying."

Schinkel shrugged his broad shoulders but did not reply.

WHEN THE MEN HAD departed to conduct their various tasks, I wrote a quick note to *Herr* Vogel. I asked him to bring all he had learned about the Krauses and urgently requested his presence that evening. Then I called for Joan.

"How are you?" I asked, noting her weary expression.

"Knackered after what went on this mornin'. Judgin' by the looks of you, you're in as bad a shape as meself."

I agreed. Then relayed in brief that there would be several people coming that evening for a meeting and asked her to convey that to the cook. A regular dinner would be unnecessary, but a cold buffet would be suitable. Then I told Joan to go and have a sleep upstairs, for she deserved the rest. I should have liked nothing better than to lay down on my own bed, but there was too much going on for me to relax.

I went into the study and pulled out all my notes. I must think clearly, and not about who murdered the nurse or who attacked me. I had to think about who had been buried under the Willow tree.

Hypothetically was the best way to do it. If my mother had indeed given birth to twins, what would justify raising one and not the other? A disability, a deformity, something of that nature, though perhaps not noticeable in a photograph? In my heart, I knew that would never have stopped my mother from loving her child. But it would not have been her decision. My father would have ruled on what my mother did or did not do.

Charles Rutherford was a man of high principles, with a keen awareness of his reputation and never allowed it to be sullied. Had he not kept me all but locked away in our house after my mother's death? If my mother had given birth to a deformed child, there was no way that poor soul would have ever graced our doorstep.

On this, I felt relatively certain that I was on the right track. Emotionally, I felt a sense of loss, especially since the unmarked grave had been found. Something unseen and unknown lurked in the margin of my memory like a whisper, a scent on the breeze.

In theory, my father could have forbidden the other child to remain in London, or anywhere she could be seen. What better place to hide her than in Germany, with a matron aunt? There she would receive better care than in an asylum, and my mother would be free to see her whenever she wished. That certainly explained the monies sent regularly. Yet the money had never been discontinued. If it was my sister buried out there, the income would have become unnecessary, and the lodge sold. I knew my father well enough to know his dislike of spending. Unless he didn't know his daughter had died. If Aunt Gisela was as shrewd as her reputation, she could have remained quiet about the loss!

My breath quickened. I had a thread of something

here...I could feel it. If my sister died, Gisela could have concealed the fact by burying her on the grounds at Lorelei to avoid anyone's knowledge of the event. If her existence had remained a closely guarded secret, who would know? My father would never have shown an interest in her, nor would he have visited. So, what if Gisela had the girl buried? Would anyone have been privy to it? The Krauses! That would explain the large sums paid to them and their leaving the area.

I opened the drawer of the desk and retrieved the old photograph. I stared at the back of it and read the name. Astrid. I turned it over to look at her face, so like my own. And then I felt it, a strong surge of love that engulfed my entire body and mind. This was my twin, the other part of me. This was my sister—Astrid Rutherford, and no one would convince me otherwise.

Chapter Twenty-Four

HERR VOGEL WAS THE first to arrive at the lodge, and he was a sight for sore eyes indeed. He looked as he always did, completely dishevelled, and bestowed a broad smile upon me as he came into the drawing room. We exchanged pleasantries until the coffee was brought in. I offered him a touch of cognac in his, which he readily accepted.

"I have heard a great many things about you lately," he said, his little eyes peering through his round glasses.

"And they are probably true. Staying here has been an experience unlike any I've ever had, *Herr* Vogel."

"I am only glad you are recovered. Baron von Brandt was most helpful whenever I telephoned to ask after your welfare."

"You called Max?"

"*Ja.* On a couple of occasions. I was concerned for your safety but did not wish to intrude. I rested easier knowing he was looking out for you."

"Thank you."

"Now then. Why don't you bring me up to date on everything, and then I can share what I have learned about the mysterious Krauses."

It took two cups of coffee to relay all I that I had learned to the scholarly lawyer. He listened intently and did not interrupt.

The Secret of Lorelei Lodge

"...and that is why the Baron, Wolfgang and the *inspektor* will be here this evening. I wanted you here in your official capacity as my family's legal counsel."

"But a twin sister? You are sure of it?" He was dumbfounded.

"Yes. Though I have yet been unable to reconcile why my aunt was receiving money from another source. Remember that ledger I showed you?"

"I do, but I do not recall when the payments began."

"I can rectify that." I left the room for my study, returning a moment later with the small book. I flipped it open to the entry where the additional amount had been included.

"Eighteen ninety-three, only two years ago," I said.

"Which coincides with when the Krauses were sent away," he said, examining his notes.

"Yes. If my sister died in ninety-three, why would anyone give my aunt money after the fact?" I looked at the older man's face while he ruminated my question.

Then it struck me. "What if Gisela was blackmailing someone because of what happened to Astrid? Maybe that person had a role in her demise?" The mental jigsaw in my mind filled in another piece, and the thrill of anticipation gripped me. I could sense we were getting close to understanding what had happened. Soon I would know so much more about my past.

"*Herr* Vogel, if we can find the source of the money, we will finally be able to unearth the truth."

"That is my job," said *Inspektor* Schinkel, joining us. He came into the room and sat down with us while I made the introductions. It seemed the two men were already well acquainted due to their respective work, and a common love of ornithology. *Herr* Vogel informed me they belonged to the same bird-watching group in *Prinzenstadt*. He then told Schinkel all I had just covered.

"Did you find out anything about the man who attacked me?" I imagined him being hung up like a ham as the *inspektor* had said he would do earlier.

"Ah," he said. "Our prisoner is being very difficult. He will not speak a word, and we have made little progress. But he will talk eventually." He pulled a folded piece of paper out of his pocket and smoothed it out. "Here is a sketch of the man. I believe it is a close likeness." He turned it to us.

The man had a thick swatch of dark hair which drew to a low point in the middle of his forehead which we British commonly referred to as a *widow's peak*. He looked like a boxer who had been in one too many fights. His nose was crooked, and his face rough. He had close-set dark eyes and thick bushy brows.

"I recognise him as the man in my room," I said. "But I have never seen the fellow before."

The lawyer did not know him either.

"That is fine," said Schinkel. "We will show this to everyone in *Linnenbrink—Prinzenstadt* too. Someone is bound to recognise him. You don't forget that sort of face." He set the paper down on the coffee table.

There was a muffled sound of talking in the hallway, and after a moment, Fritz escorted the von Brandt brothers into the room. Max had a serious expression on his face, his eyes dark and brooding. Wolfgang looked pale, not his usual buoyant self.

"Ah, *Guten Abend meine Herren,*" Inspektor

Schinkel greeted them as he got to his feet. "Thank you so much for joining us this evening." He looked over to me. "Could I use your study to have a conversation with *Herr* von Brandt, *fräulein?*"

"Be my guest. You remember where it is?"

"*Ja. Dankeschön.*" The policeman gave a nod towards the door, and Wolfgang, with a last look at his older brother, turned and walked off, the bulky Schinkel following. Once the two men had left the room Max greeted my lawyer with familiarity.

"I did not expect to see you here this evening, Vogel. But I am glad you came."

"*Danke*, Baron. My deepest condolences upon the tragic loss of your wife."

Max nodded. But before he responded a man shouted something unintelligible from the next room, and then there came a low rumble of another tone, then more shouting. It was apparent the *inspektor* was grilling Wolfgang, and it was not being received well at all. Suddenly, a door slammed, pounding footsteps retreated down the hallway and the front door was flung open and closed with a bang.

The three of us exchanged glances, and then the drawing room door opened to admit the policeman. "Your brother has decided to forgo the interview."

"I'm sorry," said Max. "He's not been himself for a while."

"And that is precisely why I wished to talk to him. But there we are. It will have to wait." The *inspektor* settled his ample body on the far end of the sofa where I sat. "*Fräulein* Rutherford tasked *Herr* Vogel with some inquiries regarding the Krause couple, Gustav and Klara. There seems to be some confusion over them, the time they worked here and then Klara's reappearance and subsequent death. May I ask you, Baron? Were you familiar with the Krauses when they worked for Gisela Bergman?"

"No," Max said. I may have spent some time here as a child, but I was sent off to school quite young and then continued my education in America. I believe my younger brothers might know more. I am sorry."

"It is of no concern," said Schinkel. "The Krauses were employed here until being paid off and sent away. The husband, Gustav, died in a carriage accident, and for some reason Klara returned to *Linnenbrink,* perhaps in pursuit of her old job. But whatever her reason, Gisela was already dead, and somehow, with your brother's assistance, she ended up becoming your mother's nurse under a false name." He paused. "If I am repeating information you already know, please forgive me. It is easier for me to keep track if I say it from start to finish."

He cleared his throat before continuing. "We assumed Wolfgang was being compassionate by helping this widow, but why she used another name we do not know. Now it begins to get complicated. Inadvertently, your mother told *Fräulein* Rutherford about Klara's true identity, and suddenly the *fräulein* began receiving threats. I believe this has something to do with your brother."

"How dare you!" Max got to his feet, his eyes blazing with anger. "You draw many conclusions based on no evidence, *Inspektor*, and no facts."

"Please, Max," I said quietly. "It helps nothing losing your temper. All we are trying to do is discover the truth. I would rather you were a part of the process than not."

"I'm sorry." He sat back down, running his fingers through his thick dark hair. "It's a trying time for us all and my patience is dangerously thin."

"I understand," Schinkel said. "I have no desire to implicate anyone in your family, Baron. But the law must be obeyed by us all. May I continue?"

Max nodded. *Herr* Vogel had not said a word.

"*Fräulein* Rutherford has explained a theory to me, and *Herr* Vogel, which we believe most credible." He then asked my permission to speak to Max in German as it would be less difficult to explain that way. I told him to go ahead.

I understood every word as he regaled Max with the main points of my argument in the reality of my having a twin sister. He elaborated a few points but emphasised the parallel between my knowing about Klara, and it putting me in harm's way. He asked if there was anything about Wolfgang he should know. If his brother had spent much time here at the lodge in the past two years. That got my attention.

In my deliberations, it hadn't occurred to me that Wolfgang could have known my sister, for I'd been too focused on his knowledge of Klara. I held the impulse to say anything as I was not supposed to understand German, but my mind started racing.

The *inspektor* said he would be requesting official permission to examine Wolfgang's finances going back three years. This was not to pry, but to find something very specific regarding payments which might have been made to Klara. I watched Max solemnly nod in agreement and was consumed with pity for him. He was Atlas, with the weight of the world on his back.

It seemed a good time to pause and I announced there was food waiting in the dining room for everyone. I planned to spend that time thinking about what I'd just overheard.

Cook had set up a selection of sandwiches, pastries, and a tureen of soup warming on a small flame. I had not realised I was hungry, and before long was seated with the others when there came more commotion in the hallway. Fritz entered the dining room looking harassed.

"What is it, Fritz?"

"The baroness calls. I have taken her to the drawing room."

I thanked him, dabbed at my mouth with my serviette and got to my feet. "Allow me to go and speak with her," I told Max. "You stay and finish your meal." He gave me a sharp nod, and I left the men to their food.

In the drawing room, Lisbeth von Brandt stood at the window, wringing her hands.

"Ingrid," said Katja, who I had not yet seen. "I'm sorry for the intrusion, but the baroness is distraught this evening. She would insist I bring her here to you. She grew hysterical until I agreed."

"The baroness is always welcome," I said, approaching Lisbeth. Her dark eyes darted between me and the window. She was definitely wound as tight as a drum.

"Come," I said quietly. "Why don't you take a seat with me here on the sofa? Then we can talk, or perhaps ring for a nice glass of sherry?"

Lisbeth nodded and allowed me to take her arm and lead her to the seat. I rang the bell for Fritz, and he arrived with a tray of sherries at the same time the men joined us from the dining room.

"Mutti," said Max. "What brings you here?"

Lisbeth did not answer. Her eyes skittered between *Herr* Vogel and *Inspektor* Schinkel. "Who are these men?" she demanded.

"They are my friends," I said quickly before anyone else could answer. "And here is Max. We have been eating supper. Would you like something to eat, Baroness?"

She glanced down at the tray of sherry and then reached down and began to slide the tray over to one side.

"What is it?" I asked. "Do you want me to move the drinks out of your way?"

She ignored the question, and I realised she was trying to see the sketch *Inspektor* Schinkel had left lying on the table.

Lisbeth picked up the sheaf of paper and stared at it. "Marta," she said to me. "Why do you have this picture of Gustav in the drawing room? The man is a brute. I told you he should not be here, yet you have not taken my advice. I am disappointed in you. He is trouble, and I don't trust him with the women."

The room fell silent. I looked at Max's mother and then pointed to the picture. "Do you know him, Lisbeth?"

She turned and stared at me as though I were an idiot. "Of course, I do. Why Gisela kept him and his miserable wife here, I don't know." She looked over at Max. "Wolfgang brought her into the palace, and she made me drink so much medicine." Her eyes began to cloud over, and I shook my head at Schinkel. I did not want him to badger the woman.

Katja busied the baroness with her drink, while I moved away to the window, followed by Schinkel, Vogel and Max. We stood close together and spoke quietly.

"I thought you said Krause was dead?" Schinkel asked the lawyer.

"There was a death certificate filed, and a report of the accident."

I chimed in. "Then it was obviously falsified. Think what you will of the baroness's mental state, I have learned to know when she is clear-headed. She does not forget people's faces. If she says that man is Gustav, then it is."

"Her word will be questioned," said the policeman. "She would not be able to testify well."

"I am afraid the *inspektor* is correct," Vogel agreed.

"You jump to conclusions, gentlemen," Max broke in. "The Krauses left two years ago when my mother was not so…ill. Unless Klara communicated recently with her husband, Gustav would not be aware of Mother's mental state. Not unless you tell him."

"I follow your thoughts, Baron. Excellent suggestion."

But I trailed behind. "What are you saying?"

"We take my mother to the gaol. We let her see Gustav. He will know she recognises him. Then his ruse of being dead is exposed and it might scare him enough to start talking."

For the first time that day, a bud of hope bloomed.

Chapter Twenty-Five

HAVING MAX AS A house-guest was not so strange as seeing two hulking dogs lope about the place. Joan still squeaked when they came close, and that seemed only to entice them even more.

We ate a companionable breakfast together. The night before had been tiring, but so productive. Max was commissioned with taking his mother to the *Prinzenstadt* Gaol. He'd explained to her that she was a guest of honour, being the highest ranked person in the area. Everything hinged upon her being clear-minded. All we needed was for her to know who Gustav Krause was.

Herr Vogel was travelling to the Krauses last known address to make enquiries about them. He intended to discover proof of the falsification of a death certificate. With that, and Gustav's attempt to either abduct or hurt me, they could easily keep him behind bars. But we needed so much more. Gustav held the key to the past. He was the only person still alive who lived at the lodge when Astrid was there. I hoped to God we could learn something today.

Max was dressed in a pewter grey serge suit. His dark hair was brushed, but there was something different about him. He had no beard!

"You have shaved off your beard," I exclaimed, staring boldly at his face. If possible, the lack of facial hair on his chin rendered him even more handsome than he already was. He'd kept his moustache, but unlike most of the German men I had seen, he'd cropped it very short.

"It was not intentional." He buttered a slice of toast. "My valet is at the palace, and he usually helps with my grooming. My attempt did not go so well. I accidentally shaved off one part of it." He rubbed his freshly exposed skin with his fingers. "Though I think I prefer it this way."

"I do." The words slipped out before I could help it. His eyes met mine. What was it I read there? Yearning? Affection? Though my mind had been suffused with so much, there in the background I could always find Max.

"Blasted dogs!" The door flew open, and Joan came in, Frido and Sascha at her feet. "Baron von Brandt, your bloomin' pets won't leave me alone. I'm trippin' over them left an' right!"

Max dabbed his mouth with a serviette and got to his feet. "I'm sorry, Joan. It's because they like you and, I suspect, you've given them treats from the kitchen?"

She had the decency to grin.

"*Komm mit Frido, Sascha. Lass uns spazieren gehen.*" He called to the dogs to take them for a walk. They bounded towards him and with a great flurry of activity, they followed him out of the room.

"Blimey," said Joan once we were alone. "Don't he look handsome with that ugly beard gone?"

I WAS GLAD TO see Susanna when she arrived later that morning. I couldn't stop thinking about the baroness and her trip to the gaol, so it was wonderful to have a distraction.

"I would have come sooner after what happened to you," she blurted. "But Saul made me stay away so you could recuperate." Susanna came straight over to me and enfolded me in her arms. "You poor, poor thing, Ingrid. You must have been terrified!"

I pulled out of the embrace and gestured for her to take a seat. We both sat down, and she pulled off her lacy gloves. Susanna had brought the sunshine into the place, dressed in a bright canary yellow gown, complete with a jolly bonnet threaded with yellow flowers.

"It was certainly something I never wish to experience again," I said. "But luckily Joan was there to rescue me, and they now have the wicked fellow in custody."

Her blue eyes were huge with interest. "Do you think it's the same man who attacked you in the village?"

"It is likely. Hopefully there aren't two people who want to hurt me."

She shook her head. "I cannot believe all that's transpired since your coming. I shall feel far safer once we're back in a city."

"Do you still plan on leaving after the funeral?"

"Yes." She fiddled with the gloves on her lap, and I realised she was nervous. I had thought it the excitement of coming to talk about my close brush with harm, but now I wasn't so sure. There was something else going on, I could sense it.

"Is everything all right, Susanna?"

Her eyes darted from me to the window and back again. "Why yes, of course. Why would you ask?"

"You seem edgy and a little subdued. I'm used to you chatting away."

She waved one hand as though brushing my comment aside. "It's all this talk of murder and mayhem. I fear it has finally got to me. As I said to you the other day, we are not all warriors like you, Ingrid."

Perhaps I was being too sensitive, hardly surprising after recent events. But I was not convinced by her explanation. Susanna was hiding something, but what? Wolfgang's face popped into my mind, and I hoped the silly girl was not still engaged in their flirtation. But knowing Susanna, it was entirely possible, especially since her remaining time here was short and she'd soon be homeward bound.

I wondered what she'd feel about Wolfgang if I told her of his relationship with Valentina. Tempted to say something, I nevertheless did not. Instead, I turned the conversation to my own plans, and whether I should stay in Germany, or go back home.

Susanna smiled at this. "You will stay because of Max." She raised one brow. "He's not married now."

"That is in poor taste, Susanna," I snapped. "His wife has yet to be buried."

"I am sorry," she said petulantly. "I meant nothing bad by it. It was just an honest statement. It's obvious the two of you care for one another. He's no longer bound to another, so why shouldn't you pursue him?"

"I do care about Max. But that has little to do with reality. He has lost a spouse. Whether they were madly in love or strangers, Valentina was his legal wife and there is a protocol that belongs there. We both have our own paths to follow. If they meet one day in the future, then so be it. But for now, they do not."

"You know, Ingrid. For a warrior, when it comes to love, you are such a coward."

It was not said with malice, and I was not offended. For once, Susanna Koppelman was absolutely right.

SUSANNA STAYED FOR LUNCHEON and then took her leave. I hoped to see her before the funeral, but we made no specific plans. It was hard knowing what would happen from one day to the next, judging by the past week.

I watched out of the window for signs of a carriage. Max had been gone hours, and I was so anxious to hear what happened with the baroness. Would the sight of her elicit the response *Inspektor* Schinkel hoped for? So much hinged upon that. For someone needed to talk, and it was blatantly apparent that whatever Wolfgang knew, he was not about to share.

Another hour passed, until I finally heard the crunch of wheels coming down the driveway. I got to the front door before Fritz and threw it wide open, then ran into the afternoon sunlight. My heart sank a little when the bulky figure of the *inspektor* opened the cab door and stepped out. I had hoped to see Max, but regardless, someone was here with news.

I ushered the man into the house without asking anything. I did not want Dieter or Fritz to overhear. Schinkel followed me in, and I asked the butler to bring him a cold drink, for it was warm outside.

As soon as we entered the drawing room and shut the door I could wait no longer. "Well? Can you tell me how it went?"

Inspektor Schinkel inclined his head for permission to be seated.

"Yes," I said quickly, "of course. Make yourself comfortable."

The policeman took off his hat and leaned back in the chair. "Thank you, *fräulein*. I know you have been waiting for news, so I shall get right to it. The baroness was in fine form. She took one look at our prisoner, and calmy said, "Gustav, what have you gone and done now?" The man was dumbstruck, and then even more shocked when she asked if he had been beating his wife Klara again."

"What?"

"The man likes his drink and had been too free with his fists from time to time. This was not well known as Klara stayed within the confines of the lodge, never venturing far. But the baroness and your own mother had chastised him before."

I sat down, my heart wild with excitement. "So, what happens now?"

"I have interviewed Krause, and with the baroness identifying him and your lawyer looking at the fraudulent death certificate, he has admitted to being Gustav Krause and that he only returned to *Linnenbrink* to find his wife, Klara. It seems the man was run down by a carriage, and in a bad way for a short time, during which, his wife took their savings and left him."

"Goodness."

"My observation is he's a man easily brought to temper, so he followed her here to confront her about the money, but insists he had nothing to do with her death."

"What about him attacking me? What does he have to say about that?"

"He won't talk about it. We caught him red-handed—he can't deny it. But he is being clever and staying quiet."

I was disappointed to hear he was not admitting to my attack. "So, what happens next?"

"I want to look at Wolfgang's finances and see if there is anything there to tie him to Gustav and Klara Krause. Whatever they've been hiding, we have to force their hand and get one of them to speak the truth."

"And how do you plan to do that?"

"Ah," said the *inspektor*. "That would be telling."

THE NEXT MORNING WAS Sunday. It was nice having Max's company for breakfast. The dogs lay under the table, ever hopeful of scraps, and we chatted comfortably about the day ahead. Max had arrived back at the lodge in time for dinner the previous evening. He'd recounted the events with his mother at the gaol in far more detail than the *inspektor* had, and I was feeling more optimistic about finally understanding what had happened to my sister, Astrid.

I thought of her often. I carried her photograph in my pocket all the time and continually looked at her face. It was just like looking at my mother. But knowing she and I had been born together, had spent time together as infants, shared the love of our mother, kept Astrid in a special place in my heart. Regardless of the outcome, I would make sure she was no longer forgotten. Everyone would know Astrid had been part of this life and not just a hidden secret imprisoned at the lodge. I desperately wanted to find her. Part of me believed she was the body buried in the garden, but what if—

The sound of a horse whinnying cut into my

thoughts. Max got up abruptly and the dogs immediately began barking. Max went to the window. "It's Saul." He sounded puzzled. "What is he doing here?"

Moments later the sound of footsteps came rushing down the hall and Saul burst into the dining room. His hair was a mess, his clothes looked as though he had slept in them, and his face was ashen.

"Whatever has happened?" I felt a stir of fear.

"It's my sister," he said in an anguished voice, his bright blue eyes staring at Max. "She has run away with your damned brother!"

THEY LEFT TOGETHER FOR the palace to use the telephone and alert the police. Saul was beside himself. While Max had readied his horse, Saul blurted out the story of discovering Susanna's note not an hour earlier. As I watched the men gallop away, I remembered Susanna's behaviour when she'd called on me yesterday. How I wish I had followed my instincts!

I called for Metzger. I wanted to go and check on Katja. She would be devastated. With Gustav in the gaol, I felt less frightened about going out, but I still preferred to be safe inside the carriage than walking there alone.

THE PALACE WAS IN an uproar. Max must have commanded those who could be spared to look for Wolfgang, as there were several men on horseback who passed us coming down the drive. I rushed into the palace and did not encounter the house servants who usually attended visitors. I knew the way to Katja's apartments, and it was there I headed. But when I arrived at the wing of the palace she and Wolfgang shared with their son, there was no answer to my knock on the door. I took the liberty of opening it anyway. There was not a soul to be seen.

Undaunted, I decided to try Lisbeth. Perhaps Katja was there. I wondered if the baroness remained ignorant of what was happening. Magda answered my knock, her face taut, her eyes large with concern, and that told me my answer. I stepped inside the room and saw Lisbeth walking back and forth in front of her window. She was wringing her hands and muttering. I turned to the nurse and in German asked her to fetch us refreshment. Once the woman had gone, I continued speaking in German.

"Lisbeth?" I said softly, "Lisbeth, tis me." I slowly approached her, and she stopped in her tracks and stared at me. A frown spread across her forehead, and I saw with disappointment her eyes were misty and unclear.

"This is all your fault," she hissed, glaring at me and pointing a gnarled finger in my direction.

"What are you talking about?" I said as gently as I could. "Let us sit down and you can tell me."

"No." She was adamant. "You had to leave her here, didn't you? Even when I told you it was wrong! But you stopped listening to me when he showed up and smiled at you." Her eyes narrowed. "How could you?"

I struggled to understand the context of her words. Was she talking to me as Marta?

"Who showed up? Who are you talking about, Lisbeth?"

"Rutherford," she spat the name as though it left a

bad taste in her mouth. "Two beautiful girls, but one a little broken. And you left her behind. That was wrong!"

This time I was speechless to respond. I caught my breath and then walked to one of the armchairs and sat down. Now I understood. She was speaking of me and Astrid. Lisbeth was finally remembering!

"I am sorry," I said, hoping to encourage the conversation and calm her. 'You are right. It was wrong for me to leave my baby behind for someone else to care for."

"Care?" Lisbeth came to sit across from me, her eyes wide with confusion and fury. "Gisela Bergman was a conniving miserable woman. You left your angel with her and went far away."

"I was wrong, Lisbeth. I should have taken Astrid home with me and her sister. But I came back to see her often."

This pacified her somewhat. "You did. And those picnics in the garden." She levelled her gaze on me and a hint of clarity appeared. "When you died, there was no one to look out for her. I tried to see her, but Wolfgang stopped me, and Max was in America. And then I kept forgetting to go and see her. Gisela locked her up. Marta, I am so sorry." A tear rolled down the older woman's face and I steeled myself to not absorb what she was saying, for to do so would break my resolve and I would crumble. I had to find out more. I took a chance.

"Don't be sorry, Lisbeth. Astrid is at peace now."

"That poor child," she said softly. "And it was all my fault."

I glanced up quickly. What was this? "I don't

understand," I said quietly. "How could it have been your fault?"

The baroness wiped away the tear and sat a little straighter. "He is my son, and he took her for his own. She didn't know any better, and because of her innocence, she died for it."

I sat forward on my chair, not believing my ears. "Who took her, Lisbeth, please tell me!" I said in English.

"Wolfgang," came the voice from behind me. I turned to see Katja standing in the doorway.

Chapter Twenty-Six

"WHAT DID SHE MEAN?" I waited until Magda had returned, then ushered Katja from the room, asking her as soon as we were in the corridor.

Katja looked at me through swollen-eyes, red from crying. "I don't know the entire story, only that there was a girl at the lodge, I thought perhaps one of the servants. I suspected my husband was going over there and spending time with her. Wolfgang cannot resist a pretty face. But just like all the others, he eventually stopped seeing her, and then one day she was gone."

"How do you know that?" I said far more urgently than necessary.

"I overheard him speaking to the *krankenschwester* when she first came to the palace. He was not going to employ her until she threatened to tell me about his affair. Wolfgang told her the girl was gone, and that I would never believe a thing she told me. Then she laughed and said something about her being gone from this world, but still close by. She demanded the job, and extra money too."

"So, Klara Krause was blackmailing Wolfgang?"

"That is what the woman threatened. I know very little about what happened after that."

Poor Katja. How horribly she had suffered from her philandering husband's wandering eye. She had known about my sister, dear God, my sister! And what about Valentina? Had Katja been aware of the humiliation both she and Max were having inflicted upon them? Now Wolfgang had run off with Susanna.

"Katja, I am so sorry you have all this to cope with. If I can be of any help—"

"Please," she said softly. "I would prefer to be left to think things out for myself."

"Mama!" A young boy's voice echoed down the hallway.

"I must go," she said and turned away. But as an afterthought she stopped and looked at me. "Thank you for your kindness, Ingrid."

"I TELL YOU, THOSE were her exact words," I informed the *inspektor*, who had come to the lodge after luncheon. '*He is my son, and he took her for his own. She didn't know any better, and because of her innocence, she died for it.*' I think Astrid was kept here by my aunt because she had some type of disability my father would not countenance. That would explain the monthly financial support sent here."

"*Ja*, that makes sense."

"Mother would bring me with her in the beginning, which is why I have a few memories, though they are vague. My nightmares always feature me seeing myself. That would be Astrid looking at me. And it also explains Wolfgang's shock when he first met me at the palace. He thought he'd seen a ghost."

"You believe Wolfgang had a relationship with your sister?"

"I do. She would have been twenty-three when the Krauses left here. I think she died, and they were paid off to keep quiet and go away."

"An excellent theory, *Fräulein* Rutherford, but how do you think she died? The pathologist has found no evidence on the body to suggest any kind of trauma."

"Perhaps she had a poor heart? Consumption? He would not be able to tell an illness, would he?"

"*Nein*, he would not." He looked at me from across my desk. "Do you think Wolfgang killed her?"

"I certainly don't want to think that, but who else could it have been?"

"So here is the evidence we have, to prove Wolfgang's connection with the Krauses," Schinkel stated. "First, we have his mother's word. By tomorrow, I will have results from the bank regarding some of his recent transactions. If Wolfgang was paying Klara or your aunt, then it proves he was being blackmailed. This all ties in with my progress concerning *Herr* Krause."

I sat forward. "What has happened?" I said, unable to constrain the excitement in my voice.

"Gustav has finally admitted to being the person who attacked you in the village, as well as climbing into your room that night. He insists he was not going to hurt you but abduct you on the instruction of his benefactor."

"Who was that?" My heart skipped a beat.

"Wolfgang."

I gasped and sat back in my chair. "But why? I had done nothing."

"We can surmise several theories. For a start, you had his mother's ear, and he could not control what she said to you. That meant you could identify Klara, the same person who blackmailed him. You were becoming a nuisance."

I nodded. "That also explains why he tried to discourage me from the work in the hidden garden." I quickly recounted the conversation we'd had a while ago, when Wolfgang said the fountain was a bad idea. "He told me the plumbing work would be problematic."

"As it would be with a body in the way," said the *inspektor* dryly. "Now the hunt continues. As we know, Wolfgang has reasons he doesn't want to be found."

"Do you think Susanna is in any danger?"

"I doubt it. Wolfgang is a narcissist. He will treat her well enough because she idolizes him." He got to his feet. "With that, I must go to the palace and see if there is any news at all." He bade me a good day and left me alone with my thoughts.

MAX ARRIVED AS IT was getting dark, the dogs close at his heels. When they came into the lodge, the massive hounds made straight for the kitchen where Joan would have a treat for them both.

Max joined me in the drawing room for a drink before dinner. He looked worn out.

"Are you sure you wouldn't be more comfortable at the palace? We are safe now Gustav is locked up, and I feel terrible keeping you away from your home and your privacy." I passed him a glass of brandy.

"To be truthful, Ingrid, I prefer being away from there—at least for the time being. Magda cares well for my mother, and Katja needs time to focus on Jackob with Wolfgang gone. The staff are probably gossiping constantly, and I would not get any rest. I'd rather be here with you." He took a sip of his drink, but his eyes, almost the colour of the brandy in his glass, were fastened acutely upon me.

I held his stare for a few seconds, and then purposefully moved away and sat down. "Have you spoken to *Inspecktor* Schinkel this evening?" I asked.

He joined me and gave a sigh as he leaned back against the cushioned sofa. "I have had that pleasure." He took another sip of brandy. "My world seems to have gone mad in this past month. My wife has died, an employee murdered and now it seems my brother is a wanted felon, who has absconded with my business partner's sister."

I grinned. "It does sound rather awful when you say it like that. If it makes you feel any better, my world has been a little mad too. My father died, I discovered not only a dead aunt I never knew existed, but Lorelei Lodge, and potentially a twin I didn't know who might have been buried in the garden. Oh, and two threatening notes, a bash on the head and I was almost kidnapped, and all down to your brother."

As ridiculous as it seemed, we both burst out laughing. Max shook his head. "We must be hysterical, Ingrid. Because none of this is a laughing matter."

"You are right. But sometimes you have to laugh at tragedy, else we would drown in our sorrows."

He regarded me once again, his stare always so intense. "How are you holding up? It has been a rotten time for you. The discovery of Astrid must have made a significant impact on you."

I raised a brow and considered his question. "There is some sort of a balance, I think. The nightmare which plagued me has faded away. The strange sense of isolation and loneliness, which I have had ever since I can remember, somehow makes sense. The feeling of loss is strong, for I want to know Astrid, to share my life with her. Yet finding out Astrid was alive, that she existed, also validates her, when others would keep her hidden away.

It's complicated and I am conflicted. But my resolve is to find out the truth about her life and likely death, and then share Astrid's existence with the world." Tears stung my eyes and I quickly dashed them away.

Max looked at me with approval. "Have you always been so sensible and thoughtful? I think you such a capable person, Ingrid. Your mother would be very proud." Our eyes met and held again, and I marvelled at this tenuous bond holding us by a tiny thread. Would it withstand all there was to come? For the reality was, I had lost a sister, and it was likely at the hands of the brother of the man sitting across from me. It did not bode well, not at all.

There was a loud crash in the hallway, followed by barking, and Joan's exclamation. "Bloody, dogs! Now look what you've made me do."

It broke the tension, and we both got up to go and see what damage had been done.

THE NEXT MORNING MAX was gone before breakfast. The following day would be Valentina's funeral, and there was much for him to attend to. The service would be held in *Prinzenstadt*, where due to her popularity, a number of people were expected to attend, especially from her peers in the operatic societies. There would also be journalists from many national newspapers. I had my own plans for the morning. I had decided to explore the attic.

Since the discovery of my having a twin, it had crossed my mind to explore that part of the house. But up until now I had not found the time. Today would be the perfect opportunity. It had started raining, and Joan was out, gone with Metzger into the village for provisions.

Dieter had already pulled down the steps for me and left two lamps burning, for which I was grateful. It was obvious by the dust and cobwebs present that the place had been untouched for a while. I hoped there were no rats or mice hiding in any of the corners.

The space wasn't as big as I expected, and I wrinkled my nose at the tangy scent of musty neglect and forgotten memories. There were a variety of objects strewn about. Several trunks, which at first glance looked full of old clothing and books, a tailor's dummy, a large, cracked mirror, and several boxes of papers. I was disappointed. I felt sure there would be stacks of items to dig into, some remembrances of my mother or my heritage. I half-heartedly examined each trunk, but they offered no treasures or hints of the past.

I had all but given up, when the light of my lamp caught something bulky, draped in a sheet over in one corner. I suspected it would be a small piece of furniture, but it drew my interest. Setting my lamp on the ground, I pulled away the sheet and my breath caught in my throat.

Untainted by the hand of age, it was a beautifully crafted doll's house. My doll's house. Astrid's doll's house. I reached out a hand and my fingertips traced the outline of the sloping roof. It stood as tall as my waist, and I squatted down low to see better. A rush of memories assaulted my mind, and with them, visions of another, just like me, a smile on her face as we played with the tiny figures inside this very house.

It was a miniature of Lorelei Lodge. Down to each detail as far as the layout of the rooms and the colours used. I peered inside the windows to see the beautiful ballroom, and there was the study, the drawing room and the kitchen. My eyes travelled up to where the bedrooms were situated, and it was here that I finally felt it, the bitter blow of grief. For there in the front bedroom, in a tiny room all in shades of pink, were two small beds set close together. And as I stared at the miniature furniture, I suddenly remembered it all. My legs weakened, my throat thickened with raw pain, and I sat down on the dusty floorboards and, finally, I wept.

I cried for my sister. I cried for the girl I found in the quiet recess of my memories. I could see that face once again, my face, yet one with dark, haunted eyes. As the tears fell down my cheeks, scenes played out before me. Jumping on our beds, running up and down the hallway, holding hands across the small gap between our beds. But there was something else too. It was the silence. For even in these memories there was no sound. And as my chest heaved under the flow of my sorrow, I understood why.

My sister, Astrid, had been perfect. But she had not had the ability to hear nor speak. There had been something else wrong with her too. A propensity to mature. And that had been an abominable flaw in the eyes of Charles Rutherford. He thought her a freak of nature.

Fragments of thoughts filtered through my mind. Snippets of conversation, more tones than words as my brain dug deeper to retrieve shards of the past for me to piece together in a haphazard puzzle. My parents had fought bitterly about Astrid, that was coming back to me. All because she was deaf and dumb, an imperfection Father would never tolerate.

I wiped my eyes. Thoughts flooded my head, and I began feeling overwhelmed, as though the attic was shrinking to the size of this doll's house and the air getting thin. I started to get up off the floor, but as I did, I noticed a small box, large enough for a pair of shoes, and not much else, that was pressed up against the doll house at the very back. It must have got caught under the sheet somehow. I scooted it closer, so it was near the light.

It was a box made from cedar, I could smell its fragrance, even amid the dust. It did not weigh much, and I picked it up to take with me. I badly wanted fresh air and good light.

I went back to the stairwell of the attic and navigated my way down, carrying the little box like it was full of eggs and I daren't drop it. When I got to the study, I rang for Fritz and asked him to have Dieter retrieve the gas lamps I had left in the attic and close it back up.

I took the cedar box to my desk, and with my handkerchief, rubbed away a thin film of dust from the lid. Then I opened it up as my tears came once again. On top of a small pile of papers was a child's drawing of two girls. I knew at once I had drawn it. At the bottom, in childish and misspelled scrawl, I had written both our names, Ingrid and Astrid and drawn a tiny heart. I placed it on the desk and went to the next item.

It was an assortment of notes and drawings, none which I recognised, other than the first. But as I got closer to the bottom, the penmanship grew better, as I imagined Astrid's command of writing improved. And then I saw the last piece was actually a sheet of paper folded up. I gasped. My heart pounded as I carefully unfolded it.

And there it was in black and white. The missing page from the big black book of my family's past. The record of my birth, and more importantly, Astrid's. But there was something else there too. I frowned. What could it be? I looked closer and a sob of anguish burst from my lips.

For underneath the record of our births was one more entry. It was just a name. But one that suddenly explained absolutely everything.

Chapter Twenty-Seven

BY THE TIME MAX arrived at the lodge after I sent for him, I was so wound up I felt like a stick of dynamite that could explode at any moment. Energy coursed through my veins and the culmination of so many days, weeks, even years of hidden memories, crashed into the front of my mind like a tidal wave of forgotten history. I was bursting with the need to tell him, share this phenomenal news and this flicker of hope which had suddenly lit up such a sad, dark past.

He arrived looking harried. I had a moment of guilt when I remembered he was burying his wife the very next day, but I shrugged it aside. After greeting him, I asked him to sit and quickly poured us both a brandy. He arched a dark brow but did not question me. He could tell I had much to say.

"Before I begin, how are you coping?" I asked.

"Besides the fact my brother is still missing and creating an absolute scandal for my family, I am well. The funeral preparations are in hand, and I have family arriving as we speak. Everything is set for tomorrow afternoon. I am more concerned about you, Ingrid? Your note was not very specific."

I took a sip of my drink and then set it down. "That is because it is too much to put on paper. I wanted to tell you myself." I began with my trip up into the attic that day. My disappointment in finding very little of interest, and then my discovery of the doll's house. I omitted my emotional reaction to finding it, though at the telling my voice cracked several times and I had to take another drink of my brandy. Then I told him about all the things I remembered. He sat back in the chair, and I watched as incredulity spread across his face.

"Astrid was mute?" he said quietly. "My God."

"Deaf and dumb, and she had other problems and was younger than her years, but she was not stupid. She was every part a healthy person, just not in the eyes of my father. That is why she was left here and hidden from the world."

"Your father was a brute," Max said with disgust. "I am sorry to insult your family, but that is horrific."

"Yes. And don't apologise, there was no love lost between us. Though now it makes even more sense to me. I was a constant reminder of Astrid, and she was his failure."

"But your mother? Marta was a compassionate woman. How could she leave her own daughter?"

"I don't know. How I wish I could ask her. Obviously it explains her frequent trips here, the money that was sent for Astrid's upkeep and why Aunt Gisela was allowed to live here. Perhaps she chose to leave her here rather than have her in a sanatorium?"

"Lack of speech and hearing does not constitute placing anyone in a barbaric institution. Astrid could have functioned normally once she learned a form of communication. Sign language has been around for a century."

I sighed. "I know, Max. I don't understand how any parent could inflict that type of isolation. But it answers many questions, does it not?"

"Indeed." His warm brown eyes assessed me. "I am sorry. This has been very upsetting for you I know. You and I seem to have had a time of it these past weeks."

"We have. And you have suffered far more than I. But that is not all the news I have."

He sat a little straighter. "There is more?"

I smiled. "I have saved the best for last, Max."

"Well don't keep me in suspense," he said. "Tell me!"

"Remember the day you rescued me when I fell from the chair trying to get those large books?"

"I certainly do."

"When I went through the family records in the books, the very last page of entries was missing, the one recording my birth."

"I don't believe you told me that."

"It probably slipped my mind with everything else I had to think about. Anyway, today I found it, Max. That very page! I can't imagine why she would have torn it out, yet Astrid must have done it, and then hidden the page with some other notes in a small box that I found tucked next to the doll house."

"Did you see your birth recorded on there?"

I pulled out the folded paper from my pocket and handed it to him. Max scanned the page, and then looked up at me with the same shocked expression I must have had when reading the words for the first time myself.

"Can you see both of our births are recorded? That is my father's hand, I would know it anywhere and it finally corroborates my sister's existence. But that last line at the bottom, it is in another's hand, and I believe

Astrid wrote that. Now I can prove Astrid was born. And that before she died, she gave birth to a son. Oskar Bergman von Brandt."

Our eyes met. His trying to contemplate the insinuation of what he had just read. Mine, acknowledging that Astrid's words were true. Max emptied his glass then got up and poured himself another. I watched as he downed it in one gulp before coming to sit back down.

"Are you all right?" I was concerned.

"*Ja*. It is just the realisation that my brother's depravity has exceeded the depths of what I already knew about him. I am appalled that he has sunk even lower in my estimations."

I was immediately defensive. "You mean that he impregnated a disabled woman?"

"God no!" His eyes blazed with sudden anger. "I would never think that! I am just disgusted that he had the arrogance and conceit to consider all women his concubines. He's collected them like the hunter who hangs his trophies on the wall. That Wolfgang could selfishly destroy the lives and happiness of so many…it sickens me to the core." He looked at me and I saw the pain in his expression. "I am so very sorry, Ingrid. I promise I will get the answers out of my brother, if it is the last thing I do." With that, he abruptly got to his feet, and without another word, walked off.

JOAN WAS STILL SLEEPING in my room. It was an odd arrangement, but it suited us both—at least for the time being. Though the threat to my safety was locked away in a gaol, the fact we were strangers in a foreign land gave strength to our unity.

I waited until we were settled in our respective beds. "Joan. I have something to tell you. I want you to listen to what I have to say, and then we can talk about it when I am finished." Joan had a propensity to interrupt at the best of times. I wanted to get this story out in one go.

"Oh, all right," she agreed reluctantly. "But I hope it isn't long, 'cos I'm right knackered."

I told her the story of Astrid. About my memories of her as far back as I could reach. What little I recalled of my parents' dispute over her coming to live in London with the family. How the poor girl had been brought up here in Germany. That she'd been locked away because she was a deaf mute and not able to learn as quickly as others without receiving the help she required to communicate. I told Joan that Wolfgang had been involved with her. And though we knew few details, at some point Astrid had borne a child. It seemed likely it was her body buried in the garden, though there was no sign of a baby buried there too. I explained that Max was trying to help resolve all the unanswered questions so we could finally lay my poor sister to rest.

When I finished, Joan didn't speak for a moment, though I heard her sniff more than a few times. It was a sad and moving story, there was no doubt.

"That poor little mite," she finally said softly. "An' when do you think this all happened, miss?"

"We think sometime in the past three years, maybe sooner."

"So that poor lass would've been twenty years old, give or take?"

"Yes, the same as me."

"That's terrible. I can't believe your mum would have left her here. But I s'ppose she had her reasons."

"Yes. My father was likely the main one. Anyway, I wanted you to know. That's why there have been so many visitors here over the past two days. Astrid was kept a secret, and the police believe it all ties in with what happened to me. I have already sent a note to the *inspektor* to update him."

"Well, I'm blowed," Joan said. "An' I thought coming to Germany was going to be dull. Who would have thought it would turn out like somethin' you'd read in one of them Penny Dreadfuls? But I am right sorry for you, miss. It's rotten that you don't have your sister here."

"But I've got you, Joan," I said quietly. "And thank goodness for that."

IT WAS TUESDAY, THE day of the funeral. Traffic into *Prinzenstadt* was diabolical as the funeral was so well attended. By the time I arrived, I only got a seat because Saul had saved one for me a few rows from the front pew.

Saul looked dreadful. His skin pallid, his eyes haunted. Even his bright golden hair was dull as dishwater.

"Has there been any news?" I whispered once I sat down beside him.

"No, not one word nor sighting."

"I am so sorry, Saul. I can't believe Susanna is putting you through this. All I can say to reassure you is I am sure she is not being harmed."

"Yes, that is something, I suppose. But if word of this gets to America, my sister will be ruined." He stopped as the booming sound of organ pipes filled every molecule of the church. We all stood as the funeral procession slowly made their way up the aisle.

There were six pallbearers. Max was in the front, and behind him were two men bearing a distinctive likeness to him. Of course, it would be his younger brothers. I had not even considered their attending. The coffin was completely covered in crimson roses, and as they passed by, I felt my grief well in sorrow for the loss of a life so young and a talent stolen.

Behind the coffin came Lisbeth with Katja, and then others who I assumed were relatives of the family as the music rose to a crescendo and then fell silent.

"Let us pray," the Bishop of *Prinzenstadt* commanded.

IT WAS A RELIEF to be back outside in the sunshine once again. Saul remained with me and together we took my carriage back to the *Safranpalast* to pay our respects to the family. We discussed the talk of a special operatic performance to be given in Valentina's memory in the next few weeks, and that being a wonderful tribute.

Arriving at the palace, we took our place in the long queue of carriages taking turns dropping their respective cargo at the front door.

Saul and I followed the other mourners down the familiar hallway. We were led through the palace and out the back of the building. Here, a massive courtyard spilled onto the lawn, where canvas awnings had been erected. Judging by the hordes of people here, catering to them all outdoors was a good idea.

"Come, Ingrid," Saul said, taking my hand to thread over his forearm. "Keep hold of me so that I don't lose you in the melee. There must be more than two hundred people here."

"It would not surprise me," I agreed. "I am sure many have come from Berlin and other cities. Valentina was much beloved."

Saul moved in the direction of the largest tent, where the von Brandts congregated. He had already told me he wanted to give his condolences and leave quickly. I felt the same way, so our mission was of mutual benefit.

By the time our turn came to greet the family, we had been waiting more than thirty minutes. I spoke with Katja first, who introduced me to the other von Brandts, Günther and Kurt. Günther favoured Wolfgang so much, he might have been his twin, but where the former was arrogant, this brother was studious, awkward and polite. Kurt was the image of Max, but with blond curly hair.

"I have heard much about you," he said in flawless English. "And I only wish we could have met under different circumstances."

"Yes, I agree. But I know your brother will feel the benefit in having you both here on such a sad occasion. It has been much for him to cope with, I fear." There was little to add as so many waited behind me, so I moved on to greet Max.

His face was solemn. Regardless of his relationship with Valentina, I knew he was devastated by her death. The ceremony must also bring back memories of his son, Nikolai. I empathised greatly with him.

"How are you bearing up?" I said, after shaking his hand and resisting the impulse not to let go.

"Better now my brothers are here." I saw his eyes

flicker to Saul who was next in line. "I will be busy the rest of today, but I should like to call on you in the morning if I may?"

"Of course," I answered and then moved on so that he could speak with Saul. The two men greeted each other and then spoke quietly for a moment.

At length, Saul and I were able to extricate ourselves, and Metzger took us back to the lodge. I invited Saul to stay on for lunch, which he accepted, and then afterwards, suggested we go out for a walk as the weather was so fine.

"I have yet to see the walled garden I have heard you speak of," he said. "Can you show it to me?"

"Yes. I think the *inspektor* is allowing us back in there now the area has been excavated." We left the lodge and headed down the path. "In some ways I worry the garden will feel morbid after what has happened. But I think my sister loved the garden, so I want to believe she was at peace here."

Saul knew some of what had happened in the past few days, but I did not elaborate nor share any details about Wolfgang's relationship with my sister. If he knew that, he would be terrified for Susanna.

The door was wide open to the garden and as we went in, I noticed everything was ready, all except the fountain. The piece had not been made yet, but the plumbing was installed, and all the turf re-laid where the ground had been dug over.

"This is lovely," Saul muttered as we walked towards the courtyard. I explained the meaning behind having so many Cornflower beds there, and I showed him my pendant so he would understand the significance of the flower, which he did. Then we strolled over to the Willow tree, and I explained that we had all played here as children, yet I had forgotten it until coming back here.

"*Fräulein* Rutherford, *Herr* Koppelman!" We turned at the sound of our names to see Dieter waving frantically at us back at the gate.

Saul and I hastened back the way we had come. Dieter met us halfway. His face was red, and he panted as though he had run a mile.

"What is amiss?" I asked.

"There is a message," he said breathlessly, staring directly at Saul. "It has come from the hotel. Your sister has returned!"

I told Saul to run on ahead and either take one of the horses or have Metzger drive him. I asked him to let me know the outcome as soon as he possibly could. But I was uptight and anxious. So, I went back and sat in the garden, too wound up to go inside. I felt safe now Gustav was in the gaol, and I had missed my time out here alone. I'd stay for a while until my mind settled.

What had happened with Susanna? I wondered, relieved she was found. I only hoped she was not hurt in any way. I'd know soon enough. Right now, I needed to think about myself, consider what I should do next with my life. But I did not get very far, for Dieter reappeared a few minutes later to announce *Inspektor* Schinkel awaited me at the lodge. I hurried back, certain it would be about Susanna, and hoped at the same time it would not be bad news.

He waited in my study, where Fritz had already brought him a cold drink. I motioned for him to remain seated as I came into the room. I took my usual place behind the desk.

"We heard Susanna was found. What has happened?" I gasped.

He held out a meaty hand to calm me. "*Fräulein* Koppelman is, as we speak, with her brother. It is not she who brings me here."

Thank goodness she was all right. "Then what is it, *Inspektor*?"

"Two things. First, thank you for your note regarding the discovery in the attic. It is partly that which brings me here. This morning, we had the opportunity to examine records of Wolfgang von Brandt's expenditures. The family has a trust, and all monies are withdrawn through their accountant."

"I see."

He pulled out his notebook and flipped to a page. "According to records here, beginning in January Eighteen-eighty-three, a sum of money was paid each month into the account of your aunt, Gisela Bergman, just as you saw in her ledger, *fräulein,* until the month of her death. We suspect that both of the Krauses were also paid by Wolfgang, but it is likely he did this with cash as the amounts would be far less."

"Then it substantiates Wolfgang was complicit in some act. Why else would he pay money to my aunt? If my sister was a secret, it would be the other way around. She would pay him for his silence."

"I agree. That would be the case, if she had still been alive."

"You think he killed her?" As much as I now loathed the man, I struggled to see him as a murderer.

"I do not," he said quickly. "But I am not yet finished. There is another regular transaction we saw in Wolfgang's records which began in August of

Eighteen-ninety-three. I might add, they only stood out to me because of your discovery yesterday."

My pulse picked up—I knew what he was going to say. Please God I was right!

"I believe your sister was delivered of a son she named Oskar Bergman-von Brandt. He was taken to a Catholic orphanage in *Aachen,* where his father, Wolfgang, has been sending a monthly donation for his upkeep."

I held my hand to my mouth to stop the cry which threatened to spill from my lips, but tears sprang into my eyes and ran down my face. I tried to compose myself, but I could not. "Please, *Inspektor*," I said between trying to gasp air. "Tell me…"

"I have a man on his way there as we speak. We will know something by the morning." Then the big bear of a man did something which shocked me. He reached across the desk and took my shaking hands in his large paws and gave them a little squeeze.

"You have been a very brave woman, *Fräulein* Rutherford. You are a credit to your family. Just hold on a little while longer." And then he smiled.

Chapter Twenty-Eight

I DID NOT SLEEP a wink that night. I tossed and turned, and finally went down to the study just after three o'clock in the morning. My mind was all over the place, my emotions too. One moment I would be in tears, crying for the sister I never got to mourn and then becoming hopeful that it was not too late to rescue her darling boy.

At dawn, I could stand it no longer. Desperate for fresh air, I went outside clad in my night attire and slippers. My body felt so wound up that even my skin made me feel trapped. I paced back and forth along the wide balcony of the second floor which overlooked the front of the house. I watched the sun slowly climb through the sky and felt my heart rise with it in desperate hope.

It was the dogs I saw first. Dark spots moving quickly through the trees, visible when they ventured out of the densest parts. I knew he would be close behind them. I raced down the stairs to the driveway in their general direction. I knew they would catch my scent and then bring Max to me.

It did not take long. For as I reached the perimeter of the trees, they came bounding towards me. I reached down to greet them both.

"Ingrid! What are you doing out here all alone?' Max rushed towards me; concern etched across his face.

"Nothing is wrong," I said quickly to abate his fears. "I have been awake all night, and I had to get some air. I saw the dogs and wanted to see you."

He stared at me, suddenly noticing my state of undress. My nightgown was cotton, but it hid very little. Hastily, he shrugged off his jacket and helped me put it on. It was much too large, but it did offer some decorum of modesty.

"Come, let us walk back to the lodge," he said.

"No. Can we go to the garden instead? I should like to be there with you for a moment."

He frowned, but nodded, and we set off in that direction, the dogs following in their meandering fashion.

"Did you hear they found Susanna?"

"Yes, but I know little other than that. I have a meeting later today with *Inspektor* Shinkel." He made no mention of Wolfgang, so neither did I.

As we walked, I glanced at his profile. I liked Max with his clean-shaven chin. "How are you feeling after yesterday? I thought the service was beautifully done, and a wonderful tribute to Valentina."

"To be honest with you I am relieved to have it behind me. It at least offers some closure to the entire ordeal, at least for my family. Perhaps we'll resume some normalcy in our lives again."

We reached the garden and walked inside. I headed straight for the little cast iron bench and sat down while the dogs investigated all the scents hidden in the grass and the bushes.

"The authorities are looking for Oskar, our nephew," I said softly. "He was placed in an orphanage in Aachen. Schinkel has sent a policeman to see if he is still there, and if he is all right."

"How did they find him?"

I knew Max would not know the progress because his day had been taken up with the funeral. "Wolfgang's finances. He'd been paying my aunt for a long time, and then for the baby's keep for the past year or more. We should know something later this morning."

Max bent his elbows on his knees, leaned forward and buried his head in his hands. He stayed that way for so long, that I automatically put my arm around him, feeling the bulk of his shoulders through the linen of his shirt. I gently rubbed the base of his neck. His muscles were as rigid as iron.

Slowly, he lifted his head and my hand fell away. He reached for it and took it in his palms, the warmth of his skin pleasant against mine.

"I have run out of words to say about my brother. I hesitate to give him that title for I am so ashamed to even know him, never mind share his blood and his name." He turned to look at me, his eyes almost black with emotion. "Ingrid, I am so very sorry for all the harm he brought to your family. I would do anything to change what happened, absolutely anything."

He pulled my hands to his mouth, and I felt the brush of his lips across my knuckles. His body moved closer to mine and, still holding my hands in his, Max pulled me closer until I could see a small cluster of freckles on the bridge of his nose.

"For just a moment, can we forget everything, Ingrid? Forget Wolfgang, Valentina, our families and all the horrible secrets? For this tiny moment, can we pretend that all there is in the world is you and me?"

I nodded.

He leaned into me, released my hands and took my face between his fingers. Then slowly, deliberately, he pressed his mouth against mine.

My lips parted and his tongue found mine, filling me with the warm taste of brandy and something new and exciting that reached into my senses and ignited them. My arms crept up to embrace him and I wrapped them around his shoulders as though if I let go I should fall a thousand feet. His arms moved to my waist and effortlessly pulled me from the bench onto his lap where my body sat sideways across him, curled into his as though we two were moulded together as one.

I heard the groan leave his throat as the kiss deepened. My fingers strayed up his neck and tangled themselves in his thick hair. Then I pulled away and leaned my head back while his mouth ravaged my skin, my neck, the hollow at the base of my throat. His hands travelled down my arms, around my waist, and up to graze against my breasts.

Suddenly he pulled back. He gently placed me back onto the bench and got to his feet. I did not move, but we stared at one another, panting like rabid dogs. He caught his breath.

"Ingrid. I must take you back to the lodge before I cannot stop myself. I think you know how much I want you, have always wanted you. But it has to be right between us. There can be no concerns, no doubts, no regrets. So, hear this now. When the time is right, when you are ready. I shall come for you, Ingrid. I shall come for you and make you mine."

I opened my mouth to respond, but there was

nothing left to say. I got to my feet, still looking at him. Then, summoning all the courage I could muster, I took a step closer.

"Don't wait too long," I said, and then walked away, leaving him where he stood.

OSKAR IS SAFE! THOSE words arrived on a telegram at eleven-twenty-five that morning. Joan brought me the missive and I read it aloud. We both cried out in delight. I immediately set about writing a note to *Herr* Vogel, I wanted to get the legalities in motion as quickly as possible.

He arrived by mid-afternoon, with drafts of documents which would begin the proceedings so that I could claim Oskar as my nephew and ward immediately.

"What about the von Brandts? Do you not think they will try for the boy also?" he asked.

"I'm not sure," I answered as honestly as I could. "There is that possibility, but based upon Wolfgang's disappearance, and his mysterious role in what might have befallen my sister, I believe my claim would be stronger. I shall have to cross that bridge when I come to it."

The lawyer packed up the papers and placed them in his briefcase. "*Fräulein* Rutherford, it is hard to believe that you have been in this country for less than two months and have uncovered the past quite brilliantly."

"I cannot take all that credit," I said. "The baroness deserves most of it, for were it not for her, I might never have learned of my sister."

"I disagree," he said with a smile. "That mind of

yours is like a dog with a bone. Once you get your teeth into it…"

He bade me a fond farewell and went on his way.

THE REST OF THE day passed painfully slowly. I received a note from Saul, asking if he and Susanna could call on me the next day. I sent a reply and asked them to wait until the day after that, as I had business to attend to. Susanna and her reputation were the last thing on my mind.

Surprisingly I slept well that night, doubtless because I had been deprived of rest, but I believe my mind, though excited, was finding peace. There were still many unanswered questions, those only Wolfgang and Gustav Krause could answer. But for now, the important thing was finding little Oskar and keeping him safe.

I WAS THINKING ABOUT asking Fritz for some coffee when I heard the carriage wheels on the driveway. I was out of the front door before it came to a halt. I knew Joan was right behind me, eager as a puppy to meet our little fellow, but I wanted to see him first.

The carriage door swung open, and the big frame of *Inspektor* Schinkel squeezed through the small doorway and onto the gravel. He gave me a wink and then turned back to the cab and gestured with his hands for the occupant to come to him.

I held my breath. And then the policeman turned, holding a small boy in his arms. I moved towards him, willing my feet not to run, for I did not want to scare Oskar, he was still so very young. When I reached him we stared at one another.

His hair was as black as my own. His eyes, the colour of the sky, inherited from my father. He reached out a little fat finger and touched the mole at the corner of my mouth, then pulled his finger back to touch the one at the corner of his own. He smiled, showing tiny white teeth.

"*Punkt*," he said.

"*Ja, liebling. Meins ist genau wie deins.*" He had told me I had a dot, and I had replied that mine was just like his.

Like his, like his mother's, like his grandmother's. There was no denying to whom this child belonged. I held out my arms and he willingly reached back.

Epilogue

IT WAS A TRADE-off. I had exchanged one male for another. Six months ago, I'd spent my time and all my thoughts with a handsome German, with dark eyes and a moody soul. Now my days were filled with grubby, sticky little boy's fingers, and walks to the park to watch the ponies.

There had been many restless nights. Evenings when Oskar wouldn't climb out of my lap, when his small, chubby arms reached around my neck and held me close. And I wouldn't have had it any other way.

Every time I looked at his lovely face, I saw Astrid, and myself as well. I watched him constantly, never letting him far from my sight. He was so precious to me. He was all the family I had. I was grateful to Max for not pressing a claim on the boy when he had every right to. For did not the man always outrank the woman in the eyes of the law?

Max's disgust with his brother tainted so much, yet I had seen his eyes soften when he'd first met Oskar at Lorelei Lodge. And in light of the loss of his own son, Max could have made it difficult for me to place my claim on the boy. But he had not.

I'd maintained communications with Katja since leaving Germany. Who would have thought I'd find such an unlikely friendship in her? It was in one of her letters that she admitted being the person who had left flowers in the garden underneath the tree. She explained she'd had only suspicions, and that her mind was confused with what was going on between her and Wolfgang. That her intentions had never been to hurt me.

I assured her there was no harm done. In essence, her silent protest against a wicked man had only helped resolve the fate of my sister. I encouraged Katja to leave the past behind, and I thanked her for becoming a dear friend. It was enough. Hadn't we all had our fill of sorrow?

The other person I wrote to was Saul Koppelman. He had finally managed to get Susanna back under the watchful eyes of her parents. Though my relationship with her would at best be tenuous because of her antics with Wolfgang, I would always maintain some affection for the silly, willful girl. For it had been Susanna who helped us finally determine what had happened to my sister two years before.

Susanna had been madly in love with Wolfgang, and too naïve to realise his request for her to run away with him was nothing more than a means to an end. He faced imminent legal reprisals, and was too much of a coward to live without having a woman under his control. Their plan was to go somewhere where they could assume new identities.

Caught up in the passion of their romance, the duo had headed first for Holland. But in Amsterdam, after a night of heavy drinking, Susanna had glimpsed the real Wolfgang and not liked what she had seen. Several episodes later, regretting her actions, Susanna had already began planning her way back to Saul. This she accomplished by walking into a police station and asking them to contact the authorities in *Prinzenstadt*.

Once she was back safely, *Inspektor* Schinkel wasted little time interviewing the young woman. At first, she'd been reluctant to share what she knew, for her shame ran deep. But with the threat of having to remain in Germany and potentially facing charges, she had capitulated.

Wolfgang had not confessed one word to her, but in his cups he'd talked freely about different subjects, often muddled and confused. Susanna had easily put some of it together.

He'd met Astrid by chance, for she was kept hidden away at all times. But apparently my sister had found a way to escape to the walled garden, and it was here their paths had crossed. Wolfgang referred to her as a quiet angel, and it appears his infatuation had grown until he had forced himself upon her, resulting in her pregnancy. This was not a surprise to learn. We had obviously arrived at that conclusion ourselves.

Yet it seemed Wolfgang had genuinely loved Astrid. My aunt allowed him to keep calling and encouraged their relationship even though Wolfgang's wife was living in full view of the lodge. But Gisela was sworn to keep Astrid hidden. In order to maintain the monies from my father, those were the terms. Father had hinted at removing my sister to an institution and selling Lorelei. Fearful of losing her comfortable situation, Gisela had kept Astrid a secret, not even seeing she had medical care during her pregnancy. Five days after giving birth to a healthy son, Astrid had died. The rest had been my aunt's wicked plan.

Concealing Astrid's death, fearful of recrimination from my father and the loss of income. Gisela must have conspired with both the Krauses, and Wolfgang to bury Astrid in the walled garden. There she would never be found, at least not in Gisela's lifetime.

This story had not answered all the questions, but in theory, it connected all the events which had occurred over those weeks. The death of Klara, the attacks upon me, and Wolfgang's strange behaviour. He and Gustav were the villains in this tale. Which man committed each crime I did not know, though Wolfgang had to have been the instigator of it all.

I did not care anymore. My concerns lay embedded in the future of a small bundle of energy, with soft skin and a ready smile.

Yet at night, when I lay alone in my bed and closed my eyes, the image of Max would always come calling. Memories filtered through my mind like postcards, offering me snaps of different scenes—a walk in the garden, the night at the opera, and of course, that passionate wild moment we had selfishly taken. How I missed him. He had become such a normal part of my daily life in Germany, that even now I would turn to speak to him only to find no one there.

Though back in my homeland, I had not settled down. Oskar was learning to speak English as well as his own native tongue, and he chattered constantly when he wasn't eating something he shouldn't. Joan was somewhat listless. Happy to be back in London, she had spent the first week reacquainting herself with friends and family, but I had noticed her smile had slipped, and her eyes no longer shone as bright. And I knew why.

It was already December, and the cold had settled in for the day. Oskar was taking his afternoon nap up in my room as he often did. The fire blazed nicely in the hearth, and I was trying and failing to engross myself in a book I had just bought. Christmas was around the corner, and I should have to get a tree this year, which would be a first.

I heard the loud knocking on the front door but paid it no mind. There were always callers here, usually well-to-do women collecting for one thing or another. Then I heard a squeal, which sounded like Joan, and I leapt to my feet and flew out of the room and to the front of the house. Expecting to see my dear Joan in harm's way, I stopped in surprise at the sight of her wrapped in the tight embrace of none other than *Herr* Metzger! She pulled away from him to look at me, tearful and joyful simultaneously.

"Metzger!" I went forward with my hand extended. He might be a servant in Germany, but here in London he was a guest in my home. He beamed at me, and with his face scrubbed clean, his facial hair neatly trimmed, it was hard to imagine he was the same man who had collected me in the carriage all those months ago.

"Welcome," I said in fluent German. "You must go with Joan and take some refreshment." I wanted to ask why he had come, but I thought it obvious by the look of adoration upon his face.

"And what of me, Ingrid. Am I welcome also?" The question was in German.

A rush of emotion flooded through my body at the sound of the voice. His voice. I looked in the doorway and he filled the space.

"Max?"

He stepped into the hallway, and I could not move a muscle. Joan and Metzger faded away, the butler, the entire universe. It was just me and Max.

"Come." He reached me and took me by the arm. "Can we go somewhere and talk?"

I came to my senses. "Of course. Sorry, you gave me such I shock that I forgot my manners," I was babbling. "The drawing room is down here."

We went into the room which now felt too warm, and Max drew off his gloves and hat, setting them down on a small table. "May I sit?"

I was being ridiculous. I snapped out of my trance. "Yes, please do. Let me ring for something. Coffee, hot chocolate?"

Max picked a chair and sat down. "Actually, I have grown quite fond of your English tea. If that is all right?"

I laughed and rang the bell. Godwin appeared within moments, and I asked for a tea tray to be brought, then I took a seat across from Max who was busy looking around the room.

"I thought we Germans were quite plain, but your home is far more understated than the lodge." He was right. The décor of the house was drab and dark.

"This is my father's home and therefore much to his tastes. It is a stark contrast to your home and Lorelei. Night and day!" The wallpaper in this room was dark green and the furniture large and ungainly in shades of deep blue. There was adequate lighting, but the dreary weather outside did not help.

Our eyes met. "You know, I always suspected you spoke my language," Max said, and a hint of a smile played around his lips. "With your mother a native German it seemed plausible. Yet you hid that from everyone, Ingrid. Why was that?"

I shrugged. "It seems foolish in retrospect. But in the beginning it was a good idea, at least until I learned more about Lorelei and my mother's history. I truly had no intention of being deceitful. Yet I enjoyed the anonymity it gave me. Once I realised the benefit of keeping it to myself, there never seemed an appropriate time to reveal it."

"Not a bad idea for a woman in a strange country without family. I commend you for it, Though I have to admit, I'm ridiculously pleased you're bi-lingual."

We made light conversation while we waited for the tea. I asked how long he had been in the country and if his family were in good health. It was strange, but though we spoke as polite friends, I felt heat radiate from his eyes as he looked at me with such force, such interest. When Godwin came into the room I gave a start. What was wrong with me?

The butler departed and I poured the tea, glad of an occupation as my hands were fidgety. I passed Max his drink. He took a sip and sighed. "This is very good. I shall have to take some back with me to *Linnenbrink.* Now I understand why Joan complained about the coffee all the time."

"It was good to see her happy just now. She has not been quite herself since we returned from Germany. Thank you for bringing *Herr* Metzger here. You did not have to do that."

"Metzger asked if I was coming to see you at any time, and if I did, he volunteered to accompany me and be my driver. I was only too happy to oblige."

I smiled. "I fear I may have lost my maid. I can't imagine Joan not wanting to return with him when you leave."

His dark eyes sparkled mischievously. "Do you want us to go back already? I have only just arrived."

"Of course not," I answered quickly.

"I am teasing, Ingrid. Please, do not be so serious. There is much for us to talk about, and I have missed being in your good company. Have I made you uncomfortable by showing up unannounced? If so, I'm sorry."

"No, don't apologise, Max. You are right, but not about my being uncomfortable, just unprepared. For the past few months my life has revolved around a small boy and his daily routine. I have forgotten how to act around adults."

"How is Oskar?"

"Thriving. He has grown so much already. His vocabulary is quite good, in both English and German. He is full of energy and so inquisitive."

"Where is he?"

"Sleeping. He usually takes an hour or two in the afternoon, by which time I am ready for a break."

"Do you have a nanny to assist you?"

I laughed. "Goodness, no. I prefer to take care of him. Joan helps tremendously, so there's no need to bring in a stranger. Oskar needs to have lots of contact with family to make up for his shaky start in life."

"He is lucky to have you."

"That is in part down to your generosity, Max. I am so grateful you are happy with our arrangement. I do not think I could ever let him go now."

"Under the circumstances I think in you, Oskar has the closest thing to a mother he can have. He is a lucky boy. Now, there are a few things I would like to discuss with you if you are willing? I thought you might like an update on the situation back home?"

"Yes," I said. "I often wonder if there has been any progress with the police."

"The most important news is that Gustav has finally admitted to helping your aunt with the burial of Astrid. This is a lesser charge for him as he was being exploited by another. He's trying to curry favour with the lawyers, in an attempt to lessen his punishment for what he did to you."

"That is good news. Now we can formally recognise Astrid's death and get a certificate so I can move forward with the guardianship of Oskar."

"Yes, I thought you would be pleased."

"Is there any news of your brother?"

At that, Max's face grew dark with emotion. "No. I live in hope he has fallen off a cliff or under a train. I cannot believe his atrocious behaviour and the devastation he left in his wake. Katja amazes me. For a woman who appeared so incapable, she has shown much resilience since Wolfgang left. Even Jakob is flourishing. They are better off without him."

I wondered if he included Valentina in that statement. Did he know the extent of Wolfgang's relationship with her? I did not want to broach that subject with Max. Some things were better left unsaid.

"How is your mother?"

He smiled. "A handful, much as your Oskar I'd wager. She still sinks slowly into that place in her mind, but she is happy, and Magda takes such good care of her. She even goes for a walk each day. You'll never guess where?"

"The walled garden?"

He nodded and I beamed with pleasure. "Oh, how I

wish my own mother was still alive. She would have loved to spend time there with Lisbeth."

"They were great friends," he said, staring at me once again.

"The best," I said returning his gaze. "Your mother was responsible for all of this finally coming out into the open, Max. I shall be forever grateful to her."

"Grateful enough to live near her again?"

His words found my ears, but before I could respond there was a knock at the door. Joan came in with Oskar holding her hand.

"Look, Oskar," I said. "You have a visitor. Your Uncle Max has come to meet you."

He blinked a couple of times and then let go of Joan's hand. Boldy, he approached Max. He stared at him for a moment and tapped him on the knee. He held out a chubby hand. "Come," he said plainly in broken English. "I have a train."

WHEN MAX AND METZGER left an hour later, I was glad of the opportunity to relax. Their sudden appearance had sent the house into turmoil. Joan was like a lovesick young girl, the staff were gossiping, and even Oskar was wound like a spinning top. Me? I felt like a small boat that had come unmoored in stormy waters.

I knew why Max was here. For had he not warned me months ago he would come for me when he was ready? The thought of it heated my blood in a way I was unused to feeling. The sight of him in my drawing room elicited such a concoction of emotions I barely knew which to pay attention to. I did not like this lack of control, this confusion. It was time for me to take this situation into my own hands.

The Secret of Lorelei Lodge

THE CAB DEPOSITED ME outside the Savoy Hotel. Acting far braver than I actually felt, I approached the reception desk and asked where I could find the rooms of Baron Maximillian von Brandt. The middle-aged man peered down at his register and told me the room number. He called over a porter and instructed him to escort me up there.

The young man tipped his cap to me and left me standing outside a gilded door with the number of the room on a plaque on the wall. I took a deep breath, raised my hand and knocked.

It took a moment for a response, and in that time I came close to fleeing. Then I heard someone approach and the door swung open.

"Metzger…" Max stopped in mid-sentence when he saw it was me standing there and not the servant he expected. My cheeks grew warm as I took in the state of his undress. He wore trousers, and nothing else. His broad chest, bare but for the dark hair which spread across it, was every part the man and not the gentleman.

"Ingrid?" Had I not been so embarrassed I should have laughed at the tone in his voice. He was completely taken aback.

"Please, come in."

I followed him in, and watched him walk over to a chair, scoop up the shirt resting there and shrug it on. He turned to me, still doing up the buttons. "I had no idea you planned to come," he said apologetically. "I would have been better prepared."

I steeled myself. It was now or never. "That was the general idea, Max."

"I beg your pardon?"

Bravely, I covered the few steps separating us.

When I was inches away, I reached up and traced the outline of his face with my fingers. He made no movement whatsoever. Slowly, I ran my hand beneath his ear to the back of his neck, which I caressed very gently. Then, with a slight tug, I pulled his face down to meet mine. With a sigh, I parted my lips and claimed his mouth.

He was warm, firm, and he was ready for me. In a moment he gathered me into his arms, crushing me against his body while his mouth plundered mine. I could not get close enough to him, I wanted to crawl inside his clothes and be against him, become a part of him. My entire being cried out to his in a desperate plea of unabashed desire.

I do not know how long we kissed one another. I do not remember unbuttoning his shirt, or how my dress slipped to the floor, nor did I care. But I tumbled onto his bed, careless of my surroundings, only mindful of the heightened arousal of my body, my senses, under his touch, his caresses.

He broke the kiss and moved his head back to look at me clearly. "Ingrid. Unless you tell me to stop, I am going to make love to you."

I had no words, but my answer came as my lips pressed hard against his.

I SAT IN THE little garden on my favourite bench, watching the boys playing chase with the dogs. Max was speaking with Wilhelm, the gardener, about building a fort over by the Willow tree for the children to play in. We were an odd family, Max, Oskar, Lisbeth, Jakob, Katja and I. Every one of us a little broken in our way, enough to know how much we needed each other.

Max and I planned to marry as soon as his year of mourning came to an end. We would live at the *Safranpalast,* and the lodge would remain in my name, to be handed down to Oskar, whenever he came of age. Lorelei Lodge would finally become part of the von Brandt estates once again.

We were happy. Jakob and half-brother Oskar became closer every day, and I was glad of it for Wolfgang's older son had borne more than anyone knew, other than Max and myself.

Unbeknownst to the world, it had been Jakob's toy automobile which had caused the death of Valentina. A little blue vehicle made of wood, which he'd left upon the stairs, causing an ankle to turn, a leg to twist, a body to unbalance and Valentina to fall down steep, marble stairs. Max had seen the toy that very morning and quickly hidden it in his pocket, desperate the child would never know.

That Wolfgang's son had inadvertently ended a long and sordid affair between his father and the opera singer was ironic. That his father had absconded was enough, but it would have been even worse had it been with his own brother's wife.

Gustav's trial had begun. As expected, he was saying nothing, but the *inspektor* assured me he would remain in the gaol for many years. And Wolfgang? No one knew his whereabouts, or whether he was alive or dead. I had a feeling he was thriving somewhere, living off another and charming his way through their money.

What a journey this had been. I had first come here so young and lonely. My maid Joan, the only person in the world who cared for me. And now? My eyes found

Max, and as always he felt my attention and turned away from Wilhelm to meet my gaze. The wave of desire and love for him filled my senses and completed me in a way I had not realised I needed. Perhaps in time, we might have our own children to add to this family who had lost so much.

My eyes shifted and moved to the boys. Jakob had forgotten the dogs and now brandished a butterfly net, racing around in pursuit of a green and blue swallowtail. Behind him, his shadow, Oskar, tried valiantly to keep up. But his little three-year-old legs could not match Jakob's pace, and he kept tripping over in the thick, green grass.

I chuckled. If only my mother could see this, how happy she would have been. And dear Astrid, my mysterious sister who had been like a fairy-tale friend in my early years, and then a mythological creature as an adult. All this time I'd yearned for her without knowing she was ever there. How cruel for us both to have been robbed of a sister's love.

Tears filled my eyes and I let them slide down my face. And as I looked up, I saw Astrid's son run towards the old lady coming into the garden. I watched as her thin arms opened wide to lift him up into a loving embrace. And I knew then, that wherever my mother and Astrid were, they were together at last, just as we were here in the special place they loved. And finally, we were going to be all right.

About the Author

Jude Bayton is a Londoner, currently residing in the American Midwest. An avid photographer and traveller, Jude loves writing about places close to her heart. To keep up with her latest releases, newsletter and monthly blog, subscribe to @judebayton.com

Find Jude Bayton at:
judebayton.com
Facebook: Jude Bayton
Twitter: @judebayton
Email: author@judebayton.com

Other Books
By Jude Bayton
The Secret of Mowbray Manor
The Secret of Hollyfield House
The Secret of Pendragon Island

The Secret of Pendragon Island
By Jude Bayton

Chapter One

May 9, 1891—Pendragon Island, Cornwall

Her name was Mrs Malahide, and by the unwelcoming expression upon her dour face, I understood immediately she was not happy with my coming. Why? I was expected. In fact, it was she who sent my travel instructions. Yet it did not make her any the friendlier. On the contrary, her dark brown eyes narrowed as she looked me up and down and her thin mouth flattened into a straight line. Then she stepped back, almost reluctant to allow me in.

"Get you inside, Miss Livingstone," she said brusquely, the Cornish lilt to her voice not unpleasant, though the tone gave her words a sharp edge. I picked up my bags and followed her in.

She was a tall, gaunt woman, dressed in dark brown serge. Thin hair, the same bland colour as her dress, was gathered into a tight bun that pulled her brow taut. A shock of white hair framed the stern face. I had never seen the like of it and fought to stop myself from staring.

"You'll be goin' right to your room," she stated. "You've missed dinner, but a light refreshment will be brought up to you presently."

We walked through the grand foyer. I stared in

fascination at the majestic staircase and several pieces of statuary, all depicting dragons in various poses. Whereupon Mrs Malahide stopped in front of an elaborate wooden panelled wall and opened a concealed door. This led to a small landing and stone staircase. I assumed the kitchen was downstairs, but the housekeeper pointed upwards.

"Your room is on the third floor of the castle, Miss Livingstone, as is mine, away from the other servants. Make sure you use this staircase and no other. The family occupy the second floor. Do not venture there under any circumstances."

I did not reply. I knew my place, after all.

I SLEPT SOUNDLY UNTIL A maid knocked upon my door, having left a breakfast tray on the landing. I ate and dressed quickly, all the while fighting my nerves. Had I made the right decision coming all this way from London to work for strangers?

Mrs Malahide collected me promptly at nine o'clock to escort me down to the ground floor, where I would meet my employer. We stood outside a set of imposing red double doors, upon which the housekeeper rapped lightly. There came a response for us to enter. I took a deep breath and followed her into the room.

"Ah, there you are." A tall, well-made man dressed in a dark grey morning coat stood with his back facing French windows. He came towards us, his hand extended. I was immediately drawn to his strikingly blue eyes. By the lines upon his face, I guessed him to be somewhere in his fifties.

"Augustus Nightingale," he said. "You must be our

new librarian. Polly, isn't it?"

I shook his hand, finding it clammy. "Poppy, your lordship."

"Poppy? Like the flower, I take it. Jolly good," he muttered, crossing a thick crimson carpet to take a seat upon a blood-red velvet sofa. "Sir Richard Barclay speaks highly of you, young lady. I understand you did an exceptional job with his library. I doubt our collection will live up to Barclay's, but I do believe we've some fine first editions here at Pendragon Castle. I look forward to seeing everything catalogued and in good order. I daresay you shall have your work cut out for you Miss...eh..."

"Livingstone, milord," I said quietly.

"Excellent. Malahide will show you to the library, and you may acquaint yourself with our collection. Lady Nightingale will meet with you sometime later this morning. I do hope—"

The drawing-room door flew open, and a young man burst into the room. Mrs Malahide stepped back in surprise.

"Father, you must come at once!" He was a younger version of his sire, blond-headed, his blue eyes bright with consternation.

"Good God, Clive. What is it?"

"The worst news," he gasped, as though he could not believe it. "Robert Penrith's been murdered."

The severity of his message brought a look of abject horror to his father's face. "What? No, it cannot be. Are you certain?"

There was a sudden tug on my sleeve. Mrs Malahide gestured with a slight nod of her head to the door. I understood her intent, and we quietly left the room to allow the gentlemen their privacy.

She marched me past several rooms, down a wide hallway towards the front of the house, simultaneously giving instructions in a firm voice. "Miss Livingstone, I shall take you to the library, and there you must remain until I fetch you. I shall be preoccupied for a time." Her countenance was shaken, her pallor pale.

"Of course," I stammered. "I am so sorry there has been such bad news."

She made no response, as though she had not even heard me, then opened a door into a room on the lower floor of one of Pendragon's two towers. "Go on in," she said. "I'll return to collect you. You'll meet the other servants then." She hurried away.

I stepped across the threshold and breathed in the intoxicating fragrance of paper, leather, and pipe tobacco. At once, everything was forgotten as my disbelieving eyes absorbed the room. Copious bookshelves teemed with books of different bindings and colours. Each wall adorned with beautifully carved mahogany shelves, packed to the gills with volume upon volume. Spellbound, I could not have been more thrilled had Miss Jane Austen been sat in one of the reading chairs waiting to greet me. I drank it in, drawing energy from the millions of words gracing thousands of hidden pages. If I had held any doubt of my coming, it was dispelled in this singular moment.

I noticed a short staircase in one corner of the room, leading up a flight to a second level. I marvelled at the intricate design of the woodwork and the elaborate golden railing of the balcony, which encircled the room's interior. Captivated, I had never before seen anything quite so magnificent. My fingers itched to touch the books. I went about the room, tracing their spines delicately. The tomes were dusty from lack of use. How could anyone neglect such a marvellous source of pleasure and knowledge? I should have been a lost soul had I not learned to read. I had the good Sisters of Loretta Convent to thank for that.

It was an immense room. A wall of windows overlooked the front driveway, while every other space was lined with bookcases—they even framed the fireplace. In its centre, a massive, thick-legged wooden table dominated the room, large enough to seat ten. It boasted grandiose chairs upholstered in a garish crimson fabric, with raised red dragons embroidered into the material. Located near the windows were two small settles and four dark red leather chairs. These were arranged so one might sit and read without being in another's direct line of vision. All the seating was placed to capitalise on the natural light coming from outside.

I could not wait to start working. At the table, I examined the stack of notepaper and several packets of notecards left in preparation for me to begin my inventory. There were several fountain pens, and a sizeable ledger with the emblem of an elaborately detailed red dragon. I found it ugly and wondered why the family had such an obsession with the colour red? It dominated Pendragon's interior, from the furnishings to the carpets on the floor—still, no matter. My job was to catalogue this extraordinary collection and ensure the books were in good condition. Judging by what I saw before me, there was much to be done.

I WAS KNEELING ON THE FLOOR, my nose buried in a

rather fine edition of Dickens's *Hard Times,* when the library door opened. I quickly got to my feet, assuming it was probably Mrs Malahide.

"Miss Livingstone?"

The autocratic voice was not that of the housekeeper but someone far more refined. A middle-aged lady entered the room, dressed in beige silk, her dark brown hair in a soft chignon. By her regal bearing, I assumed this to be Lady Nightingale. I bobbed a curtsy. "Good morning, my lady."

She came to stand before me, and my first impression was how attractive she was. Her brown eyes were kindly, her brow smooth. The light caught a prism of the garnet drops dangling from her ears.

"How do you do, Miss Livingstone." She glanced away from me and looked over at the table. "I trust you have everything you need?"

"I believe so."

"Good. Do not hesitate to ask Mrs Malahide should you require additional supplies. I fear this task has been delayed far too long, and you have much work ahead of you."

"Indeed. But I am most happy to be here, my lady. Your library is astounding. Not only is the collection impressive, but the setting is exquisite. It is like stepping into a fairyland." I bit my lip, slightly embarrassed by my outburst.

Lady Nightingale tilted her head and looked directly at my face. 'Tis heartening to see the passion in a young woman for something academic. Would that my daughter, Charlotte felt such enthusiasm for books and reading, rather than fashion and baubles. I am extremely pleased you are come to Pendragon, Miss

Livingstone. Perhaps you will be a good influence on Charlotte. Now, I must go. There has been a tragic accident with one of our workers. I have much to see to."

"I am terribly sorry to hear of it."

"It is heartbreaking." She sighed. "But unfortunately, we cannot change what has happened. I trust you know what is expected of you here. So, I shall leave you to it, then?"

"Yes, Lady Nightingale. Thank you."

She turned and left the room.

WHEN MRS MALAHIDE APPEARED, I was astonished it was time for luncheon. In her inhospitable manner, she escorted me downstairs to the kitchen.

"You may introduce yourself to the staff who are already at lunch," she declared. She pointed a long finger to what I assumed was the dining room and walked briskly away.

Fortunately, Cook observed my awkwardness and was of a friendly nature. "Come on in and sit you down," she ordered. We won't bite, dearie."

I glanced down the hall where the housekeeper had gone.

"Don't you worry 'bout 'er," she said with a grin. "She don't take her meals with the rest 'o us." The cook's name was Mrs Slade, and though short of stature and wide of girth, she exuded an energy most likely necessary to run a kitchen of this size. Her plump cheeks were flushed, and her eyes deep-set, like little blue pearls hiding in an oyster shell. She, too, was a Londoner, and though I had only been gone from the city barely two days, I relished hearing the familiar accent.

"Now, you'll not meet old Fairfax yet," she said, directing me to an empty seat. "Silly sod only went an' broke 'is arm a week ago. Fat lot of good it is bein' a one-armed butler." She laughed as though recounting a clever joke. "Come along, then. Reach over an' get a bowl. You can eat soup with the rest o' us."

I followed her lead, and when she sat at the head of the table, I stayed close, taking a place to her left. There were others still in the middle of their lunch, and we quickly introduced ourselves. Audrey was an unassertive woman in her twenties. A lady's maid, she saw to both Lady Nightingale and her daughter, Lady Charlotte. John Flannigan, who sat beside her, gave me a friendly grin. He was Lord Nightingale's personal valet and looked to be middle-aged. I liked him immediately as he seemed quite a jolly sort, judging by the laughter lines bracketing his bright eyes. Flannigan looked every bit the circus ringmaster with a bald, shiny head and thick, black handlebar moustache.

"John 'ere's been with the family since Gawd knows when," Mrs Slade declared. There isn't anythin' about this family gets past 'im." She tapped her snub nose. "Knows where all the bones got buried, does John Flannigan."

"Don't you listen to Cook, miss," the valet replied. "She's full of nonsense. Though she redeems herself as she makes the best Victoria Sandwich this side of the country." He gestured to a young man across the table from where he sat. "This here be Jarvis, our head footman. He's unofficially the substitute butler, with ole Fairfax gone."

"Pleased to make your acquaintance, miss," said

Jarvis with a grin. I smiled back and observed how attractive he was. Thick blond curls tousled loosely around his face, and his cupid mouth seemed far too pretty for a man.

"So, tell us, young lady. Where did you spring from?" Flannigan asked, dabbing his bristly moustache with a serviette.

"London," I replied. "In fact, this is my first time to have ever left the city."

"Well, I'm blowed," said Mrs Slade. "A fellow Londoner like meself." She squinted at me. "Though you sound a lot posher than me, if I do say so. You must 'ave gone to a fancy school."

I felt my cheeks warm as four pairs of eyes stared at my face. "No, quite the opposite. I grew up in a foundling home run by nuns. Near Pimlico."

"Not too far from me then," Cook said. "My family live just across the river, near Covent Garden."

A bell tinkled on the wall in the kitchen, and their heads turned in unison.

Jarvis jumped to his feet. "That's the front door. Most likely, it'll be Constable Barry," he said, quickly putting on his red livery as he walked away.

Mrs Slade finished her soup and pushed the bowl to one side. "Ooh, 'tis a shocking state of affairs if you ask me. Fancy 'aving the police come to the 'ouse. I've 'eard the poor man was stabbed. Is it true, John?"

The valet nodded. "Yes. Robert was set upon goin' home last night. They found his body on Priory Lane with a knife stuck in his back."

I shuddered and focused upon my soup.

"Oh my," Cook's voice was distressed. That's terrible. Was 'ee robbed?"

"I don't know. Though I suppose he might've had some funds from the mine on his person."

"It'll be them blasted gypsies. You mark my words. I 'eard they were back campin' in the north woods again. They'll be to blame. Stealin' from a good person like Robert Penrith is criminal enough, but to kill the man?" Mrs Slade shook her head, and her generous chins wobbled. "Those bloomin' Romany's, they should be run off the island."

Mr Flannigan turned to look my way. "Miss Livingstone, I am sorry you find us in this sorry state," he said apologetically. "We are a good bunch of folks at the castle, but I fear we've no practice dealin' with the news of a murder. The whole household is grapplin' with the terrible situation. Please forgive our manners if we seem preoccupied."

Before I could respond to his kind words, another bell jangled. This time Audrey glanced up. "That's Miss Charlotte awake then," she muttered, rising to leave.

I looked at the clock on the wall. It was well past noon, and Charlotte Nightingale was just now getting out of her bed?

As though reading my mind, Mrs Slade clucked. "That is one lazy Miss. If she were my girl, I'd 'ave 'er up with the larks every day. 'Tis shameless."

"Mrs Slade. I prefer you keep your personal opinions of the family to yourself." The distinctive voice of Mrs Malahide came from the doorway. Yet Cook seemed unperturbed by both her presence and her remark. She raised an eyebrow and leaned back in the chair, crossing her arms, but made no reply.

The housekeeper bristled. "Whenever you are

ready, Miss Livingstone." She threw me a look which I quickly perceived as an order.

I got to my feet. "Thank you so much for lunch, Mrs Slade. The soup was delicious." I turned to the valet, who stared disdainfully at the housekeeper. "It was nice to meet you, Mr Flannigan."

"Pleasure was all mine, miss."

I followed Mrs Malahide back to the library. Upon entering, she closed the door behind her. "'Tis not proper to discuss the Nightingale family downstairs, Miss Livingstone. Please do not let me ever hear *you* do so." Annoyance laced her words, yet her brown eyes were expressionless. Did the women possess any type of emotion besides irritability? If so, she hid it well.

I nodded. "Of course. I would not dream of it."

Her glance swept over my face with disapproval. She pulled a watch-fob from her breast pocket. "You are to finish for the day by four o'clock. The servants eat promptly at five, so make sure you are punctual."

Before I had time to respond, she was gone.

*****

Visit Jude's website (judebayton.com)
to find out where you can purchase your copy of

The Secret of Pendragon Island

Made in the USA
Columbia, SC
24 July 2022